ALSO BY SHANNON FAY

The Marrowbone Spells

External Forces (forthcoming)

INNATE MAGIC

SHANNON FAY

47NRTH

Text copyright © 2021 by Shannon Fay
All rights reserved.

Published by 47North, Seattle
www.apub.com

Amazon, the Amazon logo, and 47North are trademarks of Amazon.com, Inc., or its affiliates.

ISBN-13: 9781542032032
ISBN-10: 1542032032

Cover design by Faceout Studio, Jeff Miller

Printed in the United States of America

For Mom and Dad

CHAPTER 1

Thomas and I arrived at Kensington an hour late. A maid let us in, our shoes clacking against the polished wooden floor as we stepped inside. Down the hall I heard laughter coming from Andrew's party.

"Do you think Andrew's mother will be here?" I asked, scanning the wide foyer as if she might leap out.

"Well, Paul, it is her house," Thomas replied.

"She's never liked me, you know," I said. "I don't understand it. From the moment we met I could tell she didn't like me."

"Maybe she thinks you're a bad influence on her son," Thomas suggested.

"And yet she tolerates *you*," I said. "I just wish I knew what she had against *me*."

Thomas shook his head and a drop of blood hit the ground. I put a steadying hand on his shoulder. Thomas was just a little shorter than me with wild black hair and light-brown skin. He looked away, hands covering his nose.

"Your honker's bleeding," I said, then lowered my voice, aware of the young maid hovering right behind me. "Did they break it?"

"Nah, they just hit it real hard." He would have sounded a lot tougher if he didn't talk like a stuffed duck.

I was wearing a magic green-and-white herringbone suit that caused the air to swirl around me in glittering eddies. I waved my hand, the motion making the air shimmer even more fervently, then produced a grey lace cloth from my right sleeve. It was just a bit of sleight of hand, but the hazy magic sheen of my suit made it seem like I had pulled the handkerchief from the air.

Thomas, recognizing his own handkerchief, grabbed it from my hand and held it to his nose. He didn't seem too impressed by my impromptu magic trick so I turned to the maid in a bid for validation. She smiled politely.

"May I take your coats, gents?" She was a new hire: I would have remembered her dark eyes if we had met before. She had a pale-brown complexion that spoke of far-off ancestors, maybe Eastern European, maybe as far off as Africa or India. But her accent made it clear she was as much a cockney as I was a Scouser.

"Well, as long as you give them back," I said, still hoping for perhaps a genuine smile or even a laugh. I let my Liverpool accent come on strong, to show her that I was a down-to-earth lad, nothing like her posh employers.

The maid's smile was as thin as spring ice.

Thom's coat created the illusion of ravens flocking around him. Once he shrugged it off one shoulder the circuit between magic cloth and human soul was cut and the ravens disappeared like a fine mist. As Thomas struggled to get his other arm free I reached out and held the handkerchief to his nose, allowing him use of both his hands. He grunted his thanks. Once the coat was off he tilted his head forwards and I pulled the now-bloody handkerchief away.

"Looks dry," I said.

"Feels dry."

"Good." Thomas's handkerchief felt heavy in my hand. I wanted to apologize even though I wasn't the one who had bloodied his nose. On our way to the party we had run into the thugs who worked for McCormick, our "benefactor." We had managed to give them the slip but not before Thomas had gotten bopped in the face. Poor mite. Our debts and fortunes were tied up together and yet Thom seemed to be the one who always got the bad end of things.

The maid stepped forwards to take my suit jacket but I waved her off. I folded Thomas's handkerchief into a three-point pyramid. There was a large mirror hanging by the stairs and I watched my reflection carefully as I tucked the handkerchief into my breast pocket, making sure that I had hidden all the blood. Through the fabric of my coat I could feel the familiar shape of my Book, tucked into the inner breast pocket of my jacket. The herringbone suit made everything look pleasingly hazy and indistinct, adding a red shine to my brown hair while obscuring things like the light dusting of freckles across my nose. It was a somewhat silly power, the magical haze. It couldn't stop a bullet or let a man speak in tongues or any other number of actually useful things that magic clothes could do. But I always felt good when I wore it.

I smiled at my reflection, then took a step back to get an even better view. As I moved back I bumped into the maid standing behind me, causing said maid to bump into a pedestal by the door, causing a small clay horse statue on said pedestal to topple over. The statue hit the floor and broke into a dozen pieces.

The three of us looked at the broken horse in horror, our eyes locked on the shards as if we were performing some divination rite.

"Bloody hell," Thomas swore. Now his Scouser accent was coming on strong, along with a hint of worry. "That looked old. Do you think it was Greek or Mesopotamian?"

"Whatever it was, it's baroque now," I replied.

The maid looked at me as if wishing to shatter *me* into a dozen pieces.

"Sorry, that was rotten, I know," I said. "In bad situations I make bad jokes."

"I'm going to get fired for this," the maid whispered.

"No, no, it's not that bad," I said quickly. I scanned the space for some opulent rug we could sweep the pieces under, but the floor was bare—it seemed that even grand houses like the McDougals' suffered from postwar austerity. "You won't lose your job. It was an accident."

She gave me a sober look, her fear giving way to hard-eyed scepticism.

Before I could reassure her further a voice called from down the hall.

"Mr Gallagher, Mr Dawes, whatever is keeping you two out here?"

Andrea McDougal, Lady Fife, widow of the previous duke of Fife and supposedly the most powerful woman in all of the United Kingdom, appeared in the hall.

She stepped into the foyer, her deep-blue skirt swirling around her. Lady Fife was wearing a pale-blue jacket done in the style of a riding outfit but obviously tailored for social events. A normal person might not notice that it was magic but as a cloth mage I could feel the vibrations that it was giving off (or, to be more particular, the vibrations Lady Fife gave off while wearing it). A yellow lacy shirt peeked out artfully from under her jacket and I recognized Andrew's work. How sweet. He had made his mother a shirt that magically concealed the wrinkles of middle age. Andrew had once shown us pictures of his mother as a young woman: young Andrea McDougal at the 1921 Ashes, a toothy smile framed by blonde curls, white skin bright even in the sepia photograph. Thomas had said that she had been, in her time, "a tall drink of water." I wouldn't admit this to Thom or anybody else but personally I thought Lady Fife was actually more striking now. She seemed more serious, no more toothy grins, her curls pinned back in a no-nonsense style, but she had a knowing quality that I couldn't help but be drawn to.

Lady Fife came to us, smiling. Her smile dropped when she saw the shattered statue.

Whispers stated that Andrea McDougal was a scryer, a foreseer, a practitioner of the illegal art of divination. I was grimly pleased that she seemed surprised by this turn of events.

Next to me the maid sucked in her breath through clenched teeth. I certainly didn't envy her having Lady Fife as a mistress. I might have had to deal with her frosty acquaintance, but we were merely that— acquaintances. The laws of decorum demanded that we be polite and civil to each other regardless of our personal feelings. As a dear friend of her beloved only child, I got cut a lot of slack.

That line of thinking gave me an idea, my favourite kind of idea: the kind that helped and irritated all the right people.

I gave what I hoped was a comforting pat to the girl's shoulder. She looked at me, her dark-brown eyes questioning. I stepped forwards and scooped up one of the clay shards.

"So sorry, Lady Fife," I said, continuing to step closer to her. "We just had a little accident here in your foyer. I'm afraid I was a bit of a clod and knocked over your little clay horse. Dead sorry."

If I sounded flippant, it was because I was trying my best to be. The more of an ass I made of myself, the less likely Lady Fife was to cast her suspicions on the shaking serving girl.

The moment between us stretched out. I started tossing the clay piece up in the air and catching it, deftly avoiding the sharp edges. If someone didn't say something soon I was going to pick up the other pieces and start juggling.

Lady Fife gave me her usual pleasant, tight-lipped smile. She believed I had broken the statue. She just didn't believe I was sorry about it.

"How unfortunate," Lady Fife finally said. "But no matter. Tonya, clean up this mess. Mr Gallagher, Mr Dawes, you must join the rest of the party. I know Andrew is ever so eager to see you." She started to walk away from us, heading for the staircase. "I have some business I must attend to but I'll join you all shortly."

With that she disappeared upstairs in a swirl of blue-and-yellow lace. Thom and I both let out sighs of relief. We knelt down and started picking up the pieces.

"Oh, no, don't trouble yourselves," the maid, Tonya, said. We stood, moving so quickly that Thom let one of the clay shards in his hand drop. We all winced at the sound of it hitting the floor.

An uncertain gratitude clouded Tonya's face. Her gaze flitted upstairs. I got the message: she couldn't talk freely, not when her witchy employer might still be lingering on the landing or perhaps spying on us through her crystal ball or however else she did such things. "Thank you, really."

I shrugged, the motion of my suit causing the air to ripple and blur. But when I smiled at the maid it did what magic seemingly couldn't: it made her smile in return.

As we entered the room a cheer went up. Before I could take a head count of who was there Andrew bustled over. Andrew, the current duke of Fife and the day's birthday boy, had his mother's pale skin and blond hair, though his curls were far unrulier. He had blue eyes like a white Persian cat, which was fitting as he often had a kitten's mystified expression. He was wearing a light-blue shirt with filigree details. When he shook my hand it gave the illusion that little sparks were shooting off.

"Gally! Thom-Daw! The others were starting to say that you weren't going to come." Andrew's face took on a haunted visage, like a soldier recalling the theatre of war. It was gone a second later as he clapped the two of us on the backs. "But here you are! Obie, you owe me a pound."

Oberon was sitting on one of the settees, wearing a dark double-breasted suit and horn-rimmed glasses. I was always jealous that he had the broad shoulders and face to pull off that kind of masculine look. His dark hair, golden-brown skin, and smug air made it seem like he was lounging next to the Mediterranean rather than on a mate's couch.

Nonchalantly he took out his Book.

"Well, hand yours over then," Oberon said dryly, not even glancing our way. Andrew took his Book from a pocket and passed it with a wide smile to Oberon. Without a word, Oberon opened his Book, muttering under his breath as his finger first traced along a page, withdrawing the money, and then drew a line in Andrew's Book as he transferred the pound to Andrew's coffers.

"Oberon, when are you going to learn not to bet against us?" I said, leaning down over the back of the settee.

Oberon smiled laconically as he handed Andrew's Book back to him. "It's paid out in the past."

"Now, now, don't snipe, you two," Andrew said. "No birthday fighting. Let's only talk of happy things!"

On the other side of the room Gabriella Wilkes and Ralph Gunnerson were sitting by the window seat, chatting away. When they looked over I blew them a kiss. Gabs made a show of plucking it out of the air and tucking it away in her purse.

"Just how old are you, anyway?" Thomas asked Andrew.

Andrew puffed out his chest. "Well, I was born on May first, 1931, at nine forty-one a.m., which means that as of this morning I am twenty-three years of age."

"So grown up," Oberon said dryly, still idling on the couch.

"Growing older ain't the same as growing up," Ralph said. He had come over to join us while Gabs had taken a seat next to Oberon.

"Spoken like a true old man." Thomas playfully punched Ralph in the shoulder. They were the youngest and the oldest in our cloth magic class but close in a way that, frankly, made me feel like the odd man out. Even though we'd graduated last month it seemed like some dynamics within our group were here to stay. "Just how old are you anyway, Ralph? Thirty-seven?"

Ralph was tall and might have been handsome if life hadn't happened to him: he had a slight cauliflower ear on his left side, a broken nose ridge, and acne scarring across his cheeks. A childhood illness had left him with pinched red cheeks and a waxy complexion. But somehow through it all his eyes had remained kind and bright. Not even his stint on the front lines of the war had managed to dim them.

"I'm only twenty-seven! Twenty-seven," Ralph said with the mock agitation of an actor playing out a well-worn routine.

"And where would we be without you?" I said, deciding to get in on the ribbing. "Our own wise old man guiding us along—"

"Oh, I thought that was my job."

I'd know that smooth Welsh voice anywhere. With great care to act casual I turned around and confirmed that yes, the voice did indeed belong to Professor Lamb.

I tried to think of something witty to say, but in the end the best I could do was point to him and say, "*You're* here."

Lamb smiled, causing a memory to unlock in my head: a random morning from over a year ago, spent in bed together. "How is it you're so handsome?" I had asked him. He had replied that it was his "dark Welsh genes." They had given him dusky black hair, tanned skin, and his clear green eyes.

He wore a purple, heavily brocaded jacket. Lamb's one claim to fame was fixing the Purple Impurity and he never missed a chance to wear some shade of it. When he smiled wrinkles appeared on his face, but they managed to make him look dashing rather than aged, the bastard.

"Yes, Andrew invited me," Lamb said, meeting my obvious statement with one of his own.

I turned back around to face Andrew.

"Well, isn't that nice. I suppose you just decided to have a class reunion at the same time as your birthday party? Kill two birds with one stone?" There was nothing cruel in my words and yet I still managed to sound petty and bitter. I had been prepared to run into Lady Fife, but I hadn't been prepared to run into Lamb. Even worse I could feel my own agitation putting a damper on the party, but the more I tried to relax the more anxious I felt. "Jesus, Andrew, you must have other friends besides us."

A few of my classmates traded knowing, weary looks.

"Paul, don't be such an ass," Oberon said.

"What? What did I do?" It was no fun having other people voice your internal guilt.

"Please, don't snipe at each other!" Andrew pleaded. He looked around at us. "I suppose it is pretty funny that it's the whole cloth magic class here, but I really wasn't going for a theme, I promise. I just, I only wanted to invite my dearest friends, and, well, that's all of you."

He laughed but no one else joined in. I felt my heart tighten as Andrew gazed down at his feet. I stepped forwards and put a hand on Andrew's shoulder.

"Thanks for inviting us, mate. Sorry again that we kept you all waiting."

Andrew looked up, face bright again. "Oh, it's no bother! You're here now. Righto!" Andrew clapped his hands together. "Now that you're here we can eat the birthday cake!"

"Right," I said. "First I'm just going to help myself to a birthday drink."

I went over to the sideboard near the window, opened a bottle of whiskey, and poured myself two fingers. Behind me I could hear the others in various conversations: Ralph and Thomas playfully taking the piss out of each other, Gabs and Oberon debating some current event. Andrew had presumably gone to retrieve the cake. That just left . . .

Lamb came up to the sideboard and leaned against it. I could feel him staring at me but I only had eyes for the amber liquid in my hand. I didn't even like whiskey but it gave me something to look at.

"Are you and little Thom-Daw in some kind of trouble?" Lamb asked.

"What makes you say that?" Now I looked at him, giving him a far-too-wide smile.

"You were an hour late for Andrew's party and there's blood on Thomas's collar," Lamb said. "What happened?"

"I don't really think it's any of your concern." I sipped lightly from the glass, barely wetting my lips.

"Of course it is. You're my students."

"We graduated in April." It was just last month but I was eager to put the distance between us.

"Still, I worry," Lamb said smoothly. "I could help, you know. With whatever it is."

"We do not want nor need your help," I said with an almost royal crispness. Down went the whiskey—I tried not to make a sour-milk expression at the taste when I set the glass down. I was pretty pleased with how effectively I had frozen Lamb out. I moved a step to the left, away from Lamb and towards a small luncheon buffet that had been spread out. I took a plate and studied my edible options. There was not enough fruit for my liking.

Lamb slid down along the table too, standing even closer than he had been before. Back when we had been dating he had always been so careful to put space between us while in public, to make sure we never got accused of anything that might land us in prison. And yet now that we weren't even together anymore he was leaning in far too close.

"Really, Paul, don't be so stubborn," Lamb said. "Pride can be a very dangerous sin."

My plate made a slight clash as I set it down, the tablecloth muffling the sound. I looked at Lamb, not bothering to smile.

"I'm not your student anymore," I said. "And this isn't a lecture hall. So fuck off."

With that I turned my attention back to the food. I wielded the salad tongs with the precision of a brain surgeon, deftly picking out individual pieces of green. Flick! A piece of romaine went up into the air and landed on my plate. Flick! A bit of rocket followed suit. Even as I pointedly picked up leaf after leaf Lamb continued to stare at me. Eventually he spoke.

"You know, Paul, if you keep acting like a spurned lover, people are going to get the right idea."

I turned, accidentally tossing a piece of spinach onto the carpet.

"A spurned lover?" I echoed back. "Ha! *Ha ha ha!*"

The first peal of laughter came from genuine surprise. The next few chords came from a more panicked place as my brain failed to produce words.

"That's . . . they'd still have the wrong idea," I said. "Spurned lovers try to wheedle their way back. I, meanwhile, would be quite happy if I never saw you again."

"Well, that's unlikely," Lamb said easily. "Cloth magic in Britain is a very small community and I'm part of it. A pretty big part of it, in fact. So we really should be civil with each other."

I didn't have a reply for that. My mind was still processing Lamb's words. I had thought that once I graduated I could put this part of my life behind me. But Lamb would still be the one people listened to when they asked for a reference, the one who could send commissions my way, the one who could—

Thomas stepped in between us, a formidable partition despite his short height.

"Hey, Paul," he said, his voice carefully neutral. "You all right?"

I snapped my head over towards him, suddenly feeling very awake and present. "Yes, yes, I'm fine."

"C'mon. I think we'll find better company elsewhere." Thomas gave Lamb a quick once-over. "Anywhere else."

"Why, I think I've just been insulted," Lamb said lightly.

Now Thomas gave the man his full attention. "When you know for sure get back to me."

Lamb seemed mildly impressed but not intimidated. He was staring at Thomas with an expression I knew frighteningly well. It was the expression of a man going through his mental armoury and picking out the best weapon.

"Thomas." I put a hand on my mate's shoulder, ready to pull him away. I didn't want him to hear whatever put-down Lamb had at hand. "Let's go."

"Then I guess you've just wasted the last four years of your life!" Gabs said, voice rising loud enough to grab the attention of the room. She and Oberon were still sitting on the couch, but Gabs's posture was that of an angry cat, her body curled as if ready to leap at the settee's other occupant.

I have never seen another woman, not on the street, stage, or silver screen, as pretty as Gabs. She was also always the best dressed amongst us, quite the feat when your friends were all cloth mages. Today she was wearing a gold gown with rose accents. If I were closer I might have been able to twig onto what kind of magical effect it had, but from where I was standing it just looked like a beautiful dress. I knew it had to be something special, though. Gabs was probably the best cloth mage in our class, after myself. And her magical talent came in addition to her natural charms: she had blonde hair that was always styled in the latest fashion, fair skin without blemish, blue eyes that were always bright. Right now, though, they were bright with anger.

Oberon shrugged loosely at Gabs's spat words.

"No, no, not a waste. My father wanted me to get a degree, so I did. I've just no plans to waste the next forty years of my life on it. And it's not as though it can even be a stepping-stone to something else—no cloth mage has ever gone on to become Court Magician."

Oberon's words were supposed to make cloth magic sound unappealing, but they had the opposite effect on me: How amazing would it be not only to be Court Magician but to be the first one to have come up through cloth magic?

"Oberon's talking about cloth magic," she said, appealing to the room. "Says it's a foolish, dead-end trade."

"What?" Ralph said. "Jesus, mate, why didn't you tell us four years ago?"

Everyone laughed but Oberon merely shook his head.

"It's nothing to me. I just took this program on a lark, something to do. I'm not foolish enough to try to make my living out of it."

Not that I have to was the unsaid statement trailing his words. Like Andrew, Oberon was the only son of a wealthy family, his future assured by his very existence. He might not be a duke but his grandfather had been some well-to-do cotton baron.

In past years the cloth mage classes would have been full of men like Andrew and Oberon, upper-class lads whose families had all but bought them a place at school. Our year was the first time the dean had sought out so-called lower-class students, people like Ralph and Gabs and Thomas and me.

A memory flooded back of the first time Thomas and I had talked to Andrew and Oberon, back on the first day of school. Thom and I were just a couple of northern boys, seventeen and eighteen years old respectively. We'd barely been in London a week and had gotten lost taking the tube in from our crappy bedsit on the outskirts of the city. When we'd finally arrived at the college, harried and flustered, Andrew and Oberon had been sitting in the empty classroom, as calmly as if they'd been born there. When we'd introduced ourselves Andrew had been too shy to say a word, but Oberon had looked us up and down and made a comment about how cloth magic deserved better than to be the refuge of the working class.

"Paul ain't working class," Thomas had said indignantly. "His family owns a shop."

Oberon's smile had grown wide at that.

"Oh, my mistake! Wow, his family owns a *shop*. I'm sorry, I didn't realize that we were talking to the upper crust of Liverpool society. Hear that, Andrew, his family—"

At which point Thomas, embarrassed and angry, had kicked Oberon's chair out from under him.

"Ah, yes, we've all seen this from you before, Oberon," I said, walking over. It felt good to have some spat to spend my energies on rather than trying to fend off Lamb. "You're no good at something, so it must be rubbish. I beat you at Ping-Pong and it goes from being your favourite pastime to tennis for degenerates. You can't sew a passable vest so all of cloth magic is condemned. How nice it must be to have such a clear view of things."

Oberon shook his head. He was not wearing a suit of his own making but rather one of a well-known Savile Row tailor. It had no magical properties; it was just a regular (if expensive) suit. "It's not that. If I was serious about magic, I would've studied Book Binding."

The room had already been chilly but now it became positively glacial. Book Binding was an old, long-practised form of magic in England, but it had been experiencing a new golden age since the 1930s. That was when British mages brought back techniques they had discovered in India and China and from there it had become something of a national obsession. You needed a Book in order to get around, to redeem your ration coupons, to buy goods, to pay rent, basically to live in the city. Nowadays even small children were mages in miniature, able to do basic spells like transferring a few shillings. It was commonly accepted that Book Binding had won the war, scientists filling Books with numbers and calculations until they created the atomic bomb. Everyone had a Book, but only the rich could afford cloth magic.

God knows the government was only going to continue to push Book Binding. Oberon's words were a common sentiment, spoken in the House of Lords, agreed upon in shops, passed along in both public and state schools, expressed in the letters pages of the *Evening Standard*. But it was not a statement that went over well in a room of cloth mages.

Gabs spoke first. "Book Binding might be in vogue, but cloth magic is older and has the power to transform society." I was close enough now that I could feel the effects of her dress. For a moment I thought it was just her perfume: she smelled like fresh air, sunlight, and wildflowers, a scent that transported me to happy memories of living in the countryside with cousins during the war. It made me want to draw closer to her.

"I know that's the party line amongst cloth mages, but be realistic, Gabs," Oberon said with a smug smile. Gabs glared at him. *Oh, Oberon*, I thought. *Unless your deepest desire is to be murdered by a beautiful woman you best stop talking.* But he did not. "We can admit it amongst ourselves at the very least. Book Binding has already changed the world. It was Book Binders who helped create the A-bomb. And what can cloth magic claim? It's merely superficial glamour concerned with humans' most base, bare interests."

"Cloth magic has the power to alter the world!" I insisted. "You just can't see it because of your total lack."

"Of what?" Oberon said.

"Of skill," I said. "If you were any good at cloth magic, you'd be singing a different tune."

Oberon's face turned red. "Like I said, that's not it. I'm just as good as anyone in this room."

It wasn't very nice of me, but I laughed. I wasn't alone in it either. Thomas and Gabs guffawed just as loudly, and even Ralph and Lamb hid smiles.

Oberon stood, his face growing vermilion under the thick rims of his glasses. I had quickly remembered how much I disliked Oberon, but only now did I remember how much he scared me. He was one of those large, looming men in whom violence always seemed a blink away. I never liked being around blokes like that. I feared that someday I'd be killed by one. I couldn't even defend myself.

I checked over my shoulder to make sure that Thomas had my back just in case Oberon did take a swing at me.

To give Oberon credit, he didn't. He took a deep breath and his hands relaxed at his sides.

"I just think it's a shame," he said slowly, with the kind of calculated precision intended to make deeply held beliefs sound like off-the-cuff remarks, "that you've all been sold a false hope. I know being a mage must sound so glamorous when you come from a humble background, but cloth magic isn't going to change the world or your status in life."

Now, he could have been using the general *you* for that last part, but for everyone in the room it felt pretty personal. All of us at one point had been told that magic was better left to the upper class. Even Lamb had been a miner's son before he had been a college professor.

Andrew stepped through the door holding a giant Victoria sponge cake. Twenty-three candles flickered as he came into the room. "All right, everyone, start singing!"

The room was silent. Andrew took in the grim faces. Hastily he blew out all the candles and set the cake down.

"What's going on here, chaps?"

"Oberon and I were just debating the merits of cloth magic." I took a deep breath and smiled. "But I've always been a believer in works as well as faith, action rather than words. What if we have a little bet where we prove who's the better cloth mage?"

Oberon tilted his head in interest, the red flush in his cheeks fading to a manageable pink. Oberon was always up for a bet. "What did you have in mind?"

"Well." I racked my brain. "Next week is the May Gala. I assume that, even after shitting on cloth magic as a profession, you're still going?"

The May Gala was something of a graduation party for the college's cloth mages. It was a chance to show off our skills and hopefully secure a patron or two. Usually, when cloth mages were graduating, they already had jobs lined up. Ralph, for example, was going to work for a glassworks factory, making magical uniforms for its workers to help keep them safe and improve their craftsmanship to make the finished product more impressive. Another job might be working for some aristocratic family as a personal tailor, making fantastic outfits for parties and other events. Theatre companies employed cloth mages as part of their special effects teams. The military often hired cloth mages as well. Or if your family had funds, you might open your own studio and work with individual clients. But aside from Ralph, no one in my class had any work lined up. Andrew would have to focus on his duties as the duke of Fife, Gabs was planning to marry her rich German princeling boyfriend, and Oberon just seemed like he couldn't be bothered.

As for Thomas and me, we had just had no luck finding work. I'd been in a bit of a funk over the last few months, nursing my broken heart, and Thomas really wasn't a people person. The gala was perhaps our last chance to make ourselves known in London magic circles. We'd been working on our outfits for weeks, scrounging up whatever cash we could for supplies.

"Oh, right," Ralph said. "You could see who makes the better outfit for the gala. That's a good basis for a wager."

"And who would be the judge?" Thomas asked.

"Well, I could—" Lamb started to say before Oberon cut him off.

"I'm not making an outfit for myself for the gala," Oberon said. "I'm sewing a magic dress for my date." He smiled proudly.

"Who's your date?" I asked, an idea forming.

"Verity Turnboldt of the *New Revolution*," Oberon said, with the smugness of someone looking for scandal.

"You're dating a gossip columnist?" Gabs said. I couldn't tell if she was aghast or impressed. "The gossip columnist at a socialist newspaper?"

"We're keeping our relationship quiet. Not many people know about it."

"Does she know about it?" Thomas asked.

"Yes!" Oberon said, flustered. "The gala will be our first public outing together. Her debut into society, in a sense. She's a very private person."

"Hmm," I said. "And you made her a magic dress, eh?"

"That's right," Oberon said, somewhat defensively.

"All right," I said, smiling. "How about this: I'll also make her a dress, and she'll choose the one she likes better and wear it to the gala."

"Wait, so my date will also be the judge?" Oberon said.

"That's right."

Oberon chuckled. "Don't you think that gives me a rather unfair advantage?"

"No, I think it evens the playing field," I said lightly. Mirth disappeared from Oberon's eyes and I knew I had him.

"And the stakes?" he asked.

I smiled wider. "How about an exorbitant amount of money?" I said. "Say, twenty pounds?"

Twenty pounds would be a month's rent for Thom and me, and considering that for the last few months our money had gone into making clothes rather than paying said rent, we could really use the cash. Even for Oberon it was nothing to sneeze at.

"That's very dear," Oberon said, mimicking my Liverpool accent.

"You're good for it," I replied.

"You're not."

He had us there. I personally wasn't that worried about putting up our half of the bet, as I had no doubt that I would win. But obviously Oberon was not going to accept that reasoning.

"He's not good for it, but I am." Lamb put a hand on my shoulder, making me jump. "I'll put up the money for Gallagher and Dawes's side of the wager. I can't let a challenge to my trade go unremarked."

I wanted to shrug off his grip but I pressed the urge down with a deep breath. When I glanced at Lamb he smiled serenely.

I glanced over at Thomas. Thomas shook his head. *No, that look* said. *This is a bad idea.* But despite his worried face, I felt oddly reassured. Yes, Thomas might think this was a bad idea, but if he thought it was a horrible, inimitable disaster, well, he would speak up rather than just shake his head.

"That's right!" I said, attention back to Oberon. "Professor Lamb will put up the funds on our account, so you don't have to worry about being shortchanged if we lose."

Oberon tapped his foot as he thought it over.

"All right, deal," Oberon said, stepping forwards, hand outstretched. "Break a bone, make a promise."

"Cast a spell that keeps you honest," I said, completing the old rhyme. In ancient times people wouldn't just say the words. If they were serious, they would break a small bone each to magically seal the deal. But that kind of innate magic had been seemingly obsolete for centuries now, with arcane spells reduced to children's rhymes. Instead we did the modern equivalent and shook on it.

As Oberon and I shook hands, I felt a twinge in my left index finger, a rush as I felt magic circulate through me like oxygen and dissipate.

We shook hands with great magnanimity: it was clear that each of us already considered himself the victor and saw the proceedings as a mere formality. Thomas huffed but likewise shook Oberon's hand. Thomas and I always worked together, so it went without saying that if you went up against one of us you'd get both of us.

The last thing we did was combine the funds in a spell in Lamb's Book, Lamb's twenty pounds together with Oberon's to become forty pounds. The amount appeared in the Book in a fancy script before disappearing like water in the sun, the spell still there but receding into the deep recesses of the Book, waiting for the time when some reader would call it forth.

"There. Are you done now?" Andrew asked sourly, hand on his hip as he frowned down at all the half-melted candles on his birthday cake. Oberon and I replied cheerfully that yes, we were quite done, both of us chipper now that hostilities had been scheduled for another day.

Only Andrew seemed put out. He started cutting up pieces of cake with a frown and a sigh, as if it were some great chore.

CHAPTER 2

When I was a tyke living in the suburbs of Liverpool I spent most of my days in the woods, alone. I was a quiet, shy child. I had two brothers, but they were much older and I didn't like their attention when they did acknowledge my existence. My mum and dad doted on me, but even Mum would eventually shoo me out of the house when she got tired of playing piano with me.

One summer morning when I was about six I decided to dare venture onto the high street. The high street was where all the rough kids hung out, the children too young to work on the docks but old enough to roam the streets in whooping, squabbling packs. These children, boys and girls alike, raided shops, grabbing toys and candy while cussing out the shopkeepers. They ran from the police, first as a pack and then separating at the optimal moment, high-pitched laughter still ringing in the air even after they had all disappeared from sight. These ruffians terrified me, and I wanted nothing more than to be one of them. I knew, however, that I could never blend in amongst them, that I would never be one more head of their juvenile hydra. My clean face and new clothes would mark me as an outsider, a child from a loving home. Yet sometimes, when I was feeling very brave, I would walk down their patch and pretend.

This day, as I walked down the street, I noticed a crowd of people. There was a female police officer directing traffic in the middle of an intersection, though thanks to her clothes she herself was causing a commotion: drivers slowed to take a gander at her and people stopped on the pavement to gawk. She was wearing a dark long-sleeved coat that had four long trains unfurling from it, so long they trailed across the street as if they were four paths leading up to her. These long trains were yellow, the same shade as the lines painted on the roads. The officer looked more than a mite uncomfortable from all the attention she was getting. Or maybe her discomfort came from the outfit itself; the fabric weighed her down so much that she couldn't easily move and was tethered to her space in the middle of the street. Cars would actually run over the trains as they drove through the intersection. It was hard to see what magical effect the outfit actually had, but after watching for ten minutes I could see that cars would stop when the officer held out a hand, often to the surprise of the cars' drivers. The cars would then not move until she gave them the go-ahead.

"I heard it's experimental," a man in the crowd said to his mate. "If it works well here, they'll roll it out across the country."

"Hmm," his friend said, staring harder at the officer, as if he, personally, had just been asked to make a call on whether to implement the program for the whole nation. Those uniforms never would become ubiquitous: the Second World War was on the horizon, and creating such an expensive outfit for every traffic warden was beyond the reach of the nation's coffers even before cloth became scarce.

I could have watched the scene all day, but I was jostled by a couple of kids pushing their way through the crowd to get to a side street. I wanted to see where the kids were running off to, so carefully I slipped past the adults to follow them.

I got free of the crowd just in time to see the two kids dart into an alleyway. I didn't want to lose them, so I picked up my feet and ran after them, turning the corner and—

—my feet flying out from under me as something rolled under my foot. I fell back straight onto my arse. I was lucky I hadn't bashed my brain in against the brick walls of the alley or the filthy macadam of the ground.

Scattered around me were the remnants of a marble game. Facing me was a group of urchins. I knew this gang. Of all the rough kids, they were the roughest, the ones with no real adults in their lives to answer to. Shop owners would cuff their ears and they'd take it as easily as water sliding off a leaf. They wore perpetually dirty clothes and clambered over the walls and spat in the gutters and when they spoke their words were as sharp and vulgar as those of grown-ups speaking outside a pub.

This gang had won my heart because its leader was the smallest yet fiercest little blighter I'd ever seen. When the other boys started getting too rough with each other he'd set them straight with a slap to the head or a harsh word. I didn't approve of violence as a way to settle things—God knows I hated it when my brothers put the hurt on me—but I admired how this kid managed to handle himself amidst a pack of bigger boys. I'd have given anything to be that little boy's friend, but I felt I'd have a better chance at communicating with the fish in the river than talking to *him*.

There he was now, staring at me in astonishment. He had dark, wavy hair, a pointed chin, and a mouthful of crooked milk teeth. His skin was pale brown but that wasn't unusual in Liverpool—the city had not only one of the country's oldest Black communities but also Europe's oldest Chinatown. Plus, sailors from all over the world regularly made berth here. Plenty of kids I knew at school and church were mixed race.

"Oy, what's wrong with you, you git?" he said. "You just ruined our marble game!"

"I, uh, sorry," I said, which was the wrong answer. I should have said something like *What of it?* or something else confrontational, but I was a meek and shy child back then.

"I had, like, fifty marbles riding on that game!" one of the boys cried. I counted the marbles scattered about me.

"Um, I doubt it. I mean, there's only ten marbles in play . . ."

"Don't get smart with us!" another boy yelled. "First you ruin our game, then you insult us? Fuck you!"

"I wasn't—"

"Give us your marbles!"

"Yeah, give us your marbles!"

"Right, you gotta make it up to us!"

"I don't have any marbles!" I cried. I looked to the leader. One of the reasons I admired him was that even though he was just as quick to scrap as the rest of the lot, he seemed a mite more measured about it. He had a very intelligent air about him, especially for a six-year-old.

The leader stood up and the gang went quiet.

"You, come with me," he said. I got to my feet, nearly tripping once again on the marbles still scattered on the ground. He put his hand on my shoulder as if we were old friends and walked me to the mouth of the alley.

"Don't look back at 'em," he said to me quietly, just when I was about to turn my neck to glance at the rest of the gang. I did what he said and kept my gaze fixed straight ahead. Once we turned the corner he relaxed. We kept walking, all the way to where the woods bordered our little suburb.

"You better not come around by that alley again." He didn't say it like a threat but as a calm statement of fact. "If I wasn't around, those bastards would have walloped you."

"Well, thanks for saving me," I said. I took it as a good sign—if this little boy had gone so far out of his way to help me, then maybe we were kindred spirits after all.

"I didn't do it for you," the boy said, and now there was a harsh edge to his words. "If my gang roughed up a little fancy kid like you, you'd run squealing off to your ma and pa and maybe even bring down the law on us."

"I would not!" I said, aghast to be accused preemptively of squealing.

"Oh?" He punched me in the nose. It wasn't a hard punch, more like a fast bop than a solid hit, but the suddenness made me double over and clutch at my face. When I was finally able to look at the boy he stared back, daring me to say something.

I ran crying into the woods.

I made my way to what had lately become my favourite tree. There were two crooks in it, one big enough for me to sit in, the other big enough for a little bird nest. I would often spend a good hour or more in that tree, staying perfectly still, eyes locked on the nest with its three eggs nestled inside. I thought that if I could catch a glimpse of the mother bird I might be able to figure out exactly what kind of eggs they were. Sitting in the tree seemed like a good idea after the excitement of the morning. I'd be safe up there.

I had been settled in the tree for twenty minutes when there was a sound in the woods. It was just the crunching of autumn leaves, but in the stillness it sounded like stones breaking. A woman staggered towards my tree, clutching her side as she moved, her feet shuffling noisily along the ground.

She looked old to me, but I don't trust my memory on this point—I was a child and all adults were "old." The woman had curly grey hair but a youthful, unlined face. She wore dowdy clothes that were several sizes too big for her, as if she had stolen them off a washing line. She had bunched up the excess cloth of her brown cardigan and pressed it against her side. Even from my perch I could see it darkening with blood.

I did not move or speak, even when she collapsed against my tree. She let out a shuddering breath as her head fall back against the tree trunk. Our eyes met.

She blinked at me for a couple of moments before a shaky smile stretched across her face. I already suspected that this mysterious stranger was a mage, and probably a foreign one at that. The newspapers were always talking about foreign mages and how dangerous they were.

"Hello, little one." She had an Irish accent, confirming my suspicions that she wasn't from around there. I didn't say anything.

"Won't you come down?" she said. "Come down so we can be friends?"

I gave a slight shake of my head, watching her as intently as I'd been watching the bird's nest a minute ago.

The mage stopped smiling and took on a studious expression as she stared at me, trying to figure out what combination of words would unlock my fixed spot in the tree.

In the end she didn't say anything. She jackknifed forwards, clutching at the wound in her side with a loud groan.

Up until then I had felt a mix of apprehension and curiosity, but now they both gave way to an overwhelming sense of shame. There was someone hurt right below me and I hadn't even offered to help her. I jumped down into the leaves, my springy child's limbs allowing me to gracefully land on my feet.

The woman straightened up. She seemed to be in a lot less pain than she had been mere seconds ago. I had been tricked, my own good intentions used against me.

"Good boy," she said. "Can you please help me? I need some bandages and some food."

"Can you do magic?" I asked the woman. Her smile reminded me of visiting a butcher's shop and seeing the sharp tools on the wall.

"Help me and I'll show you."

I straightened up and gave her a slight, serious nod. I was still wary, still curious, but now as I ran back through the woods I was excited too.

In my house I grabbed an apple and bandages from the medicine cabinet. I was awash with guilt as I gathered up my pilfered goods. I was breaking two commandments: *Thou shalt not steal* and *Honour thy father and mother.*

Then I thought of the strange woman, blood leaking out of her side, sitting alone in the woods. If it took breaking the rules to ease another's pain, I would do it again and again. Though I was curious about how she had gotten a wound like that.

I bundled the items in an old cloth and went back to the woods. The woman had taken the cardigan off and was using it to clean her wound. When she saw me she grabbed the apple and tore into it while still keeping one hand pressed into her side. Eventually the apple was a jagged core. She chucked it over her shoulder. I was aghast—in my family we ate apples whole so as to not waste food.

"Here, wrap me up," she said and lifted her shirt up so her stomach was exposed. I was startled by this sudden display of flesh. There was a large gash in her side, long but not deep. It took me a moment to realize that *I* was meant to apply the bandages. I unrolled the long pink bandage and wrapped it around the woman's midsection. She smelled of a familiar, damp scent, and I wondered if she had gone swimming in the Mersey.

When I had clipped the dressing in place she let her blouse fall back down. She felt along her midriff, hands tracing the bandages against her skin. She nodded approvingly at my handiwork.

"What is your name, little one?"

"Paul," I said, and I thought of asking her name but shyness held my tongue. I also suspected she wouldn't tell me.

She smiled.

"Now, Paul, what would you like in return?"

My mouth opened and closed as my brain stumbled over a response. I knew what I should say—that there was no need, that one didn't do a good deed in hope of a reward. But I couldn't quite get the words out.

"As you can probably guess, I don't have much to my name," the woman said with a false, high-pitched sadness. "No gems I can give, no coins to spare." This was before the war made Books a household item, so she probably would have given me an actual physical coin. "It makes me so sad that I have so little to give to such a kind lad."

She shot a look at me out of the corner of her eye and I realized she was going to make me ask for it.

"You said that you can do magic," I said, speaking slowly and with a bit of frustration.

"Did I?"

"Yes . . ." Wait, no she hadn't. I felt my cheeks burning as the woman laughed.

"I don't know how you were able to guess, but you're right: I am a mage and I can do magic. I said I would show you, didn't I?"

She sank to the ground, her skirt swirling out around her.

"Take a seat, Paul."

I sat cross-legged about five feet away from her. She shook her head, her curly grey hair sliding back and forth over her shoulders.

"Closer."

I scooted in, still ready to jump up and run if need be.

"What do you know about magic, Paul?"

"I know that there are magic Books," I told her. "Evil Books that make you do whatever's written in them."

She cocked her head to the side and I felt as though I had said something very foolish. All my life I'd heard of enchanted Books that controlled the reader or gave forbidden knowledge. In stories these Books always came from far-off lands such as India or China, where they were used by locals to play tricks on British soldiers and missionaries who had come to their shores. Nowadays everyone in Britain has a Book, but back then they still seemed like mystical tomes rather than handy appliances.

"Um, there are also magic clothes," I added in a bid to seem intelligent.

"And what would you like, Paul?" she said. "Do you want a coat that will let you walk through the air? Or a vest that will let you memorize all your lessons? Or a suit that will let you play any musical instrument? I may not be able to give it to you today, but I promise I will come back someday and repay you."

I was quiet, not out of shyness but because as I considered her question I was starting to sour on the whole idea. I had expected so much more from her.

"What's wrong?" she asked.

"Oh, well, it's just, those things all sound grand, really," I said, trying to be polite even as I struggled with my own dissatisfaction. "But they're all just . . . things. Even if they do something amazing, they can still be taken away from you and used by someone else, so what's the point?"

I had unknowingly hit upon a major source of discourse in the mage world, but my reasoning came from a far more mundane source than the ivory towers of Oxford. I was thinking about my brothers, huge bruisers who, even though they were far too old to play with toys, still delighted in breaking mine. If I had a magic outfit, they would destroy it for no other reason than the fact that I treasured it.

The mage's eyes lit up.

"Yes, yes," she said. "They are all just things. Books can be burned. Clothes can be torn apart. That kind of magic is . . . disposable. But luckily for you, in addition to being a cloth mage, I traffic in something more permanent."

Her tone had changed, lost some of its cloying sweetness. I felt like she was finally talking to me as if I were a human being. "What kind of magic?" I asked. As far as I knew there was only one kind of magic: people picked up items crafted by mages and used them to do miracles. What else could she possibly be talking about?

"True power," she said to me, lowering her voice, "is being able to do magic *directly*. Not through an item but by directly tapping into the magical energy we ourselves generate." She leaned back. "Innate magic. The purest, most powerful magic known to mankind, and now largely lost to us. In your country, Paul, only one man may practise it—"

"George Redfield, the Court Magician!" I said excitedly. His picture hung under the king's in every civic building in the country: bespectacled but kind. During maths I would sketch him. The man might have been my first childhood crush, but I think it was more like I wanted to be him, the man a whole country loved and admired.

Her mouth twisted downwards. "Yes, that's his name."

"You don't like him?" I had never met anyone who didn't speak of Redfield in glowing terms—he was often on the wireless, speaking in calm, measured tones as he explained magic to the laypeople of England.

"It's not him I hate. I hate the idea that only one person, working directly in service to the Crown, is allowed to wield that power." Her voice had gotten more passionate as she spoke. She stopped, and when she spoke again her voice was the same calm, cloying tone it had been before. "Your government, they say innate magic is illegal, that it is dangerous. They are idiots." She looked towards me. "I can give you magic—I can *make* you magic. But it's illegal under British law. If we do this, you can never speak of our meeting, you understand?"

I thought it over. Breaking the law sounded serious, but then I consoled myself that just because I was breaking man's law it didn't mean I was breaking God's law, so perhaps it wasn't so bad.

I nodded. She scooted forwards and stared deep into my eyes.

"What do you want from this world, Paul? What do you desire? Is there anything you'd like to change about your life? Anything you'd like to change about yourself?"

It was a big question to ask a six-year-old.

"I don't like it when my brothers hit me," I said. She nodded. She reached out and felt my upper arm, squeezing and getting a feel for the bone under the skin. When she spoke, it was with a somewhat distant air, like how a doctor speaks to you while they're peering down your throat.

29

"Would you like to become stronger? So strong your brothers would scurry away like mice when they saw your shadow?"

It wasn't wholly unappealing but I shook my head.

"I often wish I knew what the birds are saying."

She nodded again. Her hand stopped gripping my arm and started to feel my jaw.

"I could make it so you'd understand every feathered fowl on God's earth. I could even make it so you could speak to them in return."

This was very tempting. My time spent alone in the forest wouldn't be so lonely anymore, once I could hear and understand the crows and wrens and starlings. But I still felt like I was skirting around the real issue, that I hadn't yet hit upon my true desire. I thought of the gangs of rough kids. Of their leader, the tough little boy who'd bopped my nose. He had acted as though he wanted absolutely nothing to do with me.

"What I'd really like," I said, eyes on the forest floor, "is to have more friends."

"More" friends. As if I had so many friends already and were just looking to boost my numbers a bit. As if my sixth birthday celebration hadn't consisted of my mum and me playing party games designed for a half-dozen children.

But if the mage saw through my words she didn't comment on it. Her hand left my face. She picked up my left hand and held it with both her hands.

"Is that what you want, Paul?"

"Yeah," I said, still not able to meet her eyes. When I eventually did so she was smiling, a close-lipped, gentle smile.

"From now on, everyone you meet will want to be your friend."

Then she took the index finger on my left hand and broke it.

I screamed. Above us the birds alighted from the trees and took off, startled away by the sound of my voice. Both my shock and pain were doubled when the mage broke *another* joint on my finger.

It hurt like nothing else, but beyond the pain was a strange discomfort. It was like a container inside of me had broken and some other liquid besides blood was running through me. My skin didn't feel big enough for whatever was flooding through my body.

I flailed about on the ground and it felt like the ocean was sloshing around within me. Eventually it all became too much and I turned on my side and vomited.

The mage stayed with me until I calmed down, even doing a very basic splint on my finger. She didn't do a great job of it—to this day there's a noticeable crook in my left index finger. The nausea soon dissipated but I still felt hot and feverish, an edge of pain making me feel more awake than I'd ever been in my life. Eventually the pain became less sharp and my mind grew fuzzy. Through the haze I could hear the mage singing to me lightly in Gaelic and rubbing my back—I don't think this was part of the spell; I think she was just trying to comfort me.

When I was lucid again it was midafternoon and the mage was gone. The birds had recovered from their shock and were once more perched in the trees.

I went home once again, this time to grab my marble collection.

The gang was still in the alleyway, a new marble game going on. When the little leader saw me he gave a huff of exasperation, as if I was causing so much trouble for him by showing my face again.

"Hey, it's that git from before!" one of the other kids yelled.

"The git has a name," I said. "I'm Paul Gallagher."

I held out my hand to the closest child, a moppet with auburn curls. She seemed confused but shook my hand. As she did I felt magic move through me, up from my left hand and over my shoulders, like a squirrel scampering over a branch. It flowed through my right arm and gave a little spark where my palm met hers. She seemed to startle at it but when she drew her hand back she looked at me with wonder.

The other kids had grown quiet. Even if they hadn't felt it directly, they seemed to sense that some kind of magic was in the air.

"I brought my marbles," I said, holding up my bag. I spoke casually, as if the marbles were no more to me than a piece of pocket lint. "You can have them, but could you let me keep three? That way I'll have a chance to win my other marbles back."

The lot seemed taken aback by my proposition, or maybe just by how smoothly I delivered it. They looked at me askew, as if unsure if I was the same child from a few hours ago. In the end they were actually quite happy to let me take part in their game. They were rough sorts, sure, but they were still kids. Most young children are happy to have one more friend to play with.

Using my three marbles I managed to win back all my others, then made a small showing of winning the others' marbles. I did well enough to win the other tykes' respect, then just as skilfully (if not more so because I had to be subtle about it) lost enough so they each won their marbles back. By the end of the game I had become a member of their little crew, nestled in close amongst them as if I'd been there the whole time.

The only one I was still nervous about was the leader. He had played a few rounds but for the most part he'd hung back, watching us with those sharp dark eyes of his. After the game ended and the others started running off to scrounge up dinner, he sidled up to me.

"Nice play," he said. "What happened to your hand?"

"Oh?" I looked at the splint on my left index finger. Usually I would have favoured my left for playing a game like marbles, but luckily I was ambidextrous. "I hurt it playing in the woods."

"Oh." The kid kicked at the ground. I was crouched down, putting my marbles into their bag. I wondered why this kid was still standing around when the others had left. Was he going to demand my marbles? Tell me to fuck off and not come near his patch again? Why was he just hanging around, scuffing up his already ragtag shoes?

No. The witch had said that everyone I met would want to be my friend. In that moment I didn't care so much about "everyone." I just cared about winning over this kid.

I stood up, offered my right hand. "My name's Paul. Paul Gallagher."

The kid seemed relieved, as if he'd been waiting for me to make the first move. "Thomas Dawes."

We shook hands, an oddly formal rite for two children to enact, but it seemed right in the moment. Once more I felt the innate magic within me unfurl, moving up through the centre of my being and into the other person, connecting us. It was like a pins-and-needles sensation, but pleasant. Thomas seemed to feel it too, though perhaps not on such a conscious level. I saw him smile for the first time, showing off his wonky grin before ducking his head shyly.

"Hey, my mum should be making supper soon," I said. "Why don't you come eat with us?"

I could see the *no* forming in his brain and making it all the way to his eyes and lips before he paused. His hand was still in mine. He shrugged and tucked his hands in his pockets.

"Yeah, sure."

I didn't know much about magic, but in that moment I knew the mage was true to her word. I was different, no longer the shy child who hid in the woods but an outgoing, charming young man. My parents were very happy that I had finally brought home a friend and I laughed and chattered more at dinner than I had in weeks. But lying in bed that night, I stared up into the darkness. How much of me had the mage changed? What exactly had been done to me?

∼

"What the hell are you thinking?" Thomas asked, stalking back and forth in the McDougals' garden. "Why do you always have to call down more trouble?"

Shortly after having some cake Thomas had pulled me outside so that he could tell me in private what an idiot I'd been. He had a lit cigarette in hand but in his irritation he had seemingly forgotten all about it, its ashy glow going this way and that as he gestured. I stayed quiet, letting him get it all out. At the edge of the McDougals' garden some indigo and purple pansies were in bloom.

"Ever think about wearing something other than black or grey?" I said. "You'd look aces in that shade of blue."

"What?" Thomas said, stopping in midstride. I plucked a flower from the ground and held it against Thomas's grey shirt.

"See?" I took in a deep breath, filling my lungs with the scent of wet soil. Spring was my favourite season: Easter, pastels, birdsong, the moment you realized winter was over. It had rained early in the morning and there was still that pleasant, clean dampness in the air, a much more palatable scent than the usual London smog.

Thomas knocked my hand away and the flower fell back to the earth.

"You can't just pick fights at the drop of a hat."

I thought it was a bit much for Thomas to be lecturing me on acting rashly. This was a man who regularly threw the first punch in a pub brawl, if only to maintain the element of surprise.

"Come on," I said incredulously. "You're yowling over nothing, mate. Lamb's the one putting up the cash."

"And if we lose?" Thomas pressed. "We already owe McCormick money—you want Lamb after us too? Do you think Lamb's just going to write off that twenty pounds?"

I put my hands in my pockets and rocked on my feet, trying to pass off my sudden shiver as bouncy nonchalance.

"No, I imagine he'd make us pay very dearly for it." I smiled at Thomas. "Or at least make *me* pay for it." I could picture it: Dinner with Lamb at some posh but private place, having to laugh at his jokes and agree with snide jabs about mutual friends always delivered with a serene but sharp smile: *Be grateful I'm talking about them and not about you.* All the while he'd watch me, waiting for me to break down and beg him to tell me why he'd dumped me. Had I clung too much? Not enough? Had he simply grown bored of me? "He'd probably let you off the hook."

"Swell," Thomas muttered, gaze dropping to the ground as he finally took a drag on his cigarette.

"You know, it's funny," I said, keeping my voice breezy. "A few months ago, I would have done just about anything to have him look my way again. And now that I want nothing to do with him, he's the one angling for me." I shrugged. Lamb flattered himself too much. Yeah, it had been a hard few months after he'd kicked me to the kerb, but it wasn't as though he were the first person I'd ever slept with. Heck, he wasn't even the first guy I'd ever slept with. If anything, I felt guilty for messing up Thomas's prospects. Because things had been strained between me and Lamb over the last few months, I hadn't gone to him for help finding work. As our prof he had a duty to help us, but the last thing I wanted was help from the man who'd dumped me.

Thomas clearly did not buy my indifference.

"Talking to you is like pounding on glass. Nothing gets through to you." His shoulders slumped and he hugged his elbows, letting out a hissed sigh. Poor mite. Even when we were kids he had always thought too much. To people who didn't know him well he often seemed short tempered, but when he lashed out his movements were born of strategy rather than panic. Even now his brain was going a mile a minute as he tried to calculate every bad possibility.

I patted his shoulder. "Thomas, don't worry!"

"Where are we going to get the fabric for this?" Thomas asked, gaze boring into me. "I've got some black jersey, but that's nothing compared to what Oberon's probably got."

"I've got some beige linen."

"Oh, beige linen. All our problems are solved then," Thomas replied with false cheerfulness. I placed both hands on his shoulders.

"Thomas," I said. "Don't you have a little voice inside your head that tells you, *Don't worry. Everything will turn out all right?*"

"No!" Thomas threw my hands off him so he could throw his own hands up in the air. "No, I don't!"

I sighed, stepped back. "What's the worst that can happen?"

"We go back to Liverpool," Thomas answered quickly and grimly, as if he had thought about this before.

"All right. Let's think about that. Let's imagine the worst, that we blow this and it's back to Liverpool," I said. "I'll start working in my father's music shop again. My brothers will put in a good word for you at the shipping company and get you a job down at the docks. Eventually my dad will retire and I'll take over as manager; meanwhile, the company men will see that you're not a half-bad Book Binder and so they hire you on as an office clerk. But you never forget the brotherhood of the docks, and on your own time and against company policy you start organizing the dockworkers into a union. I, meanwhile, have expanded my father's one measly shop into an empire, opening stores in Manchester, Cardiff, and eventually London. I grow restless, go into local politics. I have grown out of touch with the common people, campaign on an antiunion platform. You step down as union leader so you can run against me on a socialist agenda. We tear the city apart and ruin our friendship with slander and lies. A dark horse candidate wins instead of either of us. We never reconcile. We die lonely, broken men. All because we lost this one bet."

Thomas ducked his head to hide his smile. When he looked back he managed to seem serious once more.

"You remember Maggie Sullivan?" he asked. She was a cute girl who lived down the street from my parents' house. Thomas had always fancied her. "In this little scenario of yours," he said, "which one of us marries her?"

"Oh, I do, of course."

Thomas laughed.

"Well, that's not on," he said. "I guess we have to win this bet after all."

Thomas went back inside, passing me his half-smoked cigarette on his way. I wanted to take a few more moments to enjoy the garden. As I was standing there, taking in the warmth of the sun and the clean air, I heard a small cough, the kind of cough you made only when you wanted to alert someone else to your presence. Standing in the space between the house and a hedge was Tonya, the maid from before. She had a cigarette in her hand but had yet to light it. When Thomas and I had come out in the back garden she must have ducked back there to avoid being seen.

"Enjoying yourself?" I felt a little embarrassed that she had heard me talking so plainly about Lamb, but I doubted she'd run off and tell the authorities.

"Sorry." She likewise seemed abashed. "I didn't mean to listen in."

I waved it off. "No worries. It was just a lot of nonsense."

She stepped forwards and I offered her a light.

"I also heard about the bet you made with Mr Myers," she said, letting her cigarette catch fire. "Master Andrew told me."

"Mr Myers?" I said. "Oh, right, Oberon. Yes, just a bit of fun between friends."

"A twenty-pound bit of fun," Tonya said with an edge. Obviously, as far as she was concerned, anyone willing to gamble with that amount of money was just asking for trouble. I had thought she was cute before, but now that she was looking at me as though I was a proper idiot I was really falling for her.

"Don't worry. I know what I'm doing," I said.

"You're that sure you can make a better dress than Mr Myers?"

"Oh, no," I said. "For all his faults, Oberon's still a trained cloth mage at the end of the day and he's got a bigger war chest to draw from.

Whatever Thomas and I make is going to be downright plain next to whatever Oberon's cooked up."

Tonya blinked at me. "Then how can you win?"

"Because it's not about making a better dress; it's about making a dress that Verity Turnboldt prefers," I said. "Some mages get so wrapped up in making magic clothes they forget that we make magic clothes for *people*. That's the key. We'll just appeal to the judge's tastes."

"Do you even know this Verity Turnboldt character?" Tonya asked.

"No."

"And Oberon does."

"Apparently."

Tonya's crooked, incredulous smile implied that she didn't think I had much of a chance at all.

"I wish I could help you," she said, her tone of voice suggesting that we needed all the help we could get. "I owe you one for saving my arse back in the foyer."

"Forget about the foyer," I said. "Let's consider this our first meeting."

Tonya looked at me, still smiling but with a quick, reassessing quality to her gaze, as if seeing me in a new light. It must have been a favourable one because she eventually held out her hand.

"Tonya Gower," she said.

"Pleasure to meet you." As I shook her right hand I could feel a wave of magic pulse out from the break in my left index finger. *Everyone you meet will want to be your friend.* It was that act of introducing myself that put the spell upon the other person, that made them like me—no matter the situation. It only truly held for the first meeting, though. After that I was on my own.

I thought it was tied into introductions being an act of vulnerability. We made ourselves defenceless, unarmed, when we offered up our own name, put ourselves in the other person's power until they chose to meet us likewise.

That was just a theory of mine, cobbled together from reading every book I could about magic and from my own firsthand experience. But gathering info was slow going. The only one in Great Britain who truly knew anything about innate magic was the Court Magician. Only he (and it was always a he) was entrusted with the knowledge of how to practise innate magic. For every other citizen of the British Empire, this branch of magic was forbidden. It was too dangerous. Too often it killed the person it was being practised upon, or if they survived, it inflicted some curse upon them to go hand in hand with their new magical power.

I could speak from experience. The wonderful spell upon me had a rather considerable drawback: I was unable to commit an act of physical violence against another person. Even if my life was threatened, even if I would merely be acting out of self-defence, I was unable to act on it. I'd noticed it when my brothers had come home while on leave from the navy. When they'd gone to clip me around the head I couldn't bat their hands away. My limbs had stayed locked at my sides, like something else was controlling my movements. And then later on when Thomas and I would get into scraps, I couldn't throw kicks and punches at the other kids. I'd just freeze on the spot, leaving Thomas to have to do all the brawling. I didn't know if this was an accidental side effect of the innate magic cast upon me or something the mysterious woman in the woods had done on *purpose*. But why would she do that to some random child whom she'd just met? Who'd gone out of his way to help her?

Aside from the whole not being able to defend myself, sometimes I wondered what else the spell had changed about me. My desire to know people, to please them, did that tie into it too? All I wanted was to control my magic. I didn't like the idea that it was somehow controlling *me*. If I were Court Magician, perhaps I'd finally be able to suss things out.

Tonya blinked and looked away shyly.

"I might be able to help you out with your bet," she said. "I can put in a good word for you with Verity Turnboldt."

"What?" I spun towards her so quickly I dropped my cigarette. "You know her?"

Tonya grinned. "Sure. A gossip columnist needs sources all over the place, even in the servants' quarters."

"Oh." Oh shit. Andrew's newest maid was spilling secrets to a reporter for the city's leading socialist rag. I don't know who I was more afraid for: Andrew, living unknowingly with this snake in the grass, or Tonya, playing traitor while in the employ of the most powerful psychic in the country.

Tonya chuckled. "Don't worry, Lady Fife won't find me out. She thinks I'm slower than cold molasses. And I'd never rat out Master Andrew. He's the only one who's been any nice to me."

"Ah," I said, not wholly reassured. "Just . . . be careful." I picked up my cigarette. "So can you give me Verity's number?"

Tonya shook her head. "Nah, that'd be a betrayal of confidence, wouldn't it? Give me your number and I'll pass it along."

"Oh, well, there's a little bit of a trick to it," I said. "Do you know how to use the Asher Exchange?"

The Asher Exchange was a service offered by a small cabal of telephone operators. These "Hello Girls" had been given basic Book Binding training, and thanks to that they had figured out a way to anonymize the calls coming and going. Rather than tell their bosses about this innovation, they offered it as an off-the-books service to paying subscribers. If you didn't go through the Asher Exchange, the only way to get in touch with someone was to give the telephone operator their address. This was fine for most folks but when you were often ducking creditors the last thing you wanted was to be handing out your home address to people. The Asher Exchange wasn't cheap but it was one bill that Thomas and I never skipped out on.

"Of course I know about the Asher Exchange," Tonya said. "What's your code?"

"I'll write it down for you before I leave," I said. "Thanks."

"Like I said, I owe you," she said, smiling at me. The sun caught her face as she turned towards me, her skin glowing like a flower petal, strong and luminescent. She really was pretty, the warmth of her brown eyes contrasting with the coy quirk of her mouth. I could hardly believe that this was the same scared girl from an hour ago.

"Hey, are you doing anything this Wednesday?" I said. "There's a club I know that plays American rhythm and blues. You want to go dancing?"

She frowned. "I work Wednesday nights."

"Ah, right." Maids didn't get a ton of time off.

She winked at me. "But I'm really good at sneaking out."

"Oh," I said, pleased but also a little concerned. I decided to focus on the more positive emotion. "Aces! You know the big dance hall in Seven Sisters? Let's meet there at eight."

"All right," she said with a smile.

The door behind us swung open.

"Oh, Gally, there you are," Andrew said. Tonya stepped away, the hand with the cigarette dropping to her side.

Andrew came to stand with us. "I hope you haven't been leaving cigarette butts in my mother's garden, Gally," he said with no real ire.

"Of course not."

"As for you, Tonya," Andrew said, "shouldn't you be inside helping Delores?"

Tonya nodded, eyes still down.

"Of course, sir. I'll get right back to work, sir." She took a deep breath. "I just stepped outside for some air."

Andrew smiled. "Don't worry, I won't say anything to Mother. If it comes up we'll just blame Mr Gallagher here."

"Oh, thanks," I said. Tonya gulped nervously and hurried inside.

Andrew watched her go with a quizzical expression.

"Strange girl," he said. "She's new and still finding her feet, poor thing."

"Where'd you find her?" I asked.

"Oh, same old story. Someone referred her through one of Mother's charities," Andrew said. "I don't think she's getting on with the other servants. I hate having anyone in my house bullied, but I don't know what I can do for her from my side of things."

I felt a little bit guilty since I had just convinced her to shirk work and go dancing with me. I doubted that would make her any more popular with her coworkers.

"Tonya will be all right," I said. "She's tougher than she looks."

Andrew gave me a wry glance. "I didn't realize you two were so close." His smile dropped and he sighed. "I wanted to apologize, old chap. It was a wrong turn of me, inviting Lamb. I just assumed that enough time had passed that . . ."

"Don't worry your head about it. You're right," I said quickly. "I'm older and wiser now; I can't let his presence ruin happy occasions." Now it was my turn to sigh. "Really, I should apologize to you. I'm the one getting into spats on your birthday."

"Well, Oberon can be a bit much sometimes." Andrew and Oberon went way back—they'd even roomed together at Eton. But it had always seemed like a friendship born of forced circumstances rather than mutual like.

"I suppose you're also going to ask how I plan to win this stupid bet," I said.

"No," Andrew said, smiling. "I have faith in you."

I looked at him, feeling as guilty as ever. I almost preferred Thomas's and Tonya's scepticism. Sceptics made me fight harder. True believers like Andrew made me doubt myself.

"Thanks, mate," I mumbled.

CHAPTER 3

Once the other party guests had gone home, Thomas and I convinced Andrew to come out with us for a few rounds. A few rounds became many, and when Thomas and I said our God-be-with-yous to Andrew we were properly bladdered. There were no Book inspectors at the entrance to the tube station, which was lucky as we had no money to pay for the journey. Like a couple of drunk octopuses we went down the stairs and onto an empty Piccadilly train.

"Jesus, I can't wait for the May Gala," I said. "Oberon's going to have to eat his own words."

"I have a question," Thomas asked, a slur to his speech and a drunken slant to his body. The ravens appearing and dissipating around him were agitated—they hated being inside and they double hated the small confines of a tube car. "Let's say we do win this bet. What happens next?"

"Well, we take Oberon's money, we give some of it to Mrs Dylag for rent, we buy some new fabric—"

"No, not that next, I mean the bigger next," Thomas said, almost falling on me as the train pulled away from the platform. "What about after that? We can't get by on bets and scams forever."

"Ah, funny you should say that, as I do have a bigger plan. Listen to this, Thom-Daw—"

The air in front of us flickered, bits of light zipping past like the view of the tube tunnel outside the carriage window. Magic. It made both Thomas and me sober up right quick. The distortion grew more frequent and voluminous until it solidified into the shape of a person. There was one final flash of light and then a man was standing in front of us. He was in his midtwenties and wore a long grey coat that was stained with the soot and dirt of the tube tunnels.

"Evening. May I see your Books, please—" He stopped. "Oh. It's you two."

"Hullo, Edgar!" I said. "How goes it?"

Edgar sighed a sigh so deep it kicked up dust through the whole carriage car. Edgar was one of the hundred or so beleaguered and often-abused Book inspectors who worked on the London tube. Their job was to make sure the riders recorded the journeys in their Books.

Each Londoner had a Book, a slim fifty-page hardcover item that fit comfortably in a purse or coat pocket. Amongst its many uses was that it worked as a Londoner's travel card on the tube or bus. With buses you had to do the spell where you imagined your journey—the Book would then figure out how much such a ticket would cost and transfer that amount from one section to another. You showed the bus driver that you had done the proper spellwork in your Book before they'd let you on.

But with the tube it was different. There were so many stations and so many people passing through them—it would be impossible to have someone checking every single Book. So instead, the tube ran on the honour system. The expectation was that everyone (1) had a Book, (2) had loaded the proper funds onto it, and (3) was faithfully recording their journey.

But not everyone did. Thomas and I, for example, never transferred the appropriate funds when we used the tube. And I did not feel a whit of guilt about it. We ate soup made of boiled vegetable peels and chicken bones. We lined our blankets and stuffed our coats with old newspaper in the winter. We scooped half-smoked cigarettes off the pavement and snacked on bread heels tossed into the rubbish heap. You wouldn't look at me, young lad that I was with the nice hair, cheerful smile, and shiny magic coat, and think I was skint, but I was.

To catch people like me and Thom, the metro employed people like Edgar. An inspector's lot was to go from carriage to carriage and ask to see each person's Book and make sure the journey was recorded. Generally, Brits are a rule-following lot, so most people did and proudly showed off their spellwork like a child showing off their letters, but inspectors still had to take a lot of guff from ruffians and troublemakers.

"I really should check your Books to make sure you recorded your trip," Edgar said with weary trepidation.

"I'll save you the trouble: we haven't." I scooted over and patted the seat between Thomas and me. "Take a load off and chat with us."

Edgar sighed once more but sat down.

"You know, there's a poster about you in the King's Cross head-quarters," Edgar said to me. "A sketched portrait of your face, with a warning underneath telling all the Book inspectors of London not to give you any more free rides. When the city finally decides to do away with the honour system, it's going to be all your fault, Paul Gallagher."

I laughed. "When I am a rich and famous mage, I promise to pay back all the fare I've skipped out on."

Edgar gave a sceptical grunt.

"Listen, Edgar, I was just about to tell Thomas here my plan," I said. "Word is that Court Magician Redfield is compiling a list of candidates to succeed him, right? Any day now he'll have to find a successor. Why not me?"

Two very different reactions from the men next to me: Edgar gave me a look of utter disbelief, like anyone would have to be crazy to consider such a thing ever coming to pass. Thomas, meanwhile, just seemed fearful.

"You, Court Magician?" Edgar asked.

"Yes. I'm a mage. Thomas and I made that coat of yours, didn't we?" It was a third-year assignment, the aim of it to make a teleportation cloak. Teleportation is a tricky bit of magic as no one has ever created an item of clothing that grants "true" teleportation, a.k.a. the ability to go wherever you wish whenever you want. Instead each teleportation cloak needs specific parameters. The cloak Thomas and I had made for Edgar could only transport the wearer from one moving train car to another, and only to ones that had people inside. Very rigid specifications, but handy for a Book inspector.

"That's right; you did make it. And you've been squeezing free rides out of me ever since," Edgar said. He must have heard the innuendo of his own words, because a second later he blushed. It was cute. The first time we had met and he had asked to see my Book, I'd offered to buy him a drink instead. I'd stayed over at his place a few more times since then, but if he wanted to pretend that wasn't why he gave me a free pass on the tube, I'd let him have that. "Not just any mage can be Court Magician."

"Oh?" I said. "Tell me, if you're the expert then. What does it take?"

"It takes an old name, with old money," Thomas cut in. "The Court Magician has always been some bloke from the upper crust, some sacrificial third or fourth son who survives the Making by random luck."

Sacrificial was an apt word—most of the candidates for Court Magician died. Becoming the Court Magician required undergoing a magic ritual that involved innate magic. Disrupting the flow of magic in the human body was always fraught, and when you were doing something as transformative as making someone into a mage maker, well, it rarely worked. That was why there was always such a long list of candidates for Court Magician—usually at least a dozen died before the magic finally took hold with one of them.

"Well, I'm a third son, and I'm very lucky, so I tick those boxes at least," I said. "*And* I'm a damn good mage, so why not me?"

"Aren't you afraid of dying?" Edgar asked.

I shrugged, trying to seem nonchalant. "Who isn't?" Of course I was worried. I was a good Christian boy, but even with a belief in the life eternal, the soul is still always at war with one's base survival instincts. But it didn't seem outlandish to imagine that I'd beat the odds and become the next Court Magician. All my life I'd ended up in places where people never expected to see me, achieved things people would never expect from a humble Liverpool lad.

In the future it would be my portrait hanging up in schools around the country. I would be the mage maker, the font of all magic in Great Britain. I would be the one who would take the hands of young mages in training, speak with them gently, and tell them of their responsibilities before breaking their bones and making them mages.

I had a spell upon me that made everyone who met me like me, but as an adult I had found it wasn't enough. If I were the Court Magician, everyone would know and love me by default.

"It's a barbaric system," Thomas said. "Imagine killing dozens of mages just to get one mage maker."

"If we don't have a mage maker, we don't have mages." Anyone in the world could do magic: all they had to do was interact with a magical item, such as a Book or outfit. But only *mages* could make those magic items. To be a mage a person's body needed to be augmented, the magical energy flowing within them redirected. This was done through innate magic, by breaking certain bones in the body.

But the bone couldn't be broken by just anyone. It had to be done by a mage maker, someone whose body had been augmented in a way that allowed them to create more mages. In Britain that right was reserved solely for the Court Magician, who learned from the previous Court Magician the ways of innate magic. It was a very dangerous practice and even the Court Magician, for all his power, was not infallible.

The tube pulled up to the Turnpike Lane platform. Thomas and I got to our feet. The buzz from earlier was already wearing off. "Well, hope you have a quiet night, Edgar."

Edgar stepped onto the platform with us and took hold of my elbow. "Put some money on your Book, will you? The next inspector you run into may not be as forgiving as me."

I gave him a pitiful look. "I wish I could, mate, but money's been so tight lately . . ."

Edgar rubbed his temples. "Give me your Book."

I handed it over, somewhat curious to see if he was actually going to slap a citation spell in it. A spell like that would render my Book worthless, making it so I was unable to buy anything until I paid a fine and the citation was lifted. But Edgar did not fine me. Instead he took out his own Book, did a spell to remove some money from it, and then deposited that in my Book.

"There. Put some of that towards your next tube ride."

I took my Book back, squeezing Edgar on the shoulder. "Thank you, Edgar. Every time we bump into each other, I take it as a sign that someone upstairs is truly watching out for me."

Thomas was waiting by the exit. I hurried over to him while Edgar turned around to go back to the platform to wait for the next train. I put my arm around Thomas's shoulders.

"Good news, mate," I said, holding my Book aloft. "I'm treating us to another round."

~

We staggered home from the local pub, leaning against each other for support. The Harringay Ladder, or just "the Ladder," is called so because it's a collection of roughly twenty residential streets laid out neatly one after another, framed by two long perpendicular streets on either side, making the whole thing resemble a ladder when you see it from high above. Such a thing might not seem noteworthy, but if you look at a map of London you'll see that the roads all curl this way and that, like a heap of wood shavings on the floor. Amidst such disorder the Ladder does in fact stand out.

As we walked our shoulders glanced off the walls of the Harringay Passage. The Passage was a long alleyway that cut through our neighbourhood, a kind of urban footpath that went down through the middle of the ladder. It was mainly used by people as a place to toss their rubbish, or as a shortcut by locals who didn't mind the smell. Defunct Victorian stink pipes towered overhead every few yards.

". . . And once they make us Court Magician, then everyone will be like, *Fuck Books, it's all about magic clothes,*" I rambled. There was slight dampness in the air and if I focused I could just smell the moss on the stone walls and ignore the stench of the rubbish around us.

I tried to imagine what it'd be like serving King Harold. He ruled the nation like a distant father, always stern and stiff in his radio speeches. The upper class liked him—my theory was that he reminded them of their own dads, in that they only ever saw him at formal events. The public at large, however, was more enamoured with Queen Andriette, a Danish princess who had won the British over with her warmth. They also liked to read about the antics of Crown Prince Arthur and his wild parties. There was also little Princess Katherine, but the young teenager stayed out of the limelight. They would be an odd family to serve, but all families were odd in their own way. The Court Magician's main function, besides making more mages, was serving and protecting the royal family. I'd always been pretty good at dealing with people, and at the end of the day even royals were just people.

"Usually it's a post held by just one person," Thomas said. "Enough people die in the Making just getting one new Court Magician. They're not eager to push their luck to get two."

"But we'd have to do it together." I stepped in something wet and put a hand on the stone wall to keep myself upright. "Even if you don't go through with the Making, you'd have to help me. I couldn't do it without you. I mean, you're the brains *and* brawn of the operation."

"Oh yeah? And what does that leave you?"

"Plenty," I said. We stepped out under the glow of a streetlamp. "Nerves." I flexed my hands. "Vision." I touched my temple.

Thomas actually looked impressed for a millisecond before I wobbled. He stepped forwards to grab me.

"Whoa there, Galileo. We're still a long ways off from having tea with King Harold," Thomas said, still supporting me. "And you don't have to be Court Magician. We'll be fine. We'll get some work eventually. Don't you have a little voice in your head . . ." He faltered, whether because he was drunk or from something else, I didn't know.

"I don't want you to regret this life," I said to Thomas, holding on to him tight partly to show him how serious I was, and also because the ground felt like it was slipping under my feet like a loose rug. "I love you. You're my little brother. I don't want you to be unhappy because of me."

"Paul, shut up," Thomas said. "I'm only ever happy because of you."

"Jesus." I stood up straight, standing still so I could seriously look at Thomas. "That's gotta be one of the nicest things you've ever said to me. Just how drunk are you?"

Thomas stepped away and shrugged. "Not so drunk that I can't do this." He sprinted across the road towards where a Ford Pop was parked by the kerb. He jumped up and managed to slide across the bonnet. I think Thomas's plan was to jump off and stand up on the other side but instead he landed with an *oof!* on the pavement.

"Thomas?" I made a wavering line over to where he was lying on the ground, cursing as he pushed himself up.

"I'm all right."

"C'mon, you idiot." I offered him a hand and together we made our way up the street, giggling.

We shushed each other as we approached the house. When Thomas opened the door we pitched forwards, causing it to slam into the wall. We shushed the door.

It took us a second to realize there was a sound coming from within the house. The phone in the upstairs hallway was ringing.

I went up the stairs, pulling myself up the banister like a sailor pulling on a rope. Thank goodness our live-in landlady, Mrs Dylag, was away visiting a sick cousin—the ringing phone would have surely woken her otherwise. I lifted the receiver, cutting it short midring.

"Hello?" I said in my best "serious, sober young man" voice.

"Hi. I'm looking for a guy named Paul Gallagher. Do I have the right number?" The words came one after another like the clickety-clack of a train car. It was an American woman's voice. I knew from films that American accents had a north-south distinction: tilt the dial downwards and you got a southern drawl; dial it upwards and you got the clipped Yankee cadence.

"Ding ding ding!" I said as if she had just won a round on a quiz show, then remembered that I was supposed to be pretending that I wasn't actually totally pissed. I straightened up, the action making me dizzy. "Yes, that's me. And to whom am I speaking . . . to?"

"Verity Turnboldt."

I turned away from the phone so I could shout down the stairs to Thomas. "Thomas, that reporter from the *New Rev* is on the phone and she's American!"

"What the fuck!" Thomas said, alcohol doing away with his usual stoicism.

I realized that I hadn't actually covered the receiver and she had probably just heard all that. I put the phone back to my ear. "Ah, hello, Ms Turnboldt. I suppose Tonya got in touch with you?"

"That's right," she said. "Though I don't really understand what's going on. I'm supposed to be a judge or something? And who are you, anyway?"

I introduced myself and told her about how Oberon and I would each make her a dress and she would wear the winning design.

"Look, chum," she said when I had finished. Hers was a lovely voice, light yet no nonsense. "I don't know much about cloth magic, but I do know that this gala is a big deal. I don't want you to go wasting your time making a dress that no one's gonna see, okay? Because I'll tell you right now, I'm going to pick Oberon's dress."

"Ah, I see," I said. "So you two really are an item."

She barked out a laugh. "What? Not by a long shot. We've never even met in person. We've talked on the phone a few times and that's it."

I found it somewhat interesting how vehement she was that she and Oberon had never met, but I chalked it up to her not wanting rumours to get started.

"But he is taking you to the gala," I said.

"That's right. And he's already made me a dress and sent it over, and even I'm not enough of a bitch to wear something else after he put in all that work."

"He's already made it?" I said. "What does it look like?"

"Nice try, chum. No way am I telling you."

"Why not? You're not going to pick my dress anyway, right?"

The line was quiet.

"I . . . I don't know if you've ever had to fight to prove yourself," I said. "I don't mean that as an insult. I just mean that I really don't know anything about you, and I suspect that's intentional. You seem like a pretty private person. But me, I'm out here in a world full of people like Oberon Myers and the only way I can move forwards is by putting myself out there again and again and again. All I'm asking for is a chance."

Now I went quiet, berating myself for rambling on. I shouldn't have had that fifth pint.

"If you were to make me a dress," Verity said, "what would it be like?"

Thomas stumbled past me, muttering about bed as he headed up to our flat. I waited until he was gone before replying.

"Can I ask you something?" I said. "Is Verity Turnboldt a pen name?"

"Ding ding ding," she said dryly.

I smiled. "I thought so. When I first heard it, I thought that it was quite poetic, using a synonym of *truth* as a pseudonym."

"Thanks," she said. "I also thought it was pretty darn clever."

"All right then. So when you're wearing the dress that Thom and I are going to make, you will be Verity Turnboldt, reporter for the *New Revolution*, and only that. Anyone who met you before or knew you by a different name won't recognize you. It's like we're giving flesh and blood to a name on the page."

She was silent for a beat. "You can do that?"

"I guess we'll see, eh?"

"I guess so," she said, her lickety-split cadence slowing down somewhat.

"When are you free for measurements?" I said. "My business partner Thomas Dawes and I—"

"Measurements?" she said, sounding taken aback. "Is that really necessary?"

"To make clothes? Yes, it kind of is," I said. "We need to make sure it will actually fit you. And it would also be nice if it looked good as well, is my thinking."

"I'm afraid that simply isn't going to happen," said Verity Turnboldt. "I'm extremely busy and don't have time for that. I gave Oberon my measurements and he was able to make a fine dress from that, so it should do for you as well, chum. My measurements are thirty-two-twenty-six-thirty-four and my height is five foot seven. I weigh about a hundred twenty pounds. How about you start with that? You can adjust the fitting when we meet."

"You know the May Gala is this Saturday," I said.

"We'll have the fitting on Thursday, then," she said. "Is that a problem?"

I ran a hand through my hair. "No."

"Fantastic. Come to the *New Rev* office at nine on Thursday night. See you then."

She hung up. I stared at the phone for a while, my beer-soaked brain trying to make sense of the dial tone. Eventually I managed to put the phone on the cradle.

~

For Verity's dress we decided to use the black jersey Thomas had stashed away. Sunday was more or less a write-off because of how hungover we both were, but mid-Monday Thomas got to work sketching a design, a draped Greek-goddess look that would hopefully be flattering or at the very least easy to alter.

"You're good at making clothes that draw the eye and compel attention," Thomas said to me. We were lying on the floor of our attic flat, Thomas on his stomach as he sketched, me on my back as I stared out the window. We had owned a chair at one point but we had long ago pawned it. "I'm good at making clothes that help people blend in. When we combine the two you get a disconnect in the brain of the viewer. They want to look but they can't quite comprehend what they're looking at. That should help keep Verity's real identity under wraps."

"Aces," I said. "Now, how exactly are we going to get the effect?"

Thomas flung an eraser at my head. "I can't do all the work here."

I ignored him and continued to stare out the window, thinking it over. Thomas and I lived on the top floor of a home between Turnpike Lane and Manor House tube stations. Our landlady called the space a studio apartment, but really it was nothing more than a glorified attic. Not that we had improved upon the place since moving in. Against one wall were our beds, two lumpy mattresses that we pulled down or shoved aside as needed. In every corner was a bowl full of snuffed-out cigarettes and match heads. Old scraps of muslin, thread, paper, and fabric swatches spilled off our worktable to litter the floor. We didn't have a closet, so our few nice outfits hung awkwardly off a bookshelf. The shelf itself was stuffed with Thomas's collection of old *National Geographics*. My guitar lay against the shelf, gathering dust. We didn't own a sewing machine—cloth magic had to be done by hand. We still talked about getting one when we were rich. It would be nice to have it and make mundane clothes on the cheap.

The moon was hanging low in the afternoon sky, the thinnest white crescent.

I sat up straight.

"There was no moon last night, right?" I said.

"Do I look like a farmers' almanac?" Thomas replied.

"So that means tonight's moon is a newly waxing moon," I said, jabbing a finger at the window. "The second-most-mysterious moon!"

Thomas squinted at it. "You think we should try and imbue some of the moon's attributes into the fabric? That could work. Give it a nice glow as well."

"No," I said. "It's good, but it's still too straightforward. There's not enough of an illusion there, and this dress is all about creating an illusion."

We were quiet as we thought it over. A big part of being a cloth mage was figuring out how to get the desired effect in the cloth. A mage first had to find the effect they wanted somewhere in nature, even if only in the abstract. They then acted as the conduit between the natural element and the fabric, their will shaping the magical effect. It was like magic needed human sentience for it to take shape.

"The moon is the reflection of the sun's light," Thomas said. "So it's already kind of an illusion."

"It needs to be more," I said. "Like . . . like the moon on the water. You reach for it, but it's not there." That seemed to suit Verity's elusive, secretive nature.

Thomas nodded. "I like it."

And so that was how we ended up walking through Finsbury Park once all traces of the sun were gone from the sky, sitting in the trees by the lake and holding out the jersey between us like a banner, tilting it so it caught the image of the moon on the water.

When you're imbuing a cloth it is important to keep the desired effect in mind. If your mind wanders you might be in for a surprise when you actually construct the outfit. I tried to keep my eyes and thoughts on the moon rippling across the pond. I knew Thomas was doing likewise—I might have been good at coming up with natural affinities but his focus was better.

When we finally clambered down a few hours later the fabric rippled and glowed like the surface of the lake, the sliver of the new moon occasionally fluttering across its folds.

"Very nice," I said. Thomas grunted in agreement.

~

Wednesday night came and I put on a pair of trousers and a paisley shirt. I thought about wearing my magicked herringbone suit but as I was planning to dance up a sweat I didn't want to wear something so heavy. I'd just have to rely on my natural charm to win over Tonya.

She was a sweet girl but not afraid to state things plainly. Andrew had mentioned something about her not fitting in with the other servants, and I'd bet her blunt nature had a part to play in that. She didn't seem like the type to suffer fools gladly. God knows why she liked me then, but I wasn't going to question it too closely.

I could have taken the bus to meet Tonya but I took the tube instead since it was easier to avoid paying fare that way. I got off at Seven Sisters and was skipping along towards the dance hall when a man stepped out of an alleyway and punched me in the gut.

I stumbled back, bracing myself against the wall while I clutched at my stomach.

"Don't give me that. I hardly touched you," said a familiar voice. It was Davy, a slick spiv and local tough. His partner in crime, Leigh, was hulking behind him. The three of us knew each other pretty well, seeing as I owed their boss a king's ransom.

I tried to reply but my voice just came out a squeak. Davy's little love tap had knocked the wind out of me.

"Eeeeee," I managed to get out.

Leigh and Davy traded worried glances.

"Hey now, just relax," Davy said, grabbing hold of my arm so I didn't topple over. Leigh started pounding on my back, I think in an attempt to help me start breathing again. A few seconds later it was like a bubble popped inside of me and I could stand up and take air into my lungs once more.

"How'd you find me?" I asked, still slightly winded.

"You always go to the American rhythm and blues night," Leigh said.

"Ah. Nice work, lads." Damn. One more dance hall I'd have to avoid from now on. Thomas and I worked very hard to stay off McCormick's radar: we didn't have set routines, rarely loitered in the same pubs too long or regularly. But I had been too predictable, and I didn't have Thomas to save me this time.

"All right." Davy tugged my arm. "Let's go, then."

"Tonight's *really* not a good night," I said, digging in my heels. I could see the dance hall just a few streets up ahead. I was early, but maybe Tonya was already there, waiting for me. "I've got a date."

Davy smiled and patted me sharply on the cheek. "Yeah. With the boss."

The two of them grabbed my arms and we were soon in the back of a cab. Davy gave the name of McCormick's favourite pub to the driver and paid the man with an actual note. Seeing actual physical money was so rare these days; even beggars sat on the streets with their Books in hand. Cold hard cash was used mainly by criminal lowlifes to keep their transactions secret and the very wealthy as an opulent affectation.

We zoomed past the dance hall and all I could do was watch it come and go.

The cab pulled up outside a pub in East London. Davy and Leigh still had hands on me as they hustled me inside.

The place was near empty: two geezers playing darts, a bartender cleaning glasses, and Greg McCormick frowning as he stared at the newspaper.

"Hey, boss, look who we found!" Leigh said, pushing me forwards.

McCormick glanced up and his face actually brightened, as if we were in fact old friends who had just happened to bump into each other. Greg McCormick was in his late thirties but seemed ten years older. He had the squat, strong build of a rugby player and the jowly face of a dog that would snap at you if you tried to pet it. He sometimes wore a bowler hat, an accessory that accentuated the roundness of his features.

"Fancy meeting you here." I smiled back at him but apparently I wasn't happy enough for McCormick. He scowled and kicked out a chair.

"Sit."

I obediently sat at the table.

"What do you want to drink?" he asked.

"One Birra, please."

McCormick snorted. "I can't believe you always drink that Italian crap. You know we fought those bastards in the war, right?"

I shrugged. "I went to Italy on holiday a few years ago. It brings back good memories."

McCormick drummed his fingers on the table.

"A trip abroad, eh?" he said. I waited for him to make some comment about it being a waste of his money, but instead he looked wistful. "I always thought it would be nice to see Europe during peacetime."

Davy set our drinks down on the table: a Birra for me and an IPA for McCormick. For a second we just sipped our beer, going on imaginary vacations in our head.

"I really needed you last Saturday," McCormick said. "I've invested a ridiculous fucking amount in you, and you won't even come have a drink with me when I need you."

Thomas and I had run into Davy and Leigh when we had been on our way to Andrew's party. We had managed to give them the slip, but not before Thomas had gotten his nose bloodied.

"I'm sorry, Greg," I said. "It's been a really busy time. The May Gala is this weekend and I've been hard at work preparing for it. A good mage usually gets a commission or two by the end of the night. Once Thomas and I start making money, we can start paying you back."

McCormick glared at me. "Ah, you're that eager to be rid of me, are you?"

You'd think a loan shark would be happy to hear that his loanee might actually be able to pay back the outrageous amount of dosh owed to him, but the truth was McCormick didn't seem all that eager for Thomas and me to be in the black. If we ever did manage to pay him off, he'd lose the excuse to monopolize my time. "I don't ever want you to think we're ungrateful for all you've done for us."

My answer seemed acceptable to McCormick. He sighed deeply, cooling down as he switched gears. "I really needed to see you Saturday," he repeated. "I just wanted someone to talk to. I've had the week from hell."

I drank my beer. Every other week for McCormick was a week from hell. I nodded along as McCormick talked about the deals that had fallen through, how his suppliers were drying up and the buyers even more so, and the headache he'd had the whole time.

"I swear, ever since they did away with rationing it's been near impossible for an honest crook to make a living in this city," he complained. "Now that there's food in the shops again, people aren't willing to pay extra for a bit of beef. Now that you don't need to ration cloth, people aren't willing to pay top dollar for old hospital linens."

I tried not to wince. "It's quite the sorry state of the country."

"The government better watch out," McCormick said, jabbing a finger at me as though he expected me to personally relay his warnings to the prime minister. "You restrict things for years, then let it all go again, there's going to be trouble. The MPs crow about criminal empires collapsing, about undercutting the black marketeer, but they won't like the sorts rushing in to fill the void." He shook his head. "God, why can't it be like during the war when it was all lonely housewives looking to buy some watered-down brandy and nice stockings?" He took a long swig of his drink. "You know what the only profitable game in town is? Guns. And I'm not going to get into that business."

"You're a good egg, Greg," I said and meant it. He was a pain sometimes but as far as loan sharks went he was by far the best of a bad lot.

"I needed someone to talk to this week, Paul."

"I know. I'm sorry."

"I don't ask for much, do I?" he said, voice edging upwards. "Just to join me for a drink a few times a week. I've done so much for you and that little Arab."

"Don't talk about my friend like that," I said, a harder edge bleeding into my voice. Thomas had once joked that he wished he knew exactly where his father hailed from: "That way I could correct people when they use the wrong slur." No local man had claimed him, and his dad could have sailed in from just about any corner of the world. Thomas's mum was no help: she'd ditched him on a cousin's doorstep when he was three.

McCormick gave me a glare but said nothing more about Thom.

"I just don't know why I get out of bed in the morning some days, Paul," he said to me. We were both on our third beers. I nodded attentively but in my mind I thought of Tonya, waiting for me outside the dance hall. I should have told her to bring a friend and gotten Thomas to come along, make it a double date. Maybe then I wouldn't be in this mess.

"What do you think?" McCormick asked.

"Eh?"

McCormick frowned. "I *said* that sometimes I think about jumping off the top of Tower Bridge," he said, obviously peeved at having to repeat himself.

"Don't talk like that," I said. "You gotta keep going. So many people depend on you."

"Really?" He sounded sceptical but there was hope in his eyes.

"That's right," I said. "Like me and Thomas. You were there for us when we first showed up in town. Didn't know a soul, had no one to vouch for us, but you put up the money we needed to achieve our dreams. You're our hero."

I worried that last bit was a bit much but McCormick nodded.

"That's right. I don't usually do student loans but . . . well, you were becoming mages. I figured that had to pay out eventually. Of course, I didn't realize that you wanted to be cloth mages, not Book Binders . . ." He looked at me accusingly. "Plus, you talked a good game. Said that soon you'd be rich and famous."

"I'm working on it," I said. "Who knows? You might just be looking at the next Court Magician."

McCormick laughed raucously at that. "Oh sure. And why don't you marry Princess Katherine while you're at it?"

"She's, like, fourteen," I muttered, unhappy to have one more person shoot down my ambitions.

"Look, mate, the chance of you being the next Court Magician . . . well, it's just impossible, innit?"

I was silent. McCormick's brief good mood slipped away and he went back to sipping his beer moodily. He was a pain in the ass, but it still hurt my heart to see McCormick so downtrodden. The first time I had met McCormick I had fallen in love. He'd been so butch, growling out the terms of the loan and bringing his fist down hard on the table. But as time had gone on my infatuation had dwindled as I'd realized how much of the tough black marketeer act was a front, and behind it was a lonely, doubt-ridden man. I felt for him as a human being but sometimes I wished that there was actually some truth to his bluster.

On the table was a set of blue ceramic salt and pepper shakers in the shape of horses. I picked up the salt horse and galloped it over to where McCormick was staring gloomily at the table. His eyes fell upon the horse as I had it trot around the tabletop.

"Thousands and thousands of years ago, there was a city in ancient Greece that was a lot like London," I said, starting the story without any preamble. "It was a city-state called Cecropia and it had steadily grown more and more prosperous as history marched forwards. Eventually it caught the eye of the gods, and Zeus declared that if the city were to grow any bigger it needed a protector. Out of the pantheon, only two immortals stepped forwards to vie for the city's favour. They were two of the most impressive gods: Poseidon, brother of Zeus and temperamental ruler of the seas; and Athena, ever-fair and ever-calm goddess of wisdom who had emerged fully formed from the forehead of Zeus, her father.

"Rather than battle for supremacy the two gods decided that, in the spirit of good old Greek democracy, they would allow the citizens of Cecropia to choose. To sweeten the deal each god presented a gift to the city.

"Poseidon went first. From the waves Poseidon called forth the very powers of creation, pulling up the dregs of primordial soup to fashion a brand-new creature: a four-legged beast called a horse. Imagine that moment. These magnificent animals shaking their manes free from salt water as they plough through the waves, trotting up to the beach while the crowd stares with their mouths open, dumbfounded.

"Now Athena, she acknowledged that horses were a good gift but said she could do one better. For her gift she reached into the ground and summoned a seed, and from that seed she summoned a tree. The tree grew rapidly, moving as fluidly through the air as a spring of water. Its leaves were small and oval. Its fruit was black with a hard stone at its centre. Olives. Olives can be pressed to make olive oil, which in addition to making food delicious could also be used to fuel lamps. People could stay awake later, talking, loving, eating, reading, all because of Athena's gift. And so, by the light of their olive oil lamps, the citizens voted and chose Athena. And that is how the city of Athens got its name."

"Huh," McCormick said.

"Poseidon, being the type to kick off easily, was right mad. He had given them horses, after all. Horses! He flounced off in a huff, and Lord knows he carried a grudge. After that Athenian sailors always had rotten luck out on the water.

"But this wasn't the only time Athena and Poseidon faced off over the fate of a town. They followed their believers from Greece to Rome and then followed them as the Roman Empire spread out across the world. Sometimes, not all the time but sometimes, when the Romans established a new outpost the god of water and the goddess of wisdom would go to the local people and once again have them pick between the two of them."

I looked at McCormick. He was quiet now, lost to the story. *There,* I wanted to say. *Have you not for a short time forgotten your pain?*

"So when Londinium was founded, the two gods came forth once more. They didn't make a big production of it like they had back in Cecropia. There were no gifts, no ceremony. They simply went to the citizens and said 'Choose.'" I set the saltshaker horse next to its brother. "Now, you're a born and bred Londoner, so you tell me: Which god did the people pick?"

McCormick blinked, clearly surprised at being roped into the story.

"Poseidon," he said. "They chose the god of water."

"That's right!" If he had said Athena I would have rolled with that but I was delighted McCormick had chosen the more thematically satisfying answer. It was clear no matter where you went in the city. There were more statues of Poseidon than any other mythological figure. And then you looked at all the pies Poseidon had a finger in: naval warfare, commerce, horse riding, all things England had excelled at.

Though sometimes I wondered if it had been the right choice. I thought of the countless slave ships that had set out from the docks of my own hometown, of the ships returning from various colonies with stolen food and goods and knowledge. By choosing the temperamental god of water, had we as a nation chosen conquest and expansion, cruelty and greed? Was it always a choice between glory and fame versus insight and humility?

"Huh," McCormick muttered. He reached out and took the pepper shaker. He turned it around in his hand. "We got a good deal out of it," he said. "But maybe we should have chosen wisdom instead."

I was intrigued since I had just been turning over the question in my own mind. But I was tired. "Maybe we should have."

Perhaps Tonya was still waiting for me, but I doubted she'd wait much longer.

"Hey, Greg, I need to get going."

"Yeah, that's fine," McCormick said, still holding the blue horse.

"I hate to ask you this, but things have been kind of tight," I said. "Could you spare a speckled hen?"

McCormick grimaced, either at my attempt at cockney rhyming slang or because I had the gall to ask for more money. He set the horse down and took out his Book.

"This is going on your tab," he said sternly, but he hadn't scared me in years. I nodded and let him transfer ten pounds from his Book to mine, his lips pursed in concentration as he did the transference spell.

"Thanks, Greg." I could have left but McCormick was looking so thoughtfully at the horse that I felt the need to put a hand on his shoulder.

"We really are better for our association with you," I said, then grinned. "But then again, you're better for your association with *us*."

He laughed at that and that was when I knew it was all right for me to go. Leigh and Davy let me walk out of the pub. I hailed a cab and hightailed it back up to Holloway.

The dance was still going strong but Tonya was nowhere to be seen.

CHAPTER 4

With Tonya nowhere in sight, I went home and, knackered, collapsed in bed. Morning came and as soon as I woke up I started thinking about how to get in touch and apologize to her. I was a bit stumped on how to do it. It wasn't as though I could call her up. I'd have to phone the Fife residence and then ask to speak to one of the maids, but that kind of thing just wasn't done. I knew she was already having a tough go of it there and I didn't want to make things worse for her.

I could write her a letter. If I dropped it in the post before five it would be in her hands by morning. But every time I started writing an apology, it came out too florid or too curt or just nonsensical. What was I even supposed to say? That I'd been kidnapped by my loan shark's minions because their boss was in one of his blue moods again and I was the only one who could talk him out of it? Why not just tell her I'd been kidnapped by pirates?

After starting and tossing out the seventh written attempt I decided to let it lie for now. I'd make some excuse to invite myself over to Andrew's place in the coming week and I'd apologize in person.

For now, I had the gala to prepare for.

Thomas and I had been working on our projects for months and all I had left to do was the lining. My gala showpiece was a long coat made up of several triangular pieces of cloth: blood red, plum blue, mustard yellow. I was using bright-gold thread to sew the pieces together so that the whole thing seemed to shimmer as if containing a great light. It was long and went almost all the way to the ground. The cuffs and high mandarin collar of the coat were made of a similar gold fabric. This was material Thomas and I had bought in slightly more affluent times, making it all the more precious in our present penurious state.

"What does it remind you of?" I asked Thomas, gesturing to my nearly finished coat where it hung on the dress form. I could hear him hesitate as he tried to dull his usual bluntness.

"A ringmaster at the circus," he finally said. I laughed.

"I like that," I said. "But my real inspiration was going to church with Mum and Dad. It's supposed to be like a stained-glass window." Back when I was too young to understand the words the priest was saying up at the pulpit, before I could read the musical notes or lyrics of the hymnbook, I would gaze up at the stained-glass windows, enraptured by those beautiful, glowing things. They seemed so warm but at the same time so angular and sharp. I just wanted to be able to take those pictures of glass and metal and bend them around me, to wear them and have that same light.

Thomas reconsidered my coat.

"I guess I can see that," he said. "But what does it do?"

"Ah!" I swiped the jacket off the dress form. "I'll show you!" I quickly slid it on. "So, Thomas, what do you think?"

"Well, the construction's good. And you nailed that sunlight effect. It really does make it seem like there's sunlight bleeding through it. Though the primary colours, the glow, the gold thread . . . it's a lot to take in."

As Thomas was speaking I stepped away, going to the other side of the room. Behind me I left an afterimage, standing in front of Thomas with clasped hands and a calm expression.

"So you're saying you think it's a bit much?" I asked. Thomas whirled around to face me. When he looked back at the afterimage it was already fading away like fog dissipating in the sunlight. He turned back to me with an incredulous frown. "What was that?"

"I call it an afterimage," I said. "The coat demands attention, and while someone has their attention on it the real me can move around more or less unseen."

"It makes you invisible?"

"No, I'm still visible," I said. "But your attention is fixed in that one spot so you don't notice the real me walking away."

I had been sitting on the edge of our drafting table but now got up and started walking back.

"But can your afterimage actually interact with anything?" Thomas asked, still addressing the me sitting on the table.

"No," I said, causing Thomas to startle at my voice coming from right next to him. "But it can smile and nod and you'd be surprised how far that will get you."

"All right, it's a neat effect," he admitted. "Though I can't see it being good for much outside of war."

Thomas and I had very different political views, but we were both agreed that we were never going to make clothes for the military. For me it was because it went against my Christian beliefs; for Thomas it was because he had no desire to feed the capitalist machine that was modern warfare. Also, as I claimed to be a pacifist, it wouldn't be a good look for me. I say *claimed* because it was less a deeply held belief than a smoke screen to hide the fact that I was magically prohibited from physical violence. It was one more thing that drove a wedge between me and my brothers—they were proud of their naval service and thought I was just looking down on them.

There had been a few times when Thom and I had gotten into trouble and I'd had no choice but to take my licks. Thomas was always frustrated with me, but even as he lectured me I could see a glimmer of respect in his eyes, that he was impressed that I was willing to put my money where my mouth was and not fight back. I always felt like a heel when that happened.

"There are lots of other uses for it," I said. "For example, it'll be great at parties. You can go around and be everywhere at once."

"Yeah, as long as people don't notice that they're talking to a smiling, nodding mute." As Thomas spoke I started to move away. Thomas struck out with his left hand, hand going through the afterimage and making contact with my left shoulder. The afterimage rapidly dissolved in the air. "Or as long as they don't try to touch you."

"It's a start," I said, somewhat defensively. "How's your null coat going?"

Thomas's big gala showpiece was, of all things, a null coat. Null coats had a simple purpose: to nullify the effects of cloth magic. A really strong null coat could render any cloth magic in its vicinity as flat as regular cloth. Those types of null coats were incredibly rare as they took decades of practice. A slightly easier version was a null coat that protected the wearer from other cloth magics.

I'd never had the knack for null coats. As much as I hated to admit it, I was very much a traditional cloth mage who excelled in smoke-and-mirrors-type magic, making outfits that changed the wearer's appearance or subtly enchanted the viewer's mind. Mages that had a surplus of magical energy could create things that actually changed the world around them; Andrew's creations, for instance, could conjure up frost or flame. Mages who could craft clothes like that were rare though, leading many people to see cloth magic as a frivolous course of study.

But even if my style was more of the "glamour" variety, I took some comfort in that I was very good at it.

Thomas's null "coat" was a grey suit, though as a neat stylistic choice it had some of its silver lining on the outside, running up the sides and down the underside of the arms.

Thomas changed into the suit.

"All right," I said. "It's kind of simple." I started walking around him, leaving an afterimage to stand in front of him. Instead of keeping his eyes on the afterimage he turned towards me, giving me a crooked-toothed smile at my surprise.

"But it works," he said.

"Yeah." I frowned. It didn't sit well with me that his null coat could see through my own coat—that implied a level of power and craftsmanship higher than my own. A null coat, after all, was only as good as the cloth mage who made it. "But this is the May Gala. A null coat is an impressive bit of technical work, but there's no showmanship to it. People come to this thing to be razzle-dazzled! I know you think this is just ostentatious peacocking"—I gestured to my own outfit—"but it's what's going to get us jobs, not esoteric displays on arcane matters that only interest other cloth mages."

"You really think it's that bad?" Thomas said with a worried wince. I paused before speaking. Sometimes, I forgot that Thomas really did take what I said to heart.

"No," I said. "I think it's a great suit and anyone who knows a whit about cloth magic will see what an aces mage you are. But the sad fact is the crowd will always clamour for Barabbas and ignore true miracles."

"You just used up your Jesus comparison for the week," Thomas muttered.

"Well, I was comparing you to Jesus for once, so . . . shove it," I said.

Thomas laughed. "There is something else I'm working on," he said. "But it won't be ready for Saturday."

"Show me."

Thomas changed out of his suit into his regular work clothes. From the table he retrieved a cape he had been working on. It was repurposed material from old blackout curtains. Usually with cloth magic you wanted to use fabric that hadn't been used for anything yet, but sometimes you could get interesting effects from repurposed material.

The cape went down to his waist, very finely made, with a capelet for added style and a slight upturned collar. It looked like something a Victorian gentleman might have worn.

With a flourish Thomas swung it up over his shoulders.

"I have been trying to capture the attribute of darkness," Thomas said and showed me the lining of the cape. It was black silk yet oddly it didn't shimmer or catch the light the way silk usually would. Instead it had absolutely flat dimensions, just an indecipherable darkness even as Thomas swirled the cape around.

"Well, I'd say you've done that," I declared. Thomas shook his head.

"I didn't want to capture just the *look* of darkness," he said. "I'm trying to get that sense of unknowable time and space, of something infinite and borderless, how all darkness is the same no matter the time or place."

"Like the dark of the closet being the same space as the night sky," I said.

"Yes! Yes, exactly!" Thomas said.

"All right." I eyed the cape with a new curiosity. "And how's that going?"

Thomas took a deep breath. "Pick up that apple on the desk and toss it to me."

I picked it up—it fit comfortably in the palm of my hand. I lobbed it underhand towards Thomas.

Instead of catching it Thomas stepped forwards, flinging open a side of his cape. The apple hit the dark satin lining and disappeared, passing through it without coming out on the other side. It was like the cape was an open window into another world, a dark, unknowable place home to nothing but one solitary Granny Smith apple.

"Wow!" I said, genuinely impressed. "That's really amazing, Thomas! This is fantastic!"

Thomas smiled at me.

"All right." I clapped my hands together. "Now bring it back."

Thomas's smile dropped. Silently he took off the cape.

"Eh? Thomas?" I said, stepping closer.

"Like I said, I'm still working on it," he muttered.

"Eh?" It dawned on me that I wasn't getting my apple back. "You bastard! That was my lunch!"

~

We worked on Verity's dress up until the very last second. It had a sleek profile; the form was flowing rather than fitted up top like most current fashions. The sleeves, which I was particularly proud of, were draped in a way that would hang beautifully when she moved her arms.

"Something's missing," I said.

Thomas nodded in agreement. Without a word he went up and detached the right sleeve.

"Hey!" I said as the sleeve came loose. Thom merely tossed it to me.

"That's better," he said as he walked back to where I was standing. We both took it in.

"Asymmetrical?" I said. "I don't know. It seems kind of risky."

"Playing it safe can be the riskiest thing of all," Thomas said, but there was no combativeness in his voice. There were moments like this, when we'd been working hard and had just created something beautiful, where Thomas actually seemed at peace with himself and the world.

We could have stayed in Liverpool. That would have been playing it safe. But when we had realized as teens that cloth magic was something we could do for a living, that there was a school in London that taught the one thing that made both of us happy, well, there was no turning away from that.

I clapped a hand on Thomas's shoulder. "You're right. This is better."

We put the dress on a hanger and covered it with a dry cleaner's paper bag. Thom claimed he needed to stay home and work on his multidimensional cape, which was fine. I was used to being the one to handle the people side of things, and I was especially eager to meet this mysterious American.

I arrived at Fleet Street a few minutes before nine in the evening. The *New Rev* was situated in a rundown office building, alongside an optometrist and accounting firm. The door was unlocked, though it stuck a bit as I opened it. A sign said the paper's offices were one floor up, so I took the stairs.

"Hello?" I called. The lights were on but no one was there. Half a dozen desks were set up around the room. They reminded me of cluttered shrines, only instead of a saint, at the centre of each altar sat a typewriter, offerings of paper and pencils scattered around them. There was a closed door to my left, and on it was a bit of anticommunist propaganda: *IS YOUR BATHROOM BREEDING BOLSHEVIKS?* Considering the *New Rev*'s socialist leanings it was probably tongue in cheek.

"Verity?"

"Stay right there." It was the same voice from the phone, though now it came from behind the closed water closet door.

"Verity, it's Paul Gallagher," I said. "I brought your dress."

"Fantastic. Hand it over." The door opened, a sliver of yellow light spilling out into the harsh white light of the newsroom. Verity didn't step out to meet me but just held out her hand. It was a nice hand with long fingers and light-brown skin. Her nails were the short nails of a working-class woman, I noted, but I supposed a reporter had to keep her nails short so they didn't jam up the typewriter keys.

I found the whole thing a little odd but her tone brooked no argument. I handed over the dress, still in its sheath, and she promptly pulled it inside and slammed the door shut.

I undid the button on my houndstooth jacket before sitting down on a nearby swivel chair. Dimly I could hear the rustle of paper as Verity took the dress out of the dry cleaner's bag and tried it on. I spent a few minutes waiting for her, tapping out a beat on the chair's arm as I swung around.

I was in midswing when the door opened and she stepped out. My first glimpse of her was just a blur as I rotated around: dark eyes traced in kohl, hair the same colour and sheen as the dress.

I put down my foot to stop the chair and, still a little dizzy, got to my feet.

"Ms Turnboldt," I said. "What a pleasure to finally make your acquaintance."

She was beautiful, though younger than I had pictured. She looked to be in her early twenties, just like me. She was a Black woman, which I had honestly not been expecting—when I'd been imagining her in my head on the way over I had pictured a white woman, another version of Gabs. Which seemed rather silly in multiple ways the more I thought about it.

She rippled with silver in the office's dim light and set those kohl-lined eyes upon me.

"No need to be so formal," she said. "You can save yourself some time and just call me Verity."

I took a tentative step forwards, meeting her gaze. I think we were both giving each other identical looks of *Well?* It was just a matter of who would break first, either me with a compliment towards her or her with a compliment towards my dress.

I was never known for my restraint.

"You look lovely," I said.

"Yeah, yeah, I clean up nice," she replied, then added magnanimously, "and I gotta admit, it *is* a smashing dress."

"And not an easy one to pull off," I said, unable to resist a bit of boasting. "Are those the shoes you were planning to wear to the gala?"

"Yeah, I think so. Why?"

"Just checking the hem. If you're planning on wearing those heels, the hem is fine. But I'm not happy about the wrist. May I fix it?"

"Knock yourself out."

I took out a small travel sewing kit, containing some black thread, a couple of needles, and a small pair of scissors. As I stepped towards Verity she held up her hand. When she tilted her head, her hair slid off her shoulder in a movement as smooth as a piano key sinking down.

She watched while I worked. I wondered if she saw my crooked index finger and if she made anything of it. There is a stereotype about Americans that they still hold true to Puritan values and don't put much stock in magic, not of cloth or Book or any other variety. I wondered if Verity had ever even heard of innate magic.

My work done, I cut the string and took a step back.

"Well, I think it's rather good," I said. "But what do you think?"

She shrugged nonchalantly. "It's nice, but can you dance in it?"

This was obviously a rhetorical question—the design was elegant but simple and in no way would trip her up if she wanted to make a move on the dance floor. But instead of saying that I took a step forwards, gave a little bow, and then held out my right hand. Her mouth twitched and for the first time I saw her smile.

She took my hand in hers and pressed her other hand around the back of my neck. I lightly placed my other hand on her waist. And then we were off, moving in step to a simple, unheard song. In my head it was a Viennese waltz, and I wondered if it was the same for Verity. Just light steps through the desks and mess of the *New Rev.* I was barely leading, we were so in sync. I wanted badly to ask her, *Do you hear the same music as me? What song is playing in your head?* but to ask would ruin the connection, even if it confirmed that we were in fact tuning in to the same station.

The imaginary song came to an end and we came to a stop at the opposite end of the office by a large window facing the street. She slid her hands away and I took a step back. An odd feeling hung in the air, as though we were both waiting for the other person to laugh. Neither of us did.

Verity cleared her throat.

"So there's no doubt that it's a beaut of a dress," she said, "but does it work magicwise?"

"That can be a bit hard to judge," I said. "It's supposed to obscure your identity but seeing as we've never met before I can hardly say if it's worked or not."

She nodded. "That's true. Still, I'd like to know for sure before Saturday."

"You can test it out on a stranger," I suggested. "Introduce yourself under your real name, leave, put on the dress, come back, and introduce yourself as Verity Turnboldt."

"And they won't see right away that they've just met the same person twice?"

"That's right. But if *you* tell anyone who you really are, the magic won't work on them. Also if they see you getting in or out of the dress the spell will be broken then. Magic can only obscure so much."

"Gotcha. Don't worry, I don't plan on getting naked with anyone. As far as I'm concerned this gala is strictly business," Verity said.

"Then you should be fine," I said and wondered if I was included when she said *anyone*. "So why is a reporter for the *New Rev* going to the cloth mage gala?"

"I cover high society for the paper," Verity said. "And a lot of high society is going to be there."

"A society gossip column is an odd beat for a socialist newspaper."

"It's supposed to be poking fun at the idea of gossip columns in general, taking the piss as you Brits say," Verity said. "Say, you want a cup of decaf?"

"I'd love one," I said. I followed her to the staff kitchen where she bustled about, obviously well familiar with the place. The cupboard was full of mismatched cups and in the end she drank from a cheerful yellow mug and I from a slightly chipped china cup.

"So you're American," I said.

"Got it in one," she said.

"What's a Yank doing reporting on British high society?"

She smiled and sipped her drink. "Sometimes it's outsiders who have the best perspective on things. And it's fun. I've always liked writing, used to do it for the fish rags back home in New York."

"Wow. New York City?" I had visions of sailors and dames and gangsters dancing up and down Fifth Avenue while King Kong swung about overhead.

"That's the one," Verity replied. "I wrote for a few papers there and was able to use that to get this job over here."

"You've done quite a bit for one so young."

"So young?" she said. "You don't know how old I am."

"How old are you then?"

"Rude." But she was smiling.

"I promise not to tell."

"I'm twenty-three," she said.

"Oh good," I said. "I like older women."

She laughed at that. "And how old are *you*, chum?"

"I'll be twenty-three in August."

She rolled her eyes. "Only children round up. Also, I'm not too hot on younger men."

"I'm getting older every day," I said.

"Your accent," she said, changing the subject as she set down the coffee mug. "You're not from around here, are you?"

"Oh, no. I'm a Liverpudlian, born and raised," I said. "My father still lives up there. He owns a music shop. Sells instruments, gives lessons and the like." Actually, the music lessons had been more my mother's area of expertise. When she'd died Dad had tried picking up the slack, but his heart wasn't ever truly in it. "The shop has been in my family ever since my grandfather came over from Ireland and opened it up." I thought of my grandfather, a hardworking immigrant thriving in a country that would rather see the back of him. If I could rise as high as Court Magician, it felt like finally I'd be making returns on all the blood, sweat, and toil he'd suffered through to establish my family decades ago. "In America, you don't have a mage maker, do you?"

"What?" I didn't blame Verity for being confused—I had changed topics pretty abruptly. "You mean someone who breaks bones so people can become mages and serve king and country? No, that's not really a thing. If people want to become mages in the US, they track down someone who claims to be a mage maker and take their chances."

"Ah, right." I had read an article about it in *National Geographic*, how the US was awash with quacks who claimed that they could do innate magic. It led to hundreds if not thousands dead, through either medical or magical mishap. This was part of the reason that Britain only allowed one person, the Court Magician, to practise the art.

Every person in my cloth magic class had gotten their radius and ulna broken by the current mage maker, transforming each of us from ordinary person to cloth mage. Book Binders had to undergo the same process, except it was their humerus that was broken. Some cloth magicians—like Thom—got all three broken at once so they could also do Book Binding on the side. I hadn't bothered. I'd already been nervous that Redfield would notice that I already had some innate magic—I hadn't wanted to push my luck.

"It's getting late. I need to lock up this place and get home," Verity said. I took the hint and got up to go. Verity followed me to the door in order to see me out.

"I do hope we get a chance to talk more at the gala," Verity said.

"I'll cry if we don't," I said.

She shook her head. "This is why I avoid younger men."

～

As the tube car rattled homewards I thought of how the light had caught Verity's dark hair, the feel of her holding my hand as we'd danced around the newsroom. Usually, flirting gave me the same charge as feeling the sun on my face or a sip of ice water, but today I wasn't feeling it. Instead, guilt coiled in my gut like a bit of burnt incense. I couldn't help but think of another dark-haired girl I knew: Miss Tonya Gower. I still hadn't gotten in touch with her to apologize for standing her up, and the longer I let the matter lie the more insurmountable it all seemed.

The Piccadilly line was slow going as usual. The train was just doing the long stretch between Finsbury Park and Manor House when I spotted the Book inspector. She was a white woman with long brunette hair pulled back into a professional bun. As she checked people's Books she'd take time to chat with them. She seemed genuinely interested in them. I'd bet a whole pound that she wasn't a native Londoner (not that I had a pound). Londoners hated chatting on the tube.

As usual I hadn't recorded this trip in my Book. My attempt at saving a few shillings could end up earning me a fine and citation.

It would seem suspicious if I got up and moved farther down the carriage. She seemed friendly enough—maybe I could talk my way out of a fine if it came down to it. But of course, the best way to avoid that would be to avoid all talk of fines in the first place.

She stepped in front of me. She looked to be a year or two older than myself, with a gentle smile and winsome brown eyes. She opened her mouth to speak.

"Excuse me, miss," I said. "I'm in dire straits and I could really use some advice. Do you mind hearing me out?"

"Advice?" she said, puzzled.

"Yes. They say that sometimes strangers can give you better advice than your mates, as the stranger's got a more objective view of things," I said. "And, well, it's a tricky one. It's a matter of the heart."

She softened at that, as I'd guessed she would. I know a fellow romantic when I spot one. She took a seat next to me and closed her inspector's notebook.

"My name's Paul Gallagher." It always felt risky giving my name to Book inspectors, but that's part of the spell—it doesn't work if I try to hide behind a false name.

"Urszula," she said, shaking my hand. She had a Polish accent. "What's the matter of the heart that is troubling you so?"

"Well, it's like this," I said. "There's a girl I'm sweet on. We only just met, and I invited her out dancing. But then some things happened that weren't exactly my fault but . . . I stood her up. This just happened last night, but I haven't called her yet to apologize, and I'm not sure how to go about it."

"Hmm," Urszula said. "And you like this girl?"

"Yes," I said. "I mean, I don't know her all that well yet, but I want the chance to get to know her."

"Then call her up, tell her you're sorry, and ask for another chance."

"You really think that will work?" I said.

Urszula shrugged. "If it doesn't, then it wasn't meant to be." She opened her inspector's Book and I could see that she was about to shift back into work mode. We were still a minute away from Turnpike Lane.

"So I should invite her out dancing again?" I said, playing for time.

Urszula closed her Book and shook her head vehemently. "No, no, no! You can't offer up the same thing. If you want to make it work with this girl, you have to offer up something bigger!"

"Something bigger . . ." I tried to picture something bigger than a dance hall. A cathedral?

"Yes, bigger! Grander!" she said. "You need to make up for disappointing her the first time around, so you have to go above and beyond!"

Bigger than a dance. A grand gesture. What could I invite Tonya to that would fit the bill? I hardly had any time these days, as I was so busy getting ready for the gala—

I stood up and almost toppled over as the train slowed to a stop.

"That's it!" I turned to Urszula. "I know exactly what to do! Thank you!"

The doors opened and I rushed out, partly so that Urszula wouldn't ask to see my Book and also so I could get home and implement my new plan.

I'd ask Tonya to the gala! I'd apologize for standing her up the night before, I'd make her a dress, and everyone would have a good time all around.

I even knew how I'd get in touch with her: I'd call up the Fife residence and ask Andrew to discreetly get Tonya on the line. If they did it covertly enough they should be able to pull it off without arousing suspicion from either Lady Fife or the other servants.

I practically ran home from the tube station. When I opened the door to the house my landlady, Mrs Dylag, was on the phone. I made myself slow down and carefully take off my coat, trying to temper my impatience.

"Ah, Mr Gallagher!" she said, peering down at me from the top of the stairs. "There's a woman on the phone for you."

"What?" I said, thoroughly confused by such a simple phrase. I made my way upstairs and took the phone from my landlady. "Hello?"

"Oh, good, Paul!" It was Gabs. She sounded relieved and more than a little desperate. "I'm so glad you're there." She took a deep breath. "I need to make use of the Arrangement."

"The Arrangement" was a deal Gabs and I had made during college. If one of us was single or with a partner who didn't want to go to a specific social event, we'd fill in as the other's date. As two outgoing, sociable, attractive people (her more so than me on the last one) we made a good pair, even though it hadn't worked out when we had tried to date each other for real.

"Kristoff doesn't want to go to the May Gala?" Kristoff was Gabs's beau of the last year, a cloth mage a few years above us in school who was also some Prussian aristocrat. He wasn't my type—I found him dull as dishwater—but Gabs was crazy about him. He was far too accom-modating, always trying to figure out what Gabs wanted before she even wanted it.

One key way Gabs and I differed was that Gabs liked to be wor-shipped, while I preferred to be the supplicant. Once again in theory this made us the ideal pair but some sense of self-preservation held me back.

"Kristoff might still be going," Gabs said primly. "But he's not going with *me*."

"Oh no." I leaned against the wall, ready for the long haul. "What happened?"

"He found out that I'm not actually a secret Russian princess," Gabs said, somewhat reluctantly.

"Oh, Gabs," I said. "Why did you ever tell him that lie in the first place?" I'd been there for the beginning of this story, when Gabs had felt the need to invent a secret history in order to seem less common and more on Kristoff's level. I had tried to warn her against it, but she hadn't listened.

"He got mad when he learned that I'm just some commoner, just a greengrocer's daughter from Cornwall," she said. "Said things were over between us."

I sighed. "Well, first off, he's damn lucky that greengrocer's daugh-ter ever gave him the time of day," I said. "And secondly, Gabs, do you think there's any chance at all that he's not so much mad about you not being a princess as he's mad that you lied to him?"

Gabs was quiet.

"I didn't think it was so bad," she finally said.

"It's not great," I said.

"But Paul, even if it is my fault, I can't face him alone at the gala," Gabs said. "Actually, it's worse if it *is* my fault. Please, say you'll help me out, dear heart."

I hesitated, thinking of Tonya.

"Unless you already have a date," Gabs said. "Which of course makes sense. I'm sorry for calling you so last minute; it all just happened today and—"

"I don't have a date," I said. "Let's go together."

Gabs cheered up after that and we chatted for a bit. When I hung up the phone I thought of calling the Fife residence and speaking to Tonya anyway, but with my previous plan shot down, I couldn't find the courage to do so.

CHAPTER 5

Neither Thomas nor I ate the day of the gala, partly because we were too busy putting the finishing touches on our outfits and also because we had run out of money. The hunger pangs reminded me of wartime, and as that hunger grew I couldn't help but daydream about kiwi fruits. I had tasted one for the first time in the summer of '41. Thomas had been living with me and my family at that point. His blood family was scum and had kept Thomas around only because of the extra rations he'd netted them. The family had spent the rations on their own kids, leaving Thomas to wear rags and scrounge for food. He was my best mate, so I eventually told my parents we had to take him in or he'd die. Being kindhearted Christian folk, they agreed. They worked out a deal with Thomas's kin—he'd live with us and we'd take care of him but the cousins could still claim that he was a member of their household, allowing them to use his rations however they saw fit.

This deal meant that at the Gallagher household we were splitting three sets of rations four ways (my brothers were out of the house and in the navy by then). Our allotments were meagre, but not one of us complained about our share getting parcelled out further. None of us minded, even as our grumbling stomachs became a constant background noise. We'd done the right thing and that was enough.

Thomas was a smart kid, and he knew why there was so little to go around. He started to slip away and bring home fresh fruit, not just crab apples or berries that could be foraged from the countryside but exotic things like kiwis and pineapples. That first taste of kiwi was amazing. Thomas and I ate it down by the riverside, skin and all. It tasted like the freshest, most pure spring of water.

The supply of fresh fruit ended when Thomas made a gift of half a watermelon to my parents. They of course wanted to know where he'd gotten such a rarity, and they eventually shamed him into admitting that he'd been helping a local gang break into homes of wealthy shipping magnates. Not long after that Thomas, Mum, and I went out to live with Mum's relatives in the countryside. At the time I had thought it was to escape the bombs coming down on the city, but later I'd realized it was also for Thomas's sake, to keep him from falling further under the sway of the Liverpool criminal underworld.

Despite my parents' best attempts to tame him, Thomas had never lost the street smarts that had kept him alive as a child. Even now you could drop him in any city, and like a sailor following a compass needle, within an hour he could find the bar where the city's most unwanted and also most useful element congregated. He knew the bribery rates of different police officers as well as a banker knew exchange rates. I'd seen him in enough bar brawls back in Liverpool to know that he knew how to make threats—"Come near me again and I'll make you kiss the pavement." "You pull a knife on me, it's going in your eye." "Say that again and I'll mess you up so bad God won't even look at ya." Sometimes he didn't even bother with threats, just acted.

I didn't approve of violence, but my love for and trust in Thomas outweighed everything else. My little brother wasn't proud of his violent talents. Whenever we had to speak with Davy or Leigh, Thom would glare at them with such disgust. In another life, had little urchin Thomas lived that long, he could have been them, a mindless thug at the beck and call of some two-bit criminal. That look of loathing was a sharp contrast to the quiet, thoughtful gaze he had while reading or sketching, and I'd seen him gaze as tenderly upon a sewing project as a mother looking down at her sleeping child. I suspected I was one of the few people who ever got to see this side of him.

If I were Court Magician, I could give Thomas a job that would keep him out of trouble. We'd be able to eat kiwis and watermelon and every other fruit that existed in the world.

∼

The evening of the May Gala Ralph pulled up outside our door in his sputtering Ford Anglia. Gabs was already sitting in the back seat. She was wearing an astonishing dress, a poncho-like design that still managed to be formfitting thanks to artful cuts. Most eye grabbing of all was how it was festooned with mirrors that glittered even under the glow of the dim streetlamps. She was as out of place in Ralph's clunky car as Cinderella in a pumpkin.

I climbed into the car and sat down next to her. I smiled at Gabs but I was a bit frightened: all those little mirrors had sharp edges. Perhaps the beautiful dress was a statement piece: *Get too close and I'll cut you.*

Gabs smiled. "Good evening, lads. What do you think?" She gestured to her dress.

"It's a beautiful piece of work," Thomas replied truthfully. Gabs seemed somewhat disappointed by his response and turned to me. I opened my mouth to speak.

"It really is a beaut."

"It looks dangerous."

"It frightens me, Gabs."

I blinked, bright spots dancing in front of my eyes. It was as though I had spoken all three sentiments out loud, simultaneously. I loosened my jaw and pushed at my teeth with my tongue as if trying to feel traces of the words I had actually spoken. Neither Thomas nor Ralph acted as though anything strange had just happened.

Gabs laughed. "Frightened? Why would you think that, pet?"

I held my tongue. Her dress seemed to create fractals in the conversation, allowing her to pick which path the discussion went down.

And yet, despite knowing this, I felt compelled to respond.

"Not so much frightened as wary."

"Well, at least you'll make an impression at the gala."

"This is exactly the kind of thing that scared off Kristoff."

Thomas winced and through that I knew that Gabs had zeroed in on the last option. I didn't quite understand why, if she could have chosen any path, she'd chosen the one which exposed my worst side and drove a wedge between us.

"Really, Paul, like you're one to lecture me on love," Gabs said. "You'd shag a rug if there was nothing else available."

If I said anything in response I would just make things worse. I waited a moment, consolidating all my thoughts. Gabs was right in that I could be single minded at times, but I felt I could actually use that to my advantage. I held on to one thought to the exclusion of all others:

"Gabs, you are scary because you are the most talented girl I know."

"Gabs, you are scary because you are the most beautiful woman I know."

"Gabs, you are scary because you are the sharpest mage I know."

Gabs blinked, then smiled.

"That's very sweet of you to say, dear heart," she said, patting me on the knee. Some of the sharpness from earlier was gone and I felt like I could breathe again.

"I only speak the truth," I said and was startled when it was the only sentence I heard rather than one of three. Apparently Gabs's cloth magic could be turned off or on at will.

"Thomas, are you wearing a null coat?" Gabs asked idly. Thomas and I shared a small smile. Gabs was no doubt wondering why her magic hadn't had any effect on Thom.

"That's right."

"Very impressive, but might be a little too esoteric for the gala crowd, hmm?"

"Just for the record, I'm here too," Ralph said.

"Hi, Ralph!" the three of us chorused from the back seat. Ralph sighed as we laughed at his expense.

"I don't remember signing up to be your chauffeur," he said. He was wearing a suit with very clean lines made from a burgundy tweed. It was a suit he'd made for an assignment earlier in the year. If I remembered rightly it gave the wearer great physical strength. It made me sad that Ralph hadn't been able to make something new for the gala. I knew he worked hard supporting his family. His financial situation was even worse than Thom's and mine. If we were in the hole moneywise, well, only we suffered for it, but when Ralph couldn't pay the bills his wife and tykes went hungry too.

We pulled up outside Andrew's house. He was already waiting for us, standing by the kerb. Despite there being an empty seat next to Ralph he dithered on the pavement, fiddling with his top hat. Eventually Gabs leaned across both me and Thomas to open the door.

"Dawes, move your arse to the front seat," she said. Thom rolled his eyes but did as he was told. Once he was gone Gabs became sweet again, batting her eyes at Andrew. "Come sit in the back with us, pet."

Andrew happily hopped in next to me and we were off.

The May Gala was being held outside the city at Dean Abernail's massive estate southwest of London. It took over an hour just to get out of the city and into the countryside. I loved the city but it was nice to be free of it for an evening, to actually see the horizon rather than buildings towering over me.

As twilight closed in Ralph's car started making unnerving growling noises. The car bumped and juddered over the gravel country roads in a way that turned Andrew a worrying shade of green.

"No worries," Ralph told us cheerfully as we bounced around. "We'll be fine as long as we don't stop."

But the car did stop, sputtering and rolling to a slow death on the long driveway leading to the dean's house. As we got out of the car and started walking, Gabs and I traded furtive, relieved looks—it was obviously sad that Ralph's car had broken down, but better to walk than have our entrance marred by Ralph's old jalopy spitting out smoke behind us.

The mansion was a three-storey Regency-era building. From inside we could already hear music and laughter.

"Lads! Miss Wilkes!" Dean Abernail said as we stepped into the front hall. Dean Abernail was like the kindly grandfather who always had a smile and unwavering belief in your brilliance. He was already well into his cups but managed to soberly shake our hands. "Congrats on four years of hard work. Such a talented group of youngsters! You are truly a wonder to behold!"

"Thank you, Dean Abernail," Thomas and I said. The respect was genuine.

"Well, you don't want to talk to me all evening! Go! Mingle; enjoy yourselves! Oh, but Ralph, I want to introduce you to some people. They're a couple of Americans trying to figure out if cloth magic can help their factory workers . . ."

Abernail put a hand on Ralph's shoulder and led him away into the crowd, leaving Gabs, Thomas, Andrew, and me.

"Oh, I see Mother," Andrew said. He was still a little green from the car ride. "I shall let her know we arrived safely." He quickly disappeared into the throng of people.

"I'll grab us some drinks," Thomas said and left. I half suspected we wouldn't see him again, that he would hide away from the crowd somewhere for the rest of the evening.

To the left of the front hall was a ballroom. From the crush of people you could almost make a topographical map based on human density—near the middle of the floor was the raucous Crown Prince Arthur, sycophants fawning over his magical suit which made it look like waves of water were rolling about his body. In a quieter corner I saw a famous conductor talking to a few fans—it was a well-known story that the conductor had gone deaf years ago but that cloth magic made it so he could hear vibrations in the air, allowing him to continue to perform. His suit was all black and where there would usually be seams the fabric kept going, rolling into large dishes that caught sound. I saw Lamb, talking to a few graduates as well as a couple of underclassmen. There were countless beautiful people, glowing people, shining people. The mayor of London was there, as was a whole company of actors and actresses. I wondered if Redfield was in attendance, but I didn't see him.

Next to me Gabs was likewise scanning the room, obviously looking for Kristoff. When she didn't see him she gave a little sigh and squeezed my arm. She seemed both relieved and disappointed.

"Let's see what the eats are like here, eh?" I said. We made our way over to a table done up with gelled meats, prosciutto, carrots, and celery. I loaded up a plate with vegetables. "Gabs, do you want your own plate or do you just want to eat off mine—"

She squeezed my arm hard. I looked up from the table to see Kristoff standing there awkwardly. He was not wearing magic clothes but rather a simple black-tie tuxedo.

"Gabs," he said, and then with a twitchy nod in my direction, "Paul."

I nodded back. Gabs stood there silently.

Kristoff took a deep breath.

"I wish to apologize for my behaviour yesterday," he said. "It wasn't becoming of a count."

He blinked and I recognized the confused expression clouding his features. Gabs was using her magic on him, picking which of his words to become reality.

"I see," she said, still holding my arm. "Not becoming of a count, hmm? Whereas I'm just some English peasant, so nothing should be expected from *me*."

"You've done very well for a woman of your station," Kristoff said. He frowned, clearly upset and confused at the words coming out of his mouth. Gabs's face remained as placid as a porcelain doll's. She would make him suffer even if it meant ruining her own chance of happiness with him.

Like many British aristocrats who studied cloth magic, Kristoff wasn't planning to make a living of it. He had come to England to have fun, to party far from home before returning to Germany. But then he'd crossed paths with Gabs and fallen so hard that he had found multiple excuses to stick around for another couple of years while she'd finished getting her degree. I knew he cared for her, even if he was fumbling the ball here.

"Kris, I suggest you stop right there," I said, stepping forwards.

Kristoff blinked and Gabs turned towards me with surprise.

"You had your shot, mate, and you blew it," I said. "Gabriella and I are together now and we're deeply in love."

I was able to talk freely, uninfluenced by Gabs's cloth magic. Perhaps it was because I was speaking directly to Kristoff and not her. It seemed she could only dictate the conversation when she was a participant.

Kristoff seemed simultaneously doubtful and heartbroken. "Truly? But we only just quarrelled . . ."

"Like I said, you had your chance."

Kristoff turned to Gabs. "Gabriella, is this true?"

Gabs tilted her head, neither a confirmation nor a denial. Before she could speak I jumped in.

"Yes, Kristoff, it's true. I've always loved Gabs and I was just waiting for you to mess things up so that she and I could be together. I knew you could never see her for the amazing, brilliant woman that she is—"

"But I do!" Kristoff exclaimed. I held up a hand.

"I'm sorry, but it's too late. It doesn't matter what you promised her in the past or did for her or what plans you made together. I'm with her now. We have our own plans, our own promises. We have already named six of our seven future children. We're deeply in love and—"

Gabs put a hand on my shoulder. "Paul," she said, "maybe you are, but I'm not."

Damn, Gabs. Even for playacting that was rather cold.

"Gabs? Baby?" I said, trying my best to sound heartbroken.

"I'm sorry, Paul." Her voice was mournful but there was just a twitch of a smile. It was gone when she turned to Kristoff. "If you really want to talk, I'll hear you out."

He offered his hand and the two of them disappeared into the swirl of the ballroom. I couldn't help but feel a twinge of jealousy watching them go. Not because I had designs on Gabs, or Kristoff for that matter, but more because of the connection between the two of them. Thanks to the magic upon me it was easy for me to make a good first impression, but to sustain a long, deep, true love? That seemed frustratingly out of reach. Possibly my innate magic even made it impossible. It provided an instant connection but nothing more beyond that.

"Ohhh, bad luck, Casanova."

Standing next to me was Verity Turnboldt. She was wearing my dress. I let out a sigh of relief. There'd be no need to repay Lamb or listen to Oberon gloat. The dress looked even better on her under the light of the ballroom. The darkness of the fabric made her stand out amidst the colourfulness of the rest of the guests. Far from being drab, the shininess of the magicked jersey made her glow like a dark flame.

CHAPTER 6

"You look beautiful."

"Thank you." Verity gave me the once-over, observing my coat in all its patchwork, gold-threaded glory. "You look like the jack of hearts."

"I'll take that as a compliment."

"I didn't mean it as an insult."

For a moment we both stood there. There was that awkward tinge to the air, like back in the offices of the *New Rev* after we'd stopped dancing, both of us waiting for the other one to laugh or do *something*. I almost wished Verity had the power of Gabs's gown, if only so someone else could direct the conversation. *I'm not crazy, am I?* I wanted to say. *There's something there, right? Something between us?* But I couldn't think of a graceful way to phrase it.

"Ah, Verity, there you are!" Oberon joined us. I stared at him. He was wearing a very dashing black suit with wide lapels, but the fucker wasn't wearing magic cloth! He was at a cloth mage gala and he wasn't wearing magic cloth! I felt wholly frustrated with Oberon and insulted on behalf of my profession.

"Oh, hello, Paul," Oberon said. His smile faltered but returned quickly. "I suppose it's clear that you won tonight's bet." When he turned to Verity his smile took on a warmer, more genuine glow. "But I can't really be mad when I see the result. Have I told you how lovely you look tonight, Verity?"

"Only every time you look at me," Verity said, her tone caustic but her smile suggesting she didn't truly mind the attention.

Jesus Christ, I thought.

Oberon smiled at me. "I already told Lamb that you are the winner of the bet. When you see him he'll transfer the purse to your Book."

I had never seen Oberon be such a gracious loser before. I had challenged him to this bet with the tandem goal of winning his money and making him feel bad, and even though the money was mine I hardly felt like I had won anything at all. And Verity was eating it right up. She was actually looking at Oberon with respect, as if he were an admirable bloke.

Thomas appeared by my elbow, holding three drinks.

"Hey, where did Gabs go—" He stopped and stared at Verity, confusion clear in his eyes.

"Thomas, this is Verity Turnboldt," I said. "As you can see, she wore our dress tonight."

Thomas said nothing, just stayed frozen for five seconds. He then started laughing, braying more like, actually doubling over so hard he had to hold the drinks up above his head so he wouldn't drop them as his body shook.

"Oh my, I'm sorry," he said, still chuckling as he straightened up. "I just thought of something really funny and completely unrelated." He grinned and held out one of the martini glasses to Verity. It was an amber drink with three little melon balls bobbing around in the glass. "So *you're* Verity Turnboldt, eh?"

"That's right." She took the martini glass from Thomas's hand, meeting his smile with a wary look.

"I was just talking to Prime Minister Brentwood," Oberon said loftily, as if trying to regain some equilibrium.

"The prime minister is here?!" I scanned the room as quickly as I could. If I could secure the leader of the nation as a patron, maybe he could arrange a meeting with Redfield for me.

"Yeah right," Thomas said. "Prime ministers never come to the gala."

"Lady Fife probably made him come," Oberon said. "Everyone knows that Brentwood doesn't sneeze without Lady Fife's say-so."

"People are always talking up this Lady Fife, and I don't get it," Verity said. "How does one unelected official have so much power? I mean, I know this country still has a monarchy and all that, but she's not royalty. So what's the big deal?"

There was a moment of awkward silence as Verity's gaze bounced between our faces, waiting for an answer.

"She's a foreseer," I said, voice low.

"A what?" Verity said.

"A diviner. Fortune-teller, soothsayer," Thomas said.

Verity laughed. "Like, with glass balls and tarot cards? Isn't that just a party trick? And set me straight if I'm wrong, but isn't that kind of magic illegal in this country anyway? If Lady Fife is such a well-known psychic, why has no one arrested her?"

"It's very dangerous to go up against someone who knows everything," I said. "People who have tried to destroy her have not come out of it so well." Rumour was that Lady Fife had more or less decided the course of every election since the end of the war.

"So you all just let her do what she wants?" Verity said.

"Great Britain's done well under her," Oberon said. "I'm not a Labour supporter, and even I will admit that."

"Yes," Thomas said wryly. "A kinder, gentler empire."

"Ah, so she's a benevolent dictator. I see." Verity took a swig of her drink.

"You know, I didn't come to this party to talk politics," Oberon said. "Darling, would you like to take a walk in the garden?"

It took me a second to realize that "darling" was Verity.

"Actually, I wouldn't mind talking politics some more," Verity said. "Thomas, could I have a moment of your time?"

There was a forced element to her smile. Thomas met it with a gleefully sharp grin.

"Oh, sure . . . Veronica, was it?"

"Verity."

"Right." The two of them moved off to the other side of the room. Oberon and I watched them go, mired in mutual confusion.

"What do you think that's about?" Oberon said to me. I didn't have a clue, or really much to say to Oberon in general, so I quickly made an excuse to slip away.

I circled the ballroom, stopping to chat with a new face every few minutes. Even for a people person like me it was exhausting. Everyone was already drunk and dead set on getting even more sloshed. Oh, they were all perfectly happy to talk to me, but none of them were particularly interested in commissioning work. At one point I started talking to an elderly woman in a dress with a pattern that mirrored the night sky. I had had a bit to drink by then and rambled on about my dreams, how I wished to become a famous mage and how in my darkest moments I feared it would never happen. She listened intently and, when I was done, told me that if I worked very hard, I *might* be able to lose my accent.

That exchange was depressingly the closest thing I had to a conversation of substance. Everyone else was more interested in oohing and aahing over the displays of magic that would randomly break out in the middle of the ballroom. And so I settled for handing out our business card and then slipping away, leaving behind an afterimage to nod and smile as my new friends nattered on.

"What a waste of time," I muttered to myself, letting the clamour of the ballroom swallow up my words.

"Really, Mr Gallagher?"

I was near the bar when I heard Lady Fife. I turned to see her standing by the bar, French 75 in hand.

"What a marvellous coat," she said. "It allows others to pay attention to you while relieving you of any obligation to repay the favour."

Lady Fife was wearing a fabulous ball gown of robin's-egg blue and maize yellow, made with the kind of extravagance you could afford when you were able to buy bolt after bolt of fabric. The shoulders and upper arms were ornamented with yellow lilies and daffodils made out of silk. Andrew had outdone himself tonight—Lady Fife looked a shining example of both regal maturity and beauty. I could not tell what kind of magical effect the dress had, but I wondered if it allowed her to listen in on the various conversations happening around the ballroom—even as she smiled at me her head was cocked to the side as if she'd just heard a far-off sound.

I stepped up to the bar in order to stand next to her. "Lady Fife," I said, with a slight bow. "How are you tonight?"

"Very well, thank you," she said. "And how are you, Mr Gallagher?"

"Oh, never better," I said.

"Really? Because you seem unusually downhearted."

Maybe it was because I thought I'd been hiding my gloomy mood rather well. Maybe it was because I thought I heard a bit of glee in Lady Fife's voice. Whatever the reason, I bristled at her comment.

"Ah, I suppose I shouldn't think to fool someone with your abilities, Lady Fife," I said bitterly.

She smiled. "I've noticed you often speak disdainfully of divination, Mr Gallagher," she said. "Perhaps I could change your mind with a demonstration? I generally have my schedule packed with appointments, but I suppose—"

"No," I replied quickly.

"No?" she said with her chillingly polite smile.

"No," I said again. "It's true: I don't put much stock in fortune-telling. It's not that I think it doesn't work. I do, and that's the issue. I think it's better to take life one day at a time, like the little sparrows in the field and all that. Living in fear of the future just shows a lack of faith in God and a lack of confidence in oneself, and I lack for neither."

Lady Fife sipped her drink and nodded as if considering my words. "So there are no circumstances where you might ask me questions of the future?" she asked casually.

"Nope. None. Never," I replied. She nodded.

"I see." Lady Fife stepped away from the bar, the massive expanse of her dress causing me to step aside. "Enjoy the rest of the gala, Mr Gallagher."

"Hmm," a male voice murmured as Lady Fife disappeared into the crowd. I turned to see a man in formal military dress standing at the bar. It was pathetic how much better that little *hmm* had made me feel. Lady Fife might always look down her nose at me, but at least I had caught this stranger's attention. He was in his mid- to late forties, with the kind of patrician profile that wouldn't be out of place on a Roman coin. A handsome, older military man.

"My name's Paul Gallagher," I said, unbidden. I held out my hand. He seemed surprised but shook it.

"Captain Hector Hollister, at your service." As we shook hands I felt the familiar flow of magic within me—I also noticed the spark of something else, a more grounded spark of attraction. Of course, I also saw that the good captain was wearing a wedding ring. Well, all I'd done so far was look.

"It's a bit noisy here," I said over the din. "Step outside with me?"

"Yes, let's." He stood up straight and pressed his way through the crowd. The ballroom's large glass doors were open so we headed outdoors for some fresh air. Several people, especially the ones wearing more stifling outfits, were already outside, talking under the light of the moon. One bloke, a lad I recognized as having been a few years ahead of me in school, was showing how he had created a suit jacket that allowed him to stand tiptoe on a bare tree branch, the tree supporting him as if he weighed no more than a wish.

Hollister took in the scene with a wry air. "You cloth mages," he said, "you all act as if you can walk on water."

Making a suit that allows the wearer to walk on water is actually a pretty base-level assignment for most cloth mages, but I knew the captain was speaking metaphorically.

"Walk on water, huh?" I said. "You know, a lot of people abuse that parable, talk like it's about puffing yourself up too much. In the story Jesus walks out onto the water and calls for the storm raging around 'em to stop, and the storm does. Then he calls for his disciples to join him on the water, and only Peter is brave enough to give it a go. Peter's feeling good at first, feet firm on the water, but when he lets go of the boat he gets scared and sinks. Luckily his best mate Jesus grabs him out before he can drown. The point of the story isn't that Jesus could walk on water. It's that we *all* could if we had just a little more faith. That's what cloth mages do. It's not that we can walk on water; it's that we make it so that others can."

Hollister was looking at me now rather than the treetop walker. "Are you a Christian man, Mr Gallagher?"

"Yeah. Catholic." This shouldn't have been a big surprise to anybody—most of Liverpool was—but in London I was always keenly aware that it was one more thing that marked me as different.

"Ah, me too!" Hollister said brightly. "I probably should have converted to Church of England if I had wanted to rise any higher than captain, but God asks great sacrifices of us, does he not? What church do you go to?"

"Uh, it's been a while since I've been a regular churchgoer," I admitted.

Hollister lightly tsked. "My family attends mass at Sacred Heart every Sunday."

"I have to ask, Captain, if you think so badly of cloth mages, what brings you to the gala?"

Hollister shrugged. "It's part of the job." He smiled my way. "But it's not all bad. Sometimes you get to meet kindred spirits."

I fall for women more often than men. Heck, some days I think I could fall for just about any woman in the world if the circumstances were right. Blokes I don't fall for as often, but when I do I fall hard and fast, like a stone from heaven. And it had happened just now with Hollister. His contained haughtiness was like my own personal siren song. Yeah, maybe it was a bad idea for multiple reasons, starting with the ring on his finger. But I wanted to see just how far this chance encounter could go.

"You seem a bit different from the others," Hollister said.

"Well, God willing, I hope to be the first cloth mage to become Court Magician," I said, bragging about something that I hadn't even done yet. Hollister did not laugh but seemed to be appraising me. I was glad he seemed to take it seriously, but I was afraid he might ask me for concrete details, like where I was on the list of candidates.

"So what exactly is it you do, Captain?" I asked. Hollister started to answer, but my ear was caught by something else—raised voices from somewhere out in the dark. It was Verity and Oberon, obviously having some kind of heated argument. I couldn't make out the words but I could clearly make out the sharp, angry tones drifting over from amongst the hedge sculptures.

"Is something wrong?" Hollister asked.

Maybe it was just my imagination, but I could have sworn I had just heard Verity say, "Let go of me."

"I . . . I have to go but please, let's continue this conversation later," I said to Hollister and hastily walked away from the dean's house and into the dark.

When I turned the corner around a large hedge rabbit I found Verity and Oberon. They were practically snarling at each other, eyes locked and lips pulled back. What drew my eye was how Oberon had

Verity's arm in a tight grip. She glared at him with narrowed eyes, trying to jerk her arm away from him.

"You think you're the first one to make tawdry accusations against my father?" Oberon said. "Better people than you have tried to tear him down, you—"

"Hey," I said. Both of them looked over towards me, surprise replacing anger. Oberon let go of Verity and she stepped away, rubbing her arm while glaring at him. A simmering tension filled the air. It was quite the contrast to the last time I'd seen them acting all cosy in the ballroom.

"You can go, Gallagher," Verity said, still rubbing her arm. "This doesn't concern you."

"And yet I am still quite concerned," I said. "How about *you* leave, Oberon?"

Oberon took a step towards me. "This isn't any of your business, Gallagher," he said. "This woman just insulted me and my family."

"You're right," I said. "I don't know what's going on, and it's not any of my business, but whatever awful thing Ms Turnboldt said . . . I'm sure it's all true."

The comment had the intended effect, which was to take Obie's attention off Verity and put it on me. Oberon stepped towards me and managed to pop me one in the right eye. As I stumbled back I tripped over my own feet and fell onto the damp grass. Fear flared up in me when I thought of grass stains getting on my coat.

Oberon stepped forwards, his hands still balled in fists, but all I could do was press my palms to my stinging face. The innate magic within me had me all locked up, unable to do anything more than try and shield myself from more blows.

"Hey!" Verity yelled. Her voice seemed to bring Oberon back to himself. He stopped, took some deep breaths, and let his hands fall to his sides. He turned to Verity, jabbing an accusing finger in her direction.

"If you ever print a bad word about my family, I'll kill you."

With that he stomped off. I waited until his footsteps were swallowed up by the general clamour of the party before pushing myself up off the ground. I went over to where Verity was standing, a frown pulling down her face.

"You all right?"

She let out an irritated huff. "I had everything under control. You got a black eye over nothing, chum."

"Right," I said. It felt worse now, throbbing like mad.

"Damn, damn, damn." Verity stomped at the earth, the heel of her shoe digging into the ground. "This is bad. I *need* him."

I stared at her. "Oberon? Need him for what?"

"The story I'm working on," Verity said, her teeth gritted.

I rolled my eyes. "Well, in my opinion, no story is worth getting close to that git," I said.

"Well, no one asked you for your opinion," Verity snapped. I stayed quiet this time. Verity started rubbing her arms. The dress I had sewn for her wasn't exactly made for cool spring nights. I unclasped my multicolour coat and offered it to her. She looked at me as if unsure of what I was offering, then gingerly took the coat from me.

"Thanks, chum," she muttered. She wrapped the coat around her shoulders, holding it close like a blanket. For about a minute we just stood there. Finally Verity spoke.

"There's a big story I've been working on. I've been working on it for a long time." She laughed. "I suppose you could say I've been working on it my whole life."

"Is this the story you needed Oberon for?" I asked.

She nodded. "How well do you know David Myers?"

"Oberon's father?" I'd met the man a few times at various school and social events. He was a short, portly figure with a round face that reminded me of the man in the moon. A friendly, kindly man. His biggest flaw was that he tended to talk to young people as if we were patients at his paediatric hospital. "I don't know him well, but he's always been nice enough. Why?"

"He's mixed up in some nasty stuff," Verity said. "I thought maybe Oberon could help me with it, but . . ."

I shook my head. "Oberon might be an asshole, but he's not going to betray his own dad."

"That's the thing," Verity said. "David Myers isn't Oberon's father."

I stared at her. "Does Oberon know this?"

"He denies it, but I think he knows the truth."

"Jesus." I wished there was some way to go back in time, to pick up the needle on the record player and bring it back to an earlier groove. I really didn't want to get mixed up in Oberon's personal life, especially if it was going to get splashed on the front page of the *New Rev*. "I suppose it's a little scandalous that Mrs Myers cheated on Dr Myers, but she's long dead. Is it really front-page news—"

"No, no, it's not about that," Verity said. "It's much bigger. I thought Oberon would be on my side, but I was wrong."

The light from my jacket gave her skin a soft glow. I could sense her plan forming as we looked at each other.

"This story isn't just about the Myers family," Verity said. "It would expose a great injustice woven into the very fabric of this country."

"What are you talking about?" I said.

Verity shook her head. "It's too dangerous to know what I know. And just knowing isn't enough. The problem is that I don't have any actual *proof*!" She turned so she was facing me head-on. "But you could help me with that."

"Me?"

"Yes. You seem like a good guy, and—" She hesitated. "Since the moment we met I had an odd feeling, like I could trust you."

I felt a little guilty about that. Her good impression of me was a false image crafted by magic. A side effect of my innate magic was that it made me appear to be all things to all people, the God-sent solution to whatever ailed them.

I worried the spell likewise made me wish only to fulfil that desire.

"Well, I don't want to disappoint you," I said. "But what exactly would you need me to do?"

"You and Oberon are friends, right? You could get close to him and—"

"And what?" I said. "Help you air Dr Myers's dirty laundry? Mrs Myers, God rest her soul, died the day Oberon was born. What good would it do dragging her name through the mud? Even if Oberon's a prat, there's no need to out him as a literal bastard."

"I told you, there's more to it than that."

"Oh, right, some shadowy conspiracy that you can't tell me about," I said. "Look, if I truly thought you were on the side of the angels here, I'd be right with you. But you're expecting me to take a lot on trust when I don't even know your real name."

She was quiet and for a moment I thought she'd tell me her true identity. Instead she took a small notebook out of her purse—just a regular notebook, not a Book—scribbled something down, ripped out the page, and handed it to me.

"If you won't take my word for it, check it out for yourself. If you see the same things I do, leave a message for me at the *New Rev* office."

I took the scrap of paper. In the dim moonlight I could just make out what looked to be three names scribbled down in stark, printed letters.

"What is this?" I asked. Verity said nothing, just handed me my coat and headed back to the gala. For a while I stayed outside, trying to read the note in the moonlight, before tucking it in my pocket. I returned to the party, determined to find Thomas and tell him we had to get out of there before anything else happened.

CHAPTER 7

When I stepped into the ballroom I spotted Oberon standing by the bar with Hector Hollister. Obie was speaking animatedly to the captain, who was taking it all in with a neutral expression and calm bearing.

Even though I wanted to talk to Hollister more, I could tell that going over there while Oberon was still angry would be a bad idea. The party itself seemed to be winding down, the conversation less lively, people flitting about like moths. Nearly everyone here would feel awful in the morning. If you weren't accustomed to wearing magic cloth, it took a toll on your body—your limbs felt worn and tired, like you had just swum a marathon. Cloth magicians like myself spent a lot of time building up stamina to negate the effects—cold showers to help blood circulation, breathing techniques, and the like.

I couldn't find Thomas anywhere, but I did bump into Andrew, who helpfully told me that Thomas and Ralph were out on the dean's driveway, trying to fix Ralph's car.

"But don't worry, Gally!" Andrew said. "You can always get a ride with Mother and me."

Lady Fife was nearby when Andrew said this and she made a moue of distaste.

"I can give you a lift home," said Captain Hollister. I turned to find him standing behind us, back straight but a slight, uncertain shuffle to his feet as our gazes met. "I'm heading out now."

"Perfect!" I turned back to Andrew. "Thanks anyway, mate. Let's finally do that Brighton day trip soon, eh? Let's go, Captain."

Hollister drove a Vauxhall Velox, nothing flash but respectable. An uncertain silence echoed once we got in and closed the car doors.

"So," he said. "Where do you want to go, Mr Gallagher?"

Hollister gave off a strange vibe. I knew he was interested in me, but it felt like there was something more going on than a simple hookup.

Well, if he was going to be coy, so was I.

"Let's head towards London to start," I said.

Hollister nodded and started the car.

As we were making our way down the driveway I saw Ralph's broken-down heap of a car. Both Thomas and Ralph were working on it, crawling all over it like ants on a biscuit. At one point, Ralph made use of his magical strength to lift the car up so Thomas could take a look at the undercarriage.

"Hey, stop for a second," I said to Hollister. He obliged and I popped my head out the window. "Oy, Thomas!"

Thom stepped away from the car and came over. "Paul?" He glanced past me to Hollister. "Who's that?"

"This is Hector Hollister," I said. "He's giving me a drive back to London."

Thomas sighed and stepped in closer. "Well, Ralph and I are still trying to get this shit heap up and running. Might be a while yet."

I felt a pang of guilt for leaving Thomas and Ralph on the side of the road, but really, what good would I have been to them? I was no mechanic.

"I don't know when exactly I'll be home either," I said. "See you sometime tomorrow."

Thomas snorted and went back to Ralph and the car. Hollister drove on.

"I have a small pad in Central London," Hollister said. "I stay there when my work keeps me late. We could go there."

"Sure," I said, watching his face in profile. I wanted to keep talking, but those little melon-ball martinis packed quite the punch. "Mind if I rest my eyes?"

Hollister grunted. I closed my eyes and when I opened them the car had stopped and a London streetlamp was shining through the window. We were on some street in Belgravia, the poshest part of Central London. The pearly-white buildings were so pristine they almost seemed to glow—I often wondered how buildings like that could be in the middle of the city and yet stay so free of soot and grime.

Hector got out of the car and went up to a nearby town house. I hurried after him. When Hollister had said he had a pad in town, I hadn't expected something this flash.

He opened a door that led to a flight of stairs. I followed him up to a third-storey flat. It was a small space, the main room being a sitting room / office with a little kitchenette. Aside from the door we'd just come in, there were two other doors, one leading, I assumed, to the toilet and the other to the bedroom. The place seemed homey—there was a dirty cup in the sink and a sock poking out from under the couch. But even though it was obviously lived in, it had the curious feeling of being lifted from another time. Ten years ago, specifically. There was a wartime sparseness to the place even though many of the decorations spoke of old money. It was a hard space to make sense of, but one thing came through loud and clear—this was a bachelor's apartment.

"It's not actually *my* pad," Hollister said. "It belongs to a friend of mine but . . . he doesn't use it anymore and lets me have the run of the place."

"Lucky," I said, sitting on the couch. I didn't really care why Hollister had a city apartment. He was hardly the only man who had a place he kept discreetly, an apartment solely for lovers or even just for himself. I had slept with a married man before—he had been up front about it, said he loved his wife but just couldn't change this one fact about himself. Being a gay man in this country could land you in jail, or worse: you could lose reputation and employment, be shunned by family and friends, get sentenced to chemical castration by the courts. So I understood why so many gay men in the country kept a low profile. Despite my outgoing nature, I was in fact capable of keeping a secret.

"Captain, take a load off," I said, patting the couch as if it were my home and not his. Hollister took a tentative seat on the couch. Up until that point he had seemed sure of himself, but now his movements were slow, as if he was still planning them out.

I was curious about him, if only because I so rarely met fellow Christian queer men. But I was wary of prodding too much; I knew how fraught it was bearing the cross of being gay and Catholic, of having those two loves intersect. My faith had always been a comfort to me but I knew that wasn't so for everyone. I wanted to get Hollister's take on things, to see if it lined up with my own.

When I was a young lad of eleven or so the priest at my church had told me that homosexuality existed because of original sin. When Adam and Eve had eaten fruit from the tree of knowledge against God's wishes, it had thrown everything askew, ensuring their descendants would all be warped in some way, each generation growing further from God. By that point, I'd already doubted the priest's infallibility—his dentures had popped out during a sermon once and it was hard to come back from that. But I'd also suspected that I was one of those homosexuals the priest referred to: I had crushes on the girls in my class and also my fellow choirboys. And I'd known that if I had the chance to meet God face-to-face, he'd like me. So I couldn't believe that I was cast out for something inherent within me.

I did think the priest was right about it having something to do with original sin, but I had a very different take on it. If Adam and Eve had not eaten from the tree and humanity were still living in paradise, there'd still be gay people. The difference would be that no one would get bent out of shape over the fact.

"What you said at the gala, did you mean it?" Hollister asked.

"You'll have to be more specific," I said, smiling to cover up how I'd been distracted by my own thoughts.

"About being the next Court Magician."

I had been shifting over to sit closer to Hollister but this made me pause.

"Well, yes," I said, suddenly self-conscious. "I know . . . I know it sounds ridiculous. I know where I'm from—I hear my own voice when I speak. I don't have the money or the name. But all my life, I've felt like I've been destined for something more than what I'm doing."

"But you've never had the opportunity to prove it," Hollister stated.

"Yes!" I said. "If I was the one to survive the Making, I know I would be the best Court Magician this nation's ever seen. I'd make the strongest mages, open the schools wide to men and women of all races and classes. I'd start a new golden age of magic in England."

"People say we're in a golden age now," said Hollister.

I shook my head. "No. We've been able to leapfrog forwards by aping the magics of China and India, but we've only ever had a surface-level understanding of them." That was what happened when you stole something rather than tried to engage with it. "When we colonized India, we revolutionized cloth magic in this country by applying colour the same way Indian cloth mages did. When we saw how Book magic was used in China by the entire populace, not just bureaucrats, we rolled out the same system here. And to the rest of the world we presented these things as if we had created them whole cloth rather than lifted them." I was rambling but I still hadn't made my point. "But we have the chance to create new types of magic here in Britain; I'm sure of it. All we need to do is cast off old, oppressive systems, like—"

"Like the monarchy?" Hollister said. "The House of Lords?"

"Not the monarchy." I knew that would never fly—England had tried that once before and it hadn't worked then. "But maybe the House of Lords. I don't know. I just want to open the doors of magic wide."

"And what better way to symbolize that than having a common fellow like yourself as Court Magician."

"Yes, exactly," I said.

Hollister looked thoughtful.

"I think there's something to that," he said. "Magic is so regulated in this country. It could use someone to shake it up. I could arrange a meeting between you and Redfield, see if he'll put you on the list of candidates."

Hollister spoke so calmly and evenly that I almost missed the last part of his words.

"I could arrange a meeting for you with Redfield," Hollister repeated. "If he likes you, he has the power to sidestep the usual process and put you down as a candidate."

"That's really all it takes?" I wished I didn't sound so surprised.

Hollister shrugged. "Well, you'll still have to charm Redfield but . . ." He gave me a warm smile. "I'm sure you'll have no trouble with that."

I leaned in for the kiss—I couldn't help it, not after that. Hollister grabbed my shoulders and held me away from him. Panic was clear in his eyes.

"What the devil are you doing?"

"I . . . I thought that's why we came here." Also, I had figured it was what Hollister wanted, something in return for introducing me to Redfield. I didn't mind—I already found him attractive.

Hollister froze. I almost felt like I could see his whole life flashing before his eyes, projected out from his brain onto his irises like the film at a movie house. Then he broke free of it and stood up. He started pacing the length of the small room.

"No, no. I only brought you here because I wanted a private place to talk. I wasn't trying to . . . to . . . solicit you." He spoke loudly but without looking in my direction.

"All right," I said, a bit worried by Hollister's sudden frantic energy. "I'm sorry. I read the room wrong. I just figured, you brought me here and offered to do so much for me, someone who's practically a stranger . . ." I realized that maybe it wasn't a good idea to highlight that, in case Hollister realized that yeah, actually, it was a stupid idea to offer so much to someone he had just met a few hours ago.

Hollister stopped pacing to stare at me. "I meant what I said about wanting to see you as Court Magician. That's all, truly."

I felt both relieved and disappointed. I wasn't quite sure how to read Hollister, if he was lying to me about not wanting to sleep with me or not (or, for that matter, if he was lying to himself).

He coughed. "You know, the roads should be quiet this early in the morning. I should be able to make the drive up to Barnet easily enough." He glanced at his watch, seemingly just for an excuse to look away from me. "Feel free to spend the night here. There's some food in the icebox. Before you leave in the morning please write down your address so I can get in touch. The door has an automatic latch so no need to worry about a key; it will lock behind you when you go. Well, ta."

He moved towards the door like a man with flames at his back and was down the stairs before I could even say goodbye.

CHAPTER 8

The flat's tiny bedroom had a small, single bed, hardly appropriate for a secret love nest. Maybe Hollister had been telling the truth about his intentions after all. I crashed on the couch.

When I woke up the next morning a thousand anvils were striking in my head. I drank some water, helped myself to an apple in the icebox. I still felt like shit. It wasn't just the hangover—a whole storm of thoughts was swirling in my head, each one just a snowflake in a blizzard. No one at the gala had been truly interested in cloth magic, and the whole business with Verity and Oberon left a bad feeling in my stomach. Also, there was still the enigma that was Hector Hollister. What exactly was his game? My reflection in the bathroom mirror offered no answers, just a haggard expression and a burgeoning black eye from where Oberon had hit me.

There was a telephone in the flat. I picked it up and asked to be connected to a specific address in Harrow.

"Paul?" Lamb's somewhat groggy voice said over the line. "How can you be awake this early?"

"It's one p.m.," I said.

"Yes, one p.m. on the Sunday after the May Gala." Lamb sighed. "Well, you always were an early riser."

"I didn't get the twenty pounds off you last night for winning the bet," I said. "Come into town and I'll treat you to lunch." I wasn't overly eager to spend time with Lamb, but he was a good source of gossip and I had many questions to ask him.

"Oh, will you?" Lamb said. "All right then."

We made plans to meet in an hour's time.

I was still wearing my dress shirt and trousers from the night before—my stained-glass coat was hanging up by the door. The coat seemed much too ostentatious for wearing around the city on a Sunday afternoon, so I started to snoop around the closets and drawers of the flat, half looking for something to wear and half just looking. In the closet I found several suits. Much like the furniture and decor, they were at least ten years out of date. They were nice suits, well made but not showy, something a politician might wear. They were made for someone a little bit taller than me with a portly build. They would not have fit the much taller Hector Hollister. The clothes had a mustiness to them, and I couldn't shake the sense that they belonged to a dead man.

I did not find anything scandalous in the flat. In fact, there was hardly anything personal there at all. There was a locked drawer by the desk, but I had never been good at picking locks, so the contents remained a mystery to me. In the end, all I could do was shrug on my colourful coat and go meet Lamb.

"You usually know what's going on in this city," I said once we had taken our seats at a table. We were at a café at the back of a building that sat on the north bank of the Thames. It was a nice enough day that the waiter had sat us outside on the patio. "I wanted to know if you've heard any chatter about David Myers."

"Oberon's father?" Lamb said, tilting his head quizzically. Though he had sounded sleepy on the phone he now managed to have his usual look of nonchalant elegance. "Well, there's some old gossip, but nothing new."

"Then tell me the old," I said.

Lamb opened his mouth to reply but at that moment a waitress placed our food on the table. The apple had barely even hit the bottom of my stomach, and I fell upon my sandwich like a Viking raiding party descending upon a small village. It was probably four or five minutes before I noticed that Lamb hadn't even touched his food but was just watching me with a wry expression.

"You used to give me grief for not saying grace before meals," Lamb said. I dabbed my mouth with a napkin, though I feared it was too late to play the gentleman.

"I've fallen out of the habit," I admitted.

"Of praying? Or eating?"

I didn't know what to say to that, so I gestured to Lamb's plate. "Well, it's still a sin to waste food."

"Oh, I'm not that hungry," Lamb said, pushing his salad towards me. "Feel free to help yourself."

I made a point of sticking to my own food.

Lamb rolled his eyes. "I'll tell you the old gossip about David Myers, but in return you must listen to a request from me afterwards. All right, dear heart?"

I couldn't see any harm in that so I nodded, gesturing for Lamb to continue.

"In order to understand Oberon we have to go back to his grandfather, Reginald Kently."

"What? Really?" I said, nearly choking on a chip.

"Yes," Lamb said calmly. "The Kently family owned a tobacco plantation in Virginia which they managed to hold on to even after the American rebellion. In the late 1850s, young Reg went on a tour of his family's holdings. It was while he was visiting the plantation in Virginia that he fell in love with a young slave girl named Rose.

"Reginald offered her a deal: leave her friends and family to the field and come to England. All she had to do was agree to be his wife and she'd be a free woman."

"Sounds like he never freed her at all," I said. "The American Civil War was right around the corner. She would have been free if she'd just waited a few years."

"A lot can happen in a few years," Lamb said. "And who knows? Maybe she really loved dear old Reggie. Once she was in England she was a free woman according to the law of the land anyway, and yet she still went through with the marriage."

We were quiet for a moment, both taking a drink from our glasses.

Lamb soon spoke again. "Rose gave birth to three daughters, which vexed Reginald to no end. Maybe he was liberal enough to marry a Black woman, but he was a staunch supporter of primogeniture. He needed a son to whom he could leave his vast fortune. He specified in his will that only a male descendant would inherit the family money. His three daughters grew up and managed to marry well. You can perhaps see the appeal: the first couple to produce a son would win the claim to the Kently fortune. That alone is enough to overlook the colour of your wife's skin and ignore the crude comments from the rest of so-called polite society.

"Among these brave, intrepid young men was Dr David Myers." Lamb's voice rang with a mock admiration. "Myers was a bit different from the other suitors chasing after the Kently inheritance. Myers hailed from some pissant East Anglia village with a name like Dereshire or Glenhorne or Inkford. While working at St Rita's Children's Hospital, Dr Myers met Abigail Kently, the youngest Kently daughter, and they were soon married. At this point Abigail's elder sisters had borne only daughters. Reginald seemed to consider it a personal affront that the women in his family were denying him this one joy, denying his need to see his bloodline represented by a boy child. If none of his daughters could provide a male heir before his death, the money would be turned over to a distant relation.

"Oddly enough, David and Abigail did not get pregnant right away. It was four long years before they announced they were expecting. This was in 1930. Reginald was ninety-eight—"

"Ninety-eight?!" My nan had lived to eighty-five and she had been the oldest person I had ever met.

Lamb shrugged. "Bitterness can be quite the preservative. At ninety-eight Reggie still had power over the family. As the pregnancy progressed Reginald's health started to falter. The whole family held its breath, praying to every god they could that the child would be born before Reginald died, and that the child would be a masculine child. And then, one day, while Reggie was gurgling away in the critical care unit, Abigail gave birth in the privacy of the Myerses' home. And lo and behold, it was a boy! All hail King Oberon!" Lamb paused his tale to raise his teacup high in the air.

"With Oberon's birth, the family fortune was secured. Reginald died a few weeks later, leaving everything to Dr Myers to manage until Oberon came of age. Unfortunately, Mrs Myers was unable to enjoy the fruit of her labours as she died in childbirth."

"Poor woman," I said. "That's quite the family saga, but I don't quite see the scandal."

"Well, there was a lot of talk at the time about how suspicious it was that it had taken so long for the Myerses to conceive, and how they managed it just in the nick of time," Lamb said. "Some people suggested that they had gotten . . . outside help."

I remembered Verity saying that Dr Myers wasn't Oberon's father. If David Myers was infertile, the couple might have gotten someone else to father the baby.

"Still, it was awfully lucky that it turned out to be a boy," I said.

Lamb grinned. "Indeed. And that inspired some of the more outlandish rumours."

"Like what?"

"Well, as a doctor in a children's hospital, Dr Myers met many expectant and new mothers. If you needed a male child, he'd be in a good position to procure one."

"What?" I said. "That's insane! That would imply the Myerses faked Abigail's pregnancy, which is pretty outlandish considering *she died in childbirth*."

Lamb looked at me. "Did she?"

I sat there for a moment, taking his words in.

Lamb waved his hand. "Like I said, that was just some of the more extreme gossip. But nothing ever came of it, and as time moved on people became preoccupied with new scandals."

I had Verity's list of names in my pocket, but I was hesitant to show them to Lamb. Anything I gave to him was liable to become fodder for its own gossip.

"Now, as for my request," Lamb said, pressing his fingertips together. "Please stay away from Hector Hollister."

Now I really did choke on a chip.

"What?" I said. "How do you . . . I . . . you know what? It's none of your business who I spend my time with, so if you're just trying to stir up drama—"

"Don't you know what he does for a living?"

"Well, he works for the military."

"He works for the Department of Magic Regulation," Lamb said.

That shut me up. The Department of Magic Regulation was in charge of investigating improper uses of magic. Specifically, it was charged with finding people who were practising innate magic illegally or had had innate magic practised upon them.

I fell into the second category.

"So? What does that have to do with me?" I said, flippantly.

Lamb brought his tea to his mouth, pausing as if trying to cover up his lower face. When he spoke it was very quietly.

"When you're nervous you hide your left hand."

My hands were on the table, right hand resting on top of the left. I pulled them away, then felt angry at myself for further proving Lamb's words.

Lamb sipped his tea and set the cup back on the saucer.

"You know, they don't just make any idiot a professor," Lamb said. "I don't know how or where or when you got that little break in your hand or what's going on between you and Hollister, but the danger he presents far outweighs anything he can offer you."

"He just wants to help me." Even though the restaurant was near empty I still felt frightened speaking about innate magic, however obliquely. No one in my entire life had ever figured out that I had innate magic. I hadn't even told Thomas. In the back of my mind, there had always been fear of getting picked up by the Department of Magic Regulation, but they seemed so far removed from my daily life that I honestly worried more about Book inspectors on the tube.

But now I had given one of those magic regulators my name and phone number.

Lamb sighed.

"Perhaps he does want to help you. But even that could spell trouble," he said. "Paul, I sometimes think you don't understand your appeal. When people meet you, you inspire a certain feeling in them. They think, *I am the only thing that stands between this brilliant boy and his certain destruction. That* is a very heady feeling, and you should be wary of the people it appeals to."

Thanks to the food my hangover had abated but now I just felt dehydrated, like a piece of driftwood.

"You don't have to explain this to me, Christopher," I said.

Lamb had the good grace to at least look admonished.

"I'm just saying, be wary of Hollister." Lamb stared out at the Thames. "It's been at least fifty years since they hanged someone for practising illegal innate magic. But the law's still on the books. I know

when you're young, it can seem like you have nothing to lose, but . . .
you always have something to lose."

~

Once Lamb had left, I sat in the café and took out the list of names
Verity had given me the night before.

Martha Wilde

Sheldon Wood

George McKenzie

The names meant nothing to me, but Verity had given them to me
as a kind of a test. If I could figure out what these three strangers had in
common and their significance to Verity, maybe I could get past those
walls she put up.

I paid the tab for lunch and walked up to Somerset House. Somerset
House was a Book Binder's paradise, the storehouse of all official personal records in Great Britain. Births, deaths, marriages, wills, all were
stored in the building's labyrinth of a basement. If anything relevant
to your life had been put on paper and signed by witnesses, this big
hulking stone building had it in triplicate.

Somerset House was a sprawling neoclassical structure on the
Strand right next to Waterloo Bridge. Inside was a courtyard so large
the city put a skating rink in the middle of it each winter. It was right
next to my old school, University College London, and its partnership
with the school explained why so many mages worked there. When I
stepped into the records office, I counted at least eight Book Binders in
training working the front desk. Eight mages. That was more than had
been in my entire graduating cloth magic class.

Amongst the students there was one that reminded me of my
ex-girlfriend Molly. The two women didn't look anything alike: Molly
had been all smooth curves while this girl was as lean as a carrot. But
the way she talked with her hands, the little smile she had whenever

she communicated with a Book . . . that contentment and ease were bittersweetly familiar.

I went up to her.

"Hello, my name is Paul Gallagher. How are you today?" I asked. Her smile flickered once she saw me, and I didn't blame her—I was wearing a flashy, colourful coat and sported a black eye. However, her smile grew as we shook hands and my magic put her at ease.

"Quite well, thank you." Her name tag said Caroline. She had blonde hair, an inquisitive smile, and curious eyes. Freckles stood out sharply on her fair skin. I liked her. I like people who are engaged with things from the get-go. "What can I help you with?"

"I'm looking up some information on some people," I said. "I have their names but that's it."

Caroline tilted her head. "Do you know their birthdays or anything else at all?"

"Um, no," I said. "But I think they were born in this century." That was a total shot in the dark, but I felt like I had to narrow my search a little, if only so I didn't seem quite so ridiculous.

Caroline nodded. "Well, you'll still have to sort a fair bit of wheat from the chaff, but we can at least look at the twentieth-century records. Come with me."

We left the reception of the library and crossed the courtyard, then stepped into a building and down a flight of stairs into the basement.

"The post office used to be based out of here," Caroline told me as we walked, "and we handle all the marriage, birth, and death certificates in the country. We store backups of everything in Books now, but we still have the physical copies on-site too."

I nodded. I had heard this before from Molly, who had done her own stint at Somerset.

"And of course, we keep copies of every newspaper article, going back to the turn of the century!" she said. "Students here bind the newspapers daily, and we have several students whose master's project is compiling newspapers from the nineteenth century."

"Is that what you're working on?"

Caroline shook her head. "Oh, no. I'm studying to get my doctorate in chemistry, but if you want to do anything these days you have to know Book Binding. It's very useful for compiling data and logging lab results." She laughed. "I always wanted to be a scientist, but I never expected to be a mage!"

I started to think of all the ways that cloth magic could help a scientist, from a lab coat that could keep her safe from danger to an outfit that would keep her mind sharp. But I recognized that this bid probably wouldn't win me any favours, so I tried a different tack instead. "You know, you remind me of a girl I used to be in love with."

Caroline raised an eyebrow in my direction. We had come to a stop in front of a door labelled PERSONAL RECORDS. "Oh?"

"Yeah. She's a Book Binder too. Maybe you know her; she graduated just last year. Her name is Molly Evans—"

Caroline spun around to face me. "Molly Evans?" she said, smile gone, eyes wide. "You know her?"

"Well, yes. We're still good friends," I said, uncomfortable with the way Caroline was looking at me. It was a look of admiration, but it wasn't directed towards me.

"She's amazing! So young and such a brilliant mage!" Caroline said. If her eyes glowed any brighter I'd have to look away. "She got a government job straight out of school! If anyone's going to crack the transference problem, it's her."

"Yep, that's for sure." I regretted bringing up Molly. It didn't do well for my ego to be reminded that my ex was excelling far more in her field than I was in mine.

"Do you think you could give me her number? Or introduce me?"

"Uh . . ." This was not how I had pictured this going. "Are the personal records in here?" I asked, gesturing to the door that read **PERSONAL RECORDS.**

"Oh, yes! This way!" Caroline spun around. The room was full of rows of bookshelves. "All right, what name did you want to look up?"

"Martha Wilde," I said. Caroline nodded and led me deeper into the room.

"All right, here's the *Wh–Wi* Book." She opened it and I saw her eyes start to lose focus as she began to connect with the Book.

"Actually, I'll look it up myself," I said, reaching to touch the Book but not take it from her—it could be very dangerous to suddenly break someone's connection once they'd made a circuit between their soul and a Book. Luckily, Caroline was an old pro and able to break the connection easily herself, blinking at me in confusion.

"I don't mind," she said.

"Thank you, I really appreciate it, but I can take it from here." According to Verity I was on the trail of dangerous knowledge. I didn't want this helpful student to be caught in the crossfire. "All the Books are labelled, and I know how to read a Bound Book."

"Still," she said doubtfully, "usually a mage stays with visitors."

"It's all public records, right?" I said. "Don't worry, I won't cause any trouble."

She shrugged and smiled. "Well, I feel like I can trust you, so all right. Let me know when you're done."

I thanked her for her help and she left.

I opened the Book. A pure white page stared up at me. I tried to clear my mind, to focus on the sensation of the Book in my hands, to let the emptiness of the page fill my mind. For the first two minutes it was a no-go: bits of ink would bloom up and swirl away. I kept trying.

I'd never been all that hot at Book magic. Thomas said I needed to meditate more, that getting in the habit of summoning a calm mindset at will would help when I had an open Book in hand. But I just never had the patience for such things.

It didn't help that this Book, being so jam-packed with information, was a little more complicated to work than a Book you'd find in a shop. I considered getting Caroline to help me after all, secrecy be damned. I tried sitting on the floor, my back against the wall, my shoes off. After a few deep breaths and a prayer to Mary for patience I opened the Book again.

Martha Wilde, I thought as I stared at the page.

This time the information came, ink appearing and forming words and then sentences. Martha Wilde was a distressingly common name. According to the Book, in the last fifty-four years roughly 340 Martha Wildes had come into existence here in the United Kingdom. What was I even searching for?

I took a deep breath, steeling myself to break the connection with the Book. On the exhale I closed the cover and winced. Even with all my prep I'd been too hasty. The pain was like the mental equivalent of a stubbed toe.

I'd come back to Martha Wilde once I had investigated Sheldon Wood. I looked around the shelf until I found the Book containing the records of everyone with a *Wo* surname.

Sheldon Wood, I thought. The page came quicker this time. There were only three names listed, thank Jesus, and I read through them all. Each time I focused on a name, a birth certificate and any other public records of note would appear. The first Sheldon in the list had married shortly before dying in the Great War; the third Sheldon was still living and was a city councillor in Norwich. The middle Sheldon stood out to me. According to his birth certificate he had been born on December 11, 1931. The Book also had a death certificate for him, dated July 30, 1940. His obituary was included:

Sheldon Wood, beloved son and brother, died Monday while undergoing heart surgery at St Rita's Hospital. He is survived by his father, Sheldon

Wood, stepmother, Katherine Wood, and stepbrother, Benson Wood. A funeral will be held Sunday at Holy Redeemer Baptist Church. Rest safely in the arms of Jesus, dear dove.

David Myers worked at St Rita's. So far it was the only connection that I could see.

I went back to the *Wi* Book and called up the list of Marthas. By concentrating I was able to make the Book list their dates. I focused on the Marthas who had died as children. After reading about two dozen tragic childhood deaths I stumbled upon one in particular. This Martha Wilde had been born on May 24, 1936. Four years later her parents had died in a house fire. Martha had died two weeks later. Under her parents' obituary was Martha's own obit:

August 18, 1940

Martha Wilde died Thursday at St Rita's Children's Hospital, from infection after severe burns. Her guardians, Martha's aunt and uncle, Sonya and Rufus Wilde, would like to thank the doctors who tended to the girl for their dedication and care. She is predeceased by her parents, Samuel and Clementine Wilde. A service will be held on Sunday at Holy Heart Church. In lieu of flowers a donation can be made to St Rita's.

"Poor mite," I muttered. I hated hospitals. I hated the smell of disinfectant, the sight of white walls. Thinking of that poor orphan dying alone in a hospital bed of a lingering infection made me close the Book for a moment so I could collect myself.

Martha had been at St Rita's. Could Dr Myers have operated on little Martha Wilde? In which case my sympathy extended to him too. I could never work in a profession where I held someone's life in my hands, let alone a little child's. How crushing it must have been to have lost her.

I still didn't see the overall shape of Verity's investigation. I was now dreading what the last name held.

I went over to the *M* section. I grabbed the *Mc* Book off the shelf and sat down to read.

George McKenzie, I thought.

If there had been a flood of Martha Wildes, there was a deluge of George McKenzies. I tried my same trick from before of zeroing in on the ones who had died as children.

Only one had died at St Rita's during Dr Myers's tenure there. Beyond that, information on the boy was scant. There was a birth certificate, stating that little George had been born on April 19, 1923. I noted that there was an empty space where his father's name should have been. The only other logged bit of information was George's death certificate. He had died on March 3, 1927, at St Rita's of "complications."

"Complications of what?" I asked aloud. I scanned the birth and death certificates for more information. There, in the death notice, was Dr David Myers's name. He had signed off on George McKenzie's death certificate.

I closed the Book hastily, not caring about the jolt of pain that passed through me. Bits of text danced in front of my eyes as my brain tried to shake off the lingering feel of the Book's enchantment. On the surface they were all tragic stories but not sinister ones. Yet Verity had clearly put their names down for a reason. Who could have benefited from these three children dying?

Not content to leave it as a rhetorical question, I went to Caroline and asked to be shown the wills and estate records.

~

I'd listened to enough radio mystery dramas to know there was one question a sleuth always asked: *Cui bono?* Who benefits? After viewing the will and estate records that became clear. These children had been killed, murdered so their guardians could collect their money or titles. And the assassin had been the children's doctor. These kids had been betrayed at every level, by both blood and society. Just the thought of it made me want to rip pages out of the Books around me. How could people do something like that and then go on living?

The *New Rev* office was not far from Somerset House. When I arrived there was just one staff member in the office, a man wearing a beret and a very ornate moustache. He said Verity wasn't in, that she was hard at work on an undercover assignment. From his smug demeanour, I felt like she was probably just out grabbing a bite to eat and he was giving me the runaround. I left her a note asking her to call me and then went home, my mind a grey daze.

When I finally returned to my flat in North London I felt like Odysseus, unable to recognize my own home. Thomas wasn't there, which made me feel even lower. The world had changed, or maybe I had just become more aware of it. I'd been given a glimpse at the invisible strings holding the nation together, insight into how downright evil people could be if it guaranteed even just a little bit of material wealth in this world. I wanted to talk to Thom, speak about what I'd learned and get his read on it. Thomas would not be shocked by the dark deeds of powerful people—he was already quite the misanthrope. He'd be able to parse the situation without too much horror clouding his perception.

But as he wasn't around, I pulled my bed down from where it was leaning against the wall and flopped down on it. Even though it was only seven o'clock, I quickly fell into a deep sleep.

I woke to the sound of Thomas coming up the stairs.

"Paul!" he exclaimed. "I've been looking all over for you!"

"Why?" I asked, blinking awake. The clock on the wall said it was nine thirty.

"Why?! Because you never came home from the gala! You've been gone for almost twenty-four hours without a peep. I only found out you were still alive because I got in touch with Lamb."

"You worry too much." I sat up and stretched. I felt better for having a couple of hours' sleep. "I told you last night that I was going home with someone. Did you ever get Ralph's car working, by the way?"

"That's why I was worried about you." Thomas was agitated. "Don't you know who that man is? He's the military liaison for the Department of Magic Regulation."

I froze, arms still above my head. Did Thomas also know about my innate magic?

He knelt down by me. "You know that even a false accusation can ruin your life, right?" he said. "They can pick you up on little more than a rumour and then torture you until they are satisfied that you don't have innate magic. You'd end up like Johnny Simmons."

Johnny Simmons had been a sleight of hand artist back in Liverpool who had gotten picked up by the magic regulators. They'd held him for weeks before determining that he was just a regular old pickpocket and not some magically enhanced thief. He'd never talk about what had happened to him but I remembered how afterwards he needed to use both hands to pick up his pint glass.

"Hollister doesn't suspect me of something," I said. "He just . . ." I could tell Thomas that Hollister had offered to help me become Court Magician, but I knew Thomas wouldn't approve and would try to talk me out of it. "He's just a lonely guy, that's all." Heck, maybe it was even true.

Thomas narrowed his eyes. "You are courting trouble, Paul."

I snorted. "I am *not* courting trouble."

"You are *so* courting trouble!" Thomas parried. "You are sending trouble flowers! You are gingerly taking trouble's hand! You are sitting in trouble's living room, having tea with trouble's parents!"

The phone rang shrilly from downstairs. I jumped to my feet a little too fast, blood rushing to my head. "Oh, the phone! I know it's for me; I just know it!"

I quickly made my way down the stairs to where the landlady was talking into the receiver.

"All right, miss, I will go get him—"

"Him is already here!" I said, garbling my grammar as I rushed down the stairs. The landlady and I did a little awkward shuffle in the hallway as we tried to move around each other.

"If you are expecting so many calls, Mr Gallagher, I may have to add a portion of the phone bill to the rent."

"I'll try and keep it short, Mrs Dylag," I said as I took the phone from her and put it to my ear. "Hello?"

"Hi, Paul."

"Ah, hello, Verity," I said. Mrs Dylag sighed and went back downstairs. I waited until she was out of sight before speaking. "I looked into the matter we discussed before."

"And what did you find?"

"Do you have any proof of this? I mean, it's horrible, what it all suggests, but right now it's just that: suggestion."

"A suggestion of what?" she pressed. She wanted me to say it aloud.

I took a deep breath and lowered my voice. "That Dr David Myers murdered those children."

"Yes," she said simply. "That's right."

"But . . . but it's all conjecture. You could have this whole thing completely wrong." I was surprised by how much I wanted this to be the case. "Maybe you've drawn all the wrong conclusions."

"It's better to talk in person," Verity said, "Are you free?"

"Right now?" It was almost ten o'clock at night.

"That's right."

"All right, sure. Where do you want to talk?"

Out of all places, she asked to meet me by Big Ben. A very touristy destination, but then again, she was from out of town. I told Thomas that Verity had called me out for drinks and that I'd be back late.

CHAPTER 9

When I emerged from the Westminster tube station Big Ben was tolling half past ten. There are times, specifically early on a Sunday morning or late on a Sunday night, when London becomes eerily quiet. The city centre, which during the day is a compact cluster of activity, goes still. It is especially true of the area around the parliament after dark, when both sightseers and politicians are long gone from the scene, asleep in their beds elsewhere in the city. It was in this lonesome landscape that I saw Verity, standing at the base of the clock tower. I was surprised to see that she was wearing the dress Thom and I had made for the gala; then I remembered that of course she would be: it was the mask that protected her true identity. It was a chilly night so over the dress she was wearing a dark-green peacoat, unbuttoned.

She smiled as I came close.

"Good evening."

"Hi."

We stood there awkwardly for a moment. I gestured to a pub a few streets down that was still open. "Can I buy you a pint?"

She shook her head. "Oh, no. I don't want to go somewhere so public. Plus, this won't take long."

"All right." This whole meeting was rather strange so I decided to let her take the lead. I went quiet and waited for her to suggest something.

She nodded towards a bench across the bridge. "Why don't we sit there?"

And so we did. The bench was down a few steps and looked out onto the Thames. It was a dark, cloudy night, but there was some light from boats bobbing in the docks.

Verity was silent, watching the water and twisting her hands in her lap. If this were Gabs or some other girl I was close with I'd reach over and take her hand, ask her outright what was wrong. But I didn't feel like I was there yet with Verity.

"You know that statue?" I pointed to my right, back up the stairs we had just walked down. At the top of the stairs was the statue of a crowned woman riding a chariot, a spear in one hand and the other hand raised in the air. "Do you know her story?"

Verity shook her head. "I assumed it was a stylized version of Nike or Queen Victoria."

"It *is* a statue of a queen," I said. "Though not one in modern history. It's a statue of Boudicca, the queen of the Iceni, a Celtic tribe of warrior women. When the Romans came to this island, they tried to make the local people submit to their rule. They had it out for the Iceni in particular, calling their matriarchal ways unnatural. When Boudicca refused to kneel before the Romans, they assaulted her and her daughters. They thought this would break the queen, but it fortified her resolve. She led the Iceni and several neighbouring tribes in a blazing warpath across the country. When they reached Londinium, the Romans were forced to abandon the city. Boudicca's fury was so severe that when her army burned it all to the ground, it left a geological scar in the earth. Even now, when they're doing roadworks or building a new tube station, you can still see it, a vein of righteous anger."

Verity looked towards the statue. "Hmm."

I steepled my fingers. "Why have *you* come to this city, Verity?"

That caught her attention. She stopped staring at the statue to stare at me. "What do you mean?"

"You're an American with seemingly no ties to England, no friends or family here," I said. "Even if you're right about Dr Myers, I can't believe that you came all the way across the pond just because you heard a rumour about him. How did you even come to investigate him in the first place? Why do you have it out so bad for David Myers?"

Verity took a deep breath, rubbed her knees.

"David Myers is my father."

I stared at her, her face little more than a silhouette in the dark, the lights from the boats on the Thames reflecting softly off her cheeks. When would David Myers have gone overseas and fathered an American child? It just didn't make any sense. She didn't even look like him.

But then I saw the resemblance. Not to David Myers but to Abigail Myers, the dead woman whose picture hung in the Myerses' front hall.

"Oh, Jesus," I said.

Verity gave me a half smile. "You were saying you didn't even know who I was, that you didn't know my real name? I'll tell you. It's Tatianna Myers. But you can keep calling me Verity."

"Then you and Oberon . . ."

"Are *not* brother and sister," Verity said swiftly. "Dad needed a male baby to secure the family fortune, so he found one. My mom—and by that, I mean the deranged alkie who raised me—she was a maid in the Myers household. She gave birth to Oberon about twelve hours before Abigail Myers gave birth to me. Dad went to the maid, swapped kids with her, then gave her a ton of cash and shoved her—and me—onto a boat headed to NYC."

"Your mother—I mean, the Myerses' maid—she told you all this?" I said.

Verity nodded. "There's not a moment in my life where I didn't know. Mom used to rail at me, talk about the son she gave up, the friends and family she had left back home for *my* sake—"

"For your sake?" I said, anger flooding through me. "She sold her child and took you as part of a cash bribe, and she had the nerve to tell you it was all for *your* sake? What a crock of—"

"She wasn't wrong," Verity said. She turned to face me, but in the dark I could only make out the suggestion of her features. "What do you think would have happened to me if she hadn't taken me in? A child that nobody wanted?" She turned away. "Sometimes Mom would try. She'd say to me, 'You're not mine, but I still love you.' And it wasn't an easy life for her. Our white neighbours weren't always kind to her, a single white woman with a Black child. She tried to do right by me, but she couldn't even look after herself." Verity waved her hand, dismissing the past. "But I'm not here to deal with her. I'm here to deal with the snake who did this."

"Right," I said, somewhat shakily. "So how about I tell you what I *think* he did, and you can tell me how close I am."

"Go for it," Verity said.

I floundered for a second, studying her features. Did she even look like a Tatianna?

"So here's what I figure," I said. "Martha's mum and dad were middle class but pretty well off thanks to the fact that Mr Wilde had been pretty savvy with his investments. When Martha Wilde's parents died, they left everything to her, making her a rich little girl. Their will allotted some of the money to help with her upbringing, but the rest of it was tied up in a trust for when Martha turned eighteen. But Martha never turned eighteen. Instead she died from the burns she got in the fire that killed her mum and dad. Her aunt and uncle, as next of kin, inherited the full amount. Ever since then they've been faithful patrons of St Rita's.

"Sheldon came from a slightly posher family. He was the son of a lord. When Sheldon was five his mother died, and a few years later his father, Lord Wood, remarries. His second wife, Katherine Turner, was likewise a widow and also had a young son from her first marriage, a little boy named Benson." I paused, thinking about how some upper-class names sounded more like dog breeds than people, then felt bad for thinking that about little children who had no say in the matter. "Sheldon was born with a heart condition, and eventually it was considered serious enough to need an operation. Sheldon was brought in and died on the operating table. Dr Myers was one of the attending surgeons. Lord Wood mourns Sheldon but soon adopts Benson as his own son. Lord Wood didn't live too much longer after that. When he died Benson inherited his lands and titles and is currently serving in the House of Lords."

"And both Benson and his mother remain faithful supporters of St Rita's Hospital to this day," Verity said.

"The one I don't understand is little George McKenzie, the one who died long before the other two," I said. "I had to dig deep to find anything on him. He was the son of a typist. His mum was just a single, unmarried woman. The other two I could see at least a motive; people got something out of Martha and Sheldon dying. Who profited from a little urchin like George shuffling off the mortal coil?"

Verity took a deep breath. "There were rumours that his father was Prince Edward."

It was a good thing that the bench had a backing or else I might have fallen to the ground. "What?" Prince Edward had been King Harold's little brother. He had died in an automobile accident in 1927. He had never married or had any children, at least not any the public knew of.

"George's mother worked for the Royal Press Office. Supposedly she and 'Ready Eddie' had gotten close, which no one said boo about until she got pregnant. I don't know the whole story; people are very close lipped about that one. But I think that Eddie protected the mother and the boy, and it's only when he died that someone decided it was too dangerous for George to live."

"Really?" I said.

Verity shrugged. "Think about it. At the time King Harold didn't have any kids of his own, so Eddie was second in line to the throne. With Eddie dead, his bastard child could make a case that he was next in line."

"You think that the king himself . . ." King Harold was a stern man, but it was hard to picture him ordering the death of his illegitimate nephew.

"I don't know," Verity said quickly. "That one's a bit harder to pin down than the other two. But I do think that David Myers has all the answers. The rumour is that he's been blackmailing these families and that he keeps a Book which records all of his deeds. If I could just get my hands on it, I could reveal him for the rat bastard that he is."

For a moment we sat there. A drunken crew made their way across Westminster Bridge, the night eventually swallowing up the sound of their laughter.

"So you're going to tell everyone what really happened?" I said. "Publish it all in the *New Rev*? Tell them that Oberon's a changeling and you're David Myers's actual child?"

Verity laughed so hard she snorted. "No, of course not. How could I ever prove it?"

"Your mum . . ."

"Drank herself to death over a year ago," Verity said. "And no one would have believed a low-class, wayward woman like her anyway. I have no way to prove who I am. But luckily for me, Dr Myers has made other enemies. I tracked down some people who had worked with him, doctors and nurses who knew what he was truly capable of. They gave me a couple of leads, and now here I am." She took a deep breath. "I might not be able to make him pay for what he did to me, but I can at least make him pay for the other crimes he's committed."

"I want to help you." I took her hand in mine, slender bones wrapped in warm skin and muscle. Perhaps one didn't need earth-shattering magic to make things right—just a little bit of courage and resolve. Verity shifted so she was facing me. The moon emerged from behind a cloud, its light filtering through the leafy tree branches overhead. When Verity breathed out I could feel the heat from her.

"Tell me what we need to do," I said.

"I need to get into his house," she replied. "If I can get into Dr Myers's study, I know where the safe is and I know the combination. That's where he keeps the Book that has all of his blackmail material in it."

"And then you'll publish it in the *New Rev*, and he'll go to jail for all of it?"

"That's the plan."

I nodded. "Good. Let's do it."

Verity pressed in closer. "Don't worry, I'll keep your name out of my article."

"Oh? Why?"

"Well, David Myers served some extremely powerful people. They might not be too happy when their dirty laundry gets aired. I don't want you to become a target because of this."

"Verity." I waited until she met my eyes. "Do you really think I give a damn? All that matters is that this is the right thing to do. This man took sick, vulnerable children into his care, little children who had been betrayed and sold for silver by their own family, and watched as those kids bled out under his hands. If those craven bastards who paid off Dr Myers want to come at me, let them. They'll find me a bit harder to kill than some sick tot. I believe that God has set me in your path so that I can help you right this wrong. I'll walk into this lion's den with you, Verity. Let's go hand in hand into this furnace, for I know that we are in the right here, that we are under God's protection, and that there's nothing your will and mine can't do together."

She kissed me. It took me off guard since I was still thinking about dead children, but God knows I can change gears fast when need be. And aside from righting an outrageous injustice, taking up this quest would bind me and Verity together in a way that nothing else could. Perhaps it could forge a real bond, something beyond glamour and infatuation.

My hands felt the edges of her shoulder blades through her coat and I felt her hands moving along the edge of my ribs. It seemed like we kissed forever, like the stars were all blinking out around us, the Apocalypse come and gone, the Rapture over and done with, the universe slowly shutting down as we, oblivious to everything else but each other, continued to press closer to one another.

Someone walking by whistled and we were brought back to earth.

We both pulled away and I was somewhat gratified to see that Verity was blushing too.

"Good," she said, and I wasn't sure if that was a review of the kiss or a comment on what I had said prior to it.

"Do you think we could go back to your place and, um, discuss our plan further?" I suggested.

Verity grinned, making it clear that she saw right through me. "I don't think so. I need to be getting back."

"To where?" I asked. I didn't think that she had a secret husband she was keeping from me or anything, but I did wonder where she spent all her time, day and night.

"I'll call you," she said, drawing away from me. "We'll figure out what to do next then."

And with that she was gone. With nothing else to do, I turned and started the lonely walk back to the nearest tube station, still dizzy.

CHAPTER 10

Waiting for Verity's call was torture. I didn't know what exactly her plan was, but I was eager to move forwards. Plus, thinking about bringing Dr Myers down was better than worrying about Hollister. Did the captain know that the break in my finger was innate magic? Had he only brought me to his flat to try and entrap me? If we ran into each other again, would he arrest me? Or maybe he'd meant what he said about introducing me to the Court Magician—but why would he do that for me?

I did have a project to keep me busy during the week. At the gala Thomas actually had managed to score us a job—some sloppy civil servant wanted us to make him a suit that was totally water resistant. A bit of a menial task, but at least it was work. On Monday I met up with the man, got his measurements and also the cash up front. It quickly went towards materials and back rent.

As the week went on, my anxiety about everything was close to bubbling over.

"What the hell is wrong with you?" Thomas snapped on Friday morning when I knocked over a glass of water onto a design I was sketching.

"I'm fine." That wasn't entirely true, but the problem wasn't with me. It was with the world. A world that could not only let evil go unchecked but reward it.

"You look like crap," Thomas said, closing the book he'd been reading.

I shrugged. "I haven't eaten today." And even if that was an evasive answer, it was no lie. My physical hunger certainly contributed to the hollow, wary feeling in the pit of my stomach.

Thomas sighed and went to his dresser drawer. From it he removed a small tin, and from the tin he removed a piece of jerky. I was shocked that the little bastard had food squirreled away, but I really shouldn't have been so surprised. Thomas had been raised literally on the streets. He had learned to forage and hoard as easily as most tots learned to walk and talk. Even when he'd come to live with Mum and Dad and me, I'd still caught him tucking food away in his pillowcase for safekeeping.

"Here," he said as he tossed the small bit of meat to me. In my wobbly state I fumbled the catch but soon I was chewing the jerky, sitting cross-legged on the floor. I actually felt myself tearing up.

"Thank you," I said between bites.

Thomas sat down next to me. He seemed hesitant, uneasy in a way he usually only got in large crowds or when cornered by a chatty person. I silently offered him a piece of the jerky and he waved me off.

"Sometimes, when people are feeling like shit, or even when I'm feeling like shit, I'm not good at sorting it out. Not like you are," he said, and I perked up at the unsolicited compliment. "I might not know what to tell you, but if you have something you want to talk about I can at least shut my gob and listen."

I swallowed. Where to start? I knew Thomas would believe me if I told him that I thought that Oberon's father was involved in something awful. It wasn't that Thomas held a dim view of Dr Myers—he just held a dim view of humanity in general. He wouldn't struggle with it the way I was struggling.

But I hesitated. Usually I had no problem sharing things with Thomas, even when a third party had sworn me to secrecy. In my view it was their own fault: they should have known that Thomas and I were a package deal (though, hypocrite that I was, I did keep my own secrets from Thomas). But sharing Verity's secret would mean that this would no longer be a sacred trust between Verity and me. And as much as I loved and valued Thom, I wasn't ready to lose that.

So I smiled and patted my little brother's shoulder. "Thomas, you worry too much! I'm fine, so much better now that I have some food in my belly. I never knew you had some jerky squirreled away! What else you got in there?"

Thomas didn't answer right away, just frowned. "Like I said, I know I'm not good at this, but you can trust me—"

The phone rang from downstairs. A few rings later Mrs Dylag picked up and spoke a few words to whoever was on the other end.

"Mr Gallagher! It's for you!" she called up the stairs.

I stood, moving clumsily like all my limbs were asleep. Thomas looked like he wanted to say something but wasn't able to get it out before I was down the stairs.

"Hello?" I said after taking the phone from Mrs Dylag.

"Ah, Mr Gallagher," Hollister's voice said. "Glad I could get in touch with you."

My heart sank—I had hoped it would be Verity on the line. "Hello, Captain," I said.

"I'm sorry I haven't been in touch," he said. "Busy week at work. But are you free tomorrow? I was thinking we could meet for lunch."

Lunch didn't sound overly sinister—unless he was merely trying to lure me out to arrest me. As much as I didn't want to be abducted and tortured, I couldn't help but be curious if Hollister would be true to his word about helping me become Court Magician. I might never have another chance like this again.

"That sounds aces," I said. "Where would you like to meet?"

~

Hollister told me to meet him at the King's Court pub in Holborn. The place was nearly deserted when I arrived. It was one of those posh pubs in the financial district that did brisk business during the week but became a ghost town on the weekend. Hollister was sitting comfortably in a corner booth, like he was the titular king holding court.

I slid into the seat. The booth seemed much too large for just the two of us and I felt like a child sitting in an oversize chair. Hollister, however, looked at ease, arm draped along the back of the booth. I squared my shoulders, tried to make myself bigger than I felt.

"The steak here is always good," Hollister said, not bothering with the menu. The menu was a slim two-page Book. To see the different sections you merely flipped the pages back and forth, thinking hard about whether you wanted to see the appetizers, entrées, drink list, or dessert. Book menus were the norm at upscale places like this, but they were becoming more common at cheaper pubs and restaurants as well. It might have seemed ostentatious to have magic menus, but it allowed the restaurant to easily change the info inside rather than having to print out new ones whenever the selection changed. And God knows there were more and more Book Binders graduating every day, looking for work.

I made the mistake of glancing at the prices and gave a visible wince.

"This is my treat," Hollister said, considerably lightening my mood. "Order whatever you want."

"Oh, well, in that case, I'll have a cup of coffee, black," I said. Hollister ordered coffee and two medium-rare steaks. I watched him order, talking with an even-keeled haughtiness. I still found him attractive, but that kiss with Verity had pushed her to the forefront of my desires and put Hollister on the back burner. Also, Verity had been up front with me about who she was and her agenda. With Hollister I still wasn't sure what he wanted.

Once the waiter went away, Hollister smiled.

"You know, I keep thinking about how fortuitous it was that we met at the gala. A truly happy occasion." He paused. "Do you know where the word *happy* comes from?"

"No, can't say I do." Thomas would've known. For a moment I wished he were here with me, picking up on the things I was missing.

"It's from the old English tales of King Arthur and his cohorts. It meant to be aligned with one's destiny. A happy knight was not called that because he was joyful but because he was on the path he was meant to fulfil." Hollister smiled at me. "Perhaps us bumping into each other was a happy occurrence, in both the arcane and modern sense."

If his words had had just a little bit more come-hither, or if he had seemed even a little bit nervous, I would have sworn to Jesus that he was angling for me. I liked to think I was pretty good at reading men and women and knowing when they were flirting with me or not. Hollister ticked a lot of my boxes but I didn't get the sense that he was trying to pick me up, even with the expensive meal.

"I agree," I said with a smile. It wouldn't hurt to flirt a little bit, in case Hollister was just playing his cards close to his chest. It would make things so simple if all he wanted was sex.

The waiter arrived with our steaks and for a few minutes we merely cut and ate.

There are few things I hate more than persistent silence. I decided to test the waters and see just what this man thought about unlawful magic. "Captain, have you ever heard the theory of cloth magic being a decoy school of magic?"

This was a somewhat taboo subject in cloth magic classes, both because of how it devalued cloth magic as its own field and because of how outlandish it sounded. To everyone else, though, it would just seem a bit of harmless trivia.

"A decoy for what?" Hollister asked.

"For innate magic."

He was silent, waiting for me to go on.

"The idea is that when innate magic was banned back in the Dark Ages, its practitioners sought to pass on their knowledge secretly," I said. "So they co-opted cloth magic. They'd write up books detailing how to correctly put together a suit, when really they were talking about the human body. Veins became seams; skin became fabric; cuts became breaks in the bone. It's why some of the cloth magic texts from that time are so nonsensical, because they were just a smoke screen to pass on another set of knowledge."

"And that's why you studied cloth magic." It wasn't a question but a statement.

"No. Well, a little," I said. "I've always been interested in innate magic, but the only one who gets trained in it is the apprentice Court Magician."

Hollister stared at me for a moment, long enough to make me worry. In an attempt to break the tension, I carefully ate a few more pieces of steak. It did not work. There was still an awkward, taut line of silence strung between us.

"Mr Gallagher—"

"You can call me Paul," I said, cutting in. That seemed to throw Hollister. He blinked.

"Paul, I . . ." Hollister paused, gaze drifting off. "Paul. Such a common name. I had a good friend, Paul Osgood, was right with me in the Great War. He had a faulty gas mask, and when the gas flooded the trenches he threw up in his mask and choked to death on his own vomit. In the second war I had a few Pauls serve under me. One of them found an orange in a house in an abandoned French village while we were chasing after an enemy mage. Even though I'd warned the boys not to take anything he pocketed the orange, and later on when he peeled it his own skin peeled off in the same fashion. Then there was that Paul who stepped on a land mine. His guts were strewn about a bit of barbed wire like garland on a Christmas tree, though I probably only thought that because it was in fact Christmas Day."

He stopped speaking, eyes unfocused. When he finally spoke again I actually jumped in surprise.

"You don't happen to have a middle name, do you?"

"Uh, yes," I said, thrown for a loop. "James. For my grandfather."

Hollister nodded. "James. James. Jim!" His eyes lit up. Apparently the name Jim had happy connotations for him, or at the very least no graphically nightmarish ones. He looked at me with new interest, as if I had in fact transformed into a new person. "Well, Jim, I have to admit, I'm not just helping you for your sake but for the sake of the nation."

I certainly didn't know how to respond to that, so I didn't.

"See, I've been studying magic for decades. I'm not a mage—never got any of my bones broken or anything of that sort. But I've read a lot of theory," Hollister said. "I've been looking for someone who can perform a certain type of magic. Miracles. Feats of biblical proportions. The current Court Magician isn't up to it . . . but . . ."

"You think I might be?" I had a big ego but this sounded like a reach even for me.

Hollister shrugged. "I don't know. It's just a sense I got when I first met you, and talking to you has made me believe it further."

I was flattered but still wanted to know what Hollister wanted out of all of this. He seemed to sense my hesitation.

"During the wars, I saw some bloody horrible things," he said. "You know how we won the Second World War? Not us, the British, but the Allies?"

"The Americans figured out how to make atomic bombs and the Russians figured out how to make Superconductors." Superconductors had been somewhat of a myth, prior to that. Every human being on God's green earth housed a soul, and that soul was what allowed them to power up magical items, like Books or clothes. Everybody had roughly the same amount—you could train to increase your magical energy, but most people were fine with getting by with the natural amount they had within. The fluctuations within people when it came to power levels weren't that big. Except for when it came to Superconductors. Superconductors were born with overflowing magical energy. They did not need to interact with a mage-crafted item to do magic—everything they touched *turned* magic. Stories from the ancient world spoke of Superconductors who, upon their birth, melted cities and warped the humans around them into unknowable shapes. Even if they were real, they were seemingly rare. A once-in-a-generation kind of thing.

And then the Soviets had figured out how to turn normal people into Superconductors.

"I saw one of them," Hollister said. "A Soviet captain showed me. She—I . . . I think it was a woman—she was in one of those glass coffins they made for them. She was wearing this outfit designed to constrain her power long enough for us to load her onto a bomber." He went quiet for a moment. He didn't need to speak—Ralph had told me his war stories. The Allies would drop these glass coffins on German cities. The Superconductor inside would survive the fall and emerge from their glass coffin, a wretched mass of human pain and confusion, destroying everything in their path until they finally died from whatever had been done to them to make them that way.

"What . . . what did she look like?" I asked.

Hollister took a swig of his drink. "Like every bone in her body had been broken."

We were silent for a few minutes.

"And you want Britain to figure out how to do this?" I couldn't help the accusatory note in my voice—creating the Superconductors had helped swing the war in the Allies' favour, but it had been a horrific act.

"No! God, no!" Hollister said. "It's too gruesome. And costs too many civilian lives. Scuttlebutt was that for every Superconductor the Russians made, there were a hundred who simply died in the process."

Much like the process for finding the new mage maker, if on a much larger scale.

"Also, the Superconductors they were able to create were mindless," Hollister said. "Pure power with no direction. I want to discover a kind of magic that grants the user power but leaves their mind intact."

I felt a tightening in my gut.

"I should go," I said, standing up. Hollister grabbed my wrist so fast I hardly saw him move.

"What? Why?" he said, still holding on to me.

"Thanks for everything," I said. "For lunch, and for offering to introduce me to the Court Magician. But what you're talking about is creating a new weapon for the military. And I'm not interested in that. I'm a pacifist."

Hollister narrowed his eyes at me, still holding my wrist. "How old are you, Jim?"

"I'll be twenty-three in August," I said before remembering Verity's jab about how only children rounded up. "I'm twenty-two right now." *Oh my God, just stop talking, you idiot.*

"Twenty-two," Hollister repeated. "So you remember the Second World War?"

"Yes, of course."

Hollister shook his head. "I don't know how anyone could have lived through any of the wars and call himself a pacifist."

"I don't know how anyone could live through the wars and not," I said. "Look, I believe that magic is a God-given gift, and I believe he gave it to us for better reasons than finding more and more ways to murder each other."

I stopped, embarrassed to realize my voice had gotten so loud. Hollister let go of my wrist. I slumped down in my seat, ran a hand through my hair and waited for Hollister's retort.

And yet Hollister did not seem as disdainful as he had mere seconds ago. He actually looked somewhat considering.

"I do believe that England needs better magic in order to hold its own in the world," Hollister said. "The empire has all but slipped away from us and the globe is tilting towards anarchy. But the magic I'm trying to uncover, it's not for military might. It's to right a wrong, to course correct the world." He stared at me. "I swear, if you help me with this I will not let the military use it."

"All right," I said hesitantly. "But what exactly is the 'this' you want help with?"

"A new form of magic," Hollister said. "Look into it for me, and I'll arrange a meeting with George Redfield before the Making ceremony in August."

"What?!" I sat up straight. "They've already decided to have the ceremony?!"

"Oh, yes. It's not public knowledge, though, so keep it hush hush," Hollister said. "Well? What do you say, Jim? All I'm asking is for you to do some research."

Only an idiot would believe that Hollister's motivations were good. Even if he was speaking the truth of not handing over the info to the military, that still left a lot of wiggle room for him to manoeuvre.

But now that I knew the ceremony was only a few months away, there was a new sense of urgency in the air. And what Hollister said intrigued me—I couldn't help but be curious.

"Is it true the military has a copy of Aleph's *The Body Divine*?" I asked. "I've always wanted to read it."

"Oh, yes," Hollister said offhandedly. "I've read it myself. All largely nonsense." He sipped his coffee. "I can't understand why a modern mage like yourself would want to bother with it."

"Well, outdated or not, it is one of the earliest texts on cloth magic in the English language," I said.

"So you want to read it for the historical perspective?" Hollister said, then paused. "You think Aleph's book isn't about cloth magic at all. You think it is an innate magic text, one of those decoys you were speaking about."

"Yes," I said, then faltered. "Well, I think so from secondary texts that I've read about it, but without seeing it myself . . ."

"I could lend it to you," Hollister said. "Not the original of course, but the department's Book Binders have made copies."

"Really?"

"Of course." Hollister signalled to the waiter for more coffee. "If you think there is something of worth in there, I look forward to hearing about it."

~

"So he just lent it to you?"

Thomas and I were lying on our stomachs in our room, reading the copy of *The Body Divine*. Because it was merely a Bound copy it was a very slim volume with only a couple of pages. Once opened it was up to the reader to consult the index and forge a connection with the Book, a mental link that allowed the reader to summon up different chapters. There had been some trouble with both Thomas and me trying to read it at once but eventually we agreed to try and focus on the same topics at the same time.

"Yes," I said proudly. "I've always wanted to read it, so I figured why not see if he could get it for me."

"He smuggled out a book on illegal magic and gave it to a knob he hardly even knows."

"He knows me. And it's only tangentially about innate magic," I said. "There's lots here that can apply to cloth magic too."

"Don't be obtuse, Paul."

"Obtuse?" I said, smiling. "You know that's not my angle."

"I'm serious, Paul; there's something weird about this."

"Well, I'll cosine to that," I said.

"Paul, stop it and listen to me—"

"Why? You're just going to go off on a tangent."

Thomas laid his head down on the pillow, face first, as if trying to smother himself. Finally, he lifted his head, filled his lungs, and said, "Is this some kind of exchange like you had with Lamb? Because that did not—"

"What do you mean, exchange?" I said, pushing myself up on my elbows so I could better glare at him. "Just say it plainly."

"I was saying it plainly," Thomas replied, equally cross. "Don't get me wrong, Lamb shouldn't be sleeping with his students, but you worked it pretty well. Got to borrow his books, his notes, extensions on projects—"

"All of which I shared with you," I said, before it occurred to me to deny it. It was a hurtful insult, one which Oberon and Gabs and even Ralph had indirectly referred to, that by sleeping with the professor I got preferential treatment. And maybe I did get a couple of breaks and more of Lamb's time and attention, but he had said that was because I showed so much promise as a mage, not because we were sleeping together . . . but that sounded thin even to me so I didn't bother using it as a defence.

"I'm pretty sure Captain Hollister doesn't want to sleep with me," I said. "Which is a shame, as he's exactly my type." I took a deep breath. "But he does expect something in return. When I'm Court Magician, that is."

Thomas stared at me. "Are you still going on about that?"

"It's possible, Thomas," I said. "I love cloth magic, but what's the best I can do with it? Become a professor like Lamb?"

"You sound like Oberon," Thomas said.

"Why are you so against it?" I asked.

"Because I don't want you to die! It's really not that complicated!" Thomas said.

I stood up. I had let the time get away from me and I was supposed to meet Verity soon. "I won't die."

"How do you know that?" Thomas said, getting to his feet. "For fuck's sake, why do we always have to get swept up in these schemes of yours?!"

"Do you have a better idea?"

He crossed his arms. "Maybe I do. You've never asked."

I felt rightly called out on that. Thomas was so sharp tongued; I had always assumed that if he had something to say he'd say it. I figured if he was willing to go along with whatever I'd cooked up, well, those were the roles we had fallen into.

"You're right that cloth magic isn't respected in England," Thomas said. "But there are parts of the world where cloth mages are in demand. Italy. France. We could go there and set up shop." His eyes lit up. "Or we could go even farther and travel to China, apprentice ourselves to a cloth magician there, learn things that no British mages would ever conceive of—"

"All that, that's not going to happen," I said. "England's my home, Thomas. I don't want to leave it."

Thomas's shoulders slumped. But he didn't argue. Brains and brawn gave way to nerves and vision.

CHAPTER 11

Verity and I were walking through one of the more upper-middle-class areas of Islington. It was a residential street, full of town houses rebuilt after the war to mimic turn-of-the-century styles. It was a beautiful day, and occasionally people walked by with pampered poodles, or nannies passed pushing ridiculously posh prams.

"And Thomas says I'm middle class," I muttered.

"What?" Verity said.

"Nothing, never mind." We were staring at one house in particular, a grey building with well-trimmed hedges. It was where Oberon Myers and his father lived.

"You know, this has to be one of the oddest dates I've ever been on, and that's saying something," I said lightly.

"Who says this is a date?" Verity said.

"All right," I said. "Is it?"

"This is just us casing the joint," Verity said. "I've never seen the place for myself."

"I've been inside a few times," I said. "There's a parlour with a pool table there"—I pointed to the ground-floor window to our left—"and a dining room, and a kitchen which leads to the backyard. I've never been upstairs."

"I think that's where the doctor keeps his study," Verity said. "Do you know if they have any servants?"

"I think they have a cook and a maid who comes in a couple of times a week, but they don't have any live-in help."

Verity nodded. She was still wearing that black dress. It made me uneasy. We were supposed to be just two young lovers out on a midday walk, yet here she was wearing an evening dress. She already stood out in this neighbourhood thanks to her dark skin and American accent.

Also, I didn't understand why she still felt the need to wear it around me. Weren't we past disguises? Wearing cloth magic for hours at a time like she did was surely taking a toll on her. One of the dangers of cloth magic was that you wouldn't feel its ill effects until *after* you took the magical clothes off. Perhaps Verity, being an American, hadn't known that when she'd accepted a magical dress, though she'd have experienced the side effects firsthand by now: the wave of bone weariness as you peeled your clothes off, leaving you feeling as weak and powerless as a chick that had just emerged from its egg. I didn't understand why Verity put herself through that. As a cloth mage, I had long practised breathing techniques while wearing magical outfits in order to build up my endurance, but Verity was just an ordinary person. Why not wear regular clothes?

"So what's the plan then?" I asked. "Just break in and grab it?"

Verity shook her head. "A break-in's too risky. The houses are all so close together and somebody would probably call the cops on us." Verity took my arm and we started walking down towards the station. "You can get inside, can't you? You're friends with Oberon, right?"

"More like acquaintances."

"Well, I *need* you to be friends," she said. "All you have to do is make sure the front door is unlocked, then distract Oberon while I get the Book from upstairs."

"And what about Dr Myers?"

"He's going on a golf trip to Scotland next weekend. He'll be gone from the twenty-ninth to late on the thirtieth," Verity said. "If we do this carefully, we'll have the whole story splashed on the front page before Dr Myers even knows the Book's missing."

A few yards away was a tennis court, the *thok thok* of a lazy doubles game sounding like a broken metronome. A breeze flitted through the leaves overhead and through Verity's dark hair. She gave me a weak smile. "Thank you." She looked down. "I know you're risking a lot here, and I don't know how to make it up to you."

"Really?" I gestured down the road towards a cluster of restaurants on the high street. "I have no money. Buy me some food."

She laughed at that, and then it really was a date.

"Now, I'm not made of money," Verity said, taking my hand and leading me to a chip stand. "So how about we split a plate of french fries?"

"Sounds aces," I said. Verity paid with cold hard cash, which caused some people to stop and stare—it was extremely rare to see someone pay with actual coins. I supposed that, as a foreigner, she had never gotten a Book of her own. We stepped to the side and after a few minutes had a warm basket of chips. I grabbed a napkin and we took a seat on a bench shaded by a large oak. The chips were still too hot to hold so we set the little paper basket between us. I stuffed one into my mouth, not caring how it burned. Verity just frowned at the food.

"What's wrong?" I asked, my mouth still full.

"That was miserly of me, chum," she said. "What I said back there."

I was torn between comforting Verity and eating another chip. My body decided on the order of operations—it grabbed a chip, swallowed it whole, then let me focus on Verity. "Sorry, what?"

"What I said about not being made of money and only buying an order of french fries to split," Verity said. "I should have treated you to something nicer."

I felt such a rush of sympathy for Verity then. I held back from letting it all pour out, in case I seemed sentimental or saccharine.

"Are you kidding? This is great," I said.

She bit her lower lip. "No, no, it's not. I went right for the cheapest option without a second thought. That's hardly a way to repay you."

"Verity, it doesn't have to be like that," I said. "I'm very happy with these chips, all right? Here, I'll prove it. Lend me a pen, will you?"

Curious, she took out a fountain pen she had in her purse and handed it to me. I started to write on the napkin.

"I, Paul Gallagher, owe Verity Turnboldt the amount on the reverse side in return for a serving of chips," I said as I wrote. I flipped the napkin over and covered that side in a hundred little x's in neat lines.

"Wow, look at all those x's," Verity said. "That's a big sum of money."

"Really? I thought they were a hundred little kisses." I finished and held out the napkin to her. "For you."

She took it with the tips of her fingers, perhaps in an attempt not to get any more grease stains on it. "Thank you," she said. She held the napkin in her lap for a minute, then carefully folded it and put it in her purse.

"You know, I'm happy to help you, really," I said. "But I don't think you're going to get what you're owed from Dr Myers."

Verity looked at me sharply. "What?"

"I mean, as your dad, he owed you a happy life," I said. "But no matter what leverage you have over him, he won't be able to give that to you now."

Verity laughed at that—a brittle, angry laugh.

"Oh, believe me, Paul, I know that," she said. "This isn't about me getting what's due me; it's about David Myers getting *his* due."

"Oh? And what's that?"

"An unhappy life. I want to make him regret ever sending me away."

We were both quiet for a while after that. The two of us pecked at the rapidly cooling chips. Now that I was a little less hungry, I decided to ask Verity the question I'd been dreading to ask.

"And after you do that," I said, "what will you do then?"

Verity shook her head, shrugged, gave a wave of her hand, as if all these gestures could be taken together to supply an answer.

"I don't know. But I *do* know I won't know what I want to do next until I do this."

"Ah, all right," I said. "But in broad strokes, do you see yourself sticking around here in London, or . . . ?"

"Well, maybe." Verity smiled, injecting some lightness back into the conversation. "As long as I still have other debts to collect on, I guess." She patted her purse.

So no promise of anything more after we pulled this off, then. I could respect that. Even if she was only using me to bring down Dr Myers, I didn't really begrudge her that either. She had the most personal of reasons to want revenge, and I felt it was my job to get justice for those little children Myers had killed. And I enjoyed Verity's company. Maybe, given enough time, I could convince her to stay—to stay in England, to stay with me.

~

The call from Hollister came at eight on a Wednesday morning. Luckily I am a bit of a morning lark, so I was already up, washed, and dressed when Mrs Dylag called up the stairs to tell me to come to the landing. She was curious—I got lots of phone calls but generally in the evening.

"It's about some work," I said quietly to Mrs Dylag before I took the phone from her.

"I hope it's paying work," Mrs Dylag said. "I'm still waiting for you to put this week's rent in my hand." She held her empty hand out to me, palm up.

I took the phone from her and gave her a winning smile. "Oh, Mrs Dylag, you know we'll get it to you eventually," I said. She harrumphed at that but shuffled off to her room, leaving the door open a crack so she could eavesdrop.

153

"Trouble with the landlady? I remember when that was my biggest worry," Hollister asked, with a nostalgic chuckle.

The last time I had eaten was yesterday when Verity had bought those chips. I might be awake, but I was starving and not in the mood to romanticize being skint.

"Oh, no trouble," I said loudly and brightly for Mrs Dylag's benefit. "So, Captain, what can I do for you?"

"It's more about what I can do for you, Jim," Hollister said. He sounded chipper—perhaps like me, he was a morning person. "I talked to Redfield and he's willing to meet with you."

"Really?" I said, standing up a little straighter in the hallway, as if the Court Magician's eyes were already upon me. "Oh. Uh, when?"

"Today at ten," Hollister said.

"What?" Two hours from now? I'd been thinking about this hypothetical meeting for days, going over what I'd say, what I'd wear. I was even thinking of creating a new suit for it, but I hadn't decided what kind of magic effect would be best. "I'm . . . I don't know if I'm ready."

"Well, ready or not, today's the day," Hollister said. Easy for him to be cheerful—this wasn't his future hanging in the balance. "I'll come down from Barnet and pick you up. Where in North London are you exactly?"

"I—" I almost told him but stopped. When had I ever told Hollister I lived in North London? It wouldn't be like me to let something like that slip. "How about we meet at Alexandra Palace?" It was close enough to my place that I could walk there, but not so close that Hollister could pinpoint where I lived.

"All right. See you there in an hour." He hung up before I could ask any more questions.

I raced to my room and grabbed my herringbone suit off its spot where it hung askew on the bookcase. I loved that suit, it looked plenty flash, but I desperately wished I had a different outfit to wear, just so I could feel shiny and new.

Thomas was lying in bed, asleep but muttering, and I was glad that even as I clattered about he didn't wake. He'd made his objections to me becoming Court Magician well known already—I didn't need another lecture from him. I understood his fear, though—if I didn't survive the ritual, what would he do without me?

I was soon out the door and following the New River Path upstream towards Ally-Pally. I was glad I had picked the place as our meeting point—the walk gave me time to relax, to slow my beating heart.

I *had* in fact met the Court Magician once before. He was the mage maker, after all, so every student studying magic at the UCL had to visit him at one point or another. You could study the techniques of making clothes or binding Books all you wanted, but unless a mage maker laid hands on you, until he broke the bone of your arm, until the magic flowing through you was redirected, you'd never be a mage but merely a mundane craftsman.

I had made my appointment near the end of my second year, just before summer vacation—better to have my arm out of commission then rather than during school. When I first met Redfield, I felt so relieved that (1) my innate magic seemed to work even on him, the toppermost mage in the land, and (2) he didn't seem to notice anything amiss. We chatted amiably even as he strapped my arm to the chair. I had him break my right arm—I was ambidextrous anyway and wanted him to stay far away from my left hand, lest he notice my broken pointer finger.

I tried so hard to pay attention to the specifics of what he was doing, curious to see if his methods were different from those of the Irish mage I'd met as a child. He double-checked to make sure my arm was tied down, then picked up a hammer and swung it into my forearm, right in the middle of the length. I screamed—everyone screams, they tell you. Redfield didn't even seem to notice. He was so focused on his work. He let the hammer drop to the floor so he could put both his hands on my arm, shifting the pieces of bones around inside their sleeve of skin and muscle. And then, beneath the pain, I'd felt something familiar. A wave, a sensation of a current running through me, a galaxy of atoms inside me. Then it had been gone and I'd felt only the pain again, but I'd known I'd been made into a mage.

Just remembering it made my stomach do a little flip—or perhaps it was just nerves. I was more nervous now than when I had first met Redfield. There was still a chance he could see that I had illegal innate magic. Also, I couldn't rely on said magic to charm him this time—it only worked on the first meeting.

Hollister's car was waiting outside Ally-Pally.

"Why, Jim, you're white as a sheet," he said as I drew close. "You're not ill, are you?"

"No, no, no. Not at all," I said, trying to smile. Hollister didn't seem convinced but slid back into the driver's seat. I got into the passenger side, rubbed my temples.

Hollister didn't start the car immediately. I caught him looking at me with concern.

"You're worried?" Hollister said.

"Well, yes." The words came out of my mouth like a toad tumbling out. "What if I say something stupid? I could completely scuttle my chances and that's that."

Hollister smiled. "I doubt that will happen. You can be very persuasive, Jim. Besides . . ." He trailed off. Perhaps he had run out of words of comfort, or maybe he had thought better of them. "Well, we're off!" He started the automobile and pulled onto the main road.

Hollister was quiet during the drive to Buckingham Palace, which I was grateful for. What would I even say to Redfield when I saw him? How could I make my case to him? How could I win him over without magic? I was so lost in thought that when I realized we were going through the gates into Buckingham Palace, I startled as if awaking from a dream. But it was the opposite—it was like I was waking from real life into a dream. The palace was a wide, decorated building at the end of a large lawn. It was like its own park within the gates. I glanced over my shoulder—there was London with its traffic and crowds and grey buildings. But when I looked forwards it felt like we were in the countryside on the grandest estate in the country. It seemed impossible to believe we were still in the city.

Hollister drove the car around to some back building that was out of the public view and into a single-storey car park that looked a lot more utilitarian than many of the ornate buildings surrounding it.

"What if we run into King Harold? Or the queen? Or the prince or princess?" I was babbling and Hollister held up a hand to cut me off.

"The royal family is vacationing in Scotland right now," he said smoothly.

"Shouldn't Redfield be with them then?" One of the duties of Court Magician was to protect the royal family. Hollister hesitated.

"Redfield doesn't like to travel," he finally said. We got out of the car and went down into an underground tunnel. Multiple paths split off from each other, connecting the different smaller buildings that surrounded the palace. Hollister walked confidently and I tried to keep up. We passed various busy people—men in suits carrying files, servants delivering fresh linen, kitchen staff pushing carts of confectionaries. From one passing cart I managed to blag a cream puff and popped it into my mouth without thinking. It was delicious but barely made a dent in either my hunger or my nervousness.

We went up a tight stairwell and emerged back into the aboveground world. We were in what at first I took to be a hallway, because of how narrow it was, but then I saw that it was really a waiting room. One end opened out to a hallway, and the other ended with a closed door. The long wall opposite us had high, arched windows with glass and frames that were probably as old as the palace itself. The wall behind us had the door we had just emerged from, as well as painted portraits of the past Court Magicians. I didn't know which was more dazzling—the sun or the faces staring down at me, judging me.

Shannon Fay

"Now, Jim, just breathe," Hollister said, grabbing my shoulders. "You have nothing to worry about, truly. Just . . . just be yourself."

I had been hoping for better advice than a paltry cliché. But before I could ask for more, the door at the end of the room opened.

"Hello, Captain. And hello again, Paul." Court Magician Redfield stood in the doorway. He was a somewhat mousy white man, honey-brown hair and piercing blue eyes behind thick glasses, an academic, bristly moustache. He held on to the doorknob in a tight grip, his other hand holding a cane. I tried not to stare—in his public appearances I had never seen him use a cane. He wasn't even that old, only fifty-five. "Please come in and take a seat." Hollister stepped forwards with me and Redfield spoke again: "Captain Hollister, please wait out here."

I glanced to Hollister, who gave me a curt nod and smile.

Hollister had gotten me this far, done all he could. It was all on me now.

Redfield's office was perfectly square and at least two storeys tall. The wood-panelled walls covered the room and curved up top to meet in a vaulted ceiling. Flags hung from poles jutting out high up on the walls and paraphernalia was on display in every corner, bits of magic history encased in glass boxes. For a moment I felt like I was in a Catholic church rather than a mage's office.

"Please, take a seat." Redfield was still making his way towards his desk, legs moving stiffly as he used his cane to support himself. Despite his entreaty to sit down, it seemed rude to take a seat while he was still making his way there.

"May we sit by the window?" My voice had a high pitch that made it sound unrecognizable to me. The office had two large windows, side by side, facing east. There was a small, round coffee table and two moderately comfy chairs set up by it. It seemed like a less formal setup than him sitting behind his desk, me in front of it. It was also closer for Redfield.

He paused.

"Yes, let's," Redfield said. He sat in the chair on the left, settling in with practised ease. As I sat in the other chair, small clouds of dust drifted up and floated in the sunlight. Redfield was obviously used to sitting in his chair, but he rarely entertained people here, it seemed.

I waited for him to speak.

"You are wondering about my cane," Redfield said flatly. He had it in front of him, hands resting on top of it. I said nothing, knowing it would be rude to either confirm or deny it.

"The last time the winnowing was held for Court Magician, I was your age," Redfield said. "I was number fourteen on the list. I was the third son in my family. My oldest brother would inherit our father's lordship, my next-eldest brother would take over our grandfather's company, and myself, well, back then people in my situation and class were expected to die quietly in a facility somewhere or live a quiet, retiring life in the family home." Redfield reached down and pulled up the right leg of his trousers. Underneath was some kind of brace, a device made of metal and leather. I only caught a glimpse of it before he let go and cloth covered the device again. "I was born like this, but it's only gotten worse with age," Redfield said. "Both legs. But I worked hard, and I went in to study magic. I thought I could find some way to cure myself, some magic that would fix my legs, let me move about the world as easily as my brothers did."

"Did you try cloth magic?" I said and immediately hated myself for interrupting.

Redfield cocked his head and looked at me. "I did. It helped, for short bursts. I still use it when I need to make public appearances. But the way it makes me feel . . . it affects me days after the fact."

I certainly hadn't expected Redfield's candour. He spoke evenly, the way you might if you were telling your secrets to a bird or rock. Merely relating things without any emotional weight to the events.

"When I couldn't find anything in cloth magic or Book Binding to help me, I decided I would look to innate magic. But the only way to learn of innate magic is to become Court Magician, so I asked my teacher to put in a good word for me and get a place on the list of candidates. My parents and brothers saw it as a death sentence. But if I died while attempting to serve this country . . . many fine, upstanding young men die that way in this country. I think they liked the idea of me dying in a way that had nothing to do with my condition, as if that would allow them to finally erase that part of me."

"But you didn't die," I said, because I was an idiot who hated silence and had a severe addiction to stating the obvious.

"No, I did not," Redfield agreed. "The thirteen young men before me did, the ritual claiming them." He paused. "They said number seven, Peter Sampson, that his bones turned to liquid. I don't know if that's exactly true, but they did have to cremate his remains." Redfield shrugged. "No one expected me to be the one to live through the winnowing. My body, already seen as weak, was not expected to survive the ritual."

"Maybe you just wanted it more than the others," I said. That got a small smile from Redfield.

"Perhaps. I did want it very badly. I thought once I was mage maker, I would have complete control over myself. I thought I could just wish my legs to full strength. And by becoming Court Magician, in a way my wish was granted. It was decided that England's top mage could not have a physical deformity, so as far as the public was concerned, I do not. My parents destroyed any photos of me in a wheelchair. When I went out in public, I wore braces or magic clothes that gave spectators the appearance that I was walking under my own power. Just like that, I was cured!"

He fell silent and for once in my life I was wise enough to let it linger.

"I don't know what you wish to gain from being Court Magician." He held up a hand to stop me from answering. "I'll be honest: I don't really care. But I can guess—you're a working-class lad from Liverpool who's done well for yourself. Hollister is an odd duck, but he has an eye for magic. So if you survive the Making, I'm sure I could train you into a fine Court Magician. But whatever you think you can achieve, whatever changes you think you can make, I'm telling you now that you should lower your expectations."

I waited to see if there was anything more, but Redfield stayed silent.

"Get that brown Book off my desk, will you, Paul?"

I leaped into action and returned with the Book. Redfield opened it, opening a channel with the Book as easily as sipping a cup of tea. A list of names appeared on the page.

"There," he said as my name materialized on the page. "You're number eighteen on the list."

I was elated that I had seemingly passed the first gauntlet but also discouraged. "Number eighteen? That seems quite high."

Redfield closed the Book. "Not particularly. I was number fourteen, remember. I'm afraid I can't put you any lower. Politics and all that. There'd be never-ending caterwauling from the families of the other boys if I put a no-name Scouser ahead of them."

"Oh," I said. "If I'm so controversial, why put me on the list at all?"

"Well, as the current Court Magician, I do have *some* say in the matter," Redfield said. "I do like you, Paul. I remember the day of your mage making. You bore it very well. I was impressed." He got to his feet and I realized he was showing me the door. "And the boys who are number nineteen and onwards, well, they might not be happy to have you go ahead of them, but they'll understand. Most of the applicants die, after all. We need a long list."

~

I walked out of Redfield's office and closed the door behind me so I could lean back on it. I pressed into the wood, trying to reconcile the solid world with the dizziness filling my head. I was relieved, elated—I had gotten Redfield's approval! I was now one step closer to becoming Court Magician. I was sick, dread filled—I was one step closer to dying a horrible death. I already felt like my bones were turning to liquid, like poor old number seven, whatever his name was.

"Jim?" Hollister got up from where he was sitting by the wall. "Are you all right? What did Redfield say?"

"He put me on the list." A sudden migraine overtook me—I squeezed my eyes closed, as though it were something I could shut out rather than something inside of me.

"Well, that's bloody fantastic! It's what you wanted, right?"

"Yeah."

Hollister was quiet, but I could feel him staring at me.

"When was the last time you ate?" he asked.

"Oh, not long ago. I had something just before meeting Redfield." That was right—the stolen cream puff.

Hollister tsked at that.

"My place is nearby, and there should be some food in the icebox. Let's go there and you can tell me all about what happened with the Court Magician just now."

"All right." Food sounded good, but in that moment all I wanted was to have a lie-down somewhere. But it was probably against palace protocol for guests to just lie down on the carpet and sleep.

CHAPTER 12

We went back through the tunnels to the car park and it was a relief merely to sit down in the passenger seat. At least, until the car started to move. I'm normally not the type to get carsick, but my empty stomach was already feeling plenty nauseous and the events of the morning had my adrenaline pumping. I kept my eyes closed and rubbed my temple as Hollister deftly moved the car through the congested London streets. Luckily, Buckingham Palace is a stone's throw from Belgravia, and we were soon at Hollister's secret apartment.

Seeing it again was strange. I noticed new things, like how yes, the decor was old but the place was neat and dust-free even though there were clear signs of someone living there. Hollister seemed to be walking a fine line between keeping the pad's stylings as they had been ten years ago and venerating the space so much that it was untouchable.

"How often do you sleep here?" I asked, curiosity getting the better of me.

"A night or two each week," Hollister said. "Sometimes my work requires me to stay late, but I really do try and spend most of my evenings at home in Barnet." I sat on the couch. Hollister, a gracious host, went to the kitchenette to get me a glass of water and, I hoped, some food. "I have two children. A boy and a girl. Harriet, my daughter, she's a teenager now and already a young lady. A very sweet girl. My younger child, Troy, he's a good strapping young lad. Wants to be a footballer when he grows up."

"They sound like nice kids," I said. I liked children, wanted some of my own someday. I wondered if Verity did too.

"You'll have to come over for dinner and meet them," Hollister said, handing me the glass of water. "My wife, Sybil, is a serviceable enough cook."

I sipped the water and felt my stomach settle. Hollister put a plate of saltines down in front of me and I had to hold back from gobbling them all up at once.

"So what did Redfield have to say?" Hollister said once the saltines were gone.

I let out a frustrated sigh. "Not all that much, really. He didn't care about me. I didn't even make a sales pitch. He just put me on the list. He acted like I was just another piece of chaff tossed in with the wheat." I took a long drink of water. Now that I was feeling better physically frustration was seeping in. "All my life I'd thought that getting on that list meant something special, that only the best of the best can go on to become Court Magician. But that's not the case, is it? Any mage could get on the list—*does* get on the list—if they have someone vouch for them. Redfield doesn't care and the Court Magicians before him didn't care either. They just need a big enough pool to draw from so that *someone* will survive."

Hollister had pulled over the chair from the desk and was sitting across from where I was on the couch. He looked at ease, one leg crossed over the other, hands clasped loosely. It was hard to imagine him living elsewhere than here, especially a suburban home with a wife and kids.

"You're selling yourself short, Jim," Hollister said. "You're a fine candidate for Court Magician. Yes, a long list is needed, but one of those gents on the list will go on to hold one of the most powerful positions in the land—they can't just put *any* Tom, Dick, or Harry on there." Hollister leaned back in his chair. "I am relieved that you made it through, though. As charming as you are, if Redfield had spotted that you have innate magic it would have been all over."

I was on my feet so fast my head swam. Before I could make for the door Hollister was also standing, grabbing my upper arms.

"Relax, Jim, relax," he said. My eyes were still on the door—that damn automatic dead bolt lock would slow me down considerably even if I were able to close the distance. Hollister gave me a shake. "Jim!"

I stared up at him. He took a deep breath.

"I am on your side," he said. "I've been looking for someone like you for years. I promise I'm not going to arrest you."

I nodded, because agreeing with him seemed like the smartest move at the moment. Hollister firmly pushed me back onto the couch. He sat next to me, hands clasped in front of him as if ready to reach out and grab me again.

"How long have you known?" It was such a stupid thing to say, to even obliquely admit to the crime, but I couldn't help myself.

"Since the night of the gala," Hollister said, taking a key from his pocket. "Your friend Oberon told me there was a rumour that you had innate magic cast upon you, that it helped you talk your way into places above your station."

"*Oberon* said that?!" I remembered how, after I had broken up the fight between him and Verity, Oberon had gone to talk to Hollister, the man whose job it was to sniff out innate magic. To get back at me for breaking up a squabble, Oberon had tried to ruin my life. That weasel. How did he even know about me? No one knew . . . except for Lamb. Lamb, who was amazingly adept at discovering secrets but God-awful at keeping them.

"Usually, I would have just dismissed Mr Myers's words as a bit of schoolyard gossip," Hollister said. "But . . . well, when I had met you earlier that night, I just got that sense that you were the chap I needed. I've been praying hard for this, Jim. See, I need someone with innate magic, an innate magician that is more than just the standard Book Binder or cloth mage. I've been looking for someone like me, someone with a Christian worldview to help me protect this country. Magic in this country is too reliant on Book Binding. We both know that. And now we're losing our colonies one by one. America is outstripping us when it comes to technology, Russia when it comes to magic. This was supposed to be our century, Jim." At the last word he blinked and glanced around, as if suddenly lost. When he looked back at me, his face was set again, the fire back in his eyes. "I believe that you and I can do miracles. *We* need to do miracles, for the sake of king and country."

"What . . . what exactly do you want from me?" I asked.

"You've read *The Body Divine*, yes?" Hollister said. "I've been reading it too. I read it years ago and thought it was just rubbish, but talking to you has given me the lens to understand it. Do you see the same thing that I do when I reread it, Jim?"

He had the bright, clear eyes of a fanatic. He was on the edge of the seat, elbows on his knees to support his torso as he leaned in towards me. If I were to make another try for the door, his coiled body would hit me before I'd even taken the first step.

And he was right: *The Body Divine* had sparked an idea in my head. A new type of magic, or one so old it was new again.

"I don't know what you're talking about," I said, words coming hard from a dry throat.

Hollister cocked his head to the side. "I really don't think that's the truth, Jim."

We were just talking. It was just a theory. I just needed to string Hollister along until I could get out of this apartment, away from him.

"In the book of Mark," I said, "the author makes note of a young man who was nearby when Jesus was arrested. The Romans tried to grab the young man, but he fled, naked, leaving his linen cloak in the hands of the soldiers. Scholars don't rightly know why Mark included this little detail, with some saying it was that the young man was actually Mark and this was him dropping in a cheeky self-cameo. But others—me— think it's more metaphorical. The linen cloak symbolizes life. It is skin itself, the representation of the human form." The sound of my own voice was a slight comfort to me, and I felt some of my unease ebb as Hollister nodded while I spoke. "When Adam and Eve left the Garden of Eden, God sewed them skins. People usually read this to mean he made them clothing from animal skins, but what if he actually made them *skin*? That prior to the fall of man, they were like God, beings of pure energy and magic." I held out my hands, palms up. "In magic the soul is always referred to as a battery, the bones the circuit. But what if the skin is the casing?"

"In which case . . . ?" Hollister prodded.

"In which case, if you want to tap into a greater source of power than even innate magic, the trick isn't breaking someone's bones. It's skinning them."

As the words came out of my mouth it was like watching a flock of birds fly away, watching helplessly as they became smaller and unreachable. A dread came over me as I realized that I couldn't take them back.

Hollister bit his lip and nodded. "Yes."

I waited for him to say something more, but he just sat there. I eyed a clock on the wall—it was barely past noon.

"Well!" This time he did get to his feet. "I'm glad we're on the same page."

"Yes, me too," I said, because he was still very much between me and the door.

"Want me to give you a ride home?" Hollister said.

"Oh, no, that's all right." I walked towards the door in a way so that I never turned my back on Hollister. I'd be out of this room and be free of him, able to forget this unsettled feeling, the worry about what he was planning to do with the information I'd just given him.

"Why don't we have lunch Sunday?" Hollister stayed where he was, merely pivoting to face me as I sidestepped to the door. "Noon at the King Court pub?"

"Yes, sure. Bye." Once I was through the door I slammed it shut behind me and nearly fell down the stairs.

CHAPTER 13

A late-May heat wave hit London, causing a haze of petrol exhaust to settle over the city. Andrew suggested the two of us take our long-dreamt-of day trip down to Brighton to escape it all, and I thought that was an aces idea. The whole deal with Hollister had left a bad taste in my mouth, and getting out of the city, even just for a day, was too good to pass up.

I was at Andrew's house early Friday morning to save him the drive north to pick me up. I knocked lightly on the door and about thirty seconds later the door opened.

Tonya stood in the doorway, looking at me with a placid expression.

"Tonya!" I really shouldn't have been surprised to see her: I was at her place of business after all. I was ashamed to admit that I'd forgotten all about the poor girl. I had meant to call her and apologize for standing her up, but I had gotten caught up in prep for the gala and then the business with Hollister and Verity's crusade. The whole thing with Tonya had just been pushed to the back of my mind. She looked . . . tired, to be honest. Her eyes were slightly dim and there was a waxen cast to her cheeks.

But I knew it would do no good to ask what was wrong, not while things were so awkward between us. I coughed, tried to regain my composure. "Tonya, I'm sorry for leaving you high and dry the other week. I really did want to go dancing with you, but that night I was . . .

detained." Oh yes, now I remembered the other reason I hadn't been eager to call her up: I didn't have a good excuse for jilting her, or at least one that wouldn't make me sound like a deadbeat. "I'm sorry, really."

"Of course, Mr Gallagher," she said sweetly, and the *Mr Gallagher* cut deeper than any actual voiced insults would have.

"Look, I'm really sorry," I said. "It's just been a wild few weeks—"

"Don't think you've got any obligation to explain to little old me," Tonya said.

"Let me make it up to you," I said, feeling like a wilting flower under her gaze. She had mastered the art of making her eyes blank but angry at the same time. "Let me take you out to dinner."

"Thanks, but as a maid I only get so many days off, and my time is too precious," she said with a smile. She stood in the doorway, not inviting me inside. I was trying to think of what to say when Lady Fife appeared over her shoulder.

"Is that Mr Gallagher? Let him in already, Tonya. We don't keep guests waiting on the front step."

"Yes, Lady Fife," Tonya muttered, opening the door and allowing me through.

I took a tentative step into the front hall. Between Tonya being sore at me and Lady Fife being her usual aloof self, the atmosphere felt quite strained indeed.

"You look well, Lady Fife," I said and meant it. I admired the fact that she nearly always wore magic cloth—most people only do so for special occasions. That day she was wearing what I assumed was another one of Andrew's creations, a dress made from blue taffeta that had great volume but also seemed light and easy to wear. She was checking her purse, a very mundane gesture that took me off guard: Lady Fife was always so perfectly composed that it was startling to see her do something as ordinary as making sure she had her house keys. The items in her purse seemed to be free of gravity and threatened to float out, stopped only by Lady Fife snapping her purse shut.

Shannon Fay

"Thank you, Mr Gallagher."

"Is Andrew about? We're going on a day trip to Brighton."

"I'm afraid my son is indisposed. He was not feeling well last night, and he woke up this morning with a full-on summer flu."

"Oh. Well, that's bad luck." I felt for Andrew—it was no fun being sick—but I also wished that someone could have bothered to call and tell me before I had travelled all the way across the city.

"But since you are here now, Mr Gallagher, perhaps you could accompany me on an errand," Lady Fife said.

That caught my interest. "Really? What kind of errand?"

"Just a chat with a friend." She glanced at me, a slightly raised eyebrow the only change in her expression. "This meeting may prove beneficial for you."

"Oh, Lady Fife, there's no need to bribe me. The pleasure of your company is reward enough." I was rather excited to be asked along on this mysterious endeavour. Lady Fife had never seemed to have any time for me before, and I was intensely curious about what could make her thaw out now.

"Splendid." Lady Fife gave some further instructions to Tonya about watching over Andrew, and then a few minutes later we were in the back of her car, the driver taking us in towards the city centre.

"It is a short drive and I still have work to do," Lady Fife said in reply when I tried to make chitchat. She pulled items out of her purse: a newspaper clipping, an ornate pocket watch, a pen. Hurriedly she held them up and let go, leaving them to hang in the air around her as cleanly as if they'd been pinned to a board. She took out a Book and started reading the lines as they appeared on the page. Occasionally she would pluck the pen from the air and cross out a line and write something new above it. The Book would then rewrite itself, the words reforming to reflect whatever changes she had made. I myself couldn't make out Lady Fife's spidery handwriting, and I wasn't gauche enough to lean over to get a closer look.

"Lady Fife," I said. "That Book . . . is it making predictions?"

Lady Fife laughed. "No, it's making forecasts. This"—she closed and patted the Book—"is no magical divination tool. It is merely a Book I have recorded all my observations in, and based on those observations it generates theories on what will happen in the near future."

"I see." I had always thought that Lady Fife was a foreseer using some kind of ancient fortune-telling device, like tea leaves or crystal balls. Could it be that the whole time she had just been very talented at Book magic? I felt oddly disappointed.

"Ah, we're here," Lady Fife said. I had been so engrossed in watching her that I had hardly noticed where we were. Now that I did, I saw the House of Parliament towering over us.

"What? Here?" I said. Lady Fife ignored me, just gathered up the items hanging in the air and placed them back in her purse. I followed her into the building. Various MPs nodded her way as we walked through the halls. I tried not to stop and stare, but I couldn't help it: I don't think I'd ever seen ceilings so high, not even in a cathedral. The coolness of the tiled floors and stone walls gave the sense of being underground, even as daylight flooded in from the towering windows.

We eventually deviated from the crowd to go into a small stairwell, up a few storeys, and down a nondescript hall with no windows but doors on every side. Lady Fife stopped at one and, without knocking, opened the door.

On the other side was a sitting room, the far wall lined with windows that offered a view of the Thames. The room was the same size as my entire flat but compared to the grandeur of the rest of the building this room seemed small and quaint. It had plush red carpets and through an open window I could smell the river. There was a man standing by the window, and when he turned around I saw that it was Prime Minister Brentwood.

"Ah, Lady Fife," the prime minister said. He came over and gave a little bow. "I hope everything is all right. I was getting worried since you are usually so punctual."

"No need to worry, Prime Minister. I'm here now." She gestured to me. "This is Paul Gallagher, a cloth mage. He was in the same class as my son."

"Ah, pleasure to meet you." Brentwood glanced my way with a questioning look: *Who are you and what exactly are you doing here?* I decided to take a page out of Lady Fife's book: don't apologize and don't explain.

"Pleasure to meet you, Prime Minister Brentwood," I said with a wide smile.

As we shook hands I could feel my innate magic working on him. His posture relaxed and he now seemed to accept my presence there as a totally rational thing.

"Please, sit," Brentwood said. There was a small coffee table in the middle of the room with four chairs around it. To my delight there was an assortment of little biscuits on the table, as well as a pot of tea. I hadn't eaten breakfast and tried not to seem too eager as I took one of the biscuits.

Brentwood and Lady Fife started to talk about things like trade tariffs and the GDP and in general acted as if I were not there. This suited me fine as I didn't feel like there was much I could contribute; I'd never been the best at keeping up to date with politics and current events, usually counting on Thomas to read the paper and relate anything of importance. I kept busy by snagging biscuits off the plate and discreetly wrapping them in a napkin so I could eat them later.

"And how goes it with the Aldrich Report?" Lady Fife asked.

Brentwood reached out for a biscuit and frowned when he saw they were all gone. I felt guilty for taking them all, so when he turned to answer Lady Fife I stealthily slipped one back onto the plate.

"It's going well, and the findings seem to line up with your views," Brentwood said. "But even so, I don't know if there's much political capital in publishing it. What do we as a nation gain from decriminalizing homosexuality?"

That caught my attention. To cover up how sharply I had suddenly sat up in my chair I reached forwards and ate the biscuit I had just slipped onto the plate. Brentwood watched as I ate it, clearly puzzled by the biscuit's miraculous appearance.

"We gain much as a nation," Lady Fife said. "Right now, the only purpose the law serves is to give our enemies leverage to blackmail some of the greatest minds in the country. The same people who helped us fight fascism are now living in terror of their own government. No person should have to suffer like that," she said. "Backing the report may require you to show a little moral fortitude and suffer some slings, but I suppose you will have to weigh that cost against the fate of the nation."

Brentwood looked like a child who'd just been sent to the naughty step. His eyes rested forlornly on the empty biscuit plate.

They chatted about some recent question time scuffles. Soon enough Lady Fife said it was time for her to take her leave.

"I am sorry we did not get a chance to talk more, Mr Gallagher," Brentwood said to me. "But any protégé of Lady Fife's is a friend of mine. Please feel free to get in touch."

I did not correct him on being Lady Fife's protégé—it seemed as good an excuse as any for me being there.

"Thank you, Prime Minister." Brentwood always appeared pretty put together in photos, but in person he looked tired and haggard. I felt sorry for him.

Once Lady Fife and I were outside the parliament building she stood there for a minute, eyes on the bustling traffic. The smog was still thick. I took out my handkerchief and held it against my nose and mouth.

"Walk with me," Lady Fife said, turning towards the statue of Boudicca. I followed Lady Fife until we were halfway across Westminster Bridge. Being over the water helped clear up the air somewhat. I leaned against the railing and looked back at the parliament building, trying to spot the window of the sitting room we'd been in just a few minutes earlier. Cars and buses motored along. A mix of tourists, street performers, and Londoners was going to and fro, the general babble making it near impossible to hear any one voice. The sun was shining on the river.

Lady Fife seemed content just to people watch, so I was the first one who spoke.

"Will Brentwood really decriminalize homosexuality?"

"Perhaps," Lady Fife said. "He knows it's the right thing to do, but he lacks a backbone. We will see if his heart is strong enough to do the work of the spine." She turned around so that, like me, she was facing the river. "But that's not why I brought you there."

"Then why, Lady Fife?" What had prompted this quite unsubtle display of power?

"I've worked very hard for this," Lady Fife said, gesturing to the cityscape hedging in the river. "I've worked so hard to create a stable nation and hope to continue to nudge it along the right path. Before, during, and after the war we could have so easily toppled into fascism. We didn't. But for all my hard work, it is still such a fragile thing. You could easily shatter it into a hundred pieces."

"Me, Lady Fife?" I said, trying not to laugh. "How could I do that?"

"By creating a new form of magic."

I was certainly not laughing now.

"Where did you hear that?" My first suspicion was Lamb—perhaps he had inferred Hollister's true goals early on. Maybe that was truly why he had tried to warn me away from the man. It would be just like Lamb to try and manipulate things from behind the scenes and go to Lady Fife with what he knew. He could probably even justify it to himself by saying he was only looking out for me. "It was Lamb, wasn't it? That gossipy—"

Lady Fife shook her head. "Don't be so hard on him. No one needs to *tell* me these things, Mr Gallagher. That said, people do talk. They especially talk about the comings and goings at Buckingham Palace and who's been added to the list of Court Magician candidates."

That made perfect sense, but it was still odd to think that there were strangers out there gossiping and speculating about little old me. It was oddly thrilling.

"I'll be direct with you, Mr Gallagher," Lady Fife said. "Withdraw your name from the list of candidates. If you do, I promise to take you under my wing. I'll teach you everything I know about magic and about running this country. There's no need to be Court Magician when you can be my successor instead."

It was a staggering offer, one that many people would walk across hot coals for. Lady Fife spoke with a frown on her face, as if taking me on was a distasteful martyrdom she'd endure . . . for what? Just why was Lady Fife suddenly extending her hand to me? What had changed?

I'd gotten on the list of Court Magician candidates. That was what was new.

"You've seen how the Making plays out, haven't you?" I said, the gears turning in my brain. "You know which candidate will be the next Court Magician." It was me. That was what Lady Fife had foreseen and what she was working hard at now to prevent: Paul Gallagher rising up to become the most powerful mage in the country. No wonder she'd rather keep me close, under her wing so she could clip mine.

Lady Fife looked at me evenly. "Are you asking me to tell you what the future holds?"

I laughed. "Oh, no, Lady Fife. We've been over that—there's no need." I couldn't help but chuckle. I had already believed that I would survive the Making, but having some third-party proof of it was a solid relief.

"At least consider that I am trying to prevent your death," Lady Fife said through gritted teeth.

I smiled. "Of course, Lady Fife. Your concern for me is touching but unneeded."

Lady Fife turned around and pointed to St Paul's Cathedral. Its trapezoid bronze roof caught the midmorning sun.

"During the war, I knew St Paul's would get hit in the blitz," she said. "I knew exactly what night it would happen. But even knowing that, there was nothing I could do. It's not as though we could move the whole cathedral somewhere for safekeeping. It was something beyond my control." She stared at me. "Perhaps there is nothing I can do here either. In this case the responsibility rests with you, Mr Gallagher. I hope you weigh your options carefully."

I didn't have a ready reply to that. Lady Fife stepped forwards and flagged down a cab, giving the driver enough fare to get me home.

CHAPTER 14

When Sunday morning rolled around I tried to sleep in, staying in bed even after Thomas got up.

"You're not going to church?" he asked me.

"No," I said, eyes shut tight.

"Not having lunch with that military man either?"

I gave up any pretence of sleep and sat up.

"No. I'm keeping my distance from him," I said. "Lamb said I should be careful of Hollister. I hate to admit it, but maybe he has a point."

"He has a point?! *I* have a point!" Thomas said, stopping midturn to glare at me. "I told you the guy was trouble!"

"Yeah, yeah, I know," I said. I must have acted suitably shamed because Thomas likewise looked uncomfortable.

"Well, if you're not swanning about in fancy restaurants, then maybe we could actually get some work done today," he said primly. I snorted. As if he was one to lecture me on slacking off when he spent most of the day on his ass, reading.

We were still working on an outfit for one Charles Mayhew, the man who wanted the waterproof suit. We unfurled the bolt of green linen we had. There's a school of colour theory in cloth magic, that certain colours will add certain attributes to the finished project. We had chosen green hoping that the things associated with it (vitality, sharpness) would help Mayhew keep it together next time he was sloshed. We still had no clue how to make it waterproof.

"Well, oil didn't work," I said. "What else is averse to liquid?"

Thomas shrugged. "Ducks?"

I snapped my fingers. "Brilliant!"

"I was joking."

"I'm not. Let's go to the park!"

After discussing the various parks in London, we decided Regent's Park had the most waterfowl and headed down there, the two of us carrying our bolt of fabric onto the bus. Once at the park we ran into a snag. To capture the attributes of something, a piece of cloth had to be exposed to it for a certain amount of time. We had managed to make Verity's dress by exposing the jersey to the reflection of the moon, but the moon is a far more placid creature than a family of ducks.

We tried luring some ducks onto the fabric with the promise of bread, but that just led to muddy duck prints and bird shit on the fabric. We tried holding up the fabric as if it were a large screen and followed a family of ducks around the park, but all this seemed to do was amuse the other human visitors.

"All right, so it's a little trickier than expected." A picnicking family who had watched us chase birds around had given us a ham sandwich to split. We sat on the pond bank, chewing thoughtfully.

"Book Binders don't have to deal with this," Thomas muttered.

"Yes, and that's why they lead boring lives," I said. The ducks had returned to the pond and were diving down to catch fish. "We haven't tried putting it in the water yet."

"No, for two very good bloody reasons," Thomas said. "One, it would probably just take on the properties of the water, not the ducks, and two, that water is bloody disgusting."

I couldn't argue with the second one, but I took a shot at the first part. "What if we mimicked how the ducks move in the water?"

"How so?"

"Look at how fast and deep they dive! And when they come up the water just slides off them," I said, pointing to a mallard that had just bobbed to the surface. "If we could just do that, we'd be in business."

"And when our material is stained to hell because we dunked it in London pond water?"

"We'll dye it dark green."

We found a large rock and wrapped the fabric up around it. I chased down a groundskeeper, introduced myself, and asked to borrow a length of rope, which Thomas and I tied around the bundled-up rock. It almost looked as though we were fashioning some kind of Old Testament weapon.

We stood on a little bridge. The apex was about a yard over the water.

"So we'll toss this in and as soon as the rope is taut, we'll haul it up as fast as we can," I said. Thomas nodded. Around us some park visitors had stopped to watch, though in true British fashion they acted as though they were only slightly interested in whatever we were up to.

We stood, holding the rock between the two of us. Just as we hefted it up over the railing it occurred to me that maybe we should have used a lighter rock. My next thought was that we should have tied the other end of the rope to something. In a panic we both grabbed at the rope. It slid through our hands. We only held it for a second before we both let go, hissing at the pain in our palms.

Thomas jumped onto the rope with both feet. He tottered on it, waving his arms in the air as he started to fall back. Before he could I dropped down and grabbed the rope. Thomas joined me and we started hauling the rock back up.

The rock came out of the water with a large slosh. The spectators around us pressed in closer to see what magical effect had taken place upon the fabric.

All they saw was a splotchy, wet green fabric covered in pond scum.

"Shit," Thomas said. We were running low on fabric and really couldn't afford to lose this piece.

"It will be all right," I said.

Thomas nodded grimly. "Yeah. We can still wash the fabric, get it clean, and try something else."

"Try something else?" I said. "No, we just gotta try this again."

Thomas looked doubtful but he didn't say no. Once again we hefted the rock over the side, though this time we tied the end of the rope to the rail. As soon as the rope was taut we pulled it up, moving as smoothly and swiftly as a couple of old deckhands.

Once again the crowd gathered around to watch the big reveal. They saw the fabric before I did, and I heard their muttered disappointment. Sure enough the linen was the same, except now it was even more discoloured by the pond water.

"Damn," I said. I waited for Thomas to tell me that we had to pack it all in now, but he was staring at the fabric in deep concentration.

"We're not going fast enough," he said. He gestured towards the ducks paddling on the water. "We got the dive part down fine, but we're just too slow and clumsy and awkward when it comes to surfacing."

"Faster, hmm?"

I tied the rope around my waist. I might have been a short bloke but I still weighed more than the rock. "Thomas, chuck the rock in. When the line goes taut I'll jump off the other side of the bridge and bring the rock back up. You grab it when it does."

Thomas stared at me, trying to find flaws in my plan.

"If you jump when the line's taut it'd be too late. Better to chuck the rock in and then take a running jump over the opposite rail. Also, the more weight the better," Thomas said, looping part of the rope around his hand. "No way am I letting you jump in the pond without me."

"All right." In which case, we'd need someone to grab the rock for us while we were swanning about in the pond. I made eye contact with a nearby tall fella. "Hey, mate!"

He was at least a head taller than anyone else in the crowd. He wore a painter's outfit and had clearly been working that day. I had picked him because he had long arms and looked like a tough enough bloke that, if he happened to take a rock to the head, it wouldn't slow him down too much.

"Hello there. I'm Paul Gallagher, and this is my associate Thomas Dawes. We're cloth mages!"

The man nodded as if he had guessed as much.

"We're trying to do some magic here, but we need your help. When we jump off that railing here, this rock is going to come flying out of the water. We need you to grab it and hold on to it for us."

"Can do," the man said. Thomas and I exchanged one more look to make sure we were on the same page, then picked up the now-soaking-wet rock and tossed it over the side. Without waiting for it to hit the water we sprinted the ten-foot width of the bridge. I heard the rock splash into the pond as we scrambled over the railing.

When picturing this plan in my mind I had imagined Thomas and me leaping off the bridge with great grace and agility, but in reality we hastily swung our legs over the railing and fell over the side. I felt the rope go taut just as we tilted over into the air.

We hit the water, Thomas falling on top of me, and for a second both of us were thrashing around. Thomas reached the surface first, letting go of the rope. I panicked, thinking I was going to die drowning in pond scum, then realized that the water came up only to my neck.

Thomas made his way to shore. On the bridge the bystanders had given up all pretence and were straight up watching us, clapping.

I tried to wade through the water but then felt a tug around my stomach. I was still tied to the rope. "Thomas, wait for me!" My foot slipped in the pond muck and I fell back, head going under. But then

I felt another, stronger tug on the rope, and a second later I was lifted off my feet.

As I was lifted out of the pond, I finally twigged as to what was going on: the people on the bridge, in an effort to help, were pulling me up with the rope.

"No, no, it's all right!" I called up to them, but my words were hampered by the fact that I was simultaneously coughing up pond water and also laughing really hard.

When I was close enough to the railing several pairs of hands lifted me over the edge. As I stood on the wooden slats of the bridge a puddle of pond water formed around me.

Thomas, somewhat rudely, pushed through my rescuers. His worried expression melted when he reached me.

"Bloody hell, Paul," he said, but he was smiling. We clasped arms, both of us still drenched in water but feeling like mages who had just duelled Poseidon himself.

Through the crowd the house painter came forwards, carrying the rock in his hands as easily as if it were a loaf of bread.

The fabric had changed. It was no longer green but a dark, almost black blue. Thomas and I carefully undid the ropes tying it to the rock.

The people in the crowd murmured as they looked at the fabric, noting how dramatically the colour had changed. But they weren't really impressed until the sun came out from behind a cloud and a ray of light hit it: the dark linen glimmered as if it were velvet, strands of periwinkle and yellow and light green rippling across the fabric. It reflected light the same way the feathers of a mallard duck did.

"We don't know if it actually does what it's supposed to do," Thomas pointed out, totally ruining the moment.

I shrugged. "Well, there's lots of water around here. It shouldn't be too hard to prove that it's waterproof."

"We should let it settle first. We can hardly see if it's waterproof when it's just had the spell applied." His eyes went to the crowd around us, and I got his point: if the fabric failed, it wouldn't be good for it to fail in front of such a big audience.

"All right, but there's something we need to do first."

I cut out a square of fabric and handed it to the house painter.

"Here, mate," I said. "Take this as a token of our thanks. You can use it as a handkerchief, or if you don't want it then just give it to your best girl."

The man looked at the shimmery dark fabric in his hand for a moment, then nodded and tucked it into his pocket. A few people on the bridge watched enviously.

I held up my hands and addressed the crowd.

"Thank you for your help today, ladies and gentlemen. If you are ever in need of a couple of cloth mages, please get in touch with the University College of London and leave a message for either Thomas Dawes or Paul Gallagher!"

∼

When we got home we hung the fabric and played a game of odds and evens to decide who got to use the bath first. I won. Afterwards, while Thomas was taking his bath, the phone started ringing. Mrs Dylag was out, so I rushed down to the landing to pick it up. "Hello?"

"Hello, Jim."

"Oh, Captain," I said. I should have known Hollister wouldn't just let me drift away.

"We had plans to have lunch together today, did we not?" Hollister said. "I was waiting for you for a good two hours."

"Ah, right. Sorry, something came up."

"You have my number; you could have told me that you couldn't make it today."

"Yes, I guess that's true," I said, saying what I thought would make the conversation end quicker.

There was a moment of silence on the line.

"I missed you today. I don't have many people in my life I can talk to about magic. In fact, I don't really have many friends at all, full stop." He paused, as if waiting for me to apologize. Jesus, this was the problem with emotionally distant older men—once you closed that gap they got clingy. It had happened with McCormick; now it was happening with Hollister. "Jim, why don't you come over to dinner tomorrow night, hmm? Break bread with me and my family? It will make up for skipping out on lunch today."

"Oh, well, that sounds lovely, but—"

"Fantastic! Can you make your way up to Barnet around six? I'll—"

"But Captain, if I come over, I don't want to discuss magic of any stripe, understand? I just need a break from it all, just for one night." I thought this was a fair compromise. I needed to stay on Hollister's good side, at least until I was made the apprentice Court Magician. I didn't want him to arrest me or ask Redfield to take my name off the list of candidates. And it would be nice to have a sit-down family meal. Surely Hollister could deliver on that: I couldn't imagine he'd want to discuss the magical properties of torture in front of his young kids.

"Of course, Jim. No shoptalk, I swear," Hollister said quite readily. We made plans to meet at the tube station near his house and I hung up the phone, feeling as though I had made a dentist appointment rather than a dinner date.

CHAPTER 15

When I emerged from the Finchley Central tube stop it was like stepping into another world: I had left the city and reached suburbia. Instead of tall stone buildings there were quaint brick houses with actual lawns and gardens. Trees filled the empty spaces.

The Hollisters lived in a large postwar home surrounded by high bushes. Mrs Hollister was there to greet us as Hollister and I pulled up in his Vauxhall Velox. She had dark hair swept up into a bun, the tight do amplifying the pinched, worried lines of her face.

"Mrs Hollister," I said, stepping up to shake her hand. "A pleasure to meet you. That floral print is very lovely. You really wear that New Look well." She wasn't an unattractive woman but she had such a despairing air that it overshadowed her physical beauty. She took my hand hesitantly, the way you might reach out towards a feral cat, but as we shook her unease melted away as my magic flowed through us.

"My wife is a very beautiful woman, is she not?" Captain Hollister asked, standing a few feet behind us. I glanced back at him, trying to read some hints from his expression. His tone was odd. It wasn't the leering, angry tone you sometimes get from blokes when you've been chatting up their girlfriends. But there was something there, some subtle trap laid within a seemingly sweet compliment from a husband about his wife.

"Yes," I said and let go of Mrs Hollister's hand. "You make a very distinguished couple."

It was a bit of a cold-water compliment, but it did the job of making the atmosphere a little less odd.

"Where are your children?" I asked. "I brought gifts for them." From my coat pocket I pulled out a small change purse and a hand puppet. Just little things I had sewn out of scraps lying around the studio, but hopefully the kids would like them.

"The children are visiting my parents in the countryside," Mrs Hollister said, her smile strained. I stood there, gifts in hand, unsure what to say. I had gotten the impression that this was supposed to be a family dinner, but now it was just me and the adult Hollisters.

"Well, they can have them when they return," I said. Mrs Hollister nodded and took the gifts from me and left them on a little table just inside the door.

I was led through the house to the backyard. Mrs Hollister showed me around the garden, and for a few minutes her birdlike nervousness dropped away, replaced with a grounded, warm countenance as she talked of the hedges coming up along the side of the house, the climbing vine that had taken hold along the lattice on the east wall, the rosebushes framing the table in the back. But then we all sat down at the patio table and her manner changed again, reverting back to her shaky, unsure self.

Because it was such a hot evening, we ate a light supper out in the backyard. There was Waldorf salad and jellied meat and it was all perfectly adequate but the atmosphere was so odd it made chewing and swallowing a chore. Hector and I usually spent our time talking about arcane theories of magic, something that might bore even most mages and certainly seemed like it would bore Mrs Hollister. Plus, we had both decided not to talk about magic. Instead we made small talk about the weather. Hector and I sipped coffee while Mrs Hollister drank some tea from India.

"That's chai tea, right?" I said. "I've never had it, but it smells good."

"You don't have to call it 'chai tea.' *Chai* means tea, so you end up sounding quite redundant," Mrs Hollister said.

"Ah," I said, properly chastised. Mrs Hollister seemed to regret her sharp tone. She stood.

"I'll make you a cup so you can try it for yourself."

"Oh, that's really not necessary." Even though her presence put a damper on the conversation, I was still wary of being alone with her husband.

"It's no trouble," Mrs Hollister replied and disappeared inside the house.

"Sybil is quite an aficionado when it comes to teas," Hector said, and for a moment I was confused as I tried to figure out who this Sybil person was before remembering that it was his wife's Christian name.

"That's good," I said. "Everyone should have something to be passionate about."

Hector frowned and nodded shallowly. I formed an unwelcome mental image of the Hollisters being intimate. The captain struck me as the kind of man who would make love the same way someone might go about their morning commute: the same stops and turns every day to the same destination, minor irritation over delays and obstructions, perhaps taking an inconvenient long way around if there was nothing to be done for it. A joyless necessity rather than a joyful indulgence.

Mrs Hollister came out with my chai in a little bone china cup, a floral pattern on it similar to the print she was wearing.

"Thank you," I said, taking the cup and saucer from her. It was a spicy tea, reminding me of curries I had grown up eating in Liverpool. I liked it. I could see myself coming to like it even more than coffee. *When I'm Court Magician I will drink chai every day,* I thought. I'd serve it to visitors and patrons and gently correct them when they called it *chai tea.* I would seem very sophisticated and worldly.

I momentarily lost myself in my daydream. When I remembered where I was the Hollisters were watching me. It unnerved me to see the two of them sitting there silently.

"Thank you so much, it is truly delicious," I told them. Thomas often said I had no self-preservation instinct, but he was wrong. There were plenty of times when a little voice in my head whispered, *Don't go home with that girl,* or *Don't go into the back alley with that guy,* and despite my horniness I listened to it. The little voice was telling me to get out now. "I'm afraid I can't stay any longer. I have several pressing projects that I must work on."

"But there's still dessert! Besides, we haven't even had a chance to properly talk yet," Hollister said. We had talked plenty, but his meaning was clear: we hadn't spoken of magic. I gave him an annoyed glance as Mrs Hollister stood and gathered the plates. I thought of pressing the matter further, of insisting that I really had to go, but though the atmosphere was odd nothing strange had actually happened. I didn't want it to seem like *I* was the unhinged one.

Mrs Hollister collected the tea set and disappeared back into the house. The captain relaxed, as if he had only now returned home after a long day.

"How are your projects coming?"

"Rather well, thanks." I started to tell him about the waterproof fabric when he cut in.

"I wanted to ask you something," Hollister said. "Innate magic doesn't work if the skin is broken, correct? So why do you think removing the skin would accomplish anything?"

"Well, the idea is to do one or the other," I said, annoyed that Hollister had brought up the subject yet unable to keep myself from talking about it. "Innate magic is a delicate operation no matter the spell, so the last thing you want to do is pierce the skin and ruin all your work. Likewise if you are working with . . . let's call it 'deep magic,' you don't want to tamper with the magic flow."

"Hmm," Hollister said. "No wonder so many people die chasing innate magic. So finicky. This deep magic really does seem like a better alternative."

"I don't know about that," I said. "Broken bones can heal. Removing the skin . . . well, there's a lot more blood loss. And that skin, it's not coming back. You might get more out of it than if you had broken a bone, but at what cost?"

I realized that I had gotten drawn into the very conversation I had wanted to avoid. "Captain, I thought we agreed we wouldn't talk about this."

"What's so wrong with talking about it?"

"Because I think you want to do more than just talk about it." I took a deep breath. "I told you, I might come up with ideas but that doesn't mean I'm willing to put them into practice."

"Because it's against the law?" Hollister said idly. "Even if we were discovered, I have enough high-placed friends to see that we never see the inside of a courtroom—"

"Jesus Christ, man!" I said. "How can you seriously consider skinning a person alive? That's one of the worst things I've ever heard. No, I'm not worried about the law of man; I'm worried about the law of God. You'd be tampering with God's own creation."

"No, I wouldn't be the one doing it," Hollister said. "You would."

I stared at him. "What?"

"I want you to do it, Jim," Hollister said, his voice even. "I want you to do it to me."

For a moment I was shocked into silence. Finally I gulped and was able to speak. "Look, Hector, I . . ." Telling Hollister the specifics about the spell on me was a desperate move, but maybe it would finally get him to drop the matter. "I *can't* do it. The innate magic I have, it has a downside. It keeps me from doing physical harm to another human being."

I held up my shaking left hand, turned it slowly so he could see the crook in my index finger. Hollister watched me with hooded eyes.

I dropped my hand and laughed weakly. "So even if I *wanted* to be breaking bones or skinning people, I couldn't." Oh Jesus, that also meant I couldn't be Court Magician. I had never put it together before now—I had always slotted innate magic in a separate category from, say, throwing a punch, but both involved hurting people.

Hollister made a thoughtful hum, tenting his fingers. "Does a doctor commit physical violence against a patient when he cuts them open for surgery?"

"What?" I said, trying to follow his line of thought. "What does that have to do with anything?"

He unbuttoned his cuffs and started to roll up the sleeves of his shirt.

"There are many times when a doctor must commit 'physical violence' while treating a patient. Piercing the skin to stitch up a wound, cutting open the body and removing diseased organs—even giving a child a shot 'harms' them in a sense. So would all that be classified as 'violence'?"

"Well, I don't know," I said. "But intention does play a big part in magic, so perhaps because the doctor's intentions are pure it sidesteps being violence?"

Hollister nodded. "I think so too. So perhaps, even with the spell upon you, you should be able to perform innate magic."

I laughed. "I hardly think that's—"

Hollister picked up a razor-sharp cheese knife. I leaned back but he didn't slash at me. Instead he dragged the knife along the side of his left arm. It was a deep gash. Blood welled up, the line of red reminding me of the icing between the layers of a Victorian sponge cake. The blood kept coming, sliding down both sides of Hollister's arm.

"It's all right," he said to me soothingly, as though I were the wounded one. "You have a sewing kit on you, yes?"

"You need to go to a hospital," I heard myself say.

"I will, later," Hollister said. "But right now you need to do this."

I didn't really know what I was doing, but the principle seemed simple enough. I took out my sewing kit and threaded a hooked needle with silk thread, making a mental note to myself to keep breathing as I did so. I pierced the skin at the end of the cut closest to me and pulled the thread through. I was so focused on my task that it wasn't until a couple of stitches later that it dawned on me that I was sticking a needle through another human's skin.

"See?" Hollister said.

I said nothing, just continued to stitch up the wound, Hollister's blood slick on my hand as I held his arm steady. I was halfway through before I realized I hadn't sterilized the needle. Well, too late for that.

"See?" he repeated once I was done. "If you can do this you can do innate magic, or deep magic for that matter."

I stood but Hollister grabbed my wrist.

"There's no reason we can't do this," Hollister said.

"But *why would we do this*?" I said. I tried to jerk my hand free but Hollister's grip stayed tight even though it was slicked with blood.

"The rest of the world is leaving us behind, Jim," Hollister said. "The powers that be here are so thrilled with Book Binding they have turned their backs on more . . . *wild* forms of magic. Magic we will need if we are to stay toe to toe with the Russians or even the Americans," he said. "But magic in itself won't be enough. What this country will need is not only that kind of power but a true leader to wield it."

"And you think that's *you*?"

Before Hollister could answer the question the back door to the house opened and Mrs Hollister stepped out.

"Ah, Sybil," Hector said lightly, letting go of my arm. She looked between the two of us in a quick movement, her frown tightening when she saw the newly stitched-up wound on her husband's arm, his blood on both of us. Yet she said nothing, just walked over steadily. When she was close enough Hollister pulled her into his lap, a movement that startled both her and me.

"Don't I have a beautiful wife?"

There it was, that odd tone. He was looking at her with a curious gaze, as if he were bored and trying to decide for himself if she was pretty or not. She glanced away, her eyes fixed on the toe of her shoe.

"Any man would be lucky to have her." Hector looked at me. "Don't you agree?"

I felt as chilled as a stone deep underground. Was this man seriously trying to pimp out his wife to me? And why? So that I'd agree to perform magic with him? Did he really think that was my price? He had taken my measure and thought that would win me over? Mrs Hollister was beautiful, sure, but since she didn't seem too keen on the idea of having sex with me, I was likewise put off. From Mrs Hollister all I felt was at worst disdain, at best a kind of pity. Her obvious discomfort was making my own stomach flip.

An evil thought popped into my head. Hollister seemed so desperate to do this magic that if I replied to his proposition with one of my own, he'd probably sleep with me. But he was so hung up on his sexuality he'd probably insist on his wife being there, and then no one would enjoy—

What the hell was I thinking? I couldn't do this.

I had to get out of there.

"They would be very lucky, the luckiest man," I said, and just like that my voice was steady, posture strong. No matter what the situation, if I just turned on the charm it was like following a dance I knew by heart. "I was just thinking of how jealous I was of your position."

Hollister smiled, though his eyes were still hooded. "Well, perhaps we can do something about that."

"Yes," I said. "But before we take this any further, may I use the toilet?"

Hollister hesitated, and I worried he had seen through my ruse. "I just want to make myself a little more presentable," I said, trying to smile my best bashful grin. I held my palms out, Hollister's blood drying on my skin.

Hollister nodded, giving way. Mrs Hollister still hadn't looked up from the toe of her shoe. "Toilet's at the top of the stairs and to the right."

"Thank you." I stood and let myself into the house. Instead of heading upstairs I walked swiftly through the house to the front door. It would be a bit of a walk to the tube station, but better to hoof it than get drawn into some kind of entrapment. Part of me couldn't believe I was turning down a threesome, but that was drowned out by a voice screaming in my head to get out, go—

The front door was locked.

There was an inside dead bolt, the type that needed a key. I'd seen this kind of lock before, usually on the doors of new-money upper-middle-class paranoiacs. I hunted around to see if the key was hanging up next to the door or something, but there was no sign of it. I could feel some of my panic pulling on the strings in my brain, making my fingers and mouth twitch.

Lying on the table was the hand puppet I had made for Hollister's young son.

I guess they really don't want you to leave, I imagined the puppet squeaking.

I went to the kitchen to see if the key was lying on a countertop or something. Through a window over the sink I saw the Hollisters arguing. Sybil was more animated than she had been all evening, still sitting on Hector's lap but leaning away from him as she angrily exchanged words with him.

At least that meant their attention was elsewhere. There was no sign of the key. I carefully checked the drawers, only to find cutlery and clutter.

There had to be another way out of the house. There was a gate in the garden, but to get to it I'd have to go out the back door and come out right where the Hollisters were having their hushed, angry row. I could make a run for it, I thought with a dry chuckle, but the captain was still in pretty good shape and would probably tackle me before I made it to the gate.

That line of thinking raised an interesting but uneasy question: Just how far was Hollister willing to go to get what he wanted?

I thought of the chairs in the living room: I could throw one through the main window and escape that way, but then Hollister could sic the police on me.

Outside Hollister said something that made Sybil fall silent. They both looked towards the house.

I was running out of time. Any moment now they'd figure out that I wasn't using the toilet—

The toilet! Hollister had said it was at the top of the stairs and to the right. That was the side of the house facing the street, the east side with the vine climbing up a wooden lattice. I could just climb down to the street and walk away.

Hastily I made my way up the stairs. The whole house was covered in plush carpet, keeping my footfalls silent. Just as I reached the top I heard the back door open.

"Jim?"

I turned right and went to the WC. Seeing the window felt so good, like I was a damned soul catching a glimpse of heaven. There was no screen, so I lifted the window up and climbed out.

My feet easily found footholds on the wooden lattice. I lowered myself down to it, pulling the window down so that it was almost closed.

I had forgotten to lock the door after me. Just as I lowered the window I saw the door swing open. I ducked down, fingers clutching the window ledge.

Only three seconds passed as I hung there, feet on the thin wood and my fingers just barely holding on to the edge of the windowsill. I was too scared to pop my head up to see what was going on—I could sense a figure standing in the bathroom.

"He's not in there," Hector said. I heard the door swing shut.

I was just saying a prayer of thanks when the wooden lattice broke under my left foot.

"Gah!" I managed to grab hold of the window ledge with my forearm as my left leg swung out from under me. A second later I found another spot for my foot, but I still clung to the window ledge, even pushing the window up so I could pull my head and shoulders back inside. As I was trying to work up the nerve to jump into the hedge below, the door swung open once more. Sybil Hollister stood in the doorway.

She moved towards me with purpose, so intense I drew back out of the window. Before I could start climbing down she grabbed the lapels of my suit.

"You can't give my husband what he wants." She kept her voice low but I could tell she would have roared it if Hollister weren't possibly lurking around the corner.

"Yes, yes, I understand!" I said. "Mrs Hollister, I would never agree to the kind of thing Captain Hollister was offering. I respect you too much, I respect women too much—"

"That's not what I mean," she hissed. "No matter what he offers you, *you can't give him what he wants.*"

I could feel the wood of the lattice cracking under my feet.

"Yes, I understand!" I repeated.

She stared deep into my eyes.

"No, you don't."

"Sybil?" Hollister's voice came from somewhere close. Mrs Hollister and I froze at the sound of his heavy tread coming towards the bathroom.

"Here." She reached into her dress and took out some letters that had been tucked into her bra. I tried not to blush as I took them from her. "Read these. Then maybe you'll understand."

The door to the bathroom swung open. Mrs Hollister gave my shoulders a push and just like that I was falling towards the ground below.

CHAPTER 16

I tried to clean up on the tube ride home, using the dim reflection in the carriage window to pick twigs and leaves out of my hair.

My work was seemingly for nothing: when I arrived at our flat Thomas gave me an askew glance. "You look like—"

"Like I fell out of a two-storey window and into a bush?" I replied testily. I was wrung out after the evening's adrenaline rush. I flopped on the bed. Thomas managed to roll out of the way before going back to his magazine. He might have asked me something but I was already falling asleep.

~

That night I dreamt that everyone around me was in pain. Buildings and people were melting, flesh and stone running together in a slurry that filled the sewer drains. A radio blared that the Russians had dropped a Superconductor in the middle of Piccadilly Circus and nothing could save us now.

A girl stumbled towards me and I grabbed her shoulders, the flesh giving way under my hands even as I squeezed tight to keep her upright. It took me a second to realize that her slack, sloping features were those of Tonya Gower.

"Tonya!" I said. "I really am sorry we didn't go dancing."

She nodded, making more of her skin pull away. She opened her mouth to speak but I woke up just as she started to form the words.

I was alone in our attic room. The walls were solid. Sunlight was coming in through the large window.

Thomas came up the stairs.

"The baker on Green Lanes was just going to put these in the rubbish bin," he said, somewhat cheerful for once. He tossed a round bun to me. The top was pitch black but the bread inside was still good. Thomas sat beside me and we cracked open the buns and scooped out the insides as if we were eating lobsters.

"You're quiet today," Thomas said. "You sick or something?"

I shook my head. "No." I took a deep breath. My heart was still beating fast from my nightmare. "Do you believe in prophetic dreams?"

"Sure," Thomas replied. "The other night I dreamt that me and Rita Hayworth had run off to Tahiti. I'm sure it'll come true any day now."

I sighed in frustration. "Fine."

Thomas paused, bread halfway to his mouth. Now he sighed. "All right, tell me about your prophetic dream."

"I'm not saying it *was* a prophetic dream," I snapped. "But, well . . ."

I told him about the melting people and buildings, the sense of unbridled magic in the air. When I was done Thomas nodded sympathetically.

"Everyone has dreams like that," he said. "Ever since the war ended. Everyone's on edge, waiting to see what Russia or America is going to try next." He shook his head and popped part of the bun into his mouth. "America has the A-bomb; Russia has Superconductors. Humanity's odds aren't looking that good."

"And meanwhile we in the UK have nothing." Was there some validity to Hollister's paranoia?

Thomas patted me on the shoulder. "I don't think your dream was a vision, all right? I think it's probably just the subconscious working through some other tension or fears eating at you."

"That could be." I told him about my visit to the Hollister household, every sip of tea, every strange look, all leading up to me escaping from the bathroom window. I did, however, leave out Hollister cutting open his own arm, as that would lead to me telling Thomas about the spell on me and the whole bit about me on my way to becoming the next Court Magician. "And the weirdest part of all is that I don't even have a clue exactly what it was all about—"

Something crinkled in my coat pocket. It was one of the letters Sybil Hollister had given me. When I had fallen into the hedge I had only managed to keep my grip on this one. I'd been so intent on merely escaping the Hollister household I had forgotten all about it.

"What's that?" Thomas asked, leaning in.

"Something Mrs Hollister gave me," I muttered. "She said if I read it, I'd understand."

Thomas managed to look apathetic for all of two seconds. "Well? Open it up!"

The envelope was addressed to one Captain Hollister, from one James Godfrey.

November 3rd, 1939

My dearest friend,
It's always a pleasure to receive your letter, even if it is difficult to read about you being in the line of fire. I am pulling some strings to get you back on British soil. I have a project in mind that I could use your help with. I won't say too much lest the censors get too excited and start marking up this letter to the point where it becomes unreadable.

I am writing this from my temporary office in St Stephen's clock tower. Yes, there is an office in the clock tower. When MPs speak out of turn too often they get banished here—it is the parliamentary version of the naughty step. I bucked under the party leader one time too many, and so he sent me here.

I have a week left to serve out my sentence here, working amongst the tickings of the clock and the quarterly chimes of Big Ben. Joke's on them though. They must have forgotten that the first war made me deaf in my left ear, so the constant ticking is not nearly the punishment it would be for some other poor bastard.

I do regret, however, that my deafness has kept me from your side. I fought so hard for this seat, and I'd give it all up in the tick of this damn clock to be in the field with you right now. I want you to know that I am fighting hard for you and the rest of the boys here in parliament. Though I can no longer serve as a soldier, I will have to make do as a politician. And I do take some comfort knowing that I may have found my own way to help king and country, even if it is rather unconventional.

Speaking of unconventional, I have made friends with a certain witchy-woman. She has said she sees me running the country someday—flattery perhaps, but one can hope!

I must be circumspect. Funny to think that, because of my position, my letters are just as likely to be censored as yours.

Ah, the bell has just chimed quarter to noon. They collect mail at 12, so I will wrap this letter up swiftly, all in the hopes that it will get to you all the sooner.

Your friend,

Jim

I read the last word with a twist in my gut. *James. James. Jim!* No wonder Hollister had latched on to that name. When he saw me, was he thinking about this man, his old mate and pen friend? "What the hell is this?" I said. For the life of me I couldn't understand why Mrs Hollister had felt it so imperative to get this letter to me.

"James Godfrey," Thomas muttered. "He died in the war."

"What?"

"Don't you remember? He's the MP who died when the Germans bombed St Paul's."

"Oh, that was him?" I dimly remembered the incident. During the blitz the East End of London had gotten hit especially hard. There were civilian casualties of course, but two victims got more ink in the press than everyone else combined: the dome at St Paul's Cathedral, and a conservative MP who had been in the church at the time despite it being late in the evening. As a child I had been more interested in the photos of the bombed-out church than in reading the obituary of a dead MP.

"The East End was already in rough shape before it got bombed to rubble," Thomas said bitterly. "But did the press write about those people? Nah, they spent columns on this Tory politician who just happened to be in the wrong place at the wrong time."

Despite everything I smiled. "I remember you were mad about that even when we were kids."

"Honestly, the world is better off without that bloke," Thomas continued, still mad. "He was a piece of shit. One of those young conservatives who tries to be all the more hardened to make up for any youthful idealism."

"He can't have been that bad." He seemed a warm, wry presence in his letter, at the very least.

"Don't get me started," Thomas said. "The man was a hard-line eugenicist. If he'd lived and become prime minister, you'd probably already be sterilized by now."

"Hey!" I said. "And what about you?"

"Me? They'd figure out where my father was from and ship me over there," Thomas said. "And that's just what would happen in this country. The colonies would have it worse. That's all if we didn't die in a war against Russia, which he was also angling for."

"Huh," I said. "Maybe it's a good thing he didn't become prime minister then."

"It's a good thing he straight up *died*," Thomas replied.

"Died," I repeated. "He died when St Paul's was bombed."

"Yes, we've already established that."

"Lady Fife knew when St Paul's would get hit," I said. "And from this letter, it sounds like she also *knew* Godfrey." I looked to Thomas. "What could this mean?"

Thomas bit his lower lip. "I don't know, but whatever happened, Godfrey is dead now. Maybe it's better just to let him rest."

~

As the days passed Hollister called me multiple times a day. I asked Mrs Dylag to screen my calls. If Hector Hollister rang, I told her, she should say I wasn't home.

"Just who is this Captain Hollister?" Mrs Dylag asked me after the fifth call in one day.

"A covetous man with a beautiful wife," I replied, allowing her to fill in the blanks however she pleased. Mrs Dylag snorted but continued to cover for me. I think she was secretly delighted to have a part to play in such a scandal.

My plan for dealing with Hollister was simple—I'd just steer clear of him until I became the apprentice Court Magician. Once that happened, I'd be under Redfield's protection and Hollister would be unable to arrest me. Until then I had other things to worry about, like helping Verity take down Dr Myers.

CHAPTER 17

I had been in touch with Verity about the next phase of our plan and it was time to put it in action. When Wednesday rolled around I picked up the phone and asked the switchboard operator to put me in touch with the Myerses' residence.

"Hello, Oberon," I said once he picked up.

"Gally!" he said, clearly surprised. The last time we had talked had been the night of the gala and we had hardly been chummy even before he'd socked me in the eye. "Well, hello. How goes your summer?"

"Pretty grand, considering you tried to get me arrested for illegal magic." A bit of an antagonistic start to the conversation, but I felt like it had to be addressed for what followed to be believable.

Oberon tut-tutted on the line. "Ah, yes, that. Look, I was angry and drunk . . . and I've never been very good at controlling myself when I get like that." He actually sounded apologetic, even if he had somehow managed to avoid saying sorry. "Did Captain Hollister talk to you?"

"Of course he did. Luckily he was able to see that it was all rubbish, so I was spared being arrested and maimed."

"Ah, yes. Good," Oberon said.

I took a deep breath. "Hey, mate, I know we haven't always been on the best of terms, and I feel partially responsible for that." That was a lie—somewhere in heaven was a record of everything that had ever happened upon earth, and its pages would show that Oberon had been at fault each and every time we'd butted heads. "I'd like the chance to bury the hatchet."

Oberon was quiet, which was what I had expected—he wanted me to grovel and beg for his friendship, the prat. I gritted my teeth and reminded myself that I was doing this for Verity, for those kids that Dr Myers had killed, that I was only suffering a temporary pain to bring about a greater justice. Just before I was going to speak, Oberon did.

"Yes, I want that too," he said. "Do you have any plans this weekend?"

"No, I don't." Now I was the surprised one—was it really that easy? "How about this Saturday?"

"I'm busy. My father's out of town that day so I'm filling in for him at a charity event. But how about this Sunday evening you and I go out and grab a couple of pints?"

"Actually, do you think we could start the night at your place?" The plan required that I get inside the Myers home. Sunday wasn't ideal as we didn't know exactly when Dr Myers would be returning from his trip, but I figured better to make plans with Oberon now than to let this chance slip away.

"All right," Oberon said easily enough. "We can play a few rounds of pool. And since Father's away, we can drink some of his good brandy."

"Sounds aces." Part of me wished it hadn't been so easy—I was extending an olive branch to Obie but he didn't realize my other hand held a dagger.

We said our goodbyes and I hung up the phone.

～

Saturday I met up with Verity to go over the plan once more. We went down to Greenwich—Verity wanted to see the meridian line and I was happy to accompany her. Our plan was a simple one, so we spent most of the day just talking, sharing stories of our childhood, and taking in

Shannon Fay

the sprawling view of the Thames from the hills that housed the Royal Observatory.

When I got home that evening Thomas was sketching a design for Mayhew's suit.

"Where you been?" Thomas asked idly.

"On a date with Verity Turnboldt," I said. Thomas smirked the way he always did when I mentioned Verity, and this time I decided to call him on it. "What's so funny?"

He chuckled and then managed to look serious. "I didn't want to say anything before because it's not really any of my business, but well, in the end your business is my business, isn't it?"

"C'mon, mate," I said.

"Has Verity Turnboldt told you who she really is yet?"

"What?" I said, taken aback. "Yeah. Weeks ago."

"Oh." Now it was Thomas's turn to be surprised. "Oh, all right. Good."

"Wait, are you saying you knew?"

Thomas shrugged. "I've known since the night of the gala."

It hit me: "The null coat!"

Thomas nodded. "But I'm glad it's all clear between you two. I didn't say anything because at first I just thought it was funny, but if it's getting serious between you two you should know."

I checked my wristwatch. I wanted to talk more about the null coat's properties but I was running late. "Oh dear, I need to get ready."

"You just got home," Thomas said. "You got another date?"

"Yeah, with McCormick." He had called me the night before and asked to meet up.

Thomas grunted. "You know, it really doesn't pay to try and be friends with that man."

I crossed my arms. "Being friends with him is the only thing that keeps us from getting a weekly beating."

"I *know* that," Thomas said sharply. "It's just, a loan shark like him lives and dies by his reputation—"

"I like to think of McCormick as more of a loan guppy," I said.

"A loan shark needs to be feared in order to stay in business," Thomas continued. "If word gets out that he is being especially nice to one of his so-called clients, he'll lose face. Other criminals, the people he works with and works for, they won't respect him."

"All right." It was always cute when Thomas took to explaining some criminal element of society like a college professor explaining schools of thought.

"And then the only way he'll be able to rebuild his reputation is by making an example out of the people who caused him to lose face in the first place. Meaning, me and you." Thomas thought it over. "Mainly you."

"Mate, McCormick's not like that, all right?" I said. "And besides, even if he was, it's only a matter of time before we get our big break and pay him back in full."

Thomas nodded but his eyes were doubtful.

As I was washing my face I heard the phone ringing on the landing.

"Mr Gallagher!" Mrs Dylag called up.

I left the bathroom to find my landlady with the phone in hand.

"Is it you-know-who?" I asked.

Mrs Dylag gave me an incredulous look. "I wouldn't have called for you if it was," she said. "It's the other man."

"Other man?" I took the phone from her. "Hullo?"

"Paul." Speak of the devil: it was McCormick.

"Ah, hullo, Greg," I said. "How goes it?"

"Not good, Paul." He didn't sound good: his breathing was so laboured that I could practically feel it through the telephone wire. "I'm in really bad shape. Can you come right away?"

I felt a little annoyed: we'd already agreed that we were going to meet that evening; couldn't he just wait an hour? But he sounded so distraught that I took a deep breath and let my irritation fade away.

"Course, Greg, as long as the first round's on you," I said, trying to make it seem as if we were just a couple of old mates meeting for a pint, not loan shark and debtor caught up in some never-ending cycle. He laughed, and it had a cracking sound to it.

"Of course," he said. "I'm at a bar in Dalston, the Nail."

That was odd. We usually met at his favourite pub in the East End. Dalston was north, a few boroughs over from where Thomas and I lived.

"Aces," I said. "I'll be there within the hour. You just sit tight, yeah?"

"Paul—" But the line went dead before he could say more. I wondered what he was going to say. Had he hung up on himself before he said something too sappy? McCormick was an odd duck, given to moods that ranged from blue to black, but I had never heard him sound so . . . high strung before. Usually his despair was the morose, languid kind.

I debated heading right out the door to catch the next bus to Dalston, but instead I climbed the flight of stairs up to the attic. Thomas was where I had left him, lying on his belly, smoking as he reread an old magazine.

"Hey," I said. "Just got a call from McCormick. He sounded worse than usual."

"That's saying something," Thomas said. "He might seem like a tough old bulldog but that man is a bundle of frayed nerves."

"Be nice," I said, still thinking on McCormick's wrung-out voice, like something had been squeezing his heart as he'd spoken. "He asked me to meet him in Dalston. That's odd, right?"

"Dalston?" Thomas looked up from the article he was reading. "That's not his patch."

"Yeah, I know. He's waiting for me at a pub called the Nail."

"The Nail?!" Thomas got to his feet. "Holy shit! That dive is lousy with goons and thugs. It's where the worst of North London gets their rounds in after knifing their grandmas."

"So you drink there often?" I asked, jokingly.

"Sometimes," Thomas replied, not joking at all. He was quiet for a few seconds before nodding as if in reply to his own thoughts. "I'm coming too."

"Thom, I don't think that's a good idea." McCormick and his goons had no love for Thomas.

"I'm coming," Thomas replied firmly. "I don't need to make chit-chat with that bastard; I'll just be nearby with a pint at the bar."

"All right," I said, realizing that I actually did want Thomas there with me this time. It was why I had come up to talk to him in the first place, knowing he'd insist on coming along. Thomas went over to our closet and pulled out his null coat. He took off his shirt and started buttoning up the grey shirt.

"Whoa, what are you doing?" I said. Wearing a magicked suit around Kensington was one thing, but Dalston? You'd better have some pretty good antimugger spells woven into the cloth, because wearing magic clothes was a big red flag saying, *Look at me! I've got money and I don't care who knows it!* "Why the null coat?"

"There's something off about this," Thomas replied. "Better to be on our guard."

"I think you're being a little bit paranoid," I said. "But if you're right, then shouldn't we wear something with more defensive proper-ties? All your null coat is going to do is cancel out other people's cloth magic. You really think that's gonna be a problem in *Dalston*?"

Thomas gave me one of his rare grins, his crooked teeth seeming to sharpen before my eyes. "Maybe, maybe not. But I know I can beat any bastard in a straight-up, no-magic fight. This suit takes any magic outta the equation."

"All right." I didn't want to appear underdressed next to Thom, so despite my misgivings I put on my herringbone suit. "Let's go."

We went out onto Green Lanes and caught the next bus heading east. About twenty minutes later we were in the heart of Dalston. A few streets down from where we got off I saw the sign for the pub, **THE NAIL**, with a large railroad spike on it. It made me think of Christ's crucifixion. An ill omen.

It was a typical Saturday night, which meant there were lots of people on the street, mostly men, mostly drunk. Thomas strode forwards, walking through them towards the pub with a steady gait and scowl, as if daring the blokes around us to say something. One of the men took him up on it, stepping out in front of us. He had alcohol on the breath.

"You looking for the bathhouse?" he asked, staring down Thomas. Some of the lads around him chuckled. "Because you're dressed like a fop."

"You looking for the morgue?" Thomas asked. "Because you're dressed like a corpse."

The man paused and looked down at his outfit as if checking to see if he had accidentally dressed like a corpse that day. Thomas pushed past the man and I followed quickly after him. I knew better than to glance back—that was prey behaviour. Thomas had taught me that. Eventually I heard one of the drunken louts behind us crack a joke and they laughed and chatter resumed. Only then did both of us relax. Thomas sighed and ran a hand through his wild hair, making it look even more dishevelled.

We reached the Nail without further incident. Rather than a respite from the bedlam outside, the pub seemed like a contained, concentrated version of it. Men (it was all men) were talking and laughing, each word and chortle louder than the last one. The pub was a long rectangle of a room. It had red carpet that was frayed where it strained to reach the edges of the wood-panelled wall. One of its walls was just a long window, the darkness of the night and the dim lighting of the pub turning it into a weak mirror.

"Paul!" McCormick came over to us now, shoving his way through the crowd. In the heat of the pub he was sweating like a roasted pig. His eyes went back and forth between me and Thom. I waited for some kind of annoyed remark or for him to just straight up tell Thomas to fuck off, but that didn't happen.

"Oh, you're here too," he said and to my great surprise added, "Good."

"Greg, it's bonkers in here. Can we talk somewhere quiet?" I shouted over the din. McCormick didn't seem to hear me, his eyes flitting around the room as sweat rolled off his nose. It was hot in the crowded pub but not that hot—maybe McCormick was sick.

"McCormick?" I shouted, snapping my fingers in front of his face. He broke free of whatever trance he'd fallen into and looked to me.

"Right, right. I got someplace we can talk. Quiet." He turned and started heading deeper into the pub. I didn't know how it could possibly be any quieter deeper in the throng of people, but nonetheless I started after him. Something was seriously wrong with McCormick, and I wouldn't be able to live with myself if I left and he did some damage to himself. I hurried my steps so I could follow the slight parting in the crowd and Thomas followed after me.

McCormick led us to a door in the back of the pub. Through it was a steep flight of stairs that led down to a small storeroom. One wall had a shelf that contained barrels of beer. The rest of the walls were exposed stone. Most of the room was taken up by a wooden table. There was no room to pull the chairs out; we had to slide into them as if we were sitting in a booth. Thomas went in first, followed by me, followed by McCormick.

"McCormick, what is all this about?" I had called him McCormick again rather than Greg but it seemed that both of us were beyond caring. The room was silent except for the ruckus from the pub above.

Hanging from the ceiling was a single bare bulb, its light so faint it barely reached the edges of the table.

"This is all your fault." McCormick's pale, wide eyes were fixed on the darkness across from us. I shot a quick glance thataway but only saw the outline of the shelves in the gloom of the room.

"Wait, *my fault?*"

"Yes," McCormick said. "When you two came to me, I wasn't going to take you on. A couple of wet-behind-the-ears Liverpool lads who didn't know their arses from their elbows. I figured you'd be dead in a week. And besides all that you wanted the money to go to school. To school! Where's the money in that? Why would a sensible businessman like myself put down hundreds of pounds on two snot-nosed brats so they could study magic? *Cloth* magic. Fucking cloth magic!"

"Hey, don't you start in on us too," I muttered.

"But when I met you . . ." Now McCormick faltered. He turned his feverish gaze upon me. "This is all your fault. I never would have gotten mixed up in this if *you* hadn't convinced me."

"Greg." I put a hand on his shoulder. He didn't react. "I'm sorry we haven't been able to pay you back yet, but I swear—"

"It's too late for that," McCormick said, and my fingers clenched ever so slightly. This was it. This was exactly what Thomas had warned me about. McCormick was going to kill us here in this shitty little pub storeroom. We had pushed things too far and now our only use was to serve as a warning to others.

I was picturing all kinds of gory displays, like our heads on spikes outside the House of Parliament, when two men came heavily down the stairs. The man in front caught my eye. He was a big, handsome white man, strong square face with tanned, acne-scarred skin. His suit was a colourful jacket of vertical navy-blue and cherry-liquorice stripes and black trousers. It was obviously magicked cloth and as he stepped into the room I drank it in, trying to figure out its properties.

Because I was so taken with the suit I didn't notice the other man right away. He was the dictionary definition of a spiv. The sharp angles of his pale face were accentuated by his slicked-back pompadour, the dim light catching the Brylcreem in his hair. If I had to guess his age I'd guess he was the same age as my brothers, somewhere in the early to midthirties. His suit was a humble but neat brown three-piece, though little things betrayed his wealth—the glint of the watch chain, the nice Italian leather shoes.

He put his hands on the top of the chair at the head of the table and smiled down at us.

Next to me I heard Thomas give a little hiss, as though he had just burned himself. On my left I could feel McCormick shaking.

"Good evening," Mr Brylcreem said. The other man was standing across from us, leaning against the shelves. It seemed odd that one wearing such a colourful suit could blend so well into the shadows. "My name is Welcome Wheelock. It's a pleasure to meet you."

Welcome Wheelock was an infamous East End crime boss. I'd never met the man but I'd heard rumblings about him. What did he want with *me*?

I had no idea, but I did have one thing, a magic that had been a part of me since I was six years old. It wasn't much, but by Jesus, I would milk it for all it was worth.

I stood and held out my hand, leaning so far over the table the wood bit into my hip.

"Paul Gallagher," I said. "It's a pleasure to meet you as well, Mr Wheelock, though you'll have to tell us what we've done to earn such an honour." I said it with just enough bite to show that we weren't completely happy with being shuttled down to some pub's storeroom and that we did in fact expect an explanation.

Wheelock stared at my hand for a second, then smiled and shook it. "Right. I've heard a lot about you." He looked at Thomas, who had pointedly stayed seated. "Less about you. Thomas Dawes, right?"

"What do you want?" Thomas asked.

"Greg here hasn't explained it all to you?" Wheelock said. He had an unexpectedly high voice, which made his fake surprise all the more cloying. "Please, sit. Let's talk." Wheelock pulled out his chair and took a seat at the head of the table. I likewise sat back down. Wheelock turned his gaze to Greg. "Greg, why don't you get a round in for me and the lads here?" He turned to me and Thomas, a knowing smile puffing out his cheeks. "A Birra for Mr Gallagher, and a Newcastle IPA for Mr Dawes, right?"

"Yes, that's——" Before I could confirm that those were in fact our drinks of choice Thomas broke out into a round of sardonic clapping, bringing his hands far apart before crashing them together again and again, his face frozen in an apathetic cast. It was the most sarcastic thing I'd ever seen and I loved him for it.

When he stopped there was a moment of awkward silence, annoyance radiating off Wheelock like heat radiating off a chunk of rotten meat.

"I'll go get those drinks then," McCormick said, sounding calmer than he had all evening. He didn't look my way as he slid out from behind the table and headed up the stairs. *Well, that's it,* I thought as I watched his retreating back. I figured we were never going to see those beers and that we had seen the last of Greg McCormick. He had seemed pretty rattled, and I imagined at that moment he was bypassing the bar and walking out onto the street, leaving this whole mess behind. I just wished I knew what kind of mess we were in.

"So you're cloth mages, eh?" Wheelock said.

Thomas and I stayed silent in unison.

"You know, when I was a tot there was nothing more I wanted to be than a mage of some kind," Wheelock said. "I just thought how amazing it would be to have that kind of power, to make magic trinkets and the like." He sighed. "I know in theory anyone can do it, but the truth is you have to have some affinity for it, don't ya? And I don't. You know how there are those, those, whatchamacallems, people who have so much magical energy running through them it don't matter if an object is magic or not; it becomes magic when *they* touch it?"

"Superconductors," Thomas said before I could.

Wheelock nodded. "That's right. Superconductors. Well, I'm pretty much the opposite. I have next to no magical energy running through me. When I pick up a Book or put on some magicked clothes, it's a sad sight. I'm practically a nonconductor." He shrugged. "I was pretty broken up about it, but then the war started up and I enlisted to take my mind off things. And though I couldn't do magic, during the war I found the thing I was good at. I could get things for people. We'd go into abandoned villages and I'd know where to find things. Where families hid the good silver, where they buried a purse in the garden. I made a pretty good business for myself. And when the war was over and I came back to London, I had enough of a nest egg that I could keep at it. It was a good way to make a little money, being able to sell things that the ration Book wouldn't cover. But eventually I realized that the money wasn't even in that. Goods were good, but services? That was much better. I got really good at figuring out who needed what and who could give it to 'em and putting the two in touch."

"So you loan out people instead of loaning out money," Thomas said.

Wheelock paused, as if making a note of Thomas's phrasing so he could use it later.

"That's right. Now, Greg, he's a swell fella, but . . . no, actually, he's a miserable sod. And he's an idiot on top of that. He gave you a big chunk of cash to go to school and become cloth mages. And for what? So you can pay him back a pound here, a shilling there? What a waste! Why not maximize the earning potential of the situation and actually use your skills? Instead of coughing up cash, you two can just do what you'd do anyway and make magic clothes and such. That way everyone wins."

"You're suggesting we make magic clothes for Greg?" I said.

Wheelock shook his head. "No, I'm saying that you make magic clothes for *me*."

I shot a confused look to Thomas, who likewise seemed puzzled, but we both knew to stay quiet.

"Any questions?" he asked, clearly relishing our discomfort.

"A few," I said. "We owe the money to Greg, so why would we work for you?"

"Oh, don't act so sad," Wheelock said, pulling his face into a mock frown. "I'm a good employer. I'll pay as well as any other client, give you interesting work."

"Such as?" Thomas asked.

"Oh, we'll see," Wheelock said idly. "There are lots of well-connected people who would be interested in suits that make them invisible and the like."

Of course. Just as the military was often looking for ways to use cloth magic to better kill people, the criminal world often turned to it for similar reasons of ill intent. Thomas and I might skirt the edges of respectability, but we weren't ones to sell our wares to cutthroats and bank robbers. It was just bad business, bringing the cops down on you. Plus, it wasn't exactly something you could put on your résumé or brag about to the world at large.

"That's not really our line of expertise," I said.

"Well, I'm sure a couple of bright boys like you can learn," Wheelock said.

"Maybe, but that's not really any of your business," I said. "Like I said before, the one we owe our debts to is Greg McCormick."

"Yes, and he owes debts to *me*," Wheelock said. "Don't worry, lads. I'll take care of you."

I didn't have to see Thomas's face to know he was getting worried. I know I was.

Footfalls came down the stairs, married with the sound of pints clinking against each other. I looked up the stairway to see McCormick coming down with three drinks in hand, his face as pasty and pale as a kneaded ball of dough. He was sweating so much it had soaked through the pits of his jacket.

"Ah, there you are, Greg!" Wheelock said.

McCormick put the glasses down on the table with a jarring clatter, his gaze focused on the tabletop. No matter how much I mentally pleaded with him to look at Thomas and me he seemed set on ignoring us.

"I was just telling the lads that I am going to be taking over their debt collection from you," Wheelock said. "They're very happy about it."

McCormick stayed silent, watching a bead of condensation slide down the glass of Birra.

"Isn't it grand?" Wheelock pressed. "You finally get paid in full. The boys get to practise their trade. I have a couple of cloth mages on retainer. I'd say this has worked out pretty well for everyone."

"And they agreed to it?" McCormick ground out.

"Hmm?" Wheelock said, in a tone that implied that whether we agreed to it was possibly the most trivial part of the whole deal. "Oh, of course they did. I mean, why wouldn't they?"

Thomas and I traded a look of grim understanding. Thomas might not like McCormick, but he was a sight better than most loan sharks swimming around London and leagues better than Wheelock.

"McCormick has always done right by us," I said. "We'd like to stick with him."

Now McCormick finally looked at me. There was still fear on his face, but it had cracked slightly and I could see surprise in his eyes.

Wheelock huffed in irritation.

"Oh Lordy," he said in a mock American accent. "You lads gave up your say in any of this when you took that money from McCormick. At that point you stopped being individuals and became a commodity.

This isn't a negotiation, get it? It's a transaction, and the transactees have no say in it. Clear?"

I was about to disagree when Thomas nudged me in the ribs. I got the message. We were deep in enemy territory here, in the bowels of a club probably full of Wheelock's hired thugs, our only ally a man who looked as though he was going to keel over from stress any minute now. The safest, smartest thing to do was to agree with whatever Wheelock wanted of us and then, once we were out of this place, slip away. Wheelock might know our drinks of choice but he didn't know where we lived. We could pull up stakes, find a new place to live, and lie low to the ground until he forgot about us. All we had to do to keep our heads was, well, keep our heads.

"Good," Wheelock said. He leaned back in his chair. "You start tonight. Our first client is on the way right now."

"What?" Shit. I was ready to play along to survive, but I wasn't especially eager to help out with some bank robbery or assassination. "What kind of job?"

"Cool your jets, Jim," Wheelock said with a wave of his hand. "You'll find out soon enough."

Thomas said something catty, Wheelock said something threatening, but the words themselves didn't register with me. Wheelock had called me Jim. There was only one other person in the whole world who called me Jim. Hollister was coming.

"Oh, McCormick," Wheelock said, the *you're still here?* unvoiced but implied. "I'll get one of the lads to bring over the dosh tomorrow."

McCormick said nothing. His face had gone from pale to grey, features hardening. He no longer looked strung out but wrung out, tired and resigned. He took his hands off the table and straightened up, fixing the lapels of his jacket. My heart rate doubled when I realized that he was about to leave us.

"Don't!" I said, voice filling the little room. "Greg, don't leave us here!"

Greg's eyes were full of pity. How often had I looked at him like that, when he was in the clutch of his own low points? Our relationship had more strings attached than a marionette, but Jesus Christ, I had spent hours upon hours listening to and talking with this man. Was he really going to leave us here at Wheelock's mercy?

"I'm sorry," Greg said.

"No, don't be sorry," I said. "Just don't do this."

He stepped away from the table. I scooted over from my chair to the one he had been sitting in, staying close to him.

"Please, Greg, don't leave us," I said. "You know what this man is. You know what you're doing to us. You're selling us to the devil. Could you live with that? Because Thomas and I, we probably won't."

"Hey, I'm sitting right here," Wheelock said, just a few feet to my right. I ignored him to keep my gaze on McCormick. He hadn't stepped forwards but he hadn't moved away either. His face was no longer resolved but doubtful, eyes meeting mine.

"We're better for our association with you," I said. "And you're better for your association with us."

It worked. Doubt left McCormick's face and he let out a breath. When he breathed in he seemed a foot taller. He gave me a grim nod, then turned to Wheelock.

"No deal."

Wheelock cursed and rubbed his temples.

"Greg," he said. "I am trying to help you out here. You will never get your money back from these two con men. I'm giving it all to you in one go, plus interest."

"It's not about the money," McCormick said. "How I manage my business is none of your business. They made the deal with me; the debt stays with me."

"Greg," Wheelock wheedled. "Be reasonable, man. You owe me a lot. You owe me your life."

"Maybe I do," Greg said. "But I don't owe you theirs."

CHAPTER 18

If I weren't so terrified I might have cheered McCormick right there and then, but in that moment the most I could do was mutter a fervent, "Attaboy, Greg." He heard it, though, and gave me another grim nod.

Wheelock let out a long sigh.

"You stupid, sentimental idiot," he said. Wheelock turned to the man in the striped jacket. "Morris, slice this moron's tongue down the middle."

"Sure thing, guv." Morris pushed himself off from where he was lounging against the shelves. A switchblade flicked open in his hand. As he stepped behind Wheelock's chair he swung the door shut, muting the roar of the pub above and condemning the room to the bare bulb's dim light.

"Still," he said, and a shiver ran through me. I was frozen in place, unable to move a muscle. My gaze was fixed on Greg and I saw that he and Wheelock were likewise stuck in time. Under the table Thomas reached out and grabbed my wrist but otherwise didn't move. I got the message: thanks to his null coat Thomas was immune to the charms of Morris's suit.

Morris reached up and squeezed Greg's face, making him open his mouth. With his other hand he took the knife and pressed the tip down into Greg's throat. Morris flicked his wrist and a line of blood splattered the table. Greg was screaming and clutching at his mouth when I realized I could move again.

"Greg!" I jumped up and grabbed him by the shoulders. He was screaming and the act of screaming itself seemed to only bring him more pain, summoning more blood to seep between his fingers.

"Breathe, breathe!" I said, which perhaps was a mistake because when Greg took a deep breath in through his nose he stopped screaming and started making strangled, wet sounds from his throat as he choked on his own blood. I pounded him on the back, hand open and flat, giving one hard whack after another. After about five he coughed up the blood, a gob of it coming up on his hands.

"You bastard! You didn't have to do that!" I yelled at Wheelock.

"Calm down, Gallagher," Wheelock said, sounding bored. "Or next time I hurt someone you actually care about."

I felt a bit indignant about that and angry on behalf of Greg. But mostly I felt fear, for still sitting at the table, unharmed, was Thomas, my little brother, my best mate. I couldn't let anything happen to him.

I sat down, gently guiding McCormick into the seat next to me. I had a split-second thought that I should demand that they let McCormick go, but I quickly realized that, best case, they would just toss him out into a back alley to bleed to death, or—worse and more likely—Morris here would slit his throat and end it. Better to keep him with me so I could protect him.

Hollister would be here soon. I hated the thought of it, but maybe I could bargain with him to get a doctor for Greg.

Next to me Greg sat slumped forwards, elbows on the table and face in his hands. Blood dripped from his mouth onto the table in a steady tempo.

"How sad it had to come to this," Wheelock said, still sounding more bored than anything. "My client particularly asked that I try to avoid violence as much as necessary, but sometimes, well, it is in fact necessary." He smiled at me. "You're good at begging."

I said nothing, just glared at Wheelock while keeping a hand on Greg's shoulder.

Jesus Christ, heavenly Father, I prayed as I rubbed circles on Greg's back. *Please send us aid in our hour of need.*

There was a knock on the door. No one was as startled as me. *That was quick.*

Morris opened the door. On the other side was a stocky young man I recognized as one of the bartenders from upstairs. His eyes passed over the scene in the room but he said nothing about Greg leaking blood onto the table. Instead he turned to Wheelock. "Your mate's here, guv'nor."

Wheelock stood. "Perfect," he said. He straightened out his clothes and brushed a few loose strands of hair back into place. "Morris, stay with the lads, would you? I'll be back again soon and then we can talk business." He looked at the three pints on the table, the beer slowly going flat. "Goodness! You haven't even touched your drinks!"

Wheelock and the stocky bartender went up the stairs. Morris closed the door behind them and for about five seconds he just stood there, his back to us. Finally, Morris spun on his heel and walked back to his space by the shelves. He leaned against them, a half smile on his face.

"You lads like baseball?"

Greg wasn't about to answer as he was too busy trying not to choke on his own blood and Thomas wasn't going to answer as he was too busy glaring at Morris.

"Yeah," I said shakily. "When we were tykes we'd get our friends together and we'd play against the American servicemen stationed nearby. They loved baseball."

"I knew it!" Morris said. "I've met a few Scousers who liked baseball because of all the Americans stationed up there. My dad was an American airman, so it's kind of the same story with me—"

"If I had a baseball bat right now I'd cave your skull in," Thomas said.

Morris paused, tilted his head in a way that reminded me of an owl that had just spied a mouse.

"But you don't," he said, smiling. "So what are you going to do?"

Thomas stood, palms coming down hard on the wooden tabletop. "We're leaving." He looked to me. "Paul, let's go."

Leaving that tiny room seemed as possible as tunnelling to China or flying to the moon, but I trusted Thomas. If he said, *Paul, let's dig,* I'd be tearing up the earth. If he said, *Paul, let's fly,* I'd jump as high as I could. But since all he said was, *Paul, let's go,* all I did was stand, helping Greg get to his feet.

"Still." There it was again, that magical command that froze both Greg and me in place. Morris's smile grew as he looked at Thomas. "Sit down or I'll nail your hands to the table."

The spell only lasted for about five seconds, but even when it wore off I was still locked in place. Was he serious? Could he actually do it? I mean, there were three of us and only one of him. Then again, Greg was quickly going pale and I was no good in a fight, so it was more one versus one. But would he do it? I'd heard lots of colourful threats in my day, and London would be like something from a Bosch painting if even half of them were carried out. Lots of people made threats. Didn't mean Morris would actually do it.

I looked to Thomas. Thomas was always better at gauging the evil inside of people.

Thomas was still glaring at Morris, his face grim and his mouth a hard line. He believed him.

Thomas gripped the table and overturned it, sending our drinks up into the air. Before they had hit the ground he dropped his shoulder and drove it into the underside of the table. He hit Morris with it, pinning him between the shelf and the tabletop. The impact knocked all the air out of Morris's lungs and he made a strained, hacking noise.

Thomas sprang back, moving on his feet like a boxer. He launched two jabs with his right fist, one to Morris's throat, earning another choked gasp, and one to his chin, causing a loud clang as the back of Morris's head bounced off the metal shelving.

Then Thomas was hurrying towards us, nearly slipping on the broken glass and spilled beer.

"Come on!" he said, taking hold of my elbow. I seized Greg, pulling him along as Thomas yanked me up the stairs. We were halfway up when Greg stumbled behind me. Morris had grabbed his ankle, causing him to trip.

"Greg!" Before I could take a step back down Morris slammed me against the wall. His knife was in his other hand. He resembled a butcher looking over a tricky piece of meat.

"Thomas!" I yelled. But Thomas had kept going up the stairs, disappearing into the rest of the pub. I felt cast down, more alone than even in the days following my mother's death. He had left me. I couldn't believe he had left me.

"*Still,*" Morris said, and I stilled. He brought his hand to my face, thumb and index finger pressing in the soft part of my cheeks where my teeth met, squeezing so my mouth opened.

Before he could level his knife against my tongue Thomas came flying down the stairs, a large green wine bottle in his hand. He brought it across in a wide arc, from left to right, smashing it into Morris's jaw.

It's funny how sometimes, when things happen too fast for the eye to see, the brain fills in the blanks with its own little stories. When Thomas hit Morris I heard the large crack of the bottle breaking and was splattered by a spray of red wine. But then, not a split second later, I saw the intact bottle still in Thomas's hand and realized my brain had lied to me. The crack was not from the bottle but from Morris's jaw breaking. The splatter wasn't red wine but his blood.

Morris howled and dropped the knife, pressing both hands to his mouth. His face reminded me of a skull, the skin pulled downwards tight around his eyes thanks to his unhinged jaw, his eyes so wide they seemed like they were going to pop out of his head. He tried to say something, to get out a word with only his tongue and top teeth, but it just came out a garbled sound. The magic of his suit only worked if he had the power of speech, something he couldn't manage with a busted jaw.

Thomas delivered a punch right to the side of Morris's head, sending him tripping over Greg and back down into the room. Greg shakily got to his feet.

"Come on," Thomas hissed at me, once again trying to pull me up the stairs.

"Wait," I said, grabbing hold of Greg. Thomas looked thoroughly annoyed but also like he knew it would take longer to argue the point: he wasn't going without me and I wasn't going without Greg.

We reached the top of the stairs just as three men likewise approached it from the pub side. One of them was the stocky bartender from earlier, the other two a couple of rough customers. Thomas still had the bottle of wine in hand. I had seen a few films where bottles broke in pub brawls as easily as spun glass, but in real life it's skin and bone that's more likely to give way. Thomas used the forward momentum from running up the stairs to jab one man in the stomach with the wine bottle, causing him to clutch his middle and stumble back. The man closest to us was a tall bloke and I wondered how five-foot-nothing Thomas would deal with him. My question was answered when Thomas brought his foot down hard on the man's shin, a move that caused him to drop down to one knee, cutting down the height difference so Thomas could swing the wine bottle at the man's temple. The third man was already backing away, but Thomas went after him quickly: a swift punch to the nose, blood seeping out like yolk out of an egg.

We were in the pub proper by now and of course the other patrons had noticed a fight going on. There were about a dozen thugs between us and the exit.

Thomas shoved me and Greg towards the closest window and handed me the wine bottle.

"Break the window," he hissed and then, without even missing a beat, pivoted to deliver a blow to the stomach of some nearby spiv who had been about to attack.

It was mesmerizing seeing Thomas just deal out hurt after hurt but it was sickening too, like getting enjoyment from opening your own scabs.

I focused on the window. It was true that Thom and I had grown up playing baseball. I had good form: feet perpendicular to each other, good grip on the neck of the bottle, strong back. I pulled back and swung as hard as I could.

The bottle shattered as soon as it made contact. The window cracked but that was it.

"Thomas!" I yelled, wine running over my hands and soaking into my suit. But Thomas had problems of his own: one spiv had grabbed hold of the back of his jacket and Thomas was trying to shake him off while fending off blows from a thug in front of him.

I pounded on the glass, thinking I could break it the rest of the way with my bare hands. The crack had grown a few inches when some tough put an arm around my neck and squeezed. It got all the worse when he lifted me up, my feet scrambling to reach the ground as I fought for air.

And then as soon as I was up I was down, dropped to the floor as my assailant collapsed.

Standing over my attacker was Greg. He wasn't holding his mouth anymore but instead just letting blood run up and over his chin, spilling down the front of his shirt like lava making its way down the side of a volcano. In his hands he held a barstool, his grip on it so tight I thought it might snap in his hands.

With a bloody yell he lifted the stool over his head and sent it crashing through the window.

I covered my head as the glass rained down. When I looked back up Greg had grabbed the thug at Thomas's back and flung him to the ground. He then stepped towards the thug in front of Thom, popping one into the spiv's jaw.

"Greg!" I yelled, getting to my feet. Before I could come over, Greg grabbed Thomas and practically tossed him into me.

"GAH!" he yelled at us, blood and spittle spewing out with his words. He swallowed, a painful motion that caused a shudder to go through him. But despite the pain he seemed more solid and surer than he had earlier in the night. "GO!" he yelled, louder and clearer this time. He turned and grabbed a nearby stool and used it to keep the remaining thugs at bay.

Thomas pulled me towards the broken window.

"We can't leave him!" I said, eyes still on McCormick, taking on all comers.

"Yes, we can," Thomas said.

I was about to protest further when I saw a couple of figures near the end of the bar. One of them was Wheelock, watching the scene in the pub with dismay. The other figure was Hollister, watching me. He didn't seem upset, though he had a weary smile. It was the look of a disappointed but patient man.

I turned and followed Thomas out the window.

CHAPTER 19

Luckily for us London night buses will let you on even if you have blood on your shirt. It might have helped that they were nice shirts: we looked like two well-off lads who had gotten in over their heads in some criminal gambling den. The driver gave us a pitying shake of his head when we got on.

We sat down near the back.

"Are you hurt?" Thomas asked, voice low.

"I'm fine, I—"

"Shut the fuck up," Thomas said.

"You asked me a question, how am I—"

"Don't talk to me," Thomas said, hands clenched tightly in front of him.

We got off a few stops past our usual bus stop and used a secret route through the Harringay Passage and a couple of backyards to reach our home. I thought that this was perhaps being overly cautious, but Thomas was in no mood to hear it so I kept my gob shut. It was only when we were up in our attic that he turned and looked me in the eye.

"What the hell was that about?"

"How am I supposed to know—"

I felt the slap before I saw or heard it. Thomas hit my right cheek so hard I nearly fell down. For a moment I stood there, doubled over and holding my hand to my warm face.

"You know exactly what that was about!" Thomas said. "You need to come clean right now, Gallagher, before someone else gets killed because of you!"

"We don't know Greg's dead—"

"Yes, we *do*," Thomas said, "and I sure as hell don't wanna be next!"

I straightened up and took a step back, still trying to cool down my cheek and wary of getting hit again. Thomas had only hit me once before, that bop to the nose the day we had met. Once he'd come to live with me and Mum and Dad he had changed. He'd seen how I shied away from my brothers, how I didn't defend myself in a fight. He knew I hated violence. But even now I couldn't be mad at him for hitting me. I had it coming.

"How the hell did you catch the eye of Welcome Wheelock?" Thomas said. "Why would he want to buy our debt from McCormick? What did you do, Paul?"

"I didn't do anything—"

"For fuck's sake, Paul!" Thomas stared at me, eyes blazing. "Do you think I'm stupid?!"

I took a deep breath and made myself stand my ground. "No, Thomas, I think you're the smartest man I know."

The fury in Thomas's eyes dimmed. He ran a hand through his hair, breathed out. It was a few moments before he spoke again, teeth clenched. "Just tell me what's going on."

"Hector Hollister was at the bar," I said. "I think that he was the special guest Wheelock had lined up, the one we were going to work for."

"Oh, fuck me," Thomas muttered. "How does Hollister even know Wheelock? Or you know what, who gives a fuck—it's not important. What does Hollister want from you?"

"Well," I said slowly. "I still don't really know what in particular." Thomas glowered at me, so I hurried to add: "But I *might* have given him the impression that I can give him God-level powers."

I explained to Thomas the idea of deep magic and how eager Hollister had been to implement it.

"He wants you to skin him alive?" Thomas said in disbelief. *"Why?"*

"I don't know why exactly," I said. "But if we're going by God's powers as outlined in the Bible, he could destroy cities, resurrect the dead, prolong a human's lifespan, rewrite genetics as we know it—"

"Wait, what was the last one?"

"Oh, well, there was a period in the Old Testament where incest was permissible," I explained. "It's how literalists explain humanity springing forth from one family. But once there were enough people God flicked some kind of genetic marker in humanity and then it wasn't aboveboard anymore."

"Fuck me," Thomas said, shaking his head.

"It's not what I personally believe in," I said. "But—"

"But Hollister might," Thomas finished for me.

"I don't think he's planning to change humanity on that wide a scale," I said. "I highly doubt he's doing all this so he can, say, sleep with his sister."

Thomas nodded. "Yeah, I'm thinking he's more likely to turn Moscow into a big pile of salt." He glared at me. "You'll just have to explain to him that it was all a lie, that you can't do the things you said you could."

"But . . ."

"But *what?*"

"I don't think he'd believe me."

"Then you have to convince yourself that you can't do it!" Thomas said. "Look, magic is based in the theory of ideomancy—"

"No it's not!" I said. "It's a gift from God, a divine power, a signifier of the soul—"

"It is guided by the will and subconscious desires of the user!" Thomas said, cutting back in. "If you truly believe that you can't deliver on whatever Hollister thinks you can, then you won't." He stopped, waiting for my response.

My hands dropped to my sides.

"I don't think I can convince myself of that." I smiled apologetically at Thomas. "My ego's too big."

Thomas stared at me, a cold anger brewing behind his eyes.

"You know, Mary made me promise to look after you. Asked me right near the end," Thomas said.

Mary was my mum's name. When her illness was far along she got too weak to hold books so Thomas would go to the hospital most evenings and read to her. I had thought they had just spent the time rereading their favourite novels, but maybe they had also talked, talked about what would come after, what would become of me. I could picture Mum interrupting Thomas midsentence to ask this favour, and I could see young Thomas eager to agree to anything that might ease her mind and lighten his perceived debt.

"I told her she didn't have to worry, that I'd stick by you, promise or no promise—"

"Thomas, please," I said.

"But she still made me break that proverbial bone and say the words. I thought she was just worried about leaving you behind, but I get it now. She knew better than me just how hard it was looking after you. She knew you'd make it as tough as possible, that you could be so fucking frustrating, and that she needed me to swear I'd do it—"

"Thomas, please," I said again and this time it seemed to get through to him. He rubbed his temples. We were both quiet and I could see Thomas's anger draining as he slipped into tactical mode.

"Right, right," he muttered. "We have to get out of here."

"Out of this flat?" I said, looking around the attic, our various projects scattered throughout. "They still don't know where we live."

"No, out of this city," Thomas said. "Wheelock will have every gang combing North London for us before the sun's up. We've got to get out of here, go lay low in Liverpool until they lose interest."

Liverpool? I couldn't leave the city. Not when I was in the middle of my mission with Verity. If I left town I'd miss my date tomorrow night with Oberon. And what about when Redfield performed the ritual to find the next Court Magician? I didn't want to risk missing that.

"We can't go to Liverpool," I said.

Thomas looked at me wearily. He spoke gently, perhaps regretting his previous outburst.

"Paul, I know you don't like visiting home but—"

"It's not that." Well, it was and it wasn't. I loved Liverpool, but I loved it best from afar. "It's just, we don't have money to buy train tickets all the way to Liverpool."

Thomas frowned.

"Plus, we still have to finish the waterproof suit," I said, pointing to the pieces of cloth around the room. "How about this: we finish the suit tomorrow, deliver it on Monday, collect our money, and book it straight out of town?"

Thomas was still frowning.

"It would be bad to flake out on a client," I said. "Besides, where else are we going to get the money? Ralph?"

"Ralph? 'Father of two' Ralph?" Thomas said sceptically. "No, he's got enough troubles."

"Exactly. Or Andrew?" I pressed.

Thomas shook his head. "No. Andrew would want to come with us."

He went quiet, thinking it over.

"I suppose, if you really think it's that urgent, I could ask Lamb for the money," I said, trying to sound as innocent as possible.

Thomas looked up at me, then down just as quickly. He sighed and for a second I worried he was going to call my bluff. "No, we don't ask that bastard for anything. We finish the suit, get paid, and get out."

"Great," I said, suddenly feeling very tired. I took off my suit jacket. Red wine and bloodstains were splattered all over the herringbone pattern, a large rip under one arm. The fabric was stained to the point where the magic no longer worked.

I tried not to think about how most of the blood was Greg's.

CHAPTER 20

The next day was rather strained between Thomas and me. We worked on the waterproof suit in near silence. One of us would put on a record and the other would take it off. One of us would start a conversation, only to have it flounder.

Even though I was by all appearances trying to make peace, it was a duplicitous front. There's this old play we studied in school about a royal who took the throne through treachery and bloodletting. Now an elderly man, he wishes to make amends for the evil he did to gain power, but every time he seeks advice, people tell him the same thing: the only way to make amends is to give up power. Neither God nor mortal can forgive the king while he's still enjoying the worldly gains of his actions. Even as his own guilt grows and his enemies draw nearer, he just can't own up to his deeds. As a kid I was quite bored when we had to read the play, but now as an adult I felt I understood it a bit better. I hadn't told Thomas the whole truth. I had told him about Hollister, but I hadn't told him that I was now on the list of Court Magician candidates. I also hadn't told him about my crusade with Verity against Dr Myers. I knew that he would not approve. I couldn't expect him to forgive me for what had happened with McCormick and Wheelock right when I was in the middle of lying to him about even bigger things.

When the time drew near for me to go to Oberon's house, I didn't make any excuse or attempt to cover it with some story about popping out to the shop. I just left.

I was very careful, wearing a plain brown suit that hopefully wouldn't draw any attention. I reached the Myerses' house at around seven. Oberon opened the door, his smile wide. *He* was wearing magic clothes, a dark suit that, guessing from the cut, helped with concentration.

"Paul," he said with a genuine smile. "Come on in!"

A large grandfather clock tick-tocked away in the front hall and a gleaming oak banister led up to a second floor. Hanging on the wall was the painting of Abigail Myers. Verity really did take after her. I quickly looked away.

"Your dad still away playing golf?" I asked as casually as I could.

"Yes. He's supposed to be home later tonight," Oberon said.

"Oh." I hoped Oberon didn't notice how worried I sounded. All I could do was follow him into the billiards room and hope for the best.

"You know, I was quite surprised when you called me up out of the blue," he said.

I shrugged. "I just wanted to give you the chance to apologize for what happened at the gala." Oberon laughed at that. I spoke on. "Also, it occurred to me that even though we've known each other for years, we never really had the chance to spend time together without other people around."

Oberon nodded thoughtfully as he poured some of his father's brandy.

"Yes, that's true." He handed me the snifter and then poured one for himself. "Dawes and Andrew were always buzzing around, clogging up the works. Don't get me wrong, they're fine lads, but well, no offence to your boy Thom-Daw, but you'd have to travel half the globe before you'd find a more obstinate bastard. And as for Andrew . . ." Oberon sighed. "Some days I think if you opened up that boy's head, you'd find nothing more than a slab of soft cheese."

I smiled, inwardly mad on behalf of Andrew. It didn't matter that I myself might have thought the same thing at various points; that didn't mean *Oberon* could say it.

"But I did a bad turn by you, tattling to Hollister," Oberon said. "Thank God he saw that it was all rubbish. I'm really sorry about that, Gally. But no harm done, eh? Let's consider it water under the bridge."

"Yes, let's." We clinked our glasses and downed the brandy. We played a few games of pool. We were pretty evenly matched, which surprised me as I was damn good at snooker and had beaten Oberon plenty of times in the past.

"Lucky shot," I said, somewhat ungraciously as Obie pocketed another stripe.

He smiled. "It's not luck, but it's not skill either." He stood and held out his arms so I could better get a look at the seams of his suit. "This blazer, it maximizes the wearer's precision and focus. I designed it with surgeons in mind."

"Wow," I said, impressed by his practical application of cloth magic. "Your dad must have been chuffed when you showed it to him."

Oberon's smile dropped. "No. He said the cotton material was too likely to carry germs and that it wasn't sterile enough for the operating room." He chalked up the end of his cue. "But I'm working on a new design to correct that."

Obie had always been top of the class when it came to "recoup cloaks," that is, clothes with healing or medicinal properties. I hadn't cared too much about them when we'd studied them in school; recoup clothes just simply weren't sexy enough in my opinion. But now I was a little more curious. "What other kinds of recoup stuff have you made?"

Oberon puffed up proudly. "Oh, some things here or there. Items to help with circulation, to speed along bones as they mend, that kind of thing."

"That's amazing." I had never thought about how closely recoup magic mirrored deep magic: both focused on the study of human biology. "How did you get cloth to mimic the properties of a circulatory system?"

Obie hesitated and I waited for some smart-ass remark like *A magician never reveals their secrets*. But he answered me honestly: "I went up to Oxford. A tributary of the Thames runs through the town, a river they call the Isis. When you think of the Thames, you think of this massive waterway cleaving the city in two, but in Oxford there are places where it's barely a yard wide. I attached the fabric to a rod and laid the rod across the width of the river and just let it flow in the water."

"And the waterways of the world represented the circulatory system of the human body." I was impressed. That technique showed a vision and poetry that I would have never previously ascribed to Oberon Myers. I was mad I hadn't thought of it myself.

"It didn't work as well as it should," Obie said ruefully. "The patient was still anaemic."

"Maybe the sympathy between the river and human veins wasn't strong enough," I said. "Maybe it's just too big for the properties to echo. Like, if you had a more closed waterway where over time the same water would pass over the cloth, like the same blood going through the body, it would take hold better then."

"Perhaps," Oberon said in a tone that suggested he had already thought of that. "Though there are very few closed waterways like that."

"Or maybe it was the water itself," I muttered. "The Isis is fresh water, right? Maybe that's the problem. The ratio of salt in the human body is similar to the ratio found in the same amount of seawater. The cloth needs to be in a saltwater river!"

"A saltwater river?" Oberon repeated, letting his tone do all the work.

"Why not? There are many wonders on God's green earth." I made a mental note to ask Thomas next time I saw him—surely such a thing had been written about in *National Geographic*. I realized Oberon was laughing at me. "What?"

"You just never admit when something's impossible, eh?"

I wasn't sure how to take that. "Why are you so keen on recoup stuff anyway?" I asked.

Oberon stopped chuckling. He chalked up his pool cue some more, though at this point it was well and thoroughly chalked.

"When I was seventeen I was in a car accident," he said. "I was hurt, but not as badly as . . . as the other people in the car."

"I see," I replied, even though I still felt in the dark. Oberon rolled his eyes, as if I had just stomped my feet and demanded the whole truth.

"I was the driver," he admitted. "Two of my friends were with me. We were joyriding in the countryside when I hit a damn utility pole. I was lucky: the worst that happened to me was that my face slammed down onto the steering wheel." Swiftly he brought his hand to his mouth and pressed. With a pop his teeth came out. He held the partial dentures out towards me with a ghoulish grin, like an evil witch holding out a poisoned apple. "See?" His voice sounded weird with half his mouth collapsed like that, his smile lopsided.

"Jesus, mate!" I thought of Morris and his shattered jaw, my stomach churning. "Obie, put your damn teeth back in."

He did. They slid in with a squeak and a pop and then his much-too-perfect smile was perfect again. "My friends weren't so lucky. They went flying and hit the ground as hard as the car had hit that pole."

He went quiet. I wanted to ask more about his friends, how hurt they were exactly, but I was scared to hear the gory details.

"It was in the hospital that I learned that cloth magic can be used to treat people," Oberon said. "I thought that if I couldn't be a doctor, I could at least help people as a cloth mage."

"Why not just be a doctor?" I asked.

Oberon shook his head. "Even before my accident, Father always said I didn't have the aptitude for it," he said. "And after the accident

. . . he said cloth magic was a good choice as at least I'd be less likely to hurt anyone else."

I wasn't sure what to say to that. Dr Myers had always seemed like such a kindly figure; it was hard to imagine him tearing his own son down like that. Then again, this was the same man involved with the deaths of at least three children, so what did I know?

"I know this might be out of turn," I said, "but your dad sounds like kind of a prick."

Oberon let out a bark of shocked laughter. "No, no! Father was right. I could never handle the responsibility of being a doctor, of having to hold someone's life in my hands," he said. "He was just watching out for me."

"Hmm." My doubt must have shown through because Oberon was quick to placate it.

"It's always been just Father and me in this house. A couple of bachelors. We have to look after each other," Oberon said. "My mother died when I was born. She came from money, and her family has always treated my dad like little more than a gold digger. It's always been me and him against the world. Even when I really buggered things up . . . like with that automobile accident . . . he covered for me."

Oberon looked away.

"So that's why I get upset when people talk badly of him," he said. "They don't know the stresses he's under. The stresses *I've* put him under."

"I'm sorry for insulting your dad."

Oberon laughed. "No, you meant well. I actually appreciate it. Your concern, I mean." He shook his head. "I've never talked about this with anyone before. I'm sorry we waited so long to become friends."

"Obie . . ."

"I mean, I understand *why*: I was a total prat to you throughout college." He laughed. "Then again, you can be a bit of an arrogant prick yourself. But still, even after all that, you still reached out to me . . . you are the better man, Gallagher."

"Oh, come off it." I hadn't expected to feel guilty about using Oberon Myers, but here we were.

The conversation was cut short by a series of muffled bangs from the back garden. The sound of them brought me both trepidation and relief: it was time for the next phase of the plan.

"What the bloody hell?" Oberon said as the cracks echoed through the house. He left the den and I followed loosely behind. When we came to the front hall I stepped away just long enough to unlock the front door. Oberon didn't notice: he was already striding down the hall to the kitchen and out the back door.

I soon joined him, standing on the damp grass and staring down at the remains of some burnt-out fireworks.

"I can't believe this," Oberon said. "Some kids must have snuck in here and set them off."

"Young people these days," I said, shaking my head.

"This is supposed to be a nice neighbourhood, but it's just been steadily going downhill."

"Tell me about it," I said, and I meant it: the longer I could keep him outside, grousing about the downslide of Islington, the longer Verity would have to go upstairs, find Myers's safe, open it, grab the Book, and get out.

"We have delinquents going through here all the time." Oberon gestured to a shed in the corner of the backyard. "We didn't use to lock this shed, but now—" He turned towards me and paused, eyes on the second floor of his home.

"You had to put a padlock on it?" I asked, trying to keep Obie's mind centred here in the backyard. His gaze stayed on the upper floor of the house.

"I thought I saw someone up there," he said. "I think there's someone in my father's study."

"What?" I said, turning to look. "Are you sure?"

"Yes," Oberon said, his mouth a tight line.

"Then we can't go back in there; it's not safe," I said. "Let's go to your neighbour's place and call the coppers from there." I figured that by the time the police arrived Verity would be long gone. She was probably smooth enough that it wouldn't even seem like anything was out of place, at least until Dr Myers opened the safe and saw that his Book was gone.

"Good plan," Oberon said. Then, to my consternation, he walked briskly towards the house. "You go do that."

"Obie!" I said loudly as we walked through the back door, hoping that my voice would carry up to Verity and warn her. "You don't know who's up there! They could be a pack of dangerous killers!"

"As opposed to a pack of safe killers?" Instead of heading upstairs he turned and went into the den. "But you're quite right. Best to be prepared for the worst." He grabbed a pool cue off the table and tossed it to me. I caught it with both hands. Oberon picked up a cue and gave some practice swings. He was doing it wrong: I'd seen Thomas use a pool cue in a pub brawl before and he had held it in one hand, swinging it like it was an extension of his forearm.

"Oberon," I said. "This isn't . . ."

"Oh, that's right. You don't like to fight," Oberon said idly, still taking some practice swings. "Well, don't worry. I don't expect you to die helping me defend my father's home."

"No one needs to die," I said, putting the pool cue down. "Oberon, there is no one up there! You're acting like an idiot!"

That made Oberon smile. "Then I have nothing to lose by checking it out."

I was about to protest some more when there came the faintest creak from upstairs. Oberon's face turned towards the sound so fast I worried he'd get whiplash.

"Did you hear that?"

"No," I lied. Oberon walked past me, pool cue tight in his grip. I followed after him.

He went straight to his father's study. I prayed to God that Verity had found a hiding place or made it to another room.

My prayers went unanswered. Sitting in the chair by the desk was Verity Turnboldt. She sat there, back straight and chin tilted up daintily, not seeming worried in the least about being discovered.

"Hello, Oberon," she said.

"You," Oberon breathed out. "What are you doing here?"

"You know why I'm here," she said, standing up. She was still wearing the black dress Thomas and I had made for her. "You know what your father's guilty of."

"It's not true," Oberon said. "Just hateful, spiteful rumours. It shows just how low his enemies are, that they'd use the death of children to try and take him down."

"What if I could prove it?" Verity said. "What if I had records of him taking money in exchange for taking life? Would you believe it then?"

"You have proof?" he said, voice carefully clipped.

"Yes! He recorded it all in this Book so that he could use it as blackmail material." Verity held up the Book in question—a small, unassuming tome with a blue cover.

Oberon breathed in deeply. His face took on a calm cast, but I didn't trust it. It was like seeing a still ocean and ignoring the dark shape of the sharks swimming just below. He stepped into the room, pool cue still in hand. "Let me see."

"Oberon," I said, stepping in so I was between him and Verity. "Why don't we go downstairs and talk about this there? You know, sit down with a couple of fingers of brandy and—"

"Did she put you up to this, Paul?" Oberon asked, eyes still on Verity. "She's a man-eater, that one. You can't trust a single word that bitch says. She came to me at the gala, told me that my father was a paid assassin. My father! He's saved more lives than you could even count. Whatever sob story she told you was just a bluff to get you to go along with this. She only cares about carrying out her smear campaign against my father, and the rest of us can go whistle."

"Oberon . . ."

"You never wanted to be my friend, did you?" Oberon asked. "You only invited yourself over to let *her* in."

He snarled the last bit in Verity's direction. His eyes dropped down from her face to the Book in her hands.

"Give it to me," he said, hand outstretched, other hand clutching the pool cue tightly. I raised my arms, trying to shield Verity from him.

"Verity, run—" The blow was right to the head, but my arms moved of their own accord to block it. The pool cue hit my wrist. Verity rushed past us, Book in hand. I was relieved for all of half a second—instead of running down the stairs and out the door she disappeared into the dark of the master bedroom.

"Verity!" I didn't know the layout of the house very well but it seemed safe to assume that Verity's route was a dead end. Oberon delivered a hard blow to my stomach, causing me to drop to one knee. He turned and headed towards the bedroom.

"No!" I didn't have many options open to me but I made do: I scrambled forwards on my hands and knees so that I was right in front of Oberon, causing him to trip over me.

"Verity, run!" I yelled. There was silence from the bedroom. Oberon, still on the floor, delivered a blow to my stomach with his foot and it felt like a donkey had just kicked me. He got to his feet while I was still on my knees in the hallway and started bringing the pool cue down over and over again.

I tried my best to protect my head but there were just too many blows—to the crown, the temple, the back of my skull. A hard strike landed and when I came to, I saw with a shock I was lying on the ceiling. No, I realized when my eyes focused on my blood seeping into the carpet, I was lying on the floor—it only felt like I was lying on the ceiling because the rest of the world was spinning around me.

Oberon was walking towards the bedroom.

"Verity," I croaked and crawled after him, fighting both the vertigo in my head and the pain running through my torso. Every time my left ribs touched the floor it was like someone was grabbing the bones and twisting them, just pure pain radiating out from my left side that made dark spots dance in front of me.

Oberon passed through the door to the bedroom. I placed a hand on the wall and tried to stand. I had just gotten off my knees when a wave of nausea welled up through me so fast I barely even knew what was going on before I vomited there in the hall. Leaning against the wall for support I half ran, half stumbled into the bedroom.

My first thought was relief: there was no sign of Verity. Then Oberon's fist came flying at me, knocking me to the floor.

Oberon stood over me, looking around the room. I tried my best to do likewise. The curtains were wide open and the windowpane ajar—had Verity somehow slipped out the window and fallen two storeys below? Was she all right?

Oberon grunted in frustration. His grip tightened on the pool cue. My own blood was smeared near the top half. I knew that if I begged for my life it would tip him over the edge into finishing the job, so I bit my tongue, too scared to even breathe.

I let out a sigh of relief when he tossed the pool cue away. But then he was straddling my chest and the pain from the crack in my ribs made me scream. I was still screaming when Oberon closed his hands around my throat and squeezed.

This was how I'd always feared that I would die, killed brutally all because I had no way to fight back. The room was already dark and yet it seemed to still be going grey at the edges of my eyes. Pain from my ribs, pain in my lungs, pain in my throat. I'd been in scraps before but never this close to death. I had always thought that in the moments before my demise I'd get a greatest-hits highlight reel, a quick summary of my whole life up to that point. Instead the opposite happened. My life had contracted to the last thirty seconds, my world this dark room. I couldn't conceive of anything that had come before, couldn't remember feeling anything but terror. My mind had gone blank. It was like when you're trying to remember something that you know you know but it's just gone, only instead of trying to remember the capital of Paraguay I couldn't recall the face of anyone who had ever loved me. It felt like a preview of hell.

And then Oberon spoke and somehow managed to make things worse.

"I'm sorry, I'm sorry, I'm sorry . . ."

Just then a cough came from over by the window.

Oberon loosened his hands in surprise and I was able to get down a few tortured gulps of air. We both looked over to the source of the sound.

Both sides of the window were framed by heavy, floor-length curtains. Peeking out from the hem of the curtains on the left were the tips of Verity's shoes.

I made a worried noise but Oberon paid me no notice. He started walking towards the curtains, slowly and carefully so as to not make any sound.

"Verity!" I said, but my voice was barely louder than the cracking of an egg. My panicked desperation gave way to something much colder. *You stupid bitch,* I thought as Oberon crept closer to the window. *Why didn't you run out the front door?*

Later, when I had the luxury of not being in mortal danger, I was ashamed of myself, ashamed that I'd felt such anger towards Verity and not the man about to kill her. I don't think of Verity like that, I don't think of women like that, but in that moment when I was stripped down to just a ball of fear, that was who I became. It terrified me that, in what could have possibly been my last moments on earth, terror had transformed me into someone the exact opposite of who I believed myself to be.

But then that hatefulness dissipated and I was left with a neutral, detached certainty. I could see both my and Verity's future, all three minutes of it, set out like two mirrors facing each other: she would die and then I would die and then she would die and then I would die and then she would die and then I would die—

Oberon was standing in front of the curtain. With a swipe of his hand he pulled it back.

There was nothing there but Verity's empty shoes.

Verity burst forth from behind the other curtain. She had a little statue of some kind in her hand. I didn't get a good look at it before she brought it down on Oberon's head. He crumpled to the floor and Verity dropped the statue onto the carpet. I watched her bare feet come closer as she dashed over to me.

"Paul? Paul!" she said, shaking my shoulders a little too hard. She blocked my view of Oberon but I could hear him groaning, feel the vibrations through the floor as he rocked on the carpet. "It's okay!"

I managed to give a slight shake of my head. *No, it's not "okay,"* I wanted to tell her. *Kill him.* But the words couldn't come. My whole body was locked in place. Even my lungs weren't moving. It was like my brain had just short-circuited.

She slapped me and that got me breathing again.

"Come on, you have to get up!" Verity yelled. "You have to—"

Downstairs the front door opened and closed. Verity stopped shaking my shoulders but her fingers gripped tightly into my skin as her head shot up towards the doorway. Oberon groaned loudly and the sound of movement downstairs ceased. It started up again a second later as the person below made their way upstairs.

"*Shhh,*" Verity shushed me, though I wasn't making any noise. Her eyes darted around the room, searching for a place to hide.

The bedroom light flicked on and the sudden brightness made me yell, eyes squeezed shut against the light. When I finally got over the pain and opened them I looked over towards the light switch. Standing in the doorway was Dr David Myers.

CHAPTER 21

When I came to, I was sitting by the fireplace in the den. Dr Myers was standing next to me, pouring a glass of water from a pitcher. It reminded me of the time in my first year of college when Oberon had had the whole cloth magic class over for dinner. Before the meal I had fallen out of the tree in the backyard while trying to return a baby bird to its nest (and perhaps show off a bit for my classmates). Afterwards I had sat in this very chair while Dr Myers had bandaged up my ankle. Now here we were again, me in an even worse state.

Dr Myers looked over his shoulder and saw I was awake. Maybe he was also remembering the same thing because he smiled and said, "Hello, young man. How's the ankle?"

I laughed. It was a good joke: my ankle was the only part of me that wasn't hurting.

Verity came around and I realized she had been standing behind me. She placed a hand on my face—or, more accurately, the plasters covering my face. When I brought up a hand to feel it for myself Verity stopped me. She seemed relieved when I met her gaze with a wan smile. I don't think I'd ever seen her look so worried. Wordlessly she took the water from the doctor and raised it to my lips. The water felt nice but had an unpleasant metallic tang to it.

"Not too much, now," Dr Myers said. He seemed remarkably affable for a man who had come home to find a scene of violence in his bedroom. I glanced around, though the action made my head spin. The three of us were the only ones in the room.

"Is Oberon all right?" I remembered him groaning and rolling around in the bedroom, and how I'd wanted nothing more than for Verity to pick the statue back up and bash his head the rest of the way in. Thinking such thoughts now made me sick.

"He's fine," Dr Myers said. "He's resting in his room."

I nodded, relieved that he had survived but also that he wasn't down there with us. Even just thinking of seeing him made my throat close up.

"That's one of his creations," he said, gesturing to the jacket I was wearing. It was a red blazer, a harsh hue that made me blink. "It was a bit of a failed experiment, to my understanding. It was supposed to help with blood flow but instead it—"

"It slows it down." I could already feel the effect—my heart rate had slowed and there was a slight tingling sensation in my toes and fingertips. I wondered if this was the cloth that Oberon had treated in the river Isis. If so, no wonder it had failed to help an anaemic patient—it would have damn near killed them.

"It's not a good idea to wear it for a long period of time," Dr Myers said. "But I have found that it does keep the wearer calm and slows bleeding while also speeding up the coagulation of the wounds."

I nodded and made a mental note to take off the jacket when the pins and needles in my limbs got too bad.

Dr Myers sat in the chair closest to the fireplace.

"So what kind of pickle has my boy gotten himself into this time?" Dr Myers asked with mild amusement. When neither Verity nor I answered he sighed. "It's all right; you can tell me. There's very little that you could reveal about my son that would shock me. I only ask because, if he's transgressed against the two of you—which, judging from the state of young Gallagher here, seems to be the case—well, I wish to make things right." It was so hard to imagine this fatherly figure murdering a bunch of kids. Even when searching my own memories I couldn't recall him ever committing a single violent action or saying a harsh word. Doubts began to cloud my mind.

Dr Myers looked to Verity, who was still standing behind me, a hand on my shoulder.

"I'm sorry, I don't think we've been properly introduced," he said. "I'm Dr David Myers."

"Verity Turnboldt," she said.

"Ah yes, the American journalist!" Myers clapped his hands together. "I've heard Oberon speak of you, but he never mentioned how lovely you are. In fact, you remind me of—"

Myers froze, all mirth gone from his face. He stared at Verity anew, eyes searching her face.

"Verity Turnboldt," he said slowly. "I assume that is a pen name, correct? Would you mind telling me your real name?"

He looked at her expectantly but no reply came. Verity stayed quiet long enough that Dr Myers began to shift in his seat.

"My real name?" Verity repeated. There was a new solidness to her as she spoke, yet her voice also sounded somewhat rote, like a melodious recording. "That's a good question. Let's see if you know it, hmm? What *would* you have called me, had you kept me?"

"I'm sorry, what?" Dr Myers said.

Verity continued on. "Would you have named me for some long-dead queen? Mathilde, Isabella, Victoria? Or would you have named me for your mother, Susan, or the sister, little Daisy, who died from polio when you were eight and she was four?" Up until this point Verity had spoken in a level tone, as if reciting lines she knew by heart, but now her lip quivered. "Or would you have chosen to honour my mother's family, name me Abby after her, or Rose for her mother, or even Cora for *her* mother, a slave born into bondage. You couldn't name me for *her* mother, for my link to my African roots was ripped away when my family was enslaved. That whole side of my history was ripped from me, and now all I have left is *you*. So what would you have named me? What would you call me now, Father? Say my name so I know that you know who I am."

Myers was looking at Verity with dawning comprehension, a glow of wonderment coming into his face as she spoke. He stood.

"Tatianna?"

Verity's face crumpled at that. I had never seen her cry before, had never even considered it, but now that it was happening she looked like a totally different person, not the smooth, sophisticated Verity I knew but someone much younger.

"Don't come near me," she said as Myers took a step forwards. Myers stayed where he was.

"Tatianna," he said, then took a gulp of air. "No, I suppose that's not what you go by, is it? What did Shelly call you?"

"You mean my mother?" Verity said. Her tears had dried up quickly and that familiar anger at the world was back, focused in on David Myers. Myers took it calmly.

"The woman who raised you, yes."

"She told me everything. There was not a moment in my life where I didn't know the truth. I know what you did. I know how you gave me up, that you did it for money. That you bought the bastard child from a serving girl before giving me to her and sending us across the Atlantic."

"Is that what she told you?" Myers said. He spoke so calmly that I didn't even notice he had moved closer to us until it had already happened. "Tatianna, that's all codswallop. I've spent the last twenty-three years worrying about you, wondering if I would ever see you again, scared witless that you were dead or starving on the streets."

"Oh, I see, so it's all just one big misunderstanding?" Verity said bitterly.

"I don't expect you to forgive me," Myers said. "What I did was unforgivable. I did take Shelly's baby boy from her and asked her to pretend you were hers. I did do that. But it was a very dire situation.

This family, they'd run up so much debt in anticipation of the eventual payday. If Kently died without a male heir, all of your aunts and cousins would be out on the street. I had to do it to save us all."

"And I was the price you paid?" Verity spat. I felt somewhat uncomfortable being witness to all the dirty laundry being aired but neither Myers nor Verity seemed concerned with my presence.

"No, no, my darling girl!" Myers said. "I never meant to give you up forever. The plan was for Shelly to look after you for a few weeks, and then for me to formally adopt you as my daughter. In exchange I would make sure her son grew up in better circumstances and escape the servant's lot."

"That's not what she said," Verity replied. "She said you threatened her, that you'd kill her if she ever came back to England, that if she ever told anyone you'd kill her son."

Myers turned towards the fire.

"Shelly was a troubled young woman," he said. "I gave her a huge sum of money, in part to pay for your needs but also so she could straighten herself out. Instead she kidnapped you, sent a letter demanding more money. I . . ." He sighed deeply. "Oh, Tatianna, I carry so much regret. I was not myself in those weeks after you were born. My wife, my love, she was dead, and out of good intentions I had gotten myself tangled up in this duplicitous web with my own infant daughter at the centre. I realized the wrong I had done. Instead of more money, I sent word to Shelly that I would call the police and tell them everything if she did not return you. I didn't care that I would be punished; all I cared about was getting you back. But that was the wrong course of action. It spooked Shelly. She disappeared, taking you with her. I should have gone to the police then, but I was terrified that she might kill you if she thought the cops were on her trail. I never imagined that she would take you all the way to America! No wonder my private detectives couldn't find you."

"You didn't know where we were?" Verity said. "But . . ."

"Yes?" Myers said, a little too eagerly for my liking.

"But she . . . she had a receipt for passage on a boat, made out to you for a second-class berth."

Myers's expression didn't change but it was a beat before he answered.

"She must have doctored it to convince you," he said. "Oh my poor girl, I can only imagine what it must have been like for you growing up with that woman. I don't know what she was like as a mother, but the Shelly I knew was petty and vindictive, stupid in her cruelty. Nothing was ever her fault, and everyone she met she cast in the role of villain or minor antagonist."

Verity's face darkened. "Yeah. That's what she was like as a mother too."

Myers looked away, rubbed his eyes. "I can only imagine how hard it must have been for you. Between her lies and my actions, I don't blame you for hating me." He looked at us, that warm fatherly glow back in his face. "But despite that, Tatianna, I am only ecstatic that you've come into my life again. Seeing you whole and well is more than this old man deserves."

I glanced over my shoulder to gauge Verity's reaction to this bullshit only to see a soft look on her face.

You don't actually believe this creep, do you? I wanted to ask her but kept my mouth shut. It was an odd feeling, being so suspicious. I often get accused of being too naive, too trusting, of only seeing people's good side and being blind to their faults. But in that moment I felt like the only sane person in the room. Couldn't Verity see just how shifty Myers seemed? How there were so many obvious holes in his outrageous story? Was I the crazy one? Was this how Thomas felt all the time? No wonder he was such a grumpy old man.

"I don't expect you to forgive me," Myers said. "But if you can find it in your heart, I would like for us to get to know each other. If you want me in your life, I swear I will find some way to make things up to you."

Verity swallowed and seemed about to speak but was too overcome with emotion.

"You don't have to answer right away," Myers said. "But in the meantime, there are some things of your mother's that I've held on to, some things I've always wanted you to have. Can you wait here while I go get them?"

Verity gave a little nod at that and Myers left the room. I waited until I heard him heading upstairs before I turned to Verity.

"We should go. Right now."

Verity snapped out of her reverie.

"What? But he's going to bring me my mom's things."

"This is a man who killed at least three children," I said. "Remember? You're the one who convinced me of that."

Verity kicked at the carpet. "Maybe I was wrong. Maybe it was just a big misunderstanding, like he was saying."

"Verity," I said, "do you really believe that?" What had happened to the jaded, cynical New Yorker I had first met? "You know he's bad news."

"I don't know what to believe," Verity said. "I don't trust Myers, but he's right that Shelly wasn't totally on the level either. Between the two of them I don't know who's right."

"Well, maybe they're both just awful human beings." I winced at my own words but Verity didn't seem to take offence. She just nodded, as if I had made a good point.

"Yeah. That's completely possible."

"Do you still have the Book?" I asked.

She patted her purse. "Right here. Look, let me just get some of my mom's stuff from him, and then we'll go, okay?" She stared at me, her big brown eyes wide. "I might not get another chance to get something of hers."

She had a point there: If Myers went to jail for murder and conspiracy, who knew what would happen to his wife's effects? Verity would have no claim on them. I doubted Oberon would hand them over to her.

Dr Myers came down the stairs and back into the den. He had put on his flannel housecoat, which I thought was strange for several reasons, not least because it was a warm night. It hung oddly on him, as though he had something heavy in the right pocket. He held up a pair of keys.

"Everything important is out in the shed," he said. "Why don't we go and get it all right now?"

"Sure," Verity said.

"I'll come too," I said. Dr Myers shook his head.

"You should rest, Paul. It's not a good idea for you to be on your feet right now."

"I'm fine," I said, as chipper as a summer day. Verity didn't seem convinced but she nodded.

"I want him to come with us."

Dr Myers smiled thinly. "All right then."

We went through the hall and out into the backyard through the kitchen. The backyard was enclosed by a high wooden fence and several tall trees. I knew there were neighbouring yards on either side but I couldn't see them. Even the noise of the main street was muffled.

Myers was telling Verity some story about her mother, his hands in the air as he spoke. I watched how the housecoat swung with each step, the weighted item in his pocket going to and fro.

Only one way to find out what it was. I stepped up next to his right side and stumbled. Good man that he was, Dr Myers immediately grabbed me to keep me from falling. As he did so I slipped a hand into his housecoat pocket, drew out the gun, and stepped back, the barrel pointing at Myers.

Myers and Verity froze. Slowly the doctor raised his hands.

"What?" Verity asked.

"The good doctor had this on him." I wavered a little on my feet. The pins and needles were prickling all the way up my legs. Fucking Oberon and his stupid blazer. I wanted to take it off but I had to keep my focus on the man in front of me. "Care to explain, Doc?"

"It was just a precaution," Myers said. "Imagine yourself in my position: you come home to find your son beaten up and another young man injured. I grabbed it in order to protect myself." He looked to Verity. "It was before I knew who you were."

"He's lying." The gun was a slim-nosed World War I Luger, probably stripped off some dead German on the battlefield. I remembered Oberon talking about how his dad had served as a medic in the first war. "He got the gun after talking to us."

Verity was staring at her father, her face a distorted mirror image of how she had looked at him back in the den. Before it had been a look of hope. Now it was a look of disgust.

"Tatianna—" Myers started.

"Don't call me that!" Verity said. My right leg gave out from under me and I knelt down. I propped my left hand, the one holding the gun, on my knee and hoped that I looked cool, like an action star posing in a film shoot.

"Verity, what do you want to do?" I asked.

She looked at me. "What?"

"He was going to kill us, but he's your dad so it's your call." The words sounded cold even to my ears, but it was a bluff. Even without the spell upon me, I couldn't have shot an unarmed man just standing in front of me, even someone who had killed kids and would have easily done us in.

Verity stared at Myers for a long time. Myers said nothing but unflinchingly met her gaze.

"Martha Wilde, Sheldon Wood, George McKenzie," she said, speaking slowly. "Did you kill those children?"

Myers closed his eyes and took a deep breath.

"Those children were in immense pain," he said. "And my part in it was really rather minor—"

"Did you do it?" Verity repeated. "They were worth more dead than alive, right? So did you take the money and kill them?"

Myers breathed out. "Yes."

I think both Verity and I were surprised by Myers's quick confession.

"I'm only saying this because it's you, and because it's the only way to prove that I love you," Dr Myers said, speaking to Verity.

"How the fuck does it prove that?!" Verity said.

"Well." Dr Myers's eyes were wide, like a child explaining a simple fact. "You're alive, aren't you?"

Verity stared at him, totally frozen.

"What do you mean, you had a minor part in it?" I asked.

"Well, you have to understand, I wasn't just acting on my own," Dr Myers said hurriedly. "It was part of a government experiment with the Department of Magic Regulation—"

"A government experiment?" I asked. "Did you work with Hollister on them?"

"Oh, you know old Holly," Dr Myers said. "Yes, it was his and Godfrey's brainchild. They wanted to use children, as they thought they might have more luck using pure souls. We only used children who would have died anyway. But nothing came of it."

My stomach roiled and I felt very close to passing out.

"But you made sure that they were also children that nobody wanted," I said. "Or to put it another way, children whose deaths would make a lot of people rich."

"So you sold the kids to the government and then made a deal with their families to get some of the inheritance money," Verity said, having recovered the power of speech. "Though George's dates don't line up with the others. Was he part of the experiments? Or was he just a threat to the royal family?"

Dr Myers just stood there, no longer speaking.

I couldn't even stand, so I just gestured with the Luger. "Get in the shed."

Myers shook his head but obligingly used the keys to open the lock. He stepped inside. Verity clicked the padlock closed and tossed the keys over a fence. I took the bullets out of the Luger and tossed it into the corner of the yard. It had been a well-maintained weapon with no grease or rust, yet my hands felt filthy from holding it.

"Okay, *now* let's go," Verity said, helping me to my feet. The shed had a little window facing us, and from behind the dirty glass Dr Myers peered out at us like a ghost looking out from a haunted house. We turned our back on him and ran back through the house and out the front door.

CHAPTER 22

Verity hailed a cab and we piled in. It was only when the driver asked us "Where to?" that we looked at each other, at a loss for what to do now.

"Just drive," Verity told the man, who tipped his hat and took off.

Verity's eyes were on me, her gaze darting from one injury to the next.

"You look like shit," she said.

"You still have the Book?" I said, keeping my voice low. She nodded, opening her purse so I could see it nestled in amongst her eyeliner and lipstick.

"You need to go to a doctor," Verity said, still staring at me. "Or a hospital."

I reached over and took the Book out of her purse. It had a pebbled marble cover and smooth pages, but I forgot all about that as soon as I opened it and I was hit by lines of text unfolding in my brain, information coming so fast my mind couldn't parse it. New colours were bleeding into my vision. I had lost all physical sensation: no taste or smell, no sense of time or place. Even the pain that had been singing through me fell silent. The only tie I had to earth was the distant feel of Verity trying to tug the Book out of my grip. And then I was looking back at myself, my eye meeting my own eye, and I was back in the cab again, staring down at Verity's hand mirror. She had slid it onto the page right into my line of sight, breaking my connection with the Book.

"Wow," I said, shakily closing the Book. "Good thing you knew the mirror trick."

"Good thing I did." This time she managed to grab the Book out of my hand. "What happened to you?"

"This is very high-level magic," I said. "It's been wrapped up in so much security it would take a master Book Binder to get to its core."

"Well, we can find a master Book Binder *after* some master doctor looks you over," Verity said.

"I've already seen a doctor," I replied. "Dr Myers patched me up."

"Dr Myers was five minutes away from killing us, so excuse me if I want a second opinion," Verity hissed. "Did you not see what you look like?"

I had seen just a glimpse of myself in Verity's mirror: Bruises hadn't started to form yet but my face was covered in tape and gauze. I looked like I had just escaped from an Egyptian tomb.

"I'm fine." I took off Oberon's red blazer and felt a head rush as my blood started flowing again normally. I rolled down the cab window and flung it outside and watched with great satisfaction as it flapped in the air before coming to rest in the middle of the road.

"You're still bleeding from the head." To prove it she brought her hand up to my temple and pressed, making me wince. When she brought her hand away from the bandage her fingertips were red.

"Head wounds bleed," I said. "It's not anything to worry about."

Verity was about to protest more when an idea came to me.

"Driver," I said, leaning forwards. "Can you take us to Walthamstow?"

"You want to go all the way to Walthamstow?" the driver asked. "All right." He turned the car around and started heading east.

I looked sheepishly to Verity. "Can you cover the fare? There's not enough in my Book."

"What's in Walthamstow?"

"A master Book Binder."

Verity shook her head. "No, no. We're going to a hospital—"

"No hospitals!" I said. Both Verity and the cab driver startled at my outburst. "Sorry. I just hate hospitals. Look, Thomas is good at stitches. If I need 'em he can do me up later. But first we need to crack this Book. Getting the information in here is the only way we can stop Myers before he finds us and kills us."

Verity nodded. "Okay, fine. God knows I want to bring that bastard down."

I leaned back in my seat. "Great. We should be at Molly's house in about fifteen."

I was dozing off when Verity jolted forwards so suddenly it shocked me awake.

"We're going to see your ex-girlfriend?!"

CHAPTER 23

I was a bit surprised that Verity had known about Molly and me. When I teased her about snooping into my past she just rolled her eyes and said that it wasn't a big secret that we had been sweethearts. Molly and I had met early in the first years of our respective programs at the college. We had both felt an instant rapport, and because we didn't know any better, we mistook it for love. We were both young and inexperienced in the ways of how men and women carried on. Molly had never had a beau of any kind before, and I, well, I might have already had a fair number of liaisons back in Liverpool but I had never properly gone about dating a young lady. We carried out our romance in full view of our friends, walking hand in hand through the campus, pledging our love anew when we had to go to our different classes.

During that year I had gone around to Molly's home a few times for dinner with her parents. I think she had been trying to scandalize them by dating a boy from the clerk class; she seemed somewhat disappointed when they likewise fell in love with me. Their home was just a few blocks away from the William Morris museum and gardens, a detail that Verity proved to be thoroughly apathetic to when we passed the place. The Evans home was a fine two-storey house with a respectable garden surrounding it. The place was dark save for a light in Molly's bedroom. The Evanses had always liked me, but showing up at 11:00 p.m. on a Sunday night unannounced, my face wrapped up like a broken vase, was perhaps pushing my luck.

"There's a hole in the hedge here," I said once we had exited the taxi. "We can sneak through it and throw pebbles at her window."

"It sounds like you've done this before," Verity said. We found the hole and slipped into the backyard. I gathered a few small stones and lightly tossed them at the curtained bedroom window.

It took her a few minutes, but eventually Molly pulled back the curtain and peered out. I waved at her, though she didn't seem to recognize me at first. I made some vague arm motions that hopefully conveyed that it was me, Paul Gallagher, and that I needed to talk to her.

The curtain dropped and she disappeared.

"Maybe we should go," Verity said. "She might call the cops. Or release the hounds."

"They don't have hounds."

The back door opened and Molly glanced around.

"Paul?" she asked incredulously.

"Molly!" I stepped forwards and she stepped into the backyard, a smile as bright as day. Her jet-black hair was up in curlers and she was wearing a housecoat over her nightdress, the belt emphasizing her curves. My first thought when I saw her better in the moonlight was *She looks good.* Her hands went up to my face, gently avoiding my wounds, while out of habit my hands came to rest on the shelf of her hips. We embraced. It was the same embrace that we had exchanged from the day we had decided to go steady up to the day we'd decided to break up, an embrace that contained lots of warmth but no fire.

Verity cleared her throat and I hastily stepped back. "Molly, this is Verity Turnboldt."

Verity stepped forwards, looking like a ray of moonlight with her shining black dress and sleek black hair. The two women shook hands.

"So you're Molly Evans?" Verity asked.

Molly smiled. "You're surprised."

"It's just Molly Evans isn't a traditional Asian name, to my understanding."

"You're correct," Molly said. "I was born in Shanghai, but I was adopted by the Evanses and grew up here in England." She spoke with the accent of an upper-middle-class boarding school girl. "But if you want my whole biography, I suggest we step inside. It's grown quite chilly out."

She led us into the kitchen.

"Though I'd much rather hear about how you got into such a dreadful state, Paul," she said, turning on the lights in the kitchen. The light made a painful stab in my brain.

"Are your mum and dad asleep? I don't want to disturb your parents," I said, eyeing the dark hallway.

"Oh? Don't worry about that. Mother and Father are cottaging in Cornwall." Molly started bustling around the kitchen. "Cook doesn't work Sunday, so I'm afraid I don't have much in the way of leftovers to offer you. *Ah!* But here, let's see if we can't make a dent in these, shall we?" She put down a metal container of little Danish shortbreads. Molly always had the best sweets. I eagerly took one but when I chewed it I could feel anew the various cuts and bruises around my head. "Thank you," I said. I had already eaten half the biscuit and I couldn't put the rest back. I bit it, determined to eat it despite the pain.

Verity did not take a biscuit but leaned back in her chair, arms crossed.

"So," Verity said. "Why did you and Paul break up?"

I nearly choked on the dry biscuit bits in my mouth. I knew it was rarely a good idea to have your new girl meet your ex, but usually they have the decency to wait until you are out of the room before they start talking about you. Or at least wait for a time when you're not covered in plasters and sore all over.

What made it worse was I didn't know how Molly might answer. Molly and I had had an intense relationship, but the longer it had gone on the more it had become apparent that all the intensity was cerebral, that we got a charge from exchanging ideas and nothing from physical contact. I'd naturally been sad when we'd called it off, but we'd managed to stay friends.

Molly smiled at Verity as if trying to reassure a younger classmate.

"Well, we were very close," Molly said. "But in the end we were just too similar."

Verity nodded as if she had been expecting this answer but was relieved nonetheless. Molly's words were news to me: I had always thought we had broken up because of our differences. Molly gave me a look I knew well, her gracious *I've just done you a favour* look.

"So what brings you to my corner of the city?" she asked breezily. I wasn't sure how to summarize the whole thing quickly, but luckily Verity saved me from it by pulling out Myers's Book from her purse and sliding it over to Molly. Molly stared at it before placing her hand on the cover. She picked it up.

"No, don't!" I said, spraying cookie crumbs everywhere as Molly opened the Book. Her eyes took on a glassy cast as she stared at it, her body totally still. Then she let out a little huff of air through her nose and, totally unaided, closed the Book and cut the connection.

"It's very strong," I said weakly.

"Yes," Molly agreed. "But not the strongest I've ever seen. Where exactly did you get this, Paul?"

I looked to Verity, as it was her story to tell. She squared her shoulders, tilted her head so her hair slid over her shoulder and down her back.

"It belongs to Dr David Myers," Verity said.

"Oberon's father?" Molly said.

"That's right," Verity replied. "We think that Book contains evidence of him breaking the law."

"Well, you certainly don't put this much security on something just to protect your grandmother's date-square recipe," Molly said. "But what exactly do you expect to find in here?"

I said nothing, looking to Verity. I'd trust Molly with my life, but it wasn't my call to make.

"You want me to help crack this Book, don't you?" Molly coaxed. "I can do it, but it won't be easy with this many protection spells on it. And I get the sense there might be some other dangers attached to the job as well. So it's really only fair that I know what I'm getting into."

Verity nodded and started talking. She told her more than I expected her to, talking about the three suspicious deaths he had been involved in and how the Book probably contained enough evidence to serve as blackmail material against the families he had "helped." She did not talk about her own origins or how Dr Myers was her father.

"There's something else," I said. "Dr Myers said he was working on behalf of the government. That the deaths were part of experiments involving innate magic."

"Innate magic?" Molly interjected. "Really? In this day and age?"

Molly leaned back and crossed her arms.

"Well, regardless of that, this is a very tricky situation," she said. "You don't have the evidence in hand that Dr Myers killed those children, but Oberon and his father have plenty of reason to call the police on *you*."

"Only if they want all their dirty laundry aired in public," Verity snarled.

Molly nodded. "Indeed. Which means they will probably try to get this Book back through less public means. If this Book is as dangerous as you claim it is, you're in danger this very second."

"I'm sorry for bringing you into this, Mol," I said. "You were the only one I could trust."

She tilted her head. "Yes? And is that the only reason?"

I knew what she was fishing for, and luckily it was the truth: "And 'cause you're the best Book Binder in the whole United Kingdom."

She blushed but didn't deny it. We both had pretty big egos. That had been another thing that had attracted us to each other, the belief that we were the best in our respective fields and it only made sense for us to pair up.

"So how soon can you break into it?" Verity asked.

Molly ran her hands lightly over the pebbled cover. "Hmm, there's quite a few spells to unravel. I'd say about three weeks."

"Three weeks?!" Verity and I said in unison.

"Mol, that's too long!" I said. "Like you said, we're going to have assassins after us by daybreak! That Book's the only thing keeping us alive!"

"Three weeks?" Verity repeated. "After all we've done, it's going to take you three whole weeks to read a Book?"

Molly held up a hand.

"Three weeks," she said firmly. "The Book will be safe here with me. In the meantime, the two of you need to get out of the city and go to ground."

"Right," I said glumly. Thomas would not be happy when I told him about this turn of events.

"How did you get into Book Binding anyway?" Verity asked, as if checking out her credentials.

Molly shrugged. "Oh, I've always been good at it," she said. "My parents taught me some things when I was still small, so I can never remember a time where I couldn't do it. When they died in the war, a shopkeeper in Shanghai took me in because I could do his Books for him. I was working in the store when my English father—Lieutenant Evans, that is—came in to buy some cigarettes. He was so surprised to see a small child doing magic he came back the next day and arranged things with the merchant to bring me back to London. He and his wife adopted me and have been wonderful parents to me in every way."

"Wow. Good thing you're good at magic, huh?" Verity said. For a moment there was a tightness around Molly's eyes and mouth; then it relaxed back into her usual smile.

"Yes, I suppose so," she said. "It's awfully late. Would you like me to make up one of the guest bedrooms for the two of you?"

I noticed she had offered us use of only one bedroom and wondered if that was because of lack of space or if she was just trying to figure out exactly what our relationship was.

"Thank you very much, but we should go," I said. "As you said, Myers will soon be hunting us down and the sooner we are out of the city the better."

Molly nodded. She asked us to wait a moment and came back with two Books. They were only a couple of pages with a thin leather cover.

"These are clean Books," she said. "There's about twenty pounds on each of them, but they're not registered to any name. You can use them to travel around the city without leaving a record on your own Books."

"Molly, I can't take this. I should be the one paying you." Nonetheless I took one of the clean Books and put it in my breast pocket next to my personal Book. Verity nodded her thanks and put the other Book in her purse.

Molly called us a taxi and Verity went out on the front path to wait for it, rubbing her arms as she kept a lookout.

"Just be careful out there, all right?" Molly said. "I will protect you the best I can from my end, but if Myers decides to reach out to those families of the dead children . . ." She faltered. "They have considerable assets at their disposal."

"Don't worry about me," I said. "There's lots of places for me to run and hide. But what about you? Will you be all right?"

"Oh yes. It would take some sleuthing to find me," she said.

The taxi pulled up to the kerb.

"Molly, I don't know how I can ever repay you," I said. Verity called out that our ride was here, but I kept my eyes on Molly. She was one of the few girls I had dated who was shorter than me, one more cute thing about her.

She smiled up at me. "Paul, I'm not doing this for you," she said. "If Verity's right and this man is a child murderer"—her smile grew big enough to show her top and bottom teeth—"then helping to bring him down will be a pleasure."

CHAPTER 24

The driver for our return trip was a speedster who never met a curve he didn't take hard and sharp. I kept falling on my injured left rib, crying out every time my side banged against the inside of the car door. The pain was coming back. I threw up the shortbread biscuit in the back of the cab and Verity had to pay the driver extra to get him to stop yelling at us.

Luckily Mrs Dylag wasn't awake as we made our way up the stairs of the house. Verity had to support me, my right arm slung across her shoulder while my left arm lightly hugged my ribs and tried to shield them from the wall. We sounded like some kind of shuffling beasts as we plodded our way upstairs. We were halfway up the final floor to the attic when Thomas appeared at the top of the staircase. He had his hands on his hips and a stern expression on his face. He looked like a parent about to give the "I'm not angry, just disappointed" speech, except he looked plenty angry.

The anger slipped away when he saw my banged-up face.

"What the fuck, Paul?" he said, hurrying down the stairs. He made a move to support me from my left side but he ended up bumping against my ribs, making waves of pain radiate out from my torso and spread through my body. My legs buckled, though before I could collapse Thomas slipped under my left arm, and he and Verity dragged me up the rest of the way to the attic. Before I blacked out from the pain

I had just enough presence of mind to thank God for a merciful death and deliverance from torture.

When I came to I realized I had prayed too soon. I was still alive. I was on my back, and lying next to my poor, broken ribs was Mrs Dylag's frozen pot roast, wrapped up in a towel. I could just barely feel its coolness: much nearer was the pain, pulsating out from my side like a second heartbeat. But it wasn't the overwhelming sharpness from before. If I focused on my breathing I could keep it at bay, like Zeus controlling the clouds in the sky or Poseidon pacing the rhythm of the waves.

Verity was holding my right hand. She was kneeling by the bed and it was pleasant to focus on the citrus smell of her perfume—focusing on her scent kept my mind off the other, less pleasant sensations running through me. I could still taste blood in my mouth, feel the gauze on my face.

"Verity," I said, and my voice sounded odd, like when you listen to a recording of yourself. She squeezed my hand.

"Just rest," she said. "Dawes will be back soon."

"Where'd he go?" I asked. My mouth felt like it was full of cotton.

"He needed to get some things before he stitched you up."

"So I will need stitches?" I said, wondering how long I had been out. "Do you think I'll be more sexy with a scar?"

"More sexy?" Verity teased. She brushed some hair off my face.

"Right," I muttered. "Not possible." I closed my eyes so I could better feel her fingers on my skin. She had small hands and I had noticed before how cold they always were. In that moment, with my skin burning up, it was a blessing. "You must think I'm a pretty sorry excuse for a man, eh? After watching how I let Obie whale on me."

Her fingers stilled temporarily. "I don't know about that," she said. "I saw how you tried to stop him from coming after me. And you were pretty cool getting the gun off Doc Myers."

I smiled. "Yeah, I guess so."

I hadn't realized I had fallen back asleep until Verity started insistently patting my cheek. "Hey, hey! Wake up!"

"Why?" I ground out. When asleep I was aware of the pain only on a subconscious level. Awake we were like two passengers crammed into a small railway car, too close for comfort. "Can't I sleep?"

"No. I mean, maybe, but I would just feel better if you stayed awake," Verity said. "Talk to me. Tell me a story. Here, you have carte blanche to just talk and talk. How can you turn that down?"

"I'm tired." I had no stories at hand except *Once there was a young man with a set of busted ribs and all he wanted was to slip away.*

"Tell me about this room," Verity said, a desperate edge to her voice. "Tell me about the things in it." When I didn't she leaned over me to get a closer peer at the bookshelf. "Are any of these books yours?"

"Nah, they're all Thomas's."

"Even this one?" A sprinkle of dust landed on my nose as she pulled a book loose. *Illustrated Bible Stories of the New Testament.*

I opened my eyes. "That's—"

"'Presented to Paul Gallagher on July fifth, 1940. In recognition of perfect attendance. From St Joseph's Sunday School.'" She clapped the book shut with a satisfied smile.

"All right, that one's mine," I admitted.

"Perfect attendance, eh? I'm impressed by your dedication."

"Well, it's hard to skip when your ma's the Sunday school teacher," I said. Verity didn't have a quick answer for that.

"She died, right?" she said. "When did it happen?"

"Oh, a long time ago. When I was about thirteen and fourteen." It sounded odd to cite two ages, but that was just how long it had taken Mum to die. Whenever I tried to parse it, all I could imagine was a tumorous apple, Adam's and Eve's mouths closing in around it, the diseased fruit going down their throats and dissolving into their genes and being passed on to the rest of humanity. "She was in and out of the hospital for a long time."

"I'm sorry," Verity said. "That must have been hard."

"It was a long time ago . . . ," I said and closed my eyes.

"Hey, stay awake!" Verity was loud enough to be heard all the way in Finsbury Park. I winced and kept my eyes firmly closed.

Her lips touched mine. They were soft, warmer than her fingers but just as soothing. Her tongue traced the inner edge of my bottom lip and I swear I got pins and needles from the sensation, a pleasant numbness that set the rest of me on fire.

I opened my eyes.

"I'm awake," I said.

"Good," she said and leaned down for another kiss. Her black hair fell on either side of her head, a curtain that closed us off from the rest of the world. It was a slightly odd angle for kissing, as she was kneeling by my side so her face was at a cross angle to mine, but we made it work. As we kissed she'd exhale through her nose and her breath tickled my cheek. She slid her hand across my chest, stopping only when it rested over my heart. I let go of her hand so I could touch the back of her head, palm resting against the seat of the skull. She brought an arm down next to my head so she could lean in closer, and I sank deeper into that ratty old mattress as our kiss deepened. My ribs were still killing me, but I was willing to stay awake and suffer through it if it meant *this*.

Neither of us heard the front door open and close but we both heard Thomas on the stairs. Verity pushed her hair behind her ears before sitting up, trying much too hard to look nonchalant. I thought it was a pretty weak ploy but Thom didn't seem to notice anything funny when he finally emerged into the attic.

"Good, you're awake," he said. He was wearing his interdimensional cape, and with a flourish he removed a bottle of some dark liquor and a small metal tin.

"Oh my God!" I said happily. "You fixed the cape! You can actually retrieve things from it now!"

A second later he was kneeling by my left side, squeezed in between my body and the bookshelf.

"Where's my apple?" I asked.

"You don't want to see the state it was in when I finally found it." Thomas opened the little tin. There were a couple of tiny tablets inside. "You're going to have to sit up to take this," he said, sounding like a proper medical professional as he handed me one.

Verity put a hand under my back and helped me move. I almost dry heaved as the pain rippled through me, but I had nothing left in my stomach. "What is it?"

"Morphine."

"Oh, good." I swallowed it dry.

"Does it feel any better?" Verity asked.

"Give him a moment!" Thomas snapped, but the truth was that it *did* seem to work right away. Maybe it was all in the mind, but the pain felt like it had been pressed down and compacted, a tiny contained knot in my side rather than a massive thing with tendrils. I was able to breathe again.

"Yeah," I said. "It does feel better."

"Good," Thomas said. I watched with detached interest as he took out some metal sewing needles from a wet cloth bundle, the smell of rubbing alcohol filling the room. Before moving on to the next step both he and Verity took a swig from the bottle of rum, and I likewise reached out for it like an infant reaching out for milk. Like parents indulging a small child, they let me have a drink too. Thomas threaded the needle with some wire thread we had. He kind of crouched down over me before realizing that it was much too awkward to try and sew in that position, so he had me lie back down again. I didn't mind it. To me there was a kind of fairy-tale quality to it all, like I was under a spell and my best friend and true love had come to rescue me.

Thomas looked worried but his hands were steady as he started stitching up the cut on my forehead. I flinched as the needle and thread slid through me, making Thomas frown even more. Heat radiated off the needle—Thomas must have boiled it in water before coming upstairs. Verity grabbed my hand and held it tight. I wanted to tell them not to worry, that it didn't really hurt that much, that they should have some morphine too so they'd relax a little bit, but all I could do was chuckle. Thomas did a few stitches, keeping them close to the edge of the wound. It only stung a little bit.

"A kiss with teeth," I muttered.

Thomas did a final stitch and cut the thread. I reached up to touch it but he grabbed my wrist. "Leave it be."

"Will it scar?" I was less worried about it than I had been earlier; in my drugged-up state all I could manage was idle curiosity.

"Only if you poke at it," Thomas said. He put away the thread and cleaned the needle. Verity squeezed my hand.

"Thomas," I said, pushing myself up on my elbows. The motion made my head spin, but I held my ground. "We need to get out of town—"

"I know," he said coldly. "Verity here told me everything."

"Oh, good," I said. They must have had that conversation while I had been passed out. I was glad I had missed what had probably been a tense tête-à-tête. "Then we need to get to the train station and take the train up to Liverpool—"

"*She's* not coming with us," Thomas said, still angry.

"What?" I sat up fully, ignoring the lurch in my stomach. "Don't be ridiculous! She's in just as much danger as we are, if not more so—"

Thomas rounded on me, not able to keep his anger in check anymore. "It's her fault you're all fucked up, Paul! Have you even seen yourself in the mirror?!"

"A bit," I said in a small voice. I knew my looks weren't all that, but I was vain about the little I did have. I pushed that away and held tight to Verity's hand. "It was my choice to get involved with this, Thom. You can't blame Verity. Besides, she pretty much saved my life—"

"Paul, it's okay. I'll go." Verity stood, her hand slipping out of mine. I looked at her in astonishment.

"What?"

She shrugged, a rueful smile on her face. "Dawes is right. It's my fault you're all busted up like this, and hanging out with me will just get you in more trouble. Besides, I need to stay in London. Maybe Molly will break the Book early. I have to stay on this story until the very end."

"But . . . but the Myerses and Jesus knows who else will be searching all of London for you," I said.

She laughed and gestured to her dress. "That's easy. All I have to do is change my clothes and I'll become a completely different person. They won't find me." She gave me a wink. "Your magic covered that."

I didn't know how to respond to her bravado. Her reasons for staying were all solid, whereas I just wanted her to come to Liverpool because I wanted her near me.

"Great. Glad that's settled," Thomas said. "Bye, Verity. See you never."

"Thomas—" I said to him sharply but before I could reprimand him Verity leaned down and kissed a part of my face that wasn't covered by plasters. Without a word she disappeared down the stairs.

I turned to Thomas. "You didn't have to—"

"Shut up," Thomas said. "You have no right to take me to task for *anything* right now. In fact, until we are on the train to Liverpool I don't want to hear another word outta you."

Thomas spent the next twenty minutes frantically packing up our two suitcases with as much stuff from our flat as he could. I stayed where I was the whole time, sitting up on the futon. Every now and then I'd feel dizzy watching him and I'd have to close my eyes and count to thirty before the pain receded.

Once we were packed Thomas brought the suitcases down to the door and then came back up to help me down the stairs.

"It's four in the morning," I muttered. "Trains don't start running until five."

"I'd rather wait there than here," Thomas replied. Even with everything going on, I thought he was being paranoid but figured there was no arguing with him.

We made it out onto the street, each of us carrying a suitcase. As I walked, the pain in my side grew, competing with the pain in my head like siblings squabbling for their parents' attention. I was focusing on taking only slight, little breaths when there was a ringing in my ears and somehow I landed on the pavement.

"Bloody hell!" Thomas yelled, dropping his suitcase and coming over to me.

"Sorry," I muttered. "I'll be fine, just help me up."

Thomas helped me to my feet. When I tried to pick up my suitcase he snatched it out of my hand. He strode purposefully towards Green Lanes while I wobbled behind him.

"Say, Thom," I huffed out, trying to keep my breathing shallow. "Can you go a little slower?"

Thomas looked over his shoulder in exasperation: we had gone exactly ten feet. But when he saw me he slowed to a stop.

"Lean on me," he said. I came over and put a hand on his shoulder. It wasn't much support but it steadied me. We started walking again. It was slow going as I couldn't walk that fast and Thomas was carrying two suitcases. The suitcase closest to me would bang against my leg now and then, but I didn't waste my breath complaining about it.

We had almost made it to Green Lanes when the latches on Thomas's suitcase popped open and his clothes spilled out.

"Fucking hell!" Thomas yelled. He kicked at some of the clothes with a frustrated grunt, then tossed my suitcase down next to them. He knelt down and started cramming as many of his clothes as he could into my suitcase. When he was done he grabbed his nearly empty suitcase and shoved it down hard into a nearby rubbish bin. "Stupid!

Cheap! Piece! Of shit!" he hissed at it as he punched it deeper into the bin.

When he was done he stood there for a moment rubbing his temples, up to his ankles in his own clothes. I envied him being able to breathe so deeply. All I could do was lean against the wall and try to think about other things than the sharpness cutting through my sides. I tried to think about Verity. Where was she right now? Was she all right? Thinking about Verity made me hurt in a different way, so I just focused on my breathing.

"Is there a night bus that goes right to Marylebone?" I said, breaking the silence. Marylebone was the train station where we could catch a train to Liverpool.

"Fuck the night buses. We'll take a cab." Things were dire indeed if Thomas was willing to splash on a cab. Good thing I still had the dosh from Molly.

Thomas managed to flag down a cab. As soon as I was in the back seat I started nodding off.

"Hey!" Thomas said. "You took several whacks to the head! You can't fall asleep!"

"What? Ever again?" I replied.

"That's right!"

It was a quarter after five when the cab dropped us off at Marylebone. Trains hadn't left yet but the station was up and bustling. It was Monday morning and the workweek had begun. People were opening up stalls; bakers were preparing baked goods to sell to travellers. The scent made me sick. As I followed after Thom I felt such a pull within me between a tiredness throughout my limbs and the ever-present pain in my side. I wanted to sleep but felt like I would never be able to think of anything but my broken ribs.

There was already a crowd of commuters jostling to buy tickets. A man bumped into my bad side, making me cry out. Thomas spun around, murderous eyes searching for the culprit, but the commuter had melted back into the crowd, probably unaware of the pain he had caused me. I was pretty aware of it though. I dropped down to one knee, hands and arms protecting my left side, the swarm of people stepping around me like water parting around a rock.

Thomas set down our suitcase and pushed through the flow of the crowd to get back to me. "Paul, get up. You can't sit there."

I felt a bit of annoyance at that. So easy to tell someone in pain what to do. I could barely stand. When I opened my eyes blue dots danced in my vision and it felt like little needles were pricking my brain. When I breathed in deeply it caused my whole body to spasm. What else was I supposed to do but sit there?

Thomas helped me up and shielded me as we pushed our way through the crowd. We reached a large decorative pillar near the entrance.

"Just sit here for a sec, all right? I'm going to go get our suitcase." He disappeared back into the crowd. As I sat against the pillar a kindly stranger dropped a few coins in my lap, mistaking me for a beggar.

Coins. Such a rarity in a world of Books—maybe the good soul who'd gifted them to me carried them solely to give to people hard on their luck. In a daze I took the coins and made my way towards a row of public telephones, leaning against the wall for balance. I pushed into the first free phone box. The inside smelled like piss. Food wrappers crunched under my shuffling feet. I didn't want to touch the walls but I had no choice: it took all my concentration to put the coins into the pay phone and ask the operator to connect me with the Hollister homestead.

"Hello?" Hollister sounded somewhat sleepy but obviously curious about who was calling his home so early. I pictured the light on in the bedroom of his lovely home, a single light amongst the cosy streets of Barnet.

"Did you know about what your mate Godfrey did?" I said. "About him having kids killed as part of an experiment?"

A sharp breath on the line, so deep it seemed to suck the oxygen from around me.

"Jim," Hollister said. "You weren't in the wars. You don't know the horrors that are out there—"

"So you decided to recreate them here at home?" I said. "Jesus. Why? Why kids? What did you do? And what in the world could possibly be worth it?"

"I did it for you—"

"You didn't even know me then!"

"I did it for all of the British people. We were trying to find some power that would make Great Britain untouchable. We didn't find it then, but I've found it now, with you. Hearing your story, getting to know you, it solved the riddle for me. We tried to cast innate magic on children in Dr Myers's care but it never took, and yet it worked for *you* when you were a child! Do you understand what the difference was? The key to making innate magic work? You—"

I hung up the phone. It rang a few minutes later but I ignored it, leaning against the wall of the telephone box, palms of my hands pressed against my temples.

The door opened with a clatter.

"What the hell are you doing in here?" Thomas asked. "Why can't you stay where I fucking leave you?"

"Where's the suitcase?" I mumbled.

Thomas's mouth flattened into an angry line. "It's gone," he said. "Someone nicked it and I couldn't find them."

I shrugged. I would have traded just about all my worldly goods to not feel like my torso was on fire. "It's all just rubbish anyway."

Thomas didn't reply. He carefully took my arm and led me out of the phone box to a bench. I sat down and looked up at him. His face was waxy and his arms were stiff at his sides, like a mannequin's. My little brother, as tough as he was, was reaching his limit.

"We still have money, right?" I said. "All we need to do is buy our train tickets."

Thomas nodded, clearly relieved to have some kind of plan. "Right, right. I'll go buy the tickets. You just stay here, got it?"

"Yes."

"Got it?"

I pulled my right leg up so I could rest my head on my knee, careful to avoid the tender part of my forehead where the stitches were. "I'm not going anywhere," I said. Thomas disappeared into the bustle of the station.

I'll stay here and die. I hurt all over. I could feel blood pulsing through my veins and rising up against my skin, could literally feel the bruises forming. I was hungry, but the thought of food made me nauseous. It was a vicious cycle. My stomach would send out hunger pangs which would make my brain recoil in disgust which would make bile rise up in my throat. I'd swallow it back down and eventually my stomach would settle, forgetting the wave of nausea enough to remember that it was hungry and start the process all over again. All this time I had to also keep my breathing shallow, lest my lungs brush up against my busted ribs.

"Paul?"

A woman's voice. I looked up to see Tonya Gower staring down at me.

She was wearing a simple forest-green peacoat with a matching hat. At her side was a small satchel. She seemed even more worn out than the last time I'd seen her, her face wan and pinched. I wondered if she was ill, but my own pain kept me from being able to worry too much about her at the moment.

"Tonya." I sounded drunk but I was perfectly lucid. I was amazed that she had managed to recognize me even with my face all bandaged up like a mummy's.

"What happened to you?" she asked, crouching down to be eye level with me.

I smiled and learned that it hurt to smile. "Got into a bad row with a mate." Idly I wondered if Oberon was all right—would he die if Dr Myers didn't check on him? Was Dr Myers still locked up in the shed? My heart sped up at the thought of the two of them up and free, searching for Verity. "But I'll be fine. Going to get out of the city to a big fancy convalescent home. How about you? What are you doing here?"

"I'm going to visit my aunt in Dereham," Tonya said.

"Ah. Holiday from the McDougal house, eh?"

"More like a permanent holiday," Tonya replied. "They fired me."

"What?" I sat up straight at the news which made it feel like my left side had been cracked open anew. It took me a minute to get my breathing under control and to tamp down the pain enough to speak again: "Fired you? Why?"

"They had their reasons," Tonya said, eyes scanning the ceiling. "So I'm also getting out of town for a little bit, taking a breather, figuring out what my next move is." Despite her cheerful tone she wouldn't meet my eyes. "I've never been to Dereham, but I've always been curious. It's in East Anglia. It's my father's hometown. I hardly know the man, but I thought maybe if I went to the place where he was born, I might learn a little bit about him."

She spoke with a tone of wistful regret. I had no desire to dig deeper into her wounds. If she wanted to talk more about her dad, I'd be happy to listen, but I wasn't going to prod her.

"Dereham, huh?" I said. "I've never been, but I have heard that there's a holy spring in the churchyard."

"What?" she said, perking up. "Really?"

"Yeah, for such a little speck on the map, Dereham's got some amazing mythology. I once read about it in a book discussing holy sites in England. Do you know the story of how the village was founded?"

She shook her head and took a seat next to me on the bench.

"It's a fantastic tale featuring miracles, a haughty prince, greedy monks, and body snatching. The heroine of the story is Saint Withburga, a princess and later mother superior of the local convent . . ."

As I talked Tonya seemed to cheer up somewhat and I likewise forgot about my pain. Talking itself hurt my throat a little bit, but it was worth it to otherwise feel alive and connected to the human being sitting next to me.

". . . And so, even though no one knows the location of Withburga's final resting place, you can still visit the holy spring God sent in her honour."

"Amazing," Tonya said, her smile wide. At some point she had taken my hand in hers. "Thanks for the tip, mate. I'll be sure to go see this spring for myself. I don't think there's much else to do there."

The idea of Tonya on her own in a little village seemed so utterly sad to me. She was so fun and charming, and talking to her made me feel better than I had all night. As I looked at her an idea came to me.

"Why don't you come with me and Thom?" I said. She looked at me.

"What?"

"We're going to Liverpool," I said. "You can come up, meet my family. We'll show you around the town."

"I don't know. My aunt in Dereham—"

"Oh, bugger your aunt in Dereham!" I said loudly enough that a passerby glanced over. Tonya stifled a smile.

"Look," I said, "I'm in a bad way, and, well, Thomas is falling apart at the seams trying to keep it together. We could really use some help, *your* help. You and I, we haven't gotten a chance to really get to know each other, and that's my fault, but I'd really like the chance now, if you'll give it to me."

She was quiet.

"I mean, unless you've got somewhere else to go," I said.

She didn't mention her Dereham aunt. She nestled in closer, careful to avoid my left ribs.

"Okay," she said.

"Great," I said. "Liverpool is much more exciting than Dereham, even if it doesn't have such an awesome origin story."

Thomas appeared with tickets in hand. He looked down at Tonya with an arctic coolness.

"You," he said, and I was lost. As far as I knew Thomas and Tonya had hardly ever spoken to each other. So why this freezing anger from Thomas and this sly, smug air around Tonya?

"Me," she said. "I was just on my way to visit my aunt when Paul invited me to come along. We're going to Liverpool, right?"

Thomas said nothing.

"I'll help," she said, and now it sounded like she was actually asking Thomas for permission rather than just asserting facts. "I'll help look after Paul."

There was just a crack in Thomas's glacial expression, but it was enough.

"Fine," he said. He turned to go.

"Um, Thomas," I said gingerly. "She'll need a ticket."

Thomas stared at me, not angry, just disbelieving. Without a word he got back in the massive queue.

CHAPTER 25

As we approached the Lime Street train station I mentally prepared myself to come face-to-face with my brothers. We disembarked and Tonya and I sat on a bench while Thomas went to call my family and tell them about our sudden arrival.

"Who's picking us up?" I asked Thomas when he returned. "Mikey? Patrick? Oh, Jesus, don't say it's both of them—"

"It's neither," Thomas said. "They're both in Hong Kong on business."

"Oh." That put a spring in my step. "Then is Dad coming down with the car?"

"That's right."

I hadn't seen my dad since last summer when Thomas and I had come up for a visit. I had been a different person then. I'd still been together with Lamb and still had my final year of school to get through, but I had been more than confident that I'd breeze through it and emerge an acclaimed cloth mage. In short, I had been young, healthy, in love, and full of promise. Now I had returned all banged up with nothing but trouble nipping at my heels.

It wasn't long at all before Dad's old brown car pulled up to the kerb.

"Lads!" My father emerged from the driver's side. He had reddish-brown hair like mine though a few shades lighter. He had the type of round, lined face that only seemed right when it was smiling. Dad always looked like the type of old man who might show up in a fairy tale, the type to catch a magic fish by chance or steal a rose from a witch's garden, stumbling into good fortune and misadventure with the same puzzled air. I smiled to see him, but that smile fell away as he came closer, limping. Something was wrong; something was different. Half of his smile was there, but the left half of his face drooped downwards, as though something was tugging the corner of his mouth. He moved in a halting start-stop motion, the left side of his body a half second slower than the right.

Dad's smile dropped completely when he got close enough to get a good look at me.

"Oh, my poor boy." His Scouse accent was ten times stronger than mine. "What happened to you?"

I found it funny that everyone kept gawking at my face when it was my cracked ribs that were actually making me feel rotten.

"It's fine, Dad," I said. "Just got into a bit of a scrape."

My dad clasped me on the shoulder, then looked at Tonya.

"Oh, I'm sorry! I didn't realize there was a lady present." Dad made a slight bow in Tonya's direction. "How do you do, miss. As you may have guessed I'm this little rogue's old man."

"I see where he gets his good looks from," Tonya said. People always say I resemble my dad until they see a picture of my mother.

"But none of his bad habits!" Dad grinned and nodded to Thomas. "Ah, Thomas my lad, how are you, boy?"

"A'right, Sean. You?" Thomas said, his own Scouse accent already flooding back. Growing up I was always astounded by his cheek, that a little spit of a boy like him would call my parents by their Christian names. They let him get away with it, perhaps recognizing that it was a miracle this little wild child respected them at all.

"Oh, never better," Dad replied cheerfully. I couldn't believe he'd tell such a bald-faced lie; he was obviously not "never better." I shot a look at Thomas, to see if he was likewise aghast. Thomas shook his head: *Leave it be.*

"Well, what are we doing standing out here like a bunch of idiots?" Dad said. "Let's get going."

He invited Tonya to ride shotgun. As Thomas moved towards the back-passenger door I stopped him.

"I want to go home," I said.

"We are home," he replied, low voice matching mine.

"No. I want to go home to London."

I half expected and perhaps even wanted him to dress me down and tell me to not be such a child. But instead he looked at me sympathetically. He patted me on the shoulder before getting into the back seat of the car.

~

We drove through downtown Liverpool, the buildings all squatter and dirtier than even the grimiest London streets. Every third lot seemed to be empty, save for the occasional construction crew. Some buildings were little more than shells.

"Wow, so much construction going on," Tonya said, clearly reaching for a compliment.

"Liverpool got hit hard in the war," I said defensively. "It's only now that the money's there to start rebuilding." We sat in silence until we passed the Liverpool cathedral. Tonya gasped. It was a towering building, its limestone facade cutting starkly against the grey sky.

"There's this little gully around the church," I said to Tonya as we drove up the hill. "It's a cemetery actually, but on a sunny day it's a nice place to go for a walk."

She smiled at me. "First sunny day we'll have to go."

I smiled back, ignoring the pain pulsating from my ribs.

My dad lived in the same house Thomas and I had grown up in, a well-kept brick house with red shutters. The four of us went into the kitchen and Dad put the kettle on for tea. Dad did most of the talking, telling Tonya embarrassing stories from my childhood. She laughed and watched my dad in a way that made me thankful that he wasn't forty years younger.

Once it got dark Thomas announced he was going to go for a walk, maybe drop in on some old friends. Tonya said she'd go with him. Thomas didn't look thrilled by this prospect but he didn't tell her no. I watched them go.

"Don't worry, lad. Thomas would never steal your girl," my dad said. I snorted. I wasn't sure what was going on, but I was pretty sure it wasn't *that*.

Dad busied himself with cleaning up the kitchen. I watched his movements, how he did his chores with one hand, the other gripping the countertop for balance.

"Dad," I said. "What happened?"

Dad didn't turn to face me but let out a long sigh.

"In February, I had a wee fall at the store. I wouldn't have thought much about it, but Mrs O'Shea was there and she insisted that I go to the hospital. The doctors checked me over and said I could go home."

"Wait, so the fall made you like this?" I said, not quite following.

Dad shook his head. "Oh, no. See, I fell because of the stroke—"

"A *stroke*?!"

"Just a minor one," Dad said, a sheepish smile on his face. "Like I said, the doctors said the worst of it was over and—"

"And you didn't think to call me?" What if my dad had died between then and now, all without me even knowing he was at death's door?

"I talked about it with your brothers," Dad said. "And we figured since it was your last year of school, we didn't want to worry you. There was nothing you could have done, so—"

"So? So what?! I could have still come up and seen you." I wanted to keep at him, to drag him over the coals for keeping such a big secret from me. But I hadn't exactly been truthful with my dad about anything in my life, including why I had suddenly shown up on his doorstep.

"I'm fine now," Dad said. "Really."

I dropped it, and the two of us chatted half-heartedly until bed.

～

Tonya was given the guest bedroom, while Thomas and I slept in our old childhood bunk beds. The very first day I had taken Thomas home to live with us we had squabbled over who got to sleep in the top bunk. This time there was no fight over who got what: in my state I could hardly climb up and down the ladder. We had left the light on at my request—the darkness made me feel like I was choking.

As I lay in bed, I thought about my father. I could feel myself already getting used to his lopsided face, to the point where in my memories it was rewriting the smile I had grown up knowing. "I talked about it with your brothers," Dad had said. He probably just meant Mikey and Pat, but there was a chance that Thomas had been a part of their little conclave as well.

"Thomas?" I said.

"Yeah?" Thomas said from above.

"Did you know about my dad?"

He was still and silent above me.

"No," he finally said.

Prior to that day I would have accepted his words without a second thought. But he was already keeping secrets from me, like whatever was going on between him and Tonya. Who was to say he hadn't gotten word about Dad's stroke and agreed to keep me out of the loop?

"All right," I said and tried to get to sleep.

CHAPTER 26

I don't remember waking, just being barely conscious and being very, very sick. I had kicked off all my blankets in the middle of the night as the room was like an oven. I figured the house must have been on fire. I shouted, trying to warn the others, but it just came out as garbled gibberish. My father and Tonya rushed into the room and Thomas clambered down from the top bunk. Thomas hurried over to my side and my brain was sure it was Oberon moving in to kill me. I kept screaming.

Tonya pushed through and put her slim hand on my forehead. I stilled, my whole body concentrating on that hand, trying to soak up any hint of coldness from it. I drifted in and out of consciousness. The next time I was lucid, it was midday and Dr Williams was staring down at me. I'd known Dr Williams my whole life, but even when he came too close or moved too fast all my brain saw was a male figure looming over me, about to kill me. Whenever any man got too close—no matter if it was the doc, my best friend, my own father—my body went into spasms. Through my fever I could hear the doc saying he couldn't explain the fits, that it might be a sign of brain trauma, but I knew that wasn't the case. The primal, animal part of my brain wanted to defend the body from a perceived threat, but the innate magic within my bones wouldn't allow me to strike and possibly hurt my attacker. When those two warring forces came up against each other I could do nothing but watch, locked inside my own mind, as my body shook violently. This was obviously upsetting to watch, and for a while Thomas and Dad really leaned on me hard to go to the hospital. Eventually they laid off, mainly because I would get so worked up whenever they brought it up.

Tonya stayed by my side, talking to me quietly as the doc pressed at my ribs. Focusing on her was the only way to keep the rest of my brain from freaking out. I spent most of that first week in either a feverish delirium or fitful, painful sleep.

The next time I was truly lucid and aware, it was the middle of the night again and it was pitch dark around me. My first thought was that I had died. I started giving a series of barking yells, a panicked animal, and then I realized that I was in pain, so therefore I must be alive after all.

Or maybe I was in hell.

I started yelling in earnest then.

"It's okay; it's all right," a woman's voice said to my left. It took me a second to recognize Tonya's cockney accent. Tentatively she slowly patted my forehead. "You're safe."

I could just make out the light of the city coming through the gaps in the curtain and the outline of the long dresser against the wall. It was my parents' bedroom, and I was sleeping in the large double bed. I couldn't remember being moved in there.

"The light," I said, voice cracking. "Please leave the light on."

With a click Tonya turned on the bedside lamp. She was sitting in an old upholstered chair by the window. At first I wondered what the hell she had been doing, sitting in the dark; then I saw her housecoat and nightgown and realized she had been sleeping there.

"Tonya, you can go to bed," I said, proud of my coherent sentence. The world still seemed a little hazy, but like a drunk putting on a facade of sobriety I strung my words together with care. "I'll be all right."

"I don't mind," Tonya said. "I'll leave once you go back to sleep."

"Liar," I said. "I can't sleep knowing you are going to get a crick in your neck sitting there all night."

"It's no trouble," Tonya said. Never try and argue with a cockney; they are as bad as Scots when it comes to stubbornness.

"How about you sleep with me?" I said. We both looked at each other as soon as the words were out of my mouth. We laughed, my cheeks turning red.

"I just mean, there's the whole other half of the bed here," I said. "If you're going to stick around, you may as well get some rest too. You can sleep under the covers; I'll sleep on top of them."

Tonya stood. "No. You need to stay under the covers." She went to the other side of the bed and fluffed up a pillow before lying down on top of the duvet. Her deep-brown eyes were a comforting kind of darkness, a warm one I was willing to stay in.

"Good night, Paul."

"Good night, Tonya." I fell back asleep.

~

A few days later the fever broke and I was able to sit up in bed and talk to Thomas without going into convulsions at the sight of him.

"The doc says it's because you were lugging your sorry ass around London the night you got beat up," Thomas said. "He also thinks your ribs are broken, but there's no way to know without going to the hospital for an x-ray—"

"No hospitals," I said.

"I *know*," Thomas replied. "He also said there's nothing to be done for them except rest. You gotta stay in bed for a couple of weeks."

"Oh, Jesus Christ!" I'd deal with the pain, but the idea of being confined to bed for weeks made me want to claw my way out of my own skin. "Really? Seriously? Stay in bed? Can't he put a cast on it or something?"

"You can't put a cast over the ribs. You'd look like a bloody beetle." Thomas got a dreamy expression on his face. "I envy you. If I had a couple of weeks in bed, all the reading I could do . . ."

I huffed and leaned back into my pillows. Outside I could hear seagulls, their loud squawks mocking me as they flew through the air. A twinge went through my side.

"Have you heard anything from Molly?" I asked.

"It's only been two weeks, Paul," he said. "Just focus on getting better."

The problem was that the more I tried to focus on getting better, the more my mind drifted to other things, like wondering what Verity was up to. Was she all right? Was she in touch with Molly? Was she thinking about me? Occasionally Thomas was able to find copies of the *New Rev* down at the train station: *Verity Turnboldt's column is currently on hiatus,* it said in the space where her column usually ran. When I was well enough to walk around I tried ringing the *New Rev*, but they would tell me fuck all about Verity or how she was. I desperately wished for some news, any news, that she was all right.

But even though Verity was often on my mind, the fact of the matter was that Verity wasn't there and Tonya was. As the days passed she grew more lively, losing some of that faded tiredness that had clung to her back in London. She became more like that mischievous, glowing girl I had first met at Andrew's place. More than anyone she spent hours by my side, teaching me new card games and calling me out when I tried to cheat. The job fell to her partly because Tonya was the only one who didn't startle me, who didn't bring on flashbacks of the night I'd almost died. But I wasn't entirely clear why she had volunteered in the first place.

"Weren't you going to go visit your aunt in Dereham?" I asked over a game of gin rummy. It was late, the curtains drawn and everyone else in bed. Tonya and I were still up as I had yet to win a game and was determined to play until I did. I was sitting under the covers while Tonya sat cross-legged across from me.

She looked at me over her mammoth hand of cards. She had taken to wearing a headband to keep her hair back. It helped show off the delicate cheekbones of her face, her large brown eyes.

"You trying to get rid of me?" she asked.

"Not at all," I replied. "I just don't want you to think you have to hang around here, looking after my sorry arse." I smiled. The bruises on my face were mere shadows now and I'd been almost shamefully relieved to learn that the cuts wouldn't scar.

"I know I don't have to," she said. "I just don't like the idea of owing anybody anything. I want us to be square."

"What?" I said. "You don't owe me anything." I was the one who had forgotten all about her the moment something more exciting had come along.

She rearranged her cards.

"I never did repay you over that whole statue incident."

That was why she was sticking around? Because I'd saved her from getting fired? From a job she'd never liked and had eventually gotten booted from anyway?

I must have looked pretty sceptical because she quickly spoke up.

"I mean, don't get me wrong," she said. "I *do* like you. I wouldn't be hanging around if I didn't."

I set down all my cards.

"Hey now!" she said. "That's not right. You're missing the six in that run there, and those cards don't—"

"What if I don't want us to be even?" I said. "What if I want more from you?"

There was a questioning curve to her mouth, to the angle of her eyes as she looked up at me. She pressed her hands into the covers as she leaned forwards, the cards sliding every which way.

"Like what?" Her breath was warm.

Her pink housecoat was belted tightly but the neckline of her nightgown was hanging down. I tried not to let my gaze linger.

"What do you want from me?" she asked, in a voice that managed to sound both severe and inviting.

I swallowed, worried that my fever had come back. "Well, it's kind of a long list," I said. "But I'd be happy to start with us getting closer."

She pressed in, kissing me. I pulled her closer and she slid into my lap, tilting her head so we stayed locked in a kiss the whole time. I put my arms around her back while she slid one hand behind my head, braced the other against the wall. Kissing her came as easily as water tumbling down a river. She shifted so her knees were on either side of me—

She nudged my broken ribs and suddenly I was overwhelmed with pain.

"Ahhh, ahh, too close!" I said. Tonya moved off me, legs and arms scuttling like a crab's.

"Oh my God, I'm so sorry!" she said, righting herself so she could come over and put a tentative hand on my shoulder. "Are you going to be all right?"

"Yes," I said through gritted teeth. "I'll be fine. Can you hand me that glass?"

She handed me a glass of water. I let go of my poor bruised ribs to take it from her. I sipped it slowly, using it as more of a stalling technique than anything else.

"I guess you're still pretty sore there," Tonya said apologetically. "Sorry, I should have been more careful."

"It's fine, really," I said. The pain was still there but it was manageable.

"I guess we got a bit ahead of ourselves," she went on.

"A little bit, yeah," I said.

"We probably shouldn't be rolling around while you're still recovering."

"I guess you're right."

We stared at each other.

"Oh, fuck it," I said. "As long as you avoid my left side we should be fine."

"Aces," she said, giving me a wide smile. She started to come towards me but stopped when I held up a hand.

"What?" she said. "Is there something else?"

"No, it's just, well, is there anything you want *me* to avoid, or anything in particular you don't like?" I said. "I mean, we can get into what you like later, but I just like to be clear about the no-goes up front."

She stared at me for a second before smiling.

"It's okay," she said. "I trust you."

Our second kiss was slower and deeper, and soon I forgot all about my pain as Tonya and I embraced.

~

Later, when we broke apart to breathe, Tonya smiled up at me.

"Not bad, chum."

I smiled, tucking a small strand of loose hair behind her ear. Her smile faltered and she looked away, but not before I noticed that her dark eyes were sad, melancholic to the point where I saw tears welling up in them.

"You all right?" I asked, concerned. She turned her face back towards me.

"Yeah," she said. She smiled, a full, dazzling smile, and put her arms around my shoulders, pulling me in towards her. My body still felt feverishly warm and the night air unbearably cool. There was sweat gathering all over my body.

"Thanks for that," I said, swallowed. "I, uh, I haven't felt this good in a long time."

"Me either," she said, carding her hands through my hair, her hands light and gentle. Then she sat up, fixed her nightgown, and retrieved her underwear from the floor. She started heading towards the door, presumably to go sleep in the guest bedroom.

"Tonya," I said. "Don't go. You can sleep here."

She stopped and turned towards me, a quizzical look on her face.

"Hmm," she said. "But then one of us would have to sleep on top of the covers."

Before I could counter that she grinned and was gone.

CHAPTER 27

I did in fact start to feel stronger after that, though whether that was from the healing powers of love or because I was already on the mend was ambiguous. I had more energy for moving around the house and started to come down to eat meals with the rest of the household. Thomas and I sketched out some designs; I played cards with my father. One sunny day Tonya and I even had that stroll in the gully around the church. The doc wasn't too happy to see me up and about, telling me that I needed to rest in bed for at least another few weeks, but who had time for that? Maybe staying in bed would help my ribs knit together faster, but it'd drive my brain batty.

One day I was feeling well enough to sit down at the kitchen table. Dad, Thomas, and Tonya were all in town, so it was just me in the house, listening to the wireless and enjoying the sunshine coming in through the window. I was just thinking that maybe when Tonya got home we'd go for a walk when there was a knock at the door. It was a gentle, hesitant rap, but it still startled me. Probably just a neighbour looking to borrow a cup of sugar and have a bit of a gab, but just to be sure I peeked out the living room window.

Oberon Myers was standing there on the front step. Unfortunately he saw me too.

"Paul," he called out. I dropped down even though it was already too late.

"I just want to talk, I swear."

I stayed where I was.

"Please," he said, sounding sincere. "It's just me out here, all right? I'm on my own."

There was no anger or threat in his voice. He didn't say anything more, just continued to stand there.

I went to the front door and opened it.

"Hey, Obie," I said, somehow getting the words out. There he was. Just as tall and broad shouldered as ever, button-down shirt and khaki trousers. New glasses, round wire frames rather than horn rimmed. Yet he was still clearly the man who had beaten me and then nearly strangled me to death.

I shut the door, locked it, and leaned my forehead against the wood. My breathing was coming in short bursts. It'd been three weeks since Oberon had almost killed me and it felt like it had just happened. No, it felt like it was still happening.

"Paul? Paul, are you going to let me in?"

"No, actually, no." My brain felt detached from my body, as if it were moving through a haze, while my heart pounded away double time. I had gotten better over the last week, but seeing Oberon *right outside my parents' house* sent me reeling. "I changed my mind. You can stay out there."

"I'm sorry," he said. I wondered if any of my neighbours had come out to watch this man plead at the door. "I'm sorry about what happened before. I'm glad you're all right. I honestly thought you were dead."

I laughed at that. "So you came here to finish the job?"

"Jesus Christ, man, no!" Oberon said. I could hear a neighbour's window open—all the better to eavesdrop.

"I came here to talk to you," Oberon said. "Please, it's important. I think . . . I think you and Verity may be right. About him."

It seemed to me my whole street was holding its breath, waiting for my response.

With a shaking hand I unlocked the door. I still didn't feel entirely myself, but I worried about Oberon causing even more of a scene.

"Thank you—"

"Shut up." I turned and walked to the kitchen. After a second, Oberon followed me.

"Sit down." I gestured to a chair at the long end of the table. Oberon took a seat, his large frame graceful as he carefully sat in the rickety old wooden chair. He looked around at the cheap lino floor, the faded curtains, the near-empty sugar and flour pots.

"Well?" I said, sitting down at the other side of the table. "Not exactly how you expected the upper crust of Liverpool society to live?"

"I wasn't thinking anything like that," he said. "I really want to start by saying I'm sorry—"

I'm sorry I'm sorry I'm sorry

Fucker had said the same thing while choking me.

"Shut up," I snapped. "Don't say that. In fact, don't talk right now."

Oberon kept his gob shut. I took several deep breaths, reminded myself that I was in the light of my family kitchen, not in the dark of the Myerses' home. I was all right; I was going to be all right.

"What did you really come to say?" I asked.

"I've had time to think things over," Oberon said, speaking slowly. "More importantly, I've had a few very honest talks with Father. He told me about how he worked for the government during the war—"

"Did he tell you everything?" I said.

"He told me they experimented on dying children, yes," Oberon said, somewhat curtly, as if *I* were the rude one for bringing it up. "He also told me how he took a payout from several families. He also told me . . . that I am not biologically a member of the Myers nor Kently family."

He faltered there.

I sighed and rubbed my closed eyes, taking comfort in the blue shapes that formed in the darkness. "You came all this way to tell me that?"

Oberon seemed puzzled. "You don't seem very surprised."

I looked at Oberon. "In any of his come-to-Jesus confessionals, did he own up to killing Mrs Myers?"

Oberon was silent.

"It was a difficult labour," he said. "She bled out. It happens."

"It happens," I parroted, trying my best to say the words in his clipped, middle-class accent.

"I came here in the spirit of reconciliation," Oberon said, and now there was that familiar anger colouring his cheeks. "And yet you still try and drive a further wedge between me and my . . ."

He trailed off.

"All right," I said. "You said what you came here to say. What exactly did you want to come out of it?"

Oberon gazed down at his shoes.

"I was hoping we could put all past unpleasantness aside and find a way forwards through all this," he said.

"Jesus Christ, are you running for prime minister?" I said.

Oberon huffed. "My father is a flawed man, but as far as his past crimes go, well, he did them in service to the greater good, and Molly says they'll never see the light of day—"

"What what what?" I said, sitting up so quickly there was a now-familiar twang of pain in my side. I winced, clutching my ribs. "You talked to Molly?"

Oberon nodded. "She's always been a gifted Book Binder, so I figured you would take Father's Book to her. She managed to break all the protection spells on it, but she said that the information was too damaging to the government, so she handed it over to the proper authorities. Father's crimes are tied up too closely to the powers that be, so in order to protect themselves they must protect him."

I tried to process Oberon's words. Then it occurred to me—Molly had lied to him. When he'd confronted her about the Book, she'd told him a tale about getting rid of it so that he would leave her alone. That must be it. No way had she betrayed me.

"So you can tell Verity Turnboldt that she will never see my father behind bars," Oberon said. "Where is Verity, anyway? I'd have thought she'd be here with you, but I only ever see your father, Dawes, and Andrew's maid."

"Like I'd tell you anything," I said.

Oberon sighed. "Fine. But perhaps you could pass along what I've just told you. Tell Verity you both may as well drop this whole thing."

"Is this who you really want to be, Oberon?" I asked. "Being that man's goon for the rest of your life?"

Oberon stilled. "What are you talking about?"

"You don't have to throw your lot in with him," I said. "You need my forgiveness to move forwards? Then fine, you have it. If that will help you break away from him, all right. I forgive you for trying to kill me. But now that you know the truth about what he's done, if you still side with him even knowing all that . . . well, you really will become your father's son."

Oberon stared at me.

"What would you have me do?" he said. "Throw away everything I have? Turn on the one person who's looked out for me? Start over with nothing?"

"You can do whatever the fuck you want, Oberon," I said. "But if you ever decide you want to be an actual decent human being, well, come talk to me then. For now you can get the fuck out."

Oberon gave a jerky nod. "Right, well, I'll go, then," he said.

I didn't see him to the door. I stayed in the kitchen, staring at the wall, until Thomas and Tonya came home twenty minutes later.

～

"Molly, dear, I have an important thing to ask you." I was standing in my father's living room, phone to my ear and Thomas and Tonya crowded in next to me. When I had told them about Oberon's visit and his claim that Molly had turned the Book over to the authorities, Thomas had sworn but Tonya had actually given a little cry before going ashen. Even now her fingers dug painfully into my upper arm. I had a billion things running through my mind, but I couldn't help but wonder why Tonya cared so much about the state of Dr Myers's blackmail Book. "Did Oberon come and talk to you?"

"Oh, yes, he did," Molly said. She certainly sounded cheerful.

"I see. And did you tell him that you had given Dr Myers's Book over to the proper authorities?"

"Yes, that's right."

"But that was a lie, right?"

"Oh no, it was all true."

I hissed from pain as Tonya gripped my forearm even tighter.

"Molly, why would you do that?"

"You know I work for the government, right?"

"Yes, of course," I said. "But this is such a big miscarriage of power that—"

"The department I work in is MI5," Molly said. "I swore an oath to do anything to ensure the security of the nation. I might be a low-level clerk, but I still take my duty very seriously. If the information in this Book became public, public trust in the government would falter. I'm sorry things had to be this way, but this is really for the best. Don't worry, I've kept your name out of it, yours and Miss Turnboldt's."

Tonya grabbed the phone out of my hand. "You bitch! You fucking traitorous bitch!"

It wasn't her words that startled me so much as her American accent.

"Oh, hello, Verity," Molly said.

"What's the big idea?" Tonya practically spat into the phone. "We brought you that Book to unspell it!"

I only dimly heard the next few words that came over the phone line—I was still trying to process Verity's voice coming out of Tonya's mouth.

"Well, I did unspell it, but I don't remember breaking any bones regarding anything beyond that," Molly said. "There was very dangerous information in that Book and I had to decide on the most practical way forwards."

"And by helping cover this up, you also look pretty good, don't you?" Tonya said, still speaking in that foreign accent. "Not going to be a mere clerk for long, right? You backstabbing, treacherous eel. I'm sorry I ever implied you weren't British, because you are the pinnacle of this greedy country of sycophants."

I put my hand on Tonya's shoulder. She grimaced but stepped away from the phone. Thomas took hold of the receiver and started speaking to Molly. I barely heard him, all my attention on Tonya.

"Who are you?" I asked.

She took a deep breath before meeting my eyes.

"I'm Verity Turnboldt."

It was so disorienting to look at her. She still "looked" like Tonya, but now that I knew the truth I could see that they were clearly the same person. If anything, it was astounding to think there had been a time when I couldn't see that they were the same person. But that's magic for you. Now I could see the bare truth, but the spell had kept it from my eyes.

"You couldn't have told me this, I don't know, *the day we met*?"

"I hardly knew you then," Verity said—or was she Tonya? I had no idea what to call the woman in front of me, let alone what to say to her.

Thomas tapped me on the shoulder. "Molly wants to talk to you."

I took the phone and held it against my ear.

"Please, Paul, don't be mad at me. I know it seems heartless, but surely you understand."

"Why would I understand?" I asked. "Also, whatever happened to making sure that child murderers paid for their crimes?"

"If you want power in this world, it means getting your hands dirty," Molly said. "You know that. I heard that you got on the candidate list for Court Magician. Congratulations. And how, exactly, did you secure such a sought-after spot? You don't have to tell me, but think about whether we're really so different before you lecture me, hmm?"

I didn't have anything to say in reply to that, so I hung up.

I turned back to Thomas and Verity, who were looking at me guiltily.

"You knew, didn't you?" I said to Thomas as I gestured in Verity's direction.

"Yeah," Thomas admitted. "I've known since the gala."

"The null cloak!" Of course! That would have allowed Thomas to see Verity's true identity.

"Boys, we've got bigger issues to deal with," Verity said. It was so odd to hear "Tonya" speaking with a New York accent.

"Do we?" I said. "Do we really?" God, she could have at least said something before we slept together.

"Yes, we do," Verity said, voice harsh. "Thanks to your two-faced ex-girlfriend, my whole lifework's been pretty much ruined."

"You want to talk about two-faced—"

"Look, I'm sorry about how this all played out, okay?" Verity said. "I swear I wasn't trying to make you look like an idiot . . . I just . . ."

"Paul, Verity's right," Thomas said, much to my amazement. "We've got bigger fish to fry. Molly said we don't have to worry about Oberon or his dad or anyone else coming after us, as long as you drop this whole investigation into the magic experiments during the war."

"Well, fuck that," Verity said. "I'm not going to stop going after Myers now, not when I'm so close to exposing him for the bastard that he really is."

"Look, I am with you," Thomas said. "I would love nothing more than to tell the public everything you've found out, to show people the rotten core of this country. But the people in charge? They will kill us before we ever get a chance to do so. It doesn't matter that they aren't the people who committed this evil. Power protects power. The only thing keeping us alive right now is Molly's sweet spot for Paul, but don't think she won't turn him in, let alone you or me, if push comes to shove."

Verity buried her face in her hands and looked back up.

"I will never drop this," she said.

"You fucking will," Thomas said. "Paul and I aren't dying because of some pointless crusade."

"It's not pointless!"

"Please, both of you, be quiet," I said, feeling a migraine coming on. They both were silent, both of them waiting for me to talk, to share with them some brilliant plan I had. But I had no plan. All I had wanted was quiet.

Verity turned to leave. "I'm on the first train out of here tomorrow morning. You can come or stay here; I don't care," she said, tromping up the stairs.

Thomas shook his head.

"This is ridiculous," he said. "Even if it's true that we don't have to worry about Myers—which is a big *if*—what about Hollister? You know it's only a matter of time before he comes looking for us here, right?"

I did know. We'd already been in Liverpool for a few weeks, and our presence here put Dad in danger.

"Hollister won't stop," Thomas said. He looked so young. Seeing him there in the dining room reminded me of the day I had found seven-year-old Thomas hiding out in our favourite bombed-out building, making a shiv from a shard of glass, wrapping gauze around one end to serve as a handle. We had been best mates for about a year. He had always been a wild child, a biter, always ready to jump on another kid and scratch and hit. Yet even all that roughhousing hadn't accounted for the multiple bruises he'd sported day in and day out.

When I'd asked him who the shiv was for he'd just shrugged. "Whoever it needs be."

There was a reason why Thomas had always been so wary to go home each night. His home hadn't been a safe place, his family not a loving one. But he didn't have to be part of that family. He could be part of mine.

"Paul?" Thomas said, bringing me back to the present. I looked at him, comparing twenty-one-year-old Thomas to the seven-year-old boy from my memory. His skin was now free of cuts or bumps; his clothes fit him. But even though that day I had managed to convince him to put down the shiv and come home with me, I thought that nasty piece of glass was still buried deep in his heart, flesh and blood coagulating around it to the point where pulling out the weapon would hurt him as much as the person he used it on.

"I've been thinking about it these past few weeks," Thomas said, speaking carefully. "We can make magic clothes that conceal one's identity—"

"But we can't wear it all the time, and other people could create something specifically for finding us," I said. "And, well, null coats exist."

Thomas nodded shallowly.

"Yeah, I don't think we can magic our way out of this," Thomas said. "As long as Hollister is after you, the whole world is in danger."

I wanted to protest that Thomas was being hyperbolic, but then I imagined what might happen if Hollister *did* catch up with us. What if he had me skin him so that he could do something truly catastrophic, like summon a worldwide flood? I imagined the rivers of London all rising at once and washing the city out.

"Which is why we need to get far, far away," Thomas continued. "Hollister obviously has connections in this country, but the world is a big place. It should be easy for us to disappear."

I shook my head. "You know I could never live a life like that."

"You could *try*," Thomas said. "It might be our only option left."

"I just . . ."

"And if you won't do it to save your own skin, if you won't do it to save the world, then do it for me."

"What do you mean?" I asked.

"I've never felt British," Thomas said. "You complain that people treat you badly because you're the son of a shopkeeper? I'm the child of a whore and some darky sailor and no one in this country will ever let me forget it. There is so much world out there, Paul. For as long as I can remember I've wanted to go out and meet it, but I haven't, because even more than that I wanted to stay with you."

"Thomas . . ."

Thomas looked away, took a deep breath. "And if you aren't going to leave . . . I will. I'm going to leave the UK and never come back, and you can come with me or rot here—I don't care which."

That was twice in two minutes that someone had said that to me.

"You'd leave me?" I felt like I'd been punched in the gut, all the air driven out of my lungs. Thomas looked up, his eyes wide.

"I know this is all my fault," I said. "I know we can't hide out here forever. But Thomas, I'm dead if you go. You're right, of course you're right, and I'll go with you, just . . . don't leave me behind, please."

Thomas startled, a panicked look on his face, his earlier resolve gone.

"Hey, relax," he said. "Look, I didn't mean it. I was just leaning on you to get you to agree. I'm sorry."

He offered me his handkerchief and I realized I'd been crying.

"Thanks," I muttered.

"Here's an idea," Thomas said. "How about tomorrow we get on a boat. Just . . . go somewhere. We'll treat it like a holiday. Just something to give us some time and space to think. Anywhere you want. Name a place; there's no wrong answer."

I thought it over. "Well, I've always wanted to go to America."

Thomas's face fell. I guess there was a wrong answer after all.

"America, yeah, sure," he said, working himself up to it. "Travel around a bit first, maybe. Let Verity do whatever it is she wants to do here."

"No!" I said, all idle thoughts of California gone. "I can't leave her. Look, we'll go back to London, find some other way to expose Dr Myers, then leave the country, all right?"

Thomas looked doubtful. "Maybe it's not enough."

"Maybe what's not enough?"

"Getting out of the country," Thomas said. "Hollister's still going to come after us."

"We'll use our magic to stay hidden." Already I had questions about this plan—would Verity come with us?—but I didn't want to voice them while Thomas was looking so troubled.

"Yes," Thomas said. "Yes, we'll just have to trust that everything will work out."

～

The sense of relief and respite was gone as soon as I woke up. Even though I had gone to bed at around seven I had managed to sleep for a good ten hours. I went downstairs to find my dad sitting at the kitchen table with Verity. They had been talking quietly but fell perfectly silent when I came in.

"Thomas sleeping in again?" I said as I carefully sat down. My ribs were feeling better but I didn't want to chance anything. "Lazy arse."

My dad shook his head. "Thomas went back to London last night."

CHAPTER 28

I told my dad that it would be a good idea if he got out of town for a couple of days. He seemed frightened but not surprised. He helped Verity and me pack and drove us to the train station. It was awkward, both of us with frayed nerves and unsure of what to say or even how to hug goodbye.

Dad bought us a pair of second-class train tickets and when we first got on we had the compartment to ourselves. As the train pulled away the towering red silhouette of the Liverpool cathedral peaked and fell back behind the horizon.

"Paul, talk to me," Verity said. Although she was sitting across from me in the compartment, her voice was hardly louder than the rattle of the train. I thought of the portrait of Abigail Myers. Why had I never put together how much "Tonya" resembled her? Was that another aspect of the spell, that it kept such thoughts at a distance?

"Why didn't you just tell me who you were the day we met? Hell, I met you multiple times, so you had multiple chances."

"I hardly knew you back then," Verity said. "I didn't know whether I could trust you or not. I wanted an escape hatch in case things went south. And things went south. You nearly died, because of me, Paul. As Verity Turnboldt, I nearly got you killed, but as Tonya Gower, well, everything was so much simpler."

I didn't reply. Some raindrops hit the window, silently at first, then with a steady *plink!* sound as more and more of them hit the metal of the train. I stood to shut the upper window of the train compartment and winced when I felt a pain in my side—the doctor had said it would take six weeks for it to heal and I was only in week three. Verity jumped to her feet, slender arms reaching up and shutting the window with a satisfying clatter. Before she could sit back down I took her hand, my other hand still on my stinging side.

"I don't blame you for this," I said. "I don't blame you for anything. But I just don't understand why you felt the need to hide all this from me." I had thought we had forged something real together, but had I been the only one who felt that way? "Why couldn't you have just told me who you are?"

Verity shrugged, her hand loose in mine. "I don't really like who I am."

We both sat down on my side of the compartment.

"Why did Thomas hurry back to London last night?" Verity asked. "I tried to ask him about it when he left, but he wouldn't tell me."

"He's going back to kill Hector Hollister."

"Who?"

By the time the train had pulled into Chester I had told Verity my history with Hector Hollister, mainly being that he was a military man who was intent on having me perform some terrible magic for him.

"And you think he wants these powers so he can start another world war?" Verity said, a flicker of fear in her eyes.

"Something like that, yeah."

"In that case . . . why exactly are we rushing back to London?"

"What do you mean?"

Verity looked away. "Maybe Dawes has the right idea. This Hollister guy sounds like a dangerous character, and if your life is in danger as long as he's alive—"

"Verity, I'm not going to let my little brother become a murderer!" I said. "Besides, Thomas may be tough, but Hollister has some pretty dangerous people on his side. I have to find Thom and stop him before he gets hurt."

Verity looked like she was about to argue when a couple of old ladies came into our compartment, asking in one breath whether they could sit there and parking their arses down before we could answer. They were soon chatting away to each other, making it near impossible for Verity and me to keep talking about murder and the like.

Verity squeezed my arm. "Let me help you with this," she said. "I'll help you save Thom, and then we'll be even."

"Verity, I told you, you don't have to worry about us being even all the time." But I hadn't said that to Verity. I had said that to Tonya, just before we had made love. What had been a happy, healing memory was now tinged with sadness.

We were both quiet for a minute before she spoke.

"It's important to me," she said. "Let me help you with this."

Even though it was only midmorning I was tired. Dread of what awaited us in London was at war with the physical aches wearing me down.

"All right," I said.

~

When we arrived in London, I was at a bit of a loss. Thomas had left the night before, giving him a good twelve hours to do whatever it was he planned to do. And knowing Thomas, he would have had a plan. Since we didn't, Verity bought us a pasty to share and we sat on a bench outside Marylebone train station.

"What now?" Verity asked.

"Well, it would be easy for Thomas to find out where Hollister lived," I said. Would Thomas have gone straight to Hollister's home?

Jesus, I hoped not. The man had a wife and kids. Even Thomas at his most ruthless wouldn't kill a man in front of his family or leave the body in the living room for them to find when they came downstairs. "But I can't imagine him killing someone in their home like that."

"Yeah, it would be better to lure him somewhere more convenient," Verity said. "Dawes probably called up Hollister and arranged for them to meet on some flimsy pretext. And Hollister would agree, especially if Thomas made it sound like you might be there too. And when they met, Thomas would kill him. But where in the city would Thomas have asked him to go?"

It was a good question. Thomas wouldn't have wanted to commit the murder in any place that might be tied to either him or me, so our flat was out (besides, Mrs Dylag had probably already rented our room out to someone else, considering that we had skipped out on the rent and disappeared off the face of the earth). Thinking about our flat did remind me of something—when Thomas and I had fled town we hadn't been able to pack all our things. Maybe Thomas had dropped by Frobisher Road to pick something up. At the very least it would allow me to get some of my old belongings. With no better idea of what to do, we took a cab to the Ladder.

"Mr Gallagher!" Mrs Dylag exclaimed when I burst through the door. Her surprise only grew when she saw my face. I probably looked like a crazy man.

"Is Thomas here? Has he come through?" I asked.

"No! I haven't seen Mr Dawes since the two of you left without a word last month," Mrs Dylag said, some of her surprise ebbing away to make room for anger. "Just so you know, I waited for a good two weeks before I rented your room out! That's more than you had any right to expect, just skipping out like that—Mr Gallagher!" She yelled the last bit at me as I strode up the stairs, Verity right on my heels. I opened the door to our attic. The flat had been totally rearranged. Our mattresses, dress form, and workstation were gone, replaced by a double bed and a cradle. A young woman was in a chair by the window, nursing her baby, while a toddler ran around the room with a toy horse, gibbering in Polish. All three—toddler, mum, baby—stopped what they were doing to stare at us, a pair of intruders.

"Sorry," I muttered and shut the door. Verity gave my arm a comforting squeeze.

Mrs Dylag was waiting for us on the landing, a box in her arms.

"Here are your things," she said, shoving the box into my chest. "I sold that mannequin and your beds to get back some of the rent you owed me."

"Right." Honestly, the state of our flat and our stuff were the furthest thing from my mind. When I looked down into the box I was, however, relieved to see a glimpse of my stained-glass coat. Not only was it worth more than anything else I owned, but just the sight of it gave me comfort.

Verity guided me out of the flat. We stood on the pavement, silent, me gripping the box. I was surrounded by familiar sights—the long rows of identical houses, the schoolyard across the street, the mouth of the Passage—but already none of it felt like home anymore.

Verity suggested we go to the *New Rev* offices—we'd be able to make some calls, figure out our next move. I agreed, so we took the tube down to the Strand.

We stepped into the office and the same moustachioed man I'd met before came over.

"Verity! Where the dickens have you been?" he asked, staring at her with astonishment and me with suspicion.

"Working hard on a story, of course," Verity said. "It's going to be even bigger than my maid exposé, just you watch, Albert."

"Speaking of the maid exposé, the deadline for that was . . . several weeks ago . . ."

"Like I said, I've been working on something big. Now, we need to make some calls."

Albert huffed but let us work from a desk that had a couple of phones. Verity scrounged us up a couple of sandwiches. It seemed silly to think about food when for all I knew Thomas was already dead, but I made myself eat one.

I started calling everyone I knew. Andrew, Gabs, Lamb. It was slow going as they all had so many questions for me, wanting to know why I had left town so suddenly, but eventually they all said that they hadn't heard from Thomas. Then I called Ralph.

"Thom? Yeah, he came by my house last night at midnight," Ralph said, and I could hear the worry in his voice. "He asked if any of my old army mates might have a gun for sale."

"Jesus Christ!" I said. "And what did you say?"

"Well, I wasn't crazy about the whole thing, but I knew that if I told him no, he'd probably just go to even less savoury types and buy a pistol off them. So I told him we'd go in the morning. I wanted to call you and see what was going on, but I had no idea where you were and Thomas wasn't saying anything."

"Did you two go and get a gun?" I asked.

"Yeah. I was hoping he might change his mind after sleeping on it, but he was as determined as ever. So we went to my old mate Derek's place so Thomas could buy Derek's da's old service pistol."

"Jesus Christ, Ralph, why would you think that was a good idea?"

"I thought I'd just go along with it and get Thomas to tell me what was up, but the little bastard wouldn't give me anything. But I'm thinking you might know what's going on more than I do, eh, Paul?" Ralph said accusingly.

I ignored the question. "Is Thomas still with you?"

"No. He took off around three this afternoon." It was already six o'clock. "He said he had an appointment with a man in Dalston. That was about the only thing he let slip."

"Dalston," I repeated. The Nail's sign flashed in my head.

"If you need any help, you'll call me, right?" Ralph said, using the same stern voice I imagined he used when his three-year-old was acting up.

"Don't worry, Ralph, everything's going to be all right," I said before hanging up the phone. Verity had been making calls of her own, but she stopped middial to look at me.

"You got something?" she said. Around us the bustle of the newsroom continued on, reporters hustling to and fro around the honeycomb of desks, totally oblivious to what Verity and I were up to.

"What if Thomas tried to lure Hollister to a place the captain was familiar with?" I said. "A place he'd been before, somewhere he'd consider his own turf and maybe let his guard down." I picked up the phone and waited for it to connect to an operator. Once it did I asked to be put through to the Nail in Dalston.

Someone picked up on the first ring.

"Hello?" Even from one word I recognized Wheelock's voice.

"Hi," I said. "It's me."

"Hey, Captain!" Wheelock yelled, projecting his voice away from the receiver. There was a muffled sound and a second later a new voice came over the line.

"Jim!" Hollister said, sounding genuinely happy. "I knew you'd find us. Everyone else was fretting like a bunch of old women, but I knew you'd find a way to get in touch."

"I . . ." I hadn't thought through what I had planned to say to Hollister. I was partly surprised that the man was still alive, but as that news sank in it was like a hand was squeezing my heart. "Is Thomas with you?"

"Oh, yes, young Mr Dawes. He's here," Hollister said flippantly.

"I'd like to speak to him," I said.

"Of course." This time the pause was longer. In the background I could hear a few different voices: Hollister, Wheelock, Thom. They were arguing, a disagreement that came to an end with some kind of scuffle, followed by Hollister speaking in a low tone. And then Thomas himself was on the line.

"Paul," he said. "I'm sorry."

I knew that gruff tone—it was the one Thomas used when he was trying to hide that he was in pain.

"No, I'm sorry," I said.

"Look, don't—" The rest of Thomas's words were lost to me as Hollister took the phone and started talking.

"As you can hear, your friend is still amongst the living," Hollister said. "Which is pretty generous of me, considering that earlier today he tried to take my life."

I was quiet on the line, words themselves becoming a foreign concept to my brain.

"Wouldn't you say that's very generous, Jim?" Hollister prodded.

"Yes," I replied.

"I'd like to continue being generous," Hollister said. "But I'm going to need a little something from you in return. I simply want to put our theories into practice. I don't think I'm asking much."

"Not asking much?" I said. "You're asking me to come skin a man."

"From the moment I met you, I just got this feeling that you were the one who was going to help me," Hollister said. "And I was right! It's not just about the innate magic. We have the same worldview, the same conception of the cosmos, and magic is all about belief and intent, is it not? We were meant to meet. A happy accident."

"I do not have the same worldview as you," I said.

Hollister didn't seem to hear me. "How soon can you come here?"

"I . . . I don't know. I'm not in the city," I lied. I needed time to come up with some kind of a plan.

"I see," Hollister said. "Well, the sooner the better, old boy." He lowered his voice. "I'll try to watch over Mr Dawes the best I can, but unfortunately he has enemies of his own here and his pugnacious nature is not helping to keep the peace." Hollister sighed. "Don't dawdle. In the state he's in, I don't think your friend's going to make it to midnight."

To my surprise the phone went dead. I had expected Hollister to draw it out, to cajole and beg me to come. Instead he had sounded assured and certain. He knew he had me.

I hung up the phone and looked to Verity.

"So do you know where Dawes is?" she said. "Why don't we just call the cops and—"

"No," I said. "If the cops were to barge in, Hollister would kill Thomas just to spite me."

"But then . . . what are you going to do?" she asked.

"I . . ." Why was I hesitating? If I didn't go, Thomas was going to die. But to give Hollister so much power . . . how could I truly justify it if I plunged the whole world into terror and flame? Was this what my dream had warned me against? "I have to go. I owe my life to Thomas twenty times over; I can't leave him there. But . . ." I swallowed. "But if Hollister's going to start a third world war, I can't let him do that. I have to know exactly what he wants before I can decide whether it's worth Thomas's life."

Verity thought it over.

"Well, I've got no clue myself," she said. "But you and I know a lady who *supposedly* knows everything."

~

Verity and I arrived at the McDougal residence at seven o'clock.

"You don't have to come with me," I said to her. She was wearing the jersey dress from the gala. It was so odd looking at her and being able to see beyond the magic of the dress. Now I could spot the little things that had made Tonya and Verity different from each other. For one, Verity always wore heels and generally wore her hair down, while Tonya had always worn flats and kept her hair back in a ponytail or with a headband. I wondered why Verity bothered with such details: the magic of her dress would have been sufficient for keeping her true identity under wraps. Maybe these extra flourishes were for her own sake, a way to remember who she was supposed to be in any given moment.

I myself was wearing my stained-glass coat. It was not as though I expected to need its magical properties, but wearing it made me feel like I had just a little bit of control over the situation.

"I also have some things that I need to settle with Lady Fife," Verity said, in a tone that warned me against asking what exactly those things were. "Plus, you might need backup."

I could see there was no arguing with her. "Well, regardless, I'm happy you're here." I gave her a smile and then turned to the front door. I was about to knock when a manservant opened the door.

"Mr Gallagher, Ms Turnboldt," he said smoothly. "Lady Fife is expecting you."

"Show-off," I muttered very quietly under my breath as he led us into the sitting room.

Lady Fife was sitting on the settee, wearing a draped gown of powder blue. It put everything in the room into a soft focus.

"Please, sit," she said. She turned to the manservant. "Peter, please bring in some light refreshments for our guests."

We sat down and a few seconds later Peter reappeared, carrying a tray of cheese and crackers with some grapes on the side. He made a second trip to bring in a jug of pink lemonade. I made myself put some brie on a cracker and eat it. My hands were shaking from a mix of hunger and stress.

"I feel somewhat foolish making my case to you, Lady Fife," I said, "since I can only assume that, since you knew we were coming, you also know why we are here."

"Many unhappy turns are born out of assumptions," Lady Fife said. "Please, tell me what troubles you, Mr Gallagher."

I felt like a mouse walking towards a coiled cat. "I need a favour from you, Lady Fife. In order to make a decision about something, I need to see the possible outcomes."

"You wish to employ the services of a foreseer?" she said in mock horror. "Why, that is highly illegal, Mr Gallagher. Not to mention condemned in the Holy Bible."

"Well, perhaps *condemned* is a harsh word," I hedged. "Really, it merely warns against it. But I am in quite a bind, Lady Fife, and I must be sure of things before I make a move. If you aid me in this, you would forever have my friendship."

Lady Fife regarded me for a moment. "And? What else?"

"I would likewise be in your debt."

"Hmmm," Lady Fife said.

"Of course, if you need something more tangible, name your price," I said, thinking perhaps there was some problem in her life that could be solved by a skilled cloth mage. Granted, she had Andrew for that, but perhaps there was a problem she wasn't willing to share with him.

"I see," Lady Fife said. "Well, there *is* something I'd like. Something tangible, as you would say. Give it to me and I'll do the divination."

"Yes, all right," I said, sitting on the edge of my seat. "What is it?"

"I'd like my stone horse. Not a replacement or facsimile. That exact one, as it was before you broke it into a dozen pieces."

I was disappointed, partly because what she was asking for was something that no cloth magician could provide, and also because I hadn't expected Lady Fife to be so petty.

"My husband and I bought it thirty years ago, on a trip to Greece," she said, gaze sliding off us to take in imaginary azure waters. "We were in a marketplace and some shopkeeper told Geoff that this statue dated back to the time of Alexander the Great, that it once graced the hanging gardens of Babylon. I myself spotted it as a modern-day forgery, but when I tried to tell Geoff he shushed me. Shushed me and went back to talking with the shopkeeper. He had never done that to me before.

Ever. Not in front of his family, not in front of his friends. But to make himself look better to this Greek huckster he shushed me. He bought the damn horse for a king's ransom. I was furious with him. It's a wonder I didn't smash the damn thing myself when we got back to the hotel, but that would have deprived me of pointing out the obvious signs of a fake to him, how there were seams on it showing that it came from a modern mould, how the horse's saddle was from two hundred years ago, not two thousand."

I felt my heart sinking deeper down with each word. Lady Fife was not going to help me.

"Geoff was properly ashamed after that, not for being taken in but for treating me so poorly. He promised that for the rest of his life he would always listen to me. And he did. Granted, the rest of his life was only ten years on from that point, but still, they were a good ten years."

I didn't know what to say, how to apologize in a way that would convey my remorse but also convince Lady Fife to help me. It seemed like an impossible conundrum until Verity spoke up.

"Oh, for fuck's sake," Verity said. "He didn't break your stupid horse. I did."

She stood and shrugged off her dress. I stared in surprise as the fabric slid down her body and puddled in a heap on the floor. She stood there, as unabashed as a Renaissance statue, wearing nothing but her bra and knickers. I averted my eyes for modesty's sake.

"Tonya?" Lady Fife said, shock clear on her face. And then, just as quickly as someone switching masks, she started laughing, clapping her hands as her laughter died down into a chuckle.

"Oh, pardon me," she said, wiping at the corners of her eyes. "It's just that I am so rarely taken by surprise. How wonderful, Ms Turnboldt! I must commend you for your journalist fervour. All of London's high society has been gripped by your writing, wondering how you knew all the secrets and gossip of the upper class. All this time it's because you were acting as a spy in my very own home. This explains so much, including why you were such a dreadful maid."

"You're taking this well." Verity gathered up her dress and pulled it back on.

Lady Fife shrugged. "Well, I can't say I'm happy to have such a security breach in my own home. But I knew who you were when I took you in, so I really have no one to blame but myself."

"You knew I was Verity Turnboldt?"

"No. But I knew you were Tatianna Myers."

Next to me I could feel Verity tense up.

Lady Fife smiled in a way that was probably supposed to be comforting. "Don't worry, I don't think anyone else knows. I merely found out because I always do a background check on my employees. Not a traditional checking of references, but something less . . . material. When I divined your identity it told me you were the Myers baby. I was friends with your mother, and for her sake I will overlook the fact that you played the betrayer and used me to gather material for your tawdry little rag." Lady Fife took a deep breath. "Dear child, I've been waiting to meet you since before you were born."

"What?" Verity's voice wavered.

"Yes." Lady Fife cocked her head to the side. "So do you go by Tonya? Or Tatianna?"

Her hands balled into fists. "Verity's fine."

"All right. Verity. Your mother came to me a few times for consultation purposes. I'm sure you already know the sad story of your family's history, yes? The desperate need for a male heir?"

Verity's grim silence spoke for her.

Lady Fife sighed. "A dreadful business. Anyway, she came to me three times, always in the early days of her pregnancy, and asked me to divine whether the being inside her was male or female. Each time the same answer: it was a girl. The first two times she thanked me and left. After that there was no word of a pregnancy. No official announcement, no birth months later. It was as though she went straight from my house to the abortionist." I flinched at that, which made Lady Fife raise an eyebrow my way. "Which I have no qualm with, except I suspected it was her money-grubbing husband who brought her to the doctor's doorstep each time. Or who knows, maybe he performed the procedure himself. His only concern was making sure she was able to get pregnant again as soon as possible."

I shifted in my seat, causing Lady Fife to turn towards me, a sharpness in her gaze.

"I'm sorry, Mr Gallagher. Is our women's talk upsetting you?"

"No," I said, because it seemed the polite thing to say.

Lady Fife smiled. "Good man." She looked back to Verity. "The third time she came to visit me, she was different. After I told her to expect another girl she sat quietly for a long time. Finally she told me that it didn't matter, that she was keeping this one. A few days later I heard through the grapevine that Mrs Myers was finally pregnant. Would you like some water? Lemonade?"

Verity shook her head. Lady Fife refilled her glass.

"So you can imagine my surprise a few months later when the baby was a male child. I am not claiming I am *always* right, but I would never make a mistake over a simple divination like this. Compound that with the fact that Mrs Myers had died in childbirth: it seemed very suspicious indeed."

"Why didn't you tell anybody?" Verity whispered so harshly it might have been a hiss.

"Tell whom what?" Lady Fife asked. She swished her water around in her glass as if it were wine. "Perhaps, being an American, you've forgotten this, but divination is illegal in Britain. No matter how much of a public secret my talents are, I still can't rush into a police station like some kind of crazed Cassandra, screaming and shouting about all the injustices being inflicted on this little island. Besides, as personally devastating as this might all be to you, it's almost benign compared to some of the things I hear."

"My mother *died*," Verity said. "For all I know, my father himself made sure of it."

"Yes. I certainly wouldn't be surprised if that were the case," Lady Fife said. "And after your mother passed away, your father discarded you in some fashion."

"He swapped me out with a servant's male baby."

Lady Fife nodded. "I thought as much. I did try to look into it on my own initiative, but my talents lie in discerning the future, not sussing out past actions. I was able to confirm that the Myers child was alive, and so I could only comfort myself with that." Lady Fife smiled. "I also suspected you would show yourself someday and be the source of your father's downfall. How's that going?"

"I'm working on it," Verity said.

"Good girl." Lady Fife toasted Verity but set her glass down on the table without drinking from it. Her gaze roamed over Verity's face, perhaps remembering all the times her mother had sat across from her in this very room. "I'm so glad our paths crossed. I've always wanted to meet you. I don't know the particulars of your circumstances, child, but I can't imagine it's been a gilded existence. I can only imagine how it felt when you learned about what your father did—"

"I've always known," Verity said. "From my earliest memory I've always known that my father didn't want me."

Lady Fife considered this.

"But your mother did," Lady Fife said. "That's what I've been waiting to tell you for the last twenty-three-odd years. Your mother knew she was pregnant with a girl and went against your father to bring you into this world, at the cost of her own life. Your existence wasn't chance or an accident or a mistake that needed to be covered over. It was the wilful act on the part of someone who loved you. You were wanted."

Verity was silent at that. She didn't even seem to be breathing.

"Excuse me," she said in the smallest voice I had ever heard from her. She stood and slipped out of the living room.

Lady Fife and I were left staring at each other.

"Perhaps you should go comfort her? She seemed quite distraught," Lady Fife said.

"I would, Lady Fife, but you and I still have business of our own to attend to."

She sighed. "Mr Gallagher, when people seek my aid they usually offer either a large monetary contribution to the charity of my choosing or a favour in whatever their sphere of influence. You have no money or influence and therefore have nothing to offer me."

"As I mentioned before, there is something I can offer you that no one else can offer," I said. "My friendship."

Lady Fife laughed. "And what makes you think that is so appealing?"

"I suggest we make a gift to each other," I said. "A gift we can give and offer to no one else. I propose we always be honest with each other, Lady Fife. You are a lady entrusted with others' secrets, alone without any peers. I can only imagine how isolating that must be, to be the one who knows everything. You don't have to pretend with me, Lady Fife. You can act as you wish around me, say what you wish, and not fear losing face."

Lady Fife cocked her head to the side and looked at me appraisingly. "If we are to be on such close terms, perhaps you should call me Andrea, hmm?"

I sensed a trap. "I would never be so presumptuous, Lady Fife."

Lady Fife seemed to finally take pity on me. "All right, Paul. What exactly is troubling you?"

I told her a very bare-bones account of how I had gotten involved with Captain Hollister and how he now had my best friend and was probably going to kill him unless I showed myself. Lady Fife listened intently, perfectly quiet as I rushed through my summary.

"So what I need to know is what exactly will happen if I go and save Thomas," I finished.

Lady Fife looked thoughtful.

"Well, this is a bit more difficult than discerning an unborn child's sex, but I should be able to catch a glimpse of something," she said.

"All right, fine." I expected her to pull out a tarot deck or pendulum or some other illegal divination paraphernalia. Instead she held out her hand, palm up.

"Let me see your hand."

"Really?" Even amongst foreseers palm reading was seen as a charlatan's trick. Like any branch of magic, you needed both a magic item and human contact for it to work. Palms were a part of the human body and therefore couldn't operate as an object of divination.

Nonetheless I put my hand in hers.

With lightning reflexes she turned my hand over and gripped it tightly. With her free hand she picked up a cheese knife and made a small cut on my arm. I screamed at the pain and felt panic clouding the edges of my mind, a case of fits coming upon me. It only became worse when I tried to pull my hand away. Lady Fife merely tightened her grip and shook my arm so the blood dripped onto the white tablecloth. She then released my hand.

I drew my arm in towards my chest, still feeling shocked, but now that the danger had passed my panic was retreating. I had the presence of mind to make sure I didn't get any blood on my coat. The cut hurt but it was actually quite shallow but long, just a line of red on the side of my arm.

"What in Jesus's name was that for?" I asked. Lady Fife ignored me, her gaze intent on the drops of blood. Curiosity overcame me and I shuffled forwards so I was sitting on the edge of my seat.

"You can see the future in that?" I asked, amazed. "But there's no magic item. And the circuit—" I stopped and realized my mistake. There was a circuit: Lady Fife had her hands splayed out on either side of the bloodstain, creating a loop between herself and the table. But surely it was just an ordinary table, an ordinary tablecloth? How could one create magic from ordinary household items—

"Oh, Jesus, Mary, and Joseph," I said. "You're a Superconductor!"

Lady Fife arched an eyebrow. "You said we could be honest with each other, yes?" She looked back down at the bloodstain. "With most visitors I make a show of using cards or tea leaves, but the truth is I can suss out the future in everything."

I wondered if it was a slip of the tongue, if she'd meant to say *anything*, but perhaps not. I couldn't believe I was in the same room as a Superconductor. To have everything you touched become magic . . . it sounded like a heady and frightening existence.

"Is Andrew . . . ?"

"No. My dear son has a high amount of magical energy running through his bones, but he isn't at the same level as me." Lady Fife was frowning at the bloodstain. The frown stayed even when she pulled away. She leaned back, her gaze upwards, deep in troubled thought.

"Lady Fife?" I said. "Did you see the future?"

"Yes."

"Well? What is it?"

She sighed. "I shouldn't have agreed to do this reading for you. We are both sentimental fools, Mr Gallagher."

"Lady Fife?" I said, not sure what the hell she was going on about.

"I can't tell you," she said.

"What? But you just said you saw it—"

"Yes, and if I tell you, you'll do it."

"What?" I feared I was starting to sound like a parrot, capable of croaking out a select few words. "Lady Fife, I don't understand."

"What Hollister wants *cannot* come to pass," Lady Fife said, "yet if I tell you what he wants, you'll do it anyway." She rubbed her temples. "You're just going to do it anyway."

A great, frustrated anger welled up within me. "Lady Fife, please, I know you've never liked me, but please don't—"

Lady Fife cut in: "You think I'm doing this because I don't like you?"

I shrugged and let out an exasperated laugh. "Well, it's true, isn't it?"

"Have I ever given you cause to think that?" She sounded curious, as if seeking feedback on how to better mask her disdain in the future.

"No. You have always been perfectly polite to me," I admitted. "But go on; tell me I'm wrong."

She said nothing.

"I've thought about this," I said. "There's no reason you shouldn't like me. Everyone likes me."

"Because of the spell?"

My head shot up at that. Lady Fife nodded.

"Oh yes, I've noticed that you have innate magic. I'm guessing the break is the one in your left finger? Really, Mr Gallagher, you are lucky that we live in a time and place where people are largely ignorant of that field. So I take it the spell helps you win people over."

I didn't say anything but I didn't need to. I realized I was holding my left hand in my right, a dead giveaway. I made myself unclench my hands. "Do you yourself have some immunity to innate magic, Lady Fife?"

"No, Paul, but what I do have is a wealth of life experience, a deep knowledge of magic, and duties and concerns that by far outrank a child's need to be loved," Lady Fife said, each word hitting home like a judge's gavel. "I am not just a sparrow in the field, Mr Gallagher, living day to day. I can see past the edge of my own life. The things I do are not for my own betterment or even for this country's betterment but *for the continued existence of this world*. Any other concern is trivial, any cost a bargain, to achieve that."

"Please, Lady Fife," I said. "If I don't do this, they will kill Thomas. No matter how you feel about me, please don't condemn him to death."

"Ah yes, Mr Dawes," Lady Fife said thoughtfully. "He's always struck me as an intelligent young man. If he knew my reasons, he would understand."

I stood. The anger within me was close to bubbling over, but I knew it would be pointless to lash out at Lady Fife. "Then I suppose we have nothing more to discuss."

"Paul." Lady Fife hesitated. "Please don't go to Hollister. I know it will be hard—"

"Andrea," I said, her name sounding odd on my lips. "You said you'd pay any price for the sake of the world. I don't believe you. If it were Andrew, you would go."

She looked at me, her expression unreadable.

I left the sitting room. As I walked towards the front door I collided with a figure racing down the stairs.

The two of us stumbled back. The other man was the first to recover, grabbing me by the elbow to keep me from falling. The impact of the collision had sent me wheezing, pain lacing its way through my muscles as my ribs ached.

"Oh, Gally, I'm so sorry!" It was Andrew.

"Speak of the devil," I muttered.

"What was that?"

"Nothing." I had to take a seat on the stairs. Andrew stood in front of me, fidgeting as I struggled to get my breath back.

"Can I get you a glass of water?" he said.

"No," I managed to grit out.

"Some milk? A shot of sherry? A glass of wine? Or perhaps some leftovers from supper—"

"Really, Andrew, I'm fine." I looked up into his face and saw only worry.

"Oh my God, Gally! I have been so worried about you! And you hardly told me anything when you called earlier!"

"Like I said, I'm fine." Actually, my ribs were hurting something awful, but Andrew beamed at me, taking my word as the gospel truth.

"Oh, I'm so glad!"

For the first time I felt like I understood why Lady Fife coddled her son so much. How precious his obliviousness must seem when you saw nothing but bad omens and dire forecasts at every turn.

"I heard some people downstairs and was wondering who'd be visiting at such a late hour," Andrew said. "I was quite surprised to see it was you!"

"I needed to speak to your mother about something," I said. "I didn't mean to be a bother."

"Ha! I'd only be mad if you slipped away without saying hello to me," Andrew said. He frowned. "Ralph said you left town because of money problems. Is that true? You know you can always come to me if you're in a pickle, old chap."

"Yes, I know," I said. I felt strong enough to stand. "Thank you, really."

"Of course," Andrew said. "You're my dearest friend. I'd do anything for you."

"I know, Andrew." I thought of Thomas, hurt and alone amongst enemies. "I know you would."

I managed to get out the front door, Andrew following after me the whole time, gabbing away. It was a relief when I managed to close the door after me and stand alone on the quiet of the front step.

A second later I realized the night wasn't completely silent: down by the front gate stood Verity, crying softly.

"Verity." I went over and slowly took her into my arms. She grabbed onto me tightly, crying into my shoulder. After a minute she sniffed and wiped at her eyes.

"Oh, I'm sorry. It's just been quite a night."

"Yeah," I said. "It must have been a shock to hear all that stuff about your mum. I—"

"No, no, it's okay; I'll deal with it," Verity said. "My mom—both of them—are dead, but Dawes is still alive. Did Lady Fife tell you what you needed to know?"

"No," I said forlornly. "She just said it was something pretty bad. She said she wouldn't tell me, said I'd give in and do it anyway."

Verity nodded. She didn't seem surprised.

"Look," she said, drawing a breath to strengthen her voice. "I know how close you and Dawes are, but you should think carefully about going to rescue him. The last thing he'd want is for you both to die."

"Verity, he's—" *My dearest friend.* Why did that phrase ring a bell? Andrew had said it to me just a minute ago in the foyer, but it was something even deeper than that. It had been in the letter, the one to Hollister from his MP buddy.

I started laughing.

"Paul?" Verity said, giving me a very incredulous look.

"Oh, sorry," I said. "It's just I figured out what Hollister wants."

"And are you going to give it to him?" Verity asked slowly.

"Yes."

Verity took a deep breath. "Paul, I don't know if there's any weight to Lady Fife's doom-and-gloom talk, but I still think going to Hollister is the wrong move. Once he gets what he wants from you, he'll kill you."

"Well, I'm not going to do *nothing*," I said. "What do you suggest instead?"

Verity started talking about gathering up other mage friends, attacking en masse, maybe even getting the authorities involved. She kept talking even after I walked away, leaving a gilded afterimage of myself to stand there and nod as she spoke.

CHAPTER 29

"You sure about this?" the cab driver asked. The car was idling at the kerb just outside the Nail. It had been several weeks since Thomas and I had been there, but the place looked as though the brawl had just happened the other night. A large piece of plywood covered the broken window we had escaped out of, and the pub itself was dark and silent.

"It's all right," I said. "I'm meeting some friends."

The driver glanced over his shoulder, taking in my stained-glass coat, which seemed to glow in the darkness of the cab. He shook his head but held out his Book so I could pay him.

With no better idea of what to do, I went up and knocked loudly on the front door.

It opened a few seconds later. Welcome Wheelock stood there, scowling at me.

"Get in here," he said, grabbing my shoulder and pulling me inside. The pub was dark, only a bit of light from the streetlamps bleeding in past the boarded-up windows. It looked as though the inside had been cleaned up but not repaired. And yet, even though it didn't seem to be a functional bar anymore, the smell of cheap whiskey and stale beer still radiated up from the worn carpet.

"I can't believe you actually came." Wheelock sounded angry. "You stupid wanker."

"What? Of course I—"

"Jim!"

Hollister emerged from the stairs in the back and hurried over, as bright and cheerful as an Easter Sunday. He grabbed my hand and elbow, giving me his trademark strong handshake. "I'm so glad to see you."

"I wish I could say the same, Captain," I responded.

Hollister looked slightly abashed, like a child caught sneaking a biscuit before supper. "Yes, I am also sorry that it has come to this. Believe me, I never wanted anyone to get hurt."

"Hurt?" My voice shook a little bit. "You've hurt Thomas?"

"Not myself, personally. I would never resort to such brutal methods. But Mr Wheelock's associate seems to have a personal hatred for Mr Dawes, and Mr Dawes has not been helping the situation. He's been far from cooperative." Hollister managed to meet my eye. "Don't worry, he's a tough little blighter. I'm sure that given a few days' rest he'll be back on his feet."

My legs wobbled. As if sensing weakness, the pain in my ribs magnified, squeezing my torso.

"Jim?" Hollister grabbed my shoulder to steady me.

"Let's just go." My only thought was getting to wherever Thomas was and making sure my little brother was all right.

We walked over to the stairs leading down to the basement. Hollister gestured for me to go first, partly out of politeness and partly I suspected so I wouldn't make a run for it. I felt my heart sink with each step.

When I opened the storeroom door the light from the bare bulb jabbed into my brain. It took me a second to blink away the blue dots clouding my vision. The table that had been in here before had been removed, as had the metal shelves lining the walls. But Thomas was there. He sat against the far wall, slumped down on the floor. He looked like he was melting, beads of blood sliding down his face like condensation running down a glass of water.

"Thomas!" I stepped into the room but was stopped by a large hand. The hand belonged to Morris. The man had undergone quite a change since I had last seen him. His jaws were wired shut, bared teeth kept between steel wire like a caged animal. As if to make up for his immobilized mouth his eyes were frantic. It was a startling contrast to the chilled, heavy-lidded gaze he had worn before. He no longer wore a magic jacket but rather a plain white shirt.

"Let him be, Morris," Wheelock said. As soon as Morris took his hand off me I was on the other side of the room, kneeling down next to Thomas.

"Hey, Thom? Mate, speak to me."

Thomas gave a little cough before glaring at me accusingly. His left eye was already swollen shut and the right eye was bloodshot.

"Damn it, Paul. Why'd you come?"

I took out a handkerchief and carefully wiped at the blood on his face.

"Hey," I said, with a weak smile. "Remember when Johnny Flynt and his mates beat us up when we were kids?"

Thomas snorted. "Yeah, you said something stupid and ticked them off."

"Do you remember what it was?"

Thomas shook his head.

"Johnny and the rest of them were mad because we weren't hanging out with them anymore," I said. "When they asked us to be a part of the gang again, I told them that it was pointless, that you were the only one worth talking to."

Thomas laughed weakly. "And look where it got me."

I patted his shoulder. "Yeah." There was an ugly gash on his head, which seemed to be the source of the blood sliding down his face. There were cuts on his clothes and blood soaking through his shirt, but they all seemed to be shallow slashes rather than stab wounds. He was wearing his dimensional cloak, the darkness of the fabric absorbing the blood into its inky blackness.

I stood and turned. Hollister was standing in the doorway, Morris to his left and Wheelock on his right.

"You didn't have to hurt him," I said.

Hollister stepped forwards, hands out in a conciliatory gesture. "I'm sorry, Jim. But I promise that no more harm will come to him."

Morris grunted, a frustrated sound sealed in behind his wired-up teeth.

"Well, Jim," Hollister said with a slight smile, "this is your show. Just tell us what you need."

"Right," I said, trying to sound as sure of myself as Hollister did. "Well, first of all I want some bandages for Thomas. I'm not having my best mate bleed out while we do this."

"All right," Hollister said. "What else?"

"Drugs." Going down the stairs to the storeroom had made my ribs scream in pain and they hadn't stopped since. "Morphine would be good. We'll need a chair for you to sit on. I'll need a couple of knives, I guess." The words came out of my mouth easily but they reminded me that I was in fact going to slice the skin off the man in front of me. Bile rose up my throat.

"Jim, relax," Hollister said. He looked at me with that steady gaze that, in other situations, would make me fancy him anew. "I know this is frightening, but we're achieving something great here. When things get too hard, just cling to that."

"Where am I supposed to get all that at this hour?" Wheelock complained, but he didn't seem altogether upset. It seemed to me like he somewhat relished any excuse not to go ahead with things.

"Wheelock," Hollister said. "Just do it."

Wheelock huffed but disappeared up the stairs along with Morris. Morris was back in a few minutes, lugging down a chair. He had a bottle of rum with him, and I watched with a kind of morbid fascination as he tilted his head back and poured the rum into his mouth, the liquid leaking through his braces like water going down a sewer drain. When he caught sight of me watching him he handed the bottle over. I took a swig of it to be polite.

Wheelock arrived back much more quickly than I expected. He lobbed a roll of bandages over to Thom, who quickly began bandaging up the worst of his cuts. To me he gave a small paper bag of pills. I took one and chased it down with rum.

Hollister was watching me, a pitying expression on his face. "Since when do you do drugs?"

I shook my head. "I'm not a junkie. I just need it for the pain." I put my hand against the wall to help myself stand up. "I got mixed up in some bad business, but it's nothing you need to worry about."

Hollister had a melancholy expression on his face. "You could have come to me for help, Jim. I would have helped you."

At what price? But I didn't say so aloud as the answer was all around us.

"Here are your stupid knives," Wheelock said petulantly, handing me a collection of three small, thin daggers.

"Had to get old man Peterson out of bed and open up his curio shop for that, I did," Wheelock said.

Each knife had a sharp tip but dull sides.

"I can't use these," I said. "These are for stabbing, not skinning."

Morris made a grunting noise, and as we all watched he mimed sharpening the knives on a whetstone.

"Oh, that's right! We have a block upstairs for sharpening the blades!" Wheelock said, happy for a moment to have figured out Morris's pantomime. His smile soon turned to a scowl. "Give me those." He grabbed the daggers from my hands and disappeared upstairs.

Hollister and I looked at each other. We were both imagining the same thing: those small blades slowly peeling away Hollister's skin.

"You don't have to do this," I said. "You really don't."

Hollister sighed. "It's not what you think. I'm not seeking power for its own sake or even the righteous destruction of my enemies. It's just something that mortal men can't achieve. That's why I need the power of God."

"I know," I replied. "I know you want to bring back James Godfrey." Hollister's shocked face told me I was right, so I pressed on. "You wish to be like Christ and wake Lazarus from the dead, right? A Judgement Day for one. I get it; I truly do. I know what it's like to lose someone you love. When my mother died, I felt like I'd been hollowed out. Like nothing would ever be good again."

"It is devastating to lose a parent," Hollister said, having recovered from his surprise. "But Jim, while I don't mean to belittle your pain, it is natural for a parent to die before their child. But James was a young man in the prime of his life, with so much still to give."

I knew I sounded like a broken record but I'd be remiss if I didn't give Hollister a last chance to back down. "I don't know what will happen. It might not even work. It will hurt. It will hurt a lot. You could die."

"He's right, Captain." I hadn't expected help from Wheelock but there he was, walking into the room with the sharpened daggers, an uncharacteristically subservient expression on his face. "Sir, I don't know what makes this Godfrey bloke so great, but he's not worth—"

"Don't question me, Wheelock," Hollister said. Wheelock stepped back, a soldier falling in line. Hollister looked back to me, his gaze changing from that of a superior to that of an equal.

I was only half listening. I had taken the daggers from Wheelock. I held one in my right hand and eyed the finger joints on the left index finger. How hard would it be to sever that main joint? If I cut out my innate magic, then I'd be no use to Hollister, unable to be part of his dammed plan.

"You won't do it," Hollister said. I met his eyes. "Even if you were able to sever your finger before someone stopped you, then what? You think the two of you could take on the three of us? And even so, you wouldn't do it. Because if you did it wrong, you'd die, and if you did it correctly, you'd lose the one thing that makes you special."

The knife was shaking in my hand but the rest of me was frozen still.

"Do you know why the innate magic took with you and not with those poor wretches from St Rita's?" Hollister said. "We had thought children would be a good candidate for innate magic because they were pure, without sin. But that doesn't matter. What matters with magic is will and intention. It didn't work for them because they weren't willing. You were." He smiled. "I am."

I thought this was a simplification. The innate magic had taken hold within me because the person who had done the ritual—that mysterious Irish woman—was in fact a practitioner of innate magic. Godfrey, Hollister, and Myers had just been torturing children to see what would happen.

"Excuse me," Thomas said as though he were a schoolboy. He even raised his hand. "But if this whole spell only works with willing participants, then it's not going to come off. Paul isn't doing this willingly. He's doing it because you're making him do it."

Hollister had a hearty chuckle at that. "You're not a Christian man, are you, Mr Dawes?"

Thomas scowled. "What's that got to do with anything?"

"It means there's always a choice," I said tiredly. "There's no such thing as extenuating circumstances in God's book."

Thomas scowled. "Then your God is a prick."

I thought Hollister might take issue with that but to my surprise he laughed. He saw me staring at him and stopped.

"Are you ready now, Jim?"

I took a deep breath.

"Take off your shirt," I said to Hollister. He did so, shrugging off his coat so it landed on the floor and unbuttoning the white shirt he was wearing underneath. For a man in his late forties he had stayed in shape. Most of the time it would seem perverse to ogle a man before I maimed him, but the drugs had done a good job at squashing down my inhibitions.

"Take a seat," I said, removing my stained-glass coat so it would not get blood on it. Hollister sat down in the wooden chair, his arms resting on the chair's arms. I turned to Wheelock and Morris. "I need your belts."

"What? Why?"

Though Wheelock was the one asking the question I turned to address Hollister. "To tie you down."

Hollister laughed. "I'm not going to fight you, Jim. I want this."

"Yeah, yeah, the spirit is willing, I know," I said, "but the body has its own set of instincts, and when it feels it is in danger it will try and defend itself no matter how much you'd will it otherwise."

Hollister considered this and nodded. Morris and Wheelock undid their belts and handed them over to me. I went over to Hollister and knelt down, strapping down first his left and then his right forearm. He watched me with a slight air of amusement.

That done, I stood. I closed my eyes. It felt like there was some force just waiting for me to open a door, which even in my hazy state I found ridiculous: I hadn't even truly started the ritual yet.

But the moment had come. I picked up a knife. On the ivory handle someone had carved a little design: a family of elephants—mama, papa, and baby—walking along.

Hollister's eyes showed a flicker of doubt but he soon steadied himself.

"Just remember, you must keep your will and intention steady as I do this, or it will all be for nothing," I told him. He nodded.

"And don't even think of trying anything funny, love," Wheelock said from behind me. I turned. He had puffed himself up but his words had the frantic edge of someone desperately trying to stall for time. He pulled a small revolver out from his jacket pocket. "If that antique even goes near the captain's throat, I'll plug you faster than you can whistle."

"Could you put that away?" I said. "This is a delicate ritual and I can't do it under the gun."

"Wheelock, it's all right. Stand down," Hollister said. Wheelock frowned but stepped back, tucking the gun out of sight.

I took a deep breath and turned to face Hollister. Thomas was behind him just off to the left, still slumped against the wall. Our eyes met and he gave me a grim nod.

I stuck the knife into Hollister's right arm and slid it downwards.

I felt nauseous from the first bead of blood. It was such an odd sensation, the wetness of the blood mixed with the resistance of the muscle. My right hand was holding Hollister's forearm, and it felt so normal to feel another human being's skin against mine, but already the river of blood was sliding over it all, turning the familiar into something horrible. Hollister hissed a little as the knife cut through him but he didn't start screaming until I started peeling the skin away from muscle. True to his word though he stayed in his seat, feet planted firmly against the ground.

I was the one who cracked first.

"I can't," I said, stepping away, letting the knife clatter onto the floor. Hollister sat in the chair, breathing deeply. Down his arm was a series of red strips, glistening in the dim light of the room. I found I could only breathe in quick little panicked huffs with no release. "I'm sorry, I can't do this. I just can't."

Wheelock sighed. "Well, can't say I'm surprised. I never knew magic was such a gory business! I guess we should just call this whole thing off before we go too far—"

"Morris," Hollister said. "Take out one of Dawes's eyes."

"What?" I said. Morris strode forwards and picked the knife off the floor. Thomas tried to get to his feet but Morris was on him quickly, hand grasping his hair and pulling his head back.

"Stop!" I yelled, then turned back to Hollister. "I'm sorry! I didn't mean it! Let's keep going. I won't stop again, I swear to Jesus!"

Morris stilled, I think only because I sounded so unhinged. If Morris had in fact plunged that knife into Thomas's eye I am sure I would have just fallen apart.

"Morris, wait," Hollister said. Morris stayed still but continued to stare at Thomas's eyes, as if they were just a couple of grapes he wanted to pluck.

"You won't stop again?" Hollister said, managing to sound patronizing even as sweat rolled down his pale face.

"I won't," I said. "I swear I will see this through to the end."

Hollister chuckled at that. "Break a bone, make a promise . . ." He glanced over his shoulder. "Morris, let him go."

Morris gave Thomas a little shake but dropped him to the floor. Thomas glared at him as he walked away but kept his mouth shut.

With a shaking hand I grabbed one of the other knives. For a moment I met Wheelock's eye and we shared a look of mutual disbelief that we were in this situation.

I started cutting again, trying to keep my hand steady as I slid the blade down Hollister's arm again and again. There were odd sights emerging around us, swirls in the wall that curled through the air. What fascinated me though was how the straight lines of Hollister's muscles curled under my gaze, breaking away from Hollister's earthly form to connect with the curlicues circling us. With a flick of the knife I was able to connect them, meld the joint between body and spirit.

The air around us began to glow. I had removed all the skin from Hollister's right forearm. It hit the ground with a soft slap, blood pooling around my feet. So much blood already.

"Keep going," Hollister said between gritted teeth.

"Captain!" Wheelock said. "Captain, stop!"

But I was already slicing the skin off his other forearm. It was a messy, shoddy job as I'd never even skinned an animal, let alone a human being. At one point I had to dash into an unoccupied corner and throw up, but I just as quickly ran back to Hollister, terrified that if I stalled for too long he'd sic Morris upon Thom. Under the pulse of Hollister's bloody limbs I could see light shining through the sinews of his muscle, like when you covered the front end of a torch with your hand and the thin bits of your fingers glowed.

The glow in the air was growing stronger too, like a cloud being lit from within by lightning. The light from the bare bulb was swallowed up, its harsh brightness stifled by the purple-and-blue ambient lighting from the cloud that had engulfed us. I couldn't see the walls anymore. Hollister was thrashing in his seat, legs kicking out even as he made himself stay seated, trying to keep his arms as still as possible for my knife.

I couldn't stop. It was working; we were actually summoning some new magic into the world, as sure and as tangible as the blood running over my fingers. The ground was shaking under our feet and the mist was consolidating, the colours banding together to become soft hands that traced my cheek before disappearing back into the darkness. Hollister, both his arms degloved of skin, was glowing. A bare bulb.

"It's not enough!" Hollister yelled, and I had never heard so much despair and frustration in a human voice. He locked eyes with me. "Do my face."

An odd request—there were better places to carve off skin—but in the moment it felt right. There was more power to it.

"No!" Wheelock yelled. "Captain, you've already lost too much blood. Stop! Stop!"

Thomas stood up suddenly. I followed his terrified gaze to see that Wheelock had pulled out his gun. My first thought was that he was going to shoot Hollister and end the nightmare around us. Then I realized that he was aiming at *me*.

Before Wheelock could squeeze the trigger Hollister raised his hand, snapping the large leather belt that had been holding him down.

With his right hand he made a fist. Wheelock made a choking sound and then his body crumpled in on itself, as if being sucked into some internal black hole. His ribs speared inwards and his arm and leg joints cracked as his limbs were sucked in. He dropped to the floor, a dead, crumpled heap.

Morris was left standing there, even more wide eyed and crazed looking than before. His eyes slid down to Wheelock's body and then over to the revolver.

He had only just squatted down to pick it up when Thomas flew past me. Thom grabbed Morris's head and smashed it into the wall, skull giving way like a ripe gourd.

The sound and sight made bile rise up in me, which might sound weird since at that moment I was already surrounded by gore of my own making. I dry heaved as my stomach had nothing left to give.

"Paul, please," Hollister said. His face was pale: he *had* lost lots of blood.

I paused. I could have perhaps waited a few moments, let Hollister pass out and even die from blood loss. But even if he wasn't at full God level yet, he still had lots of power. If I showed hesitancy, what would stop him from killing Thomas or me the same way he had killed Wheelock?

Behind me I heard Thomas kicking Morris's prone body. I brought the knife up to Hollister's face.

If skinning an arm was tough, it was nothing compared to the intricacies of the face. There was an extra challenge in it for Hollister as well as he now had to keep his head still as I brought the knife around his eyes, under his cheeks, through his nose. His body shook as he went into shock and his teeth were clenched as hard as a cadaver's, but he kept his head as straight as if he were a lowly private on parade.

I stepped back and tried to recognize the man in front of me. The only bits of pale, beige flesh on his face were his eyelids. They were closed, two little patches of pink in a sea of red.

His chest barely rose and even the flow of blood had slowed to a stop. The exposed muscles on his arms and face glistened.

I looked over to see that the glowing purple-and-blue light had condensed down into one humanlike figure.

Then the bulb overhead shattered and we were plunged into darkness.

CHAPTER 30

There was blood on my cheek. Once I got past that sensation I could feel the grit of the concrete floor. I was lying in the storeroom. My whole left side was pressed into the puddle of blood that had pooled around Hollister's chair.

There was the merest apparition of grey daylight coming into the room through the open doorway.

"Thomas?"

I heard a groan from the other side of the room and a shambling sound. Through the dim light I saw Thomas get to his feet.

"What happened? Did we pass out?" I asked.

"I think so," Thomas replied. Now that my eyes were adjusting to the gloom I could make out Morris's body at Thom's feet. Lying near the doorway was Wheelock's twisted corpse. Thomas was searching for something, and after pushing aside Morris's body he found it. It was the gun that Wheelock had been waving around earlier. Thomas lifted up a wing of his capelet and deposited it inside his little interdimensional storage room.

I knew if I turned my head I would see Hollister's mangled, grisly remains. On some level I felt like I needed to look at them, to acknowledge what I had done. Yet now that it was morning and I felt sickeningly sober I couldn't bring myself to do it.

A hand reached up and grabbed my arm.

"Waaaaahh!" I jumped so high it was a miracle I didn't hit my head on the ceiling. As soon as my feet hit the ground I was by Thomas's side, my back pressed into the wall. I fully expected to see Hector Hollister staring back at me.

Hector's corpse was there but it stayed where it was, slumped in its chair. There was another man standing next to him, his arm still reaching out towards me. He was naked, and as he stepped forwards into the ash-grey light he held up both hands as if to further assure us of his defencelessness. He was in his late thirties, straw-coloured hair. Round face, blue eyes. Totally unremarkable in every way.

"Hello," he said, speaking slowly. "Perhaps you could explain what exactly is going on here?"

It took a moment but I recognized his plain face from the newspaper clippings.

"You're James Godfrey," I said, dumbfounded.

"That's right." Godfrey glanced around the room. Every time his eyes fell upon a body I could see cracks growing in his calm facade.

"Hey! Hey! Look at me," I said, snapping my fingers. James Godfrey's head snapped towards the sound. "It's all right. You're safe here. I know this all looks rather bad, but . . ." I faltered there, as it was hard to be reassuring in a room of mangled corpses. "Let's get you some clothes, eh?" In the corner was Hollister's shirt. He had bothered to fold it neatly before setting it down, a military man to the end. I eagerly grabbed it and held it out to Godfrey. "Here, you can wear this, it's clean." Only it wasn't anymore—my bloody hands had left red smears all over it. I looked into Godfrey's wide eyes and saw myself reflected there, covered in blood. And yet he still took the shirt from me, tugging it on like an automaton.

"My name is Paul Gallagher," I said, holding out my hand. Godfrey shook it, and as he did something strange happened—I didn't feel my innate magic spark within me. When I met someone new there was a moment when it felt like our souls connected, just a brief flash, but I didn't feel that with Godfrey. Was the magic within me broken? Or was there something broken within Godfrey? Had I not brought back a human being at all but some biological facsimile?

"Oh, Jesus," I said. Godfrey stared at me, eyes worried and questioning. Regardless of what was going on, I needed to take charge of the situation. "How about we go upstairs? I can wash up and we can get you a glass of water or something?"

Godfrey nodded mutely and we both turned towards the stairwell.

"Wait," Thomas said, holding out a hand to stop Godfrey before turning to me. "We need to talk."

"We can't leave him down here." I wouldn't have left my worst enemy to stew amidst that slaughter. Thomas huffed but let us go upstairs. Once we were in the bar Thomas pushed Godfrey towards the gents' toilets.

"Go wash your face, and don't come out until we say so," he said. We watched as Godfrey walked towards the toilets. He gazed at everything as though he were a *National Geographic* reporter exploring a strange new world.

The Nail wasn't any prettier in the daytime. Sunlight managed to work its way in around the boards in the windows, glinting off the dust motes in the air.

Thomas grabbed a stool that had been knocked over and sat it upright by the bar. He patted the seat. I sat down while he went around behind the bar.

"Ah," he said after a few seconds of searching. He put a bottle of some amber liquid on the counter and filled two shot glasses. "Drink this."

We clinked glasses out of habit and downed the alcohol. It was watered-down scotch but it still hit hard. Once I swallowed it I found my stomach was a little more settled and my head a mite clearer.

"It worked, it actually worked, it brought a man back to life," I rambled on. For a moment I felt utter elation. Then came the crushing despair. "Oh my God, it worked. I brought a man back to life. I'm going to hell."

"What?" Thomas said. "How do you figure that?"

"I've perverted God's will," I said. "I not only desecrated his creation by killing a man and slicing up his body, I went against natural law and brought a dead man back to life. I'm going to hell."

I set my head in my hands, my body rocking back and forth so hard the stool legs clattered against the floor.

"Hey, we can't lose our heads right now," Thomas said sharply.

"Forget about our heads; I am talking about my everlasting *soul*, Thomas," I said. "I can't undo this. I'm fucked."

"Paul. Paul. Listen to me. Heaven and hell? They're not real. God isn't real. When you die, regardless of any of the shit you've done, you're gonna get the same big blank nothing as everyone else."

"Even if I could believe that I just can't believe that," I rambled. No matter how long the rest of my life was, at the end of it would be an eternity separated from all forms of love. Even the concept of love and happiness would become foreign to me, pain and torment the only constants.

Thomas let out an exasperated sigh. "Fine, then we'll get you to a priest and you can confess and say ten Hail Marys or whatever. Then everything will be square, right?"

I laughed. "It's not that easy."

"Why the fuck not?!" Thomas said. "What good is all that pomp if it doesn't work? You're sorry, right?"

"It's not enough to be sorry," I said. "You have to *repent*."

"What's the difference?"

I hesitated even though the explanation was right on the tip of my tongue. You could be sorry about something but still justify it to yourself, but an attitude like that would never merit God's forgiveness. To repent meant that, if in the same situation, you would not sin in such a way again. Even as I felt like throwing up the scotch in my belly, even as I regretted going against God, I couldn't say that I truly repented my actions. I'd done what I'd done because it was the only way I could have saved Thomas, and no matter what else had happened I didn't regret that. My love for my friend barred me from God's love.

"It's fine, it's all fine," I said shakily, sitting up straight, palms pressed into the sticky bar top. "I'll be fine; just give me a moment."

Thomas poured me another shot. As I drank it I could see the wheels turning in his head, his lips pressed tightly into a frown.

"We need to think very carefully about what we do next," he said. "We can't ever let anyone know about this." Thomas looked down at the backs of my bloody hands. "It would be very bad for you."

"What? Why?" My head was still a little fuzzy and my stomach churning, my mind still trying to fathom eternity.

"It could ruin your life," Thomas said.

I laughed. What did it matter? What did *this life* matter?

Thomas had been pouring himself a shot, but at my laugh he brought the bottle down hard on the bar. "Paul, listen to me," he said sharply. "Do you want to spend the rest of your days skinning people alive?"

I stared at him, horror filling me. Apparently there were still some things in this world that could scare me. Hollister was hardly the only person with seemingly impossible desires and a strong will. Hell, that was the very definition of a fanatic. If people learned about deep magic, they'd be liable to try it themselves or start beating down my door every day to have me do it. And if I told them no, they'd do exactly what Hollister had done and try to use the people I loved as leverage.

"Oh, Jesus," I said. "No, I don't want that."

"Then no one can ever know about this," Thomas said. With his left hand he rubbed his forehead. "Fucking hell, Paul, if you were so interested in innate magic, why did you have to go to Hollister? Why didn't you just come to me?"

"I didn't think I could," I said. "I was scared that if I told you, I'd lose you." I started rolling the shot glass between my palms. "I never told you this but I have a spell on me—"

"That makes you worthless in a fight? Yeah, I've noticed," Thomas said.

My head shot up. "You knew?"

Thomas shrugged. "Not the particulars, but I could guess the broad strokes from living with you for the last fifteen-some years. Do you think I'm an idiot?"

"No," I said, smiling. "I think you're the smartest man I know." I looked away. "But there's another part of the spell. It makes people want to be friends with me. It made you want to be friends with me."

I couldn't bring myself to meet Thomas's eyes.

"Paul," Thomas said. With a slow turn I faced him. I had never seen him so at a loss for words, so frustrated for not knowing the right thing to say. Finally he let out a sigh. "You really are the biggest idiot I know."

I laughed at that. "What are we going to do about Godfrey? He's literally living proof of what happened here."

Thomas sighed and rubbed his forehead. "I don't even know where to start with him."

"I mean, what can he tell the world? How can he explain himself just showing up in the middle of London, alive and unaged? People will ask questions. Is it even legal for him to exist? I mean, what we did was illegal, but . . ."

"Whatever he tells people, he needs to keep our names out of it," Thomas said.

I nodded. "He's probably got some questions of his own. We'll tell him the truth. That his friend loved him so dearly he sacrificed himself to bring him back to life."

Thomas sighed. "It's the best we got, I guess." He offered the bottle to me but I waved him off. Thomas looked as though he was considering taking another swig but he put the bottle away.

"You know, I . . . ," he started to say, then stopped. "I . . ."

I couldn't just let the silence hang there. "If you had managed to kill Hollister," I said, "were you really planning to leave England afterwards?"

Thomas gave me a wry smile, half apology and half admonishment for being so naive.

"But you're not going to go now, right?" I said.

Thomas didn't answer my question, just tugged at the edges of his magic cape. "Go wash the blood off you; then we'll talk to Lazarus."

"Wow, a biblical reference from you?"

Thomas shrugged as he came out from behind the bar. "Even I know that one."

~

Godfrey and I sat on a couple of stools while Thomas went back to standing behind the bar. Godfrey was still wearing nothing but Hollister's bloody shirt, but he seemed much more composed than he had been.

"Gentlemen," Godfrey said, a bemused look on his face. "I fear I am very much in the dark here. I must rely on you to fill me in on what exactly is going on."

I waited to see if Thomas would take point on this but he stayed silent.

"What's the last thing you remember?" I asked.

Godfrey frowned. "I was meeting someone at St Paul's Cathedral. I was waiting there for them when the air raid siren went off. I tried to get to a shelter but . . . ." He stopped, blinked. "I remember the roof coming down and that's it."

The bombing of St Paul's. An event that Lady Fife could not prevent, but one she could use to her advantage.

"Were you supposed to be meeting Lady Fife?" I asked.

Godfrey blinked in surprise. "Yes, actually." He frowned, deep in thought. I imagined we were coming to the same conclusion: Lady Fife had set him up to die. But why? Had she seen a future where he gained power and wanted to prevent it? I remembered Thomas's harsh words regarding Godfrey's death: *It's a good thing he straight up died.* Maybe Lady Fife had felt the same way.

Godfrey smiled. "Did you lads rescue me from the wreckage?"

"No," Thomas said shortly.

Godfrey sighed. "I didn't think so." He was quiet for a long time. "What year is it?"

"Nineteen fifty-four," I said.

Godfrey let out a shocked laugh at that, clapping his hand over his mouth in surprise. We waited in silence for him to recover.

"Who is prime minister?"

"Uh, Brentwood."

"Brentwood," Godfrey said with a roll of his eyes. "That spineless backbencher is in power?" Suddenly fear filled his eyes. "Did we win the war?"

"Yes," I replied hastily. Godfrey relaxed.

"What about—"

"Can I ask you something?" I cut in. "Do you . . . do you remember anything from your time . . . not on earth?" It seemed rude to call him *dead.* "Do you remember anything of heaven? Or, um . . ."

Godfrey cocked his head. "No."

"I know this is a lot to take in," I said.

"How did I even . . . how did I get here?" Godfrey said, seemingly speaking to the dust motes floating around.

"You remember your friend Hector Hollister?"

"Of course."

"Well, after your death he dived deep into the world of arcane magics in search of a way to bring you back."

"To bring me back?" Godfrey said, a puzzled smile on his face.

"That's right." *Because he loved you.* "Because he thought you were worth more to the world than he was."

Godfrey's smile took on a rueful quality. "Poor Holly. It's rather ironic. When we were both alive, we worked so hard to find some new form of magic, a new weapon to ensure Mother Britain's glorious future. I had thought that together we could grasp it, but it seems it was my death that gave him the motivation he really needed."

"A new weapon?" I said. I thought of Verity's list of murdered children. Those three names were probably only the tip of the iceberg. "You mutilated children for *that*?"

Godfrey looked at us with surprise and then a slanted smile. "Oh, yes, that was a nasty business, I admit." He gestured towards the stairwell. "But it seems like you lads are no strangers to magic and the cost it takes."

"And to what end?" I said. "Why would you do something so horrible, and do it to bring something awful into the world?"

"Well," Godfrey said slowly, "I suppose more than anything, we just wanted to do it before someone else did."

Thomas clucked his tongue. "All right, we've heard enough."

I was turning towards Thomas when there was a loud bang and Godfrey was knocked off his stool. My head whipped back to Godfrey to see him lying on the floor, more blood already seeping into Hollister's shirt. I looked back to Thomas. He was standing there with a gun in hand. He stepped out from behind the bar and stood over Godfrey. He fired one more bullet, this time into Godfrey's head.

"Jesus Christ!" I said, leaping off the stool so fast my legs got tangled up. I hit the ground hard, the dead man right in front of me. I could see inside Godfrey's head, bits of blood and bone and brain, and now the iron scent of blood was so strong that it mixed with the rotten smell of the carpet under my cheek.

Thomas reached into the dark lining of his cape and deposited the gun back into some other dimension. He reached down to grab my

Shannon Fay

arm and help me up, but I yanked it away from him and scuttled back until I hit the bar.

"What in Jesus's name have you done?" I said.

"I did what I had to do," Thomas said. "If he lived, word would get out about our part in this and we'd be arrested for having practised illegal magic. They'd hang us. Or worse, we'd be made to do it over and over again."

"You just killed a man in cold blood!" I said, anger rising. "A totally defenceless man!"

"A man who died over a decade ago already," Thomas said. "And who was a right bastard the first time around at that. You know what he's done."

"He should have been made to answer for his crimes in a court of law! Everyone involved in the whole God-awful affair could have been brought down with his testimony. Verity could write an exposé, and—"

"And once again, our names would get dragged into it," Thomas said. "Nothing would have happened, Paul. Nothing would have changed."

"That's just cynicism."

"Doesn't make it less true," Thomas said. "This was the only way to keep us safe." He glared at me. "And don't look at me like that. You killed a man just a couple of hours ago."

"I did that to save us!" I said.

"Right, same." Thomas turned away. When he spoke he sounded tired. "I think I've gone above and beyond the call of duty here. Next time you get into this deep of a mess, you're on your own, Gallagher."

"What?" I got to my feet.

"I'm leaving. I'm getting out of this country," Thomas said. "There are a lot of places on this planet that don't shit on cloth magic, places with more sun than rain, places where I might actually be happy. All my life I've put off looking for them, but that stops now."

"But . . . what about me?" I asked. "You'd leave me behind?"

Thomas shrugged. "Would you come with me?"

I didn't say anything, didn't move. My best friend was making me choose between him and, well, everything.

Thomas shrugged. "I didn't think so." He then grabbed the edges of the dimensional cape and twirled it around him, his body disappearing as it hit the dark fabric until both man and cape had blinked out of existence. I was left alone in the bar with only the dead for company.

CHAPTER 31

Even in a neighbourhood as rough as Dalston it wasn't a good idea to linger after gunshots had been fired. The cops were probably already on their way. I had managed to wash off most of the blood I'd been covered in, and my stained-glass coat covered my bloody clothes. I flagged down a taxi and went to Ralph's place. Once there I took a long shower. Ralph even lent me new clothes, though I had to roll up the sleeves of the shirt and trouser legs several times. Poor long-suffering Ralph obviously wanted to know what was going on, but all I could tell him was that both Thomas and I were all right.

"Then where *is* Thomas?" Ralph asked.

I didn't have an answer for that. Already I missed him. I had always thought that Thomas would leave if he found out that magic had been responsible for us becoming friends. But he had always known and been my friend anyway. I'd lost him thanks to my own stupid actions. In a way it was grimly comforting, to know that I had the agency to fuck up one of the most important relationships in my life. My innate magic drew people to me, but whether they stuck around or not depended on me.

With that in mind, I went down to the *New Rev*.

"Verity?" I said, pounding on the door. When no one answered I tried a different tactic: "Tonya?" A businessman walking by on the street gave me an odd look. I waited until he was gone before pounding on the door again. "Verity?"

The door jerked open so suddenly I fell forwards half a step. Verity stood there, wearing a simple green dress with a Peter Pan collar, her hair pulled back in a ponytail. I thought she had never looked so beautiful.

"Paul!" A carousel of emotions ran across her face, anger followed by relief followed by anger. "You've got some nerve, chum, showing up after walking off on me."

"I know," I said. "I'm sorry."

She crossed her arms. "Since you survived, I'm guessing you're here to tell me that there was nothing to worry about, that you had everything under control."

"No," I said. "I wanted to say sorry and also thank you. Thank you for your help last night. And for taking care of me back in Liverpool."

Her face softened at that. "Well, you helped me plenty, so . . ."

"There you go again, pinning it all on us being even." I thought back to that night in Liverpool, the night we'd made love, and for the first time I was truly able to consolidate Tonya and Verity into one entity. "You'll exhaust yourself if you try and keep score like that all your life. When we do something for each other, I want it to be because we're in this together, not because there's some invisible ledger we're checking in on."

She thought it over.

"Come in; we need to talk," she said. We went up the stairs to the floor where the *New Rev* office was already in the middle of a busy news day. Some of Verity's colleagues looked up from their work to send questioning glances our way, but I followed Verity's lead and ignored them. We ducked into a small meeting room. Verity closed the door and stood there, her back to me. I leaned against the table in the middle of the room.

"Verity?" I asked when she stayed silent.

"I really was scared you were dead," she said quietly. "When I realized I was talking to an apparition, it hit me that I'd never see you again."

I went to stand by her.

"I'm here," I said, putting a hand on her shoulder. She turned to face me.

"What happened?"

I told her in broad strokes, leaving out the gory details. I told her how I had brought a man back to life and how Thomas had killed him.

She nodded, closed her eyes.

"Verity, talk to me," I said, scared by her stillness.

"I'm just glad you're all right." She opened her eyes and they were shiny with tears. "I don't know what to do, Paul. About my father. I came here to show everyone what a monster he is, but they already knew. They already knew what he is and they want to *protect* him. What's the point? Why did I even come here?" I felt her shoulders shaking. "I may as well have stayed in New York! I've done nothing! Nothing's changed!"

I took her hands in mine.

"Verity, can you really say that?" I said. "Do you really think *nothing's* changed? I've changed because of you."

She looked at me, eyes searching my face to see if it was just a line.

"I used to be just like your father," I said, "looking for any way to move forwards in the world without considering the cost. Meeting you saved me."

She leaned into me and I pulled her close. We stayed there like that for a few minutes before Verity spoke, her words slightly muffled.

"I'm going back to New York."

I turned my head to look at her. "What? Why?"

"I miss it," she said simply, lifting her head. "It's my home. Plus, in the latest issue of the *New Rev* we're going to reveal that I've been

Innate Magic

working as a maid and it will be this big tell-all. Everyone in this country is going to hate me, aristocrats and servants alike."

"You're a gossip columnist!" I said. "Being hated is a sign of success! Why would you go back to New York where no one hates you? You'll have to start all over again!"

She chuckled at that.

"And, well, we've barely gotten the opportunity to know each other," I said. "So maybe you could stick around and give us a chance to do that?"

Verity looked at me, a hopeful gleam in her brown eyes.

"I want to get to know you better," I said. "Jesus, I'm still not even sure what to call you."

She took a deep breath.

"Can you try calling me Tonya again?" she said.

"Tonya," I said. "Tonya, Tonya, Tonya! What a brave, nervy woman. There's no other girl I want by my side. Please say you'll stay. You and I both know there's so much the two of us could still do in this country. We'll find some other way to take down your dad without becoming him."

It seemed like she was considering it.

"Stay and I'll give you a reason to stay every day," I said.

She brushed some hair out of my eyes. As her hand fell she leaned in for a kiss. I wrapped my arms around her and we stood there, the room silent save for the muffled bustle of the newsroom just beyond the door. I never wanted to break away but I also felt another compulsion building up within me.

"Is there a phone I could use?" I asked.

~

"Hello, Court Magician Redfield?" I said. "It's Paul Gallagher."

"Ah, hello, Paul," Redfield said, cheerfully. "What can I do for you?"

I was in a corner of the *New Rev*, tucked out of the main fray, but I still felt exposed.

"I wanted to be taken off the candidate list for Court Magician," I said.

"I see," Redfield said slowly. "It's not uncommon to get cold feet. But once you're off the list, it's nigh impossible to get back on. Are you sure this is what you want?"

"Yes."

"All right, then. It's perfectly understandable," Redfield said. "The fear of dying is a hard one to ignore."

"I'm not afraid of dying," I replied. "I'm afraid that the ritual will work."

"What?" said Redfield. "Afraid of becoming the next Court Magician?"

"Yes. I've been thinking about what you said, about how you thought you could use the position to change things, to make things better, but you couldn't." There was a good chance that Redfield knew about the experiments Godfrey and Myers had run—even if he hadn't taken part directly, it was hard to believe that he hadn't been consulted. And yet he hadn't put a stop to them. I never wanted to be that man. "I believe you now."

Redfield was quiet for a beat.

"Well, then I'm glad you took my words to heart," Redfield said graciously. "Goodbye, Paul, and good luck."

The line went dead. And just like that, I was without any patrons or prospects. I didn't even know where I'd be laying my head that night. But I felt oddly free—not happy per se, but no longer weighed down with worry.

Tonya came over.

"What was all that about?" she said.

"Nothing, really," I said. "But if you want the whole story, you'll have to treat me to lunch."

"All right," she said, smiling. "Let's go."

CHAPTER 32

Gabs and Kristoff hosted the reception to their wedding on a lake in Switzerland, and when I say *on a lake* I mean literally on a lake. Gabs had instructed the guests months beforehand to create or commission magic clothes that would allow one to walk on water. In the middle of the lake the tables were set upon small floating docks. The guests who had heeded Gabs's instructions could get up and mingle, but the few who had forgone cloth magic were stuck with their tablemates.

Tonya and I were up and about. We were both wearing clothes made from the material Thom and I had used to make Mayhew's coat. A hundred other people were likewise walking around on the lake's surface, chatting and socializing as if they were in a common reception area rather than employing magic in one of the most picturesque vistas I had ever witnessed. Yet even with the mountains towering overhead, I couldn't keep my eyes off the other guests. I had never seen so many different magic outfits all dedicated to the same goal.

It was thrilling to meet so many new people from all around the world. Every time I introduced myself I felt a rush of magic as we shook hands. Whatever had happened back in Dalston, my innate magic was intact. I still didn't know what Godfrey was exactly, but it didn't matter now. The Nail had burned down that day, a clear case of arson according to the papers. Four unidentified bodies had been found inside. I suspected that Thomas was the culprit, that he had returned to the scene after I'd left to burn it down and destroy any evidence of what we'd done. A smart but dangerous move—what if the fire had spread to nearby houses? If I ever saw Thomas again I'd ask him if he'd thought about *that*.

"Paul, move!" Tonya grabbed my elbow and pulled me back. I had been so busy gawking at all the different techniques on display I hadn't seen the rowboat coming through. The boat was laden with dishes that had been cooked in the chalet on the shore. The waiters strained at the oars, struggling to get the food to the table while still hot.

"They're the ones who should have the ability to walk on water, not us," Tonya said as the rowboat passed by. The water rippled in its wake and we bobbed along with it.

"Well, magic cloth doesn't come cheap," I said.

Tonya snorted. "I think Gabs and Kristoff are good for it."

"Good for what?" Gabs said behind us. Tonya and I turned around, careful to keep both our feet on the water. Our outfits allowed us to walk on water, but it only worked if we glided, keeping both feet in contact with the water's surface. Lifting one foot even a little was liable to send us plunging under the surface.

Gabs's dress, as far as I could see, held no such flaw. It was pure white, except for the parts that were festooned with little mirrors. The little mirrors caught the setting sun in a way that made the white of the dress seem even brighter. The skirt was a large hoop skirt with little mirrors hung off the hemline, reflecting the surface of the lake back and forth to eternity.

"Paul! I am so delighted you came all this way!" Gabs said, kissing me on both cheeks.

"Is that some German custom you've picked up?" I asked.

"Hardly! It's just my custom." She turned to Tonya. "Your turn."

"I—what?" But Gabs was already kissing Tonya's left and then right cheek. When she drew back she held Tonya's hands in hers.

"Oh, Verity! I am so glad you could make it. You will write about my wedding for your paper, won't you?"

"I don't think your crowd reads the *New Rev*," Tonya said, blushing somewhat.

"Don't be ridiculous! Months later and everyone in England is *still* talking about your undercover-maid series." Gabs turned to me. "And how your magic allowed Verity to conduct such a sting operation."

It was true. When Verity had published her series about life as a maid for a high-society lady, she'd been very fastidious about name-dropping me as much as possible, noting that she couldn't have gone undercover without the aid of my cloth magic. Since then I had been getting more and more business. Granted, most of the time it was men looking to buy magic disguises so they could meet their mistresses in secret, but some of the work had been interesting.

Something else new was that Tonya and I were living together. We'd pooled our meagre funds to rent a flat on Holloway Road. It was a bit beyond our means but we were both the type who did our best work hungry. It felt quite racy, shacking up with an American girl. But we had a nice domesticity going on, cooking awful meals together and going to the cinema on the rare occasion when we were both free in the evening. Sometimes I'd worry that Tonya regretted staying in the UK, but I was too cowardly to ask her. When she looked at me with one of her dazzling smiles, I felt incredibly happy and just a little bit guilty.

"You must publish a book! I always enjoy reading your writing, Verity," Gabs said.

"Well, thanks," Tonya replied.

Gabs stepped in closer, a conspiratorial grin on her face. "And if you ever want dirt on the European bigwigs, just let me know. I'll give you an in anytime." She added a wink, which actually made Tonya flustered.

"Gabs, can I talk to you alone for a sec?" I said.

"Oh? Sure!" Gabs let go of Tonya's hands.

"I'll be just a moment," I told Tonya.

She waved away my concern. "Don't worry, I'm perfectly capable of mingling solo." She took off towards a crowd admiring the wedding cake on one of the little floating docks.

"I like her," Gabs said, sliding her arm through mine.

"I noticed," I said. "God damn it, Gabs, are you trying to steal my girlfriend?"

"I can't help it! I'm just so happy!" Gabs said, laughing. She looked at me. "Are you happy, Paul?"

It was a surprisingly earnest question, so I took it seriously.

"Yes, I am."

Gabs squeezed my arm. "I wish Thomas was here."

As far as I knew, no one had seen Thomas for months. He had sent Ralph a postcard from Calcutta, but beyond that he had been totally radio silent.

I had told everyone that we had had a falling-out, that we disagreed about our future, that he wanted to travel while I wanted to stay in London. I think everyone knew it was a load of bullshit, or at least not the whole truth. No one pressed me on it, though Gabs looked sorely tempted.

"You know Thomas hates parties." Thinking about Thomas summoned up a displaced feeling, like a phantom itch. I worried about him out there in the world. I at least had Tonya. Who did he have now that we weren't together? I smiled and endeavoured to change the subject. "I think I figured out how your dress works," I said. "The mirrors are key. It's all about the tension between reflections and how—"

Gabs put a finger to my lips. "Paul, it's my wedding day. I *really* don't feel like talking shop." She spotted someone over my shoulder. "Ah, Liebling! Warte, bitte!"

With that she was gone, walking across the lake to talk to a young couple.

A man came to stand next to me.

"For what it's worth, I think you're right about the dress." The newcomer had an upper-middle-class British accent, broad shoulders, and dark hair. He was wearing a tuxedo, and I immediately grasped that it was a disguise, that he was using the ubiquity of the tux's design as a magical element to hide his real identity. He gestured towards Gabs. "The thing about reflections is that they can never meet, so the fact that Gabs has a reflection is what's keeping her this side of the surface. If we were on choppy waves with no reflection, the magic would falter."

"I guess that's why she chose a lake rather than the ocean," I said. "I'm sorry, I don't think we've met. I'm Paul Gallagher." I held out my hand but the man merely shook his head.

"Sorry, I am here somewhat incognito. My presence would cause a scandal if it got out."

"Oh, really?" I said, interested. I noticed that the man's reflection in the lake was muddled and grey, as if his identity needed to be obscured even there. "Can you at least tell me how you know the bride?"

"We dated briefly during college."

"Oh, same here!" I said. "I thought I knew all of Gabs's college beaus . . . let's see: in first year of school, she and Andrew were an item, then in the summer between year one and two Gabs and I made a go of it, and then in year two she dated Oberon—"

"Yes," the man said. "That's when we dated."

"Ha!" The man's magical disguise made a little more sense to me now. Lots of our upperclassmen were rich young Fauntleroys who wanted to avoid scandal. I could believe that Gabs might have dated one of them on the sly, and that he might feel wistful enough to don a magic tux and attend her wedding secretly. "Well, don't let Oberon know. The man has a nasty temper and he might kill you." The words came so easily but once they were out of my mouth I frowned. The man looked likewise ill—perhaps my warning had come too late and he had already had his own run-in with Oberon Myers. I tried to think of some other topic of conversation.

I was not quick enough.

"I hear that no one has seen Oberon Myers in months," the man said.

"Yeah. Word is that he took a ferry to Calais and disappeared into the wind." A passing boat had a tray of drinks. I grabbed one. "Good riddance."

"I'm sure it wasn't easy leaving everything behind," the man said.

"Yeah, sure." I found myself subconsciously rubbing my collarbone. I could still feel Oberon's hands around my throat, shutting off life itself. I had hoped that by forgiving him I could stop having these flashes of anger and fear, that I could wean myself off the various painkillers I was still taking for my ribs, but some days it was just so hard. I made myself stop, reminded myself to breathe. "I never thought he'd be capable of it, to be honest."

"Maybe," the man said slowly, "once he had a chance to really think it over, he realized that if he stayed on his path, he really would become his father's son."

I gave the man another look. That was much too canny a guess for a mere acquaintance.

"Have you talked to him?" I said. "It sounds like you know him quite well."

The man smiled. "I know him better than most people, yes. But . . . recent events have made him question everything he thought he knew. His plan is to travel, and maybe by seeing more of the world he'll figure out who he really is."

I sighed. "Well, good luck to him with that. I can understand wanting to get away from the people and forces that made you . . . but in the end you're still you, and you need to reckon with that."

The man had a worried look on his face. I felt bad for bringing the mood down and clapped him on the back.

"This is much too serious talk for a wedding! Hey, let me introduce you to my girlfriend! You must have heard of Verity Turnboldt—"

"No," the man said quickly. "That's all right."

"Oh, right. You're not supposed to be here. Sorry, I forgot." I finished my drink, grabbed two champagne flutes off a boat. "Here!" He took one of the glasses from me and watched with a somewhat mystified expression as I clinked our glasses together. "I respect the need for secrecy but look me up in London sometime. Next time we meet, let's be friends instead of strangers!"

The man frowned at his champagne flute. "I think that may be overly optimistic."

I froze and a hot rush of embarrassment coloured my cheeks. This man was probably some ridiculously overtitled rich kid, someone so high up he couldn't even be seen at some German princeling's wedding. Of course he wouldn't deign to hang out with a commoner like me.

I was also angry at myself, for being so willing to befriend some random man I'd met at a party. I had learned the hard way with Hollister how dangerous it was to trust too easily, and yet I had almost done it again. I had come to think that maybe it was the innate magic within me. Perhaps it was what made me so quick to trust and so eager to please. But if I was at least aware of this aspect within me, I could try and temper it. I'd been trying to do that over the last few months, but it didn't come easy.

"I'm sorry, I didn't mean it like that," the man said. He sighed. "If you knew who I was, you wouldn't want to be friends with me. And quite rightly."

"Well, I appreciate your honesty," I said, still feeling a bit mad at the both of us.

"Let me introduce myself," the man said, holding out his hand. "Or at least give you my first name."

"Okay," I said, an Americanism I had picked up from Tonya. The man and I shook hands. I was not surprised when there was no frisson of magic between us. I had suspected that we had met before.

"My name is Michael," the man said. "It's the name my mother gave me." He let out a nervous exhale. "I've never had the chance to use it before now."

I let go and stepped back, trying once more to see past the magic and remember the man. He seemed like quite the odd duck.

"Michael," I repeated. "Well, it's nice to meet you."

He gave a wan smile at that, as if to acknowledge that we both knew it wasn't our first meeting.

"I don't know if it was a good idea for me to come here," he said, "but I'm glad we got to talk. I'm glad that you and Verity are well. Now that I've seen that for myself, I think I can move forwards. I hope you can do likewise."

"Michael, mate, what are you going on about?" I said.

"Paul! There you are!" Tonya called out to me. I turned towards her voice a little too quickly, and as one foot of mine lifted off the surface of the lake the heel of my other foot tilted back into the water. I started to sink, my whole left foot going under before Tonya grabbed my arm and pulled me up.

"Whoa! Careful!" she said, helping me right myself.

"Thanks." I looked over towards Michael but he had left. I caught a glimpse of him before he was swallowed up by the crowd. "That bloke I was talking to, did you recognize him?"

"The guy in the tux? No, but I chatted with him earlier."

"What? Really?"

"Yeah. Weird guy. We talked very briefly—he shook my hand and told me he wished me only happiness and stuff like that." She laughed. "You'd think it was my wedding, the way he talked."

"Hmm," I said, trying to catch another glimpse of him in the crowd. "I don't like it. He seemed to know far too much."

"Look at you, being all suspicious," Tonya said, playfully tapping my nose. "I approve of your vigilance, but I think he's harmless. People just tend to get a little weird at weddings."

"Yeah," I said, still somewhat doubtful. "Yeah, that's probably all there was to it—oh Jesus Christ, that was Oberon Myers!"

"What?" Tonya said, puzzled.

"He was wearing a magic tux, but now that he's out of sight its effect has probably worn off or something," I said. "Damn. I should go after him and—"

"No, let him go," Tonya said. "He said what he came to say. Do you have anything else to say to him?"

I thought it over. "I guess not."

The sun had ducked down behind the mountains. The staff had brought out several floating bonfires to light up the surface of the lake. On a floating dock, a band played a slow song. Tonya and I held each other close as we swayed to the music.

"I don't know what the future holds," I said. "I never have, but for the first time in my life, not knowing scares me."

"Hmm. Then just hold me," Tonya said, her head on my shoulder, "and don't be scared."

I turned my head so I could better breathe in the scent on her skin. In this moment at least, I was happy.

"All right, I will."

EPILOGUE

Thomas stepped off the train to Frankfurt and felt like he could breathe again now that he was in a new city. But that feeling soon gave way to the physical reality of the place. The air was dirty, the sky grey, the buildings even more so. The whole place felt so industrial, like a punch-clock hell.

Perhaps that was a good thing: he wouldn't be tempted to stay.

His plan was to travel. He'd head eastwards until he hit China. Once there, he'd find some cloth mage master and pledge his service in return for the chance to learn from them. Who knew how long it would take to learn the language, let alone another country's magical tradition? A long time, but Thomas wasn't daunted. He liked to think that, unlike other young people, he had a grasp on the scope of time. When he was a child he'd occasionally worked down on the docks as a runner to earn some coin. He'd seen how the men unloaded heavy boxes and barrels day in and day out. One day, Frank Smith had tried to pick up a box and collapsed on the ground, yelling in pain about his back. He'd died later that day of a heart attack. The other workers had talked about how Frankie shouldn't have tried to lift the box on his own, that the heavy load had killed him, but Thomas knew it wasn't the one box's doing: it was the decades prior spent loading and unloading cargo. A little bit every day might not seem like much in the moment, but given time it'd be the thing that killed you.

Or saved you. Thomas took note when he was heading eastwards, even if it was just a step—*one step closer to China.*

He walked down the city streets, grimly pleased at how no one around him gave him a second look. Paul would surely have a running commentary going if he were beside him. Thomas often thought it was no wonder Paul prayed so much—he probably loved the thought of being able to communicate without having to deal with such physical necessities as vocal cords and breathing. His prayers to God were probably one long stream of consciousness, never letting God get a word in edgewise:

HelloheavenlyFatherpeacebewithyouitisyourchildPauland I'mintroubleagain.

Without Paul here, Thomas was able to dwell on his own thoughts . . . which were, frustratingly, often about Paul.

Well, even if inside he was still missing his best mate, on the outside he was self-sufficient. Yes, he thought as he walked through the orderly yet grimy streets of Frankfurt, he was his own man. Alone in a city where no one knew his name or his history. A lone wolf. Just a solitary traveller, as anonymous as the paving stones under his feet—

"Oy! Thom-Daw!"

Thomas froze. There was only one person who called him Thom-Daw, or at least only one person who did so in such an unironic, joyful tone. He pivoted on his heels to see Andrew McDougal rushing over to him.

Despite the fact that the sky was soot grey, Andrew's blond curls still somehow managed to catch the nonexistent sunlight. Likewise the light-blue corduroy blazer he was wearing seemed to shimmer, and the locals who walked past Thomas and Andrew scowled as if a bright beam had been shoved in their faces.

"Andrew?" Thomas said, flabbergasted. "What are you doing here?"

"Well, looking for you, of course!" Andrew replied, still lightly winded from running over. Thomas had always liked Andrew, even if he knew he shouldn't on principle. Andrew was the duke of Fife and something like 153rd in line for the throne. Thomas believed that one of the best things that could happen in the United Kingdom would be to set up a guillotine at every subway station entrance and get a-chopping.

The aristocracy was holding the nation back, landed gentry hoarding power rather than dispersing it amongst the people.

Still, despite that, he couldn't bring himself to wish decapitation on Andrew. The bloke was just too good natured and in rare moments actually seemed smarter than his bemused air would let on.

"Looking for me?" Thomas echoed back.

"Yes. Mother knew you were in this city, so then it was just a matter of finding you. She sent me out with very little direction, so I'm happy I came upon you when I did!" Andrew said, smiling widely. That tracked—Thomas knew that Andrew was often sent out on strange errands at his mother's request, a faithful dupe who unwittingly carried out her plans. "Well, shall we go talk to her? It's almost teatime!" Andrew looked around furtively and leaned in. "Do they even *do* teatime here? I don't want to seem like a yokel."

"There's no danger of that, Andrew." Thomas sighed. "Well, let's go see your mother, then." He wasn't going to try and fight fate, at least not when the personification of it on this earth was Lady Fife. She was another noble that was spared an imaginary beheading—not out of any love Thomas bore her but because even in his idealized, perfect revolution, Lady Fife seemed like she'd still find a way to survive.

Thomas and Andrew walked away from the red-light districts of the city into a more upscale part of town. Andrew nattered on while Thomas kept watch out of the corner of his eye. He didn't think Andrew would knowingly lead him into a trap, but if he was just a pawn in a larger scheme then Thomas had to stay on his toes. Nothing seemed amiss and they soon reached a stately hotel. Thomas was suddenly aware that he had slept in the clothes he was wearing—everything in the lobby was so clean and ornate, he felt like a chimney sweep in the middle of a palace.

Lady Fife was apparently presiding over the fifth-floor penthouse.

"No elevators, so I hope you're good for a climb!" Andrew said, a hint of trepidation colouring his cheer. Andrew was huffing and puffing by the second floor. Thomas's heart was likewise pounding, but not from physical exertion. Finally when they reached the third floor he asked the question he'd been holding on to since he'd first seen Andrew.

"How's Paul?"

"Oh, he's good," Andrew said between huffs.

"Really?" Thomas couldn't help but feel disappointed. He'd left partly because it felt like what he said or did hardly impacted Paul. He hated to have confirmation that he was right.

"Well, he has been spending a lot of time with that American woman, so honestly I have not seen much of him lately." And here Andrew's tone lost its cheerful edge. Thomas decided to drop the subject. He knew better than anyone how easy it was to get wrapped up in Paul's orbit, to have your self-worth depend on him looking your way. It would be all the worse if you harboured a secret fancy for the man, like Thomas suspected Andrew did.

They reached the hotel room and Thomas gave Andrew a minute to catch his breath. Once he had his pep back, Andrew opened the door with a wide smile.

"Mother! I found Mr Dawes!"

Lady Fife was standing by the window, smoking. Thomas had never seen her smoke before. She hastily stubbed out her cigarette. She seemed surprised to see them—he had rarely ever seen her be surprised either.

"Good work, love," she said. Thomas had always liked her Scottish accent. "It's almost teatime. How about you go to the bakery around the corner and fetch us some strudel?"

"I daresay, Mother, if we call down we can ask one of the hotel staff to do so," Andrew said.

"I daresay that is true. But I'd like you to do it, please," Lady Fife said.

Andrew glanced between her and Thomas until he seemed to understand something.

"Ah, yes, of course, Mother. I shall leave you two alone."

He slipped out the door and Thomas was left alone with Lady Fife.

"Care to take a seat, Mr Dawes?" She got up from her perch on the windowsill to sit on one of the couches in the front half of the room. Thomas sat on the couch facing her. Sitting down was a mistake. He immediately felt a wave of tiredness wash over him.

"You're a ways from home, Lady Fife," he said.

"So are you, Mr Dawes."

"No, I'm not," Thomas said with more heat than he meant to. He sighed. "I could ask *how* you found me, but I don't really care about the how so much as the *why*."

Lady Fife smiled. "Let's talk about your why first, Mr Dawes. Why leave England so suddenly? What exactly are you searching for?"

"Well, I'll know when I find it," Thomas said cagily.

"I could hazard a guess," Lady Fife said. "More than that, actually. I could hazard an answer."

"Oh?" Despite himself, he was curious. Lady Fife was stringing him along for something, but what, he couldn't tell. What could he possibly offer Lady Fife? Why come all the way to Germany to speak face-to-face?

"You're searching for your father, correct?" she said.

Thomas froze up at that.

"That's why you came to a port city like Frankfurt," she said. "The rumours you heard growing up were that he was a sailor, correct? I don't know what intelligence you have, but you're on the wrong track. I can help you. We can help each other."

"You know who my father is?" Thomas managed to get out.

"I do," Lady Fife said. "I looked into it, used some of my less savoury connections."

Thomas felt a flush of anger rising up within him. "Fucking hell," he muttered.

Lady Fife raised an eyebrow. "Not the reaction I was expecting, admittedly," she said.

"If you've been digging up the past, now all of Liverpool probably knows," Thomas said, trying to keep his temper in check.

"I assure you, that is not the case," Lady Fife said. "After all, this information is only valuable if it is secret. But it sounds like this might not be such a revelation to you after all."

"Joshua Erlich," Thomas said. "Old Jewish man who ran a candy store in downtown Liverpool. Mum pointed him out to me, told me he was my father." Thomas often wondered if this was an invented memory: he would have only been around two when his mother had told him this. But there was enough resemblance between him and old man Erlich that it seemed plausible. "Mum told me not to tell anyone, that it would ruin his life. So I kept it to myself." But it seemed to Thomas that Erlich himself had known. On rainy days he'd let Paul and Thomas sit behind the counter and help them with their homework and give them free candy. Thomas had never dared mention his mother. He hadn't wanted to risk losing this small bit of intimacy that they'd had.

"If you knew," Lady Fife said slowly, "why repeat that rumour about your father being a foreign sailor?"

Thomas shrugged. "Give myself an air of mystery, I suppose." Erlich had died when Thomas was twelve. He'd watched the mourners file into the synagogue—Erlich's brothers and sisters, his nieces and nephews. His wife. Thomas had known he couldn't join them. His mother's last instruction to Thomas had been to keep his parentage a secret. He couldn't dishonour both his mother and father. Even after the old man had died, he'd kept silent on the matter. Until now. "Sorry to ruin your big reveal, Lady Fife. If you really wanted to impress me, you should have tracked down my mother." He said it lightly but he couldn't keep the hope out of his voice.

"I did try," Lady Fife said, her voice gently even. "I couldn't find any trace of her after she left you. I'm sorry."

"Don't be. It's not like I asked you to look into it." Every couple of years the police up in the Liverpool area would pull a body from the

Mersey. Sometimes no one recognized the corpse. Maybe his mother was one of those unidentified women. Until he knew for sure, it felt like she was all of them.

Lady Fife seemed somewhat unsure of what to say next and Thomas was in no hurry to help her. Before she could speak Andrew opened the door.

"Barp-ba-ba-baaa!" Andrew said, mimicking a trumpet as he held aloft a brown paper bag of pastries. He placed it on the coffee table and ripped the bag open with the kind of flourish usually reserved for great feats of strength. "You ask and I deliver!"

"Those look delightful," Lady Fife said. Thomas couldn't wait—he reached forwards and grabbed a pastry. It was pretzel shaped but flaky instead of solid. It seemed to crumble in his mouth before he could even swallow it.

"Andrew, can you please go and fetch some tea to go with this?" Lady Fife said.

Andrew was kneeling by the coffee table and had raised a pastry halfway to his mouth. "Mother, surely we could just call down—"

"Surely. However—"

"However, you want me to do it. Yes, of course." Andrew stood and brushed the crumbs off his corduroy jacket. He cast a glance out the window, perhaps thinking about jumping rather than taking the stairs again. "I shall endeavour to return shortly with tea."

"Coffee, black, for me," Thomas said and felt guilty for giving Andrew more work.

Andrew nodded, his smile tight lipped, and left.

"All right, so even if you've got nothing to offer me, I'll still hear ya out, Lady Fife." He felt fortified having eaten something, enough to put him in a generous mood.

"I need your help," Lady Fife said. "I've always had operatives in my employ who helped me shape the future of this world. But now I need such people more than ever." She clenched and unclenched her hands before flattening them in her lap. "I've lost my power of foresight."

Thomas had been halfway through a second pastry but this made him stop. Not only was this news staggering, it was staggering that Lady Fife was sharing it with *him*.

"How?" Thomas said.

Lady Fife made a dismissive wave with her hand. "I'm not sure. My power is innate. It shouldn't be something that one can *lose*, like a stray earring or pocket watch. But a week ago, all my visions grew cloudy to the point where I can't see any possible futures."

A week ago. She'd lost her powers a week ago. A week ago Thomas had watched in a dark Dalston basement as his best mate had raised a man from the dead. Two extraordinary magical events happening at the same time? That seemed too much to be a coincidence.

"I know you and I don't see eye to eye on many political issues, Mr Dawes," Lady Fife said. "But I think there's enough overlap that we could still work together. If we don't, I fear for the future of not only Britain but the world."

Thomas put down the half-eaten pastry.

Don't, a voice in his head said. *Don't backtrack. Keep heading east.*

He felt no loyalty to the country of his birth. Even if he and Paul had something to do with Lady Fife's loss of foresight, he was not responsible for the fallout. The problems of the British Empire were hundreds of years in the making and not his doing. Still, some sense of self-preservation told him that walking away now would be the wrong call in the long term. If word got out about Lady Fife, there could be a power struggle within the nation, resulting in some new puppet master pulling the strings, one even less palatable.

If he turned his back on the UK now, it might very well become an even greater monster. And he had learned at a very young age not to turn his back on monsters.

"All right," Thomas said. "When do we start?"

ACKNOWLEDGMENTS

A debut novel carries with it a lifetime's worth of debts.

I am so grateful to my agent, Rebecca Strauss, who believed in this book even when I didn't. I'm so glad to have made this journey with you.

To Adrienne Procaccini and the team at 47North, including Tegan, Laura, Riam, and Susan, thank you for making this book a real thing and bringing it to the world. Big thanks to the talented artists at FaceOut Studio for the astoundingly awesome cover.

To the various readers who have given me feedback on early drafts of *Innate Magic*, thank you. In particular, thanks to Bruce Delo, Stewart Delo, Jennifer Giesbrecht, Jane Scott, Michael Matheson, and Kathryn Johnson. I'd also like to thank the writing groups and communities that have helped me grow as a writer: to the members of Write Club and Draft Zero, thank you for looking over the first couple of chapters of this book (multiple times!). Thank you also to my Clarion West 2014 classmates for your friendship and support.

Thank you to Dan and Brenda Fay, the best parents anyone could ask for. To my siblings, Rourke, Genny, James, and Zachary, I am who I am because of you. I've been able to succeed knowing that all of you have my back.

And finally, thank you to my partner, Chris. Every day with you is an adventure and I look forward to each one.

ABOUT THE AUTHOR

Photo © 2020 Rourke Fay

Shannon Fay is a writer living in K'jipuktuk/Halifax, Canada. She attended the Clarion West Writers Workshop in 2014 and has a day job editing manga. She lives with her biggest critic (a very vocal, very fluffy white cat) and her biggest supporter (a very kind human). When not writing novels and short stories, she likes to go ice-skating (in the winter) and play board games (year-round). *Innate Magic* is her first novel.